CW00645749

displacement

ANNE STORMONT

Rowan Russell Books

Displacement
Copyright © 2014 Anne Stormont

The moral rights of the author have been asserted.
Published in 2014 by Rowan Russell Publishing

All Rights reserved. No part of this publication may be reproduced, distributed, or transmitted, in any form or by any means, including photocopying, recording, or other electronic or mechanical methods without the prior written consent of the publisher, except in the case of brief quotations embodied in critical reviews and certain other non-commercial uses permitted by copyright law.

Cover design and formatting www.jdsmith-design.com

Published by Rowan Russell Publishing
Printed by CreateSpace

All enquiries to rowanrussellbooks@gmail.com

First printing, 2014

ISBN 978-0-9929303-3-2

For Revital, a brave and tireless worker for peace,
and wonderful friend.

Acknowledgements

Thank you to all family and friends who have offered encouragement and support to me and my writing – you know who you are.

Special thanks to Margaret Bainbridge for reading early drafts and offering encouragement.

I'd also like to thank my wonderful alchemist editor, John Hudspith, who accepts nothing but the best, Perry Iles that most pedantic and pernickety of proofreaders who patiently encourages perfection, and book designer, Jane Dixon-Smith, who has ensured that the book looks good both inside and out.

Chapter One

Rachel

Snowmelt and recent heavy rainfall meant the normally tame burn was now a forceful and rapid river. The water was up to my waist. I was stuck, held fast by the mud, trapped in darkness. The flow pushed hard against me. I no longer had the strength to free myself.

It was January on the island of Skye and the wind-chill meant the temperature was probably below zero. I no longer shivered. I didn't feel cold. I didn't feel anything. The ewe had stopped struggling a while ago but I kept my arms around her neck.

I'd gone out at around seven that evening to check the sheep. Bonnie, my sheepdog, was with me. It had already been dark for hours. I'd normally have been out much earlier than this, but the last of the mourners hadn't left until around six so I'd been delayed. There'd been a wake in the hotel immediately after the burial, but a few friends and neighbours had accepted the invitation to come back to the house afterwards.

When everyone had gone, Morag helped me clear up. She offered the services of her husband Alasdair to check the animals. But I declined the offer.

Morag shook her head as she wiped down the kitchen worktop. "It's a pity your brother isn't staying here tonight. You shouldn't be on your own."

"Jonathan offered to stay. But he's been here every night since Mum died and this was the only chance for him and Alec to have a few beers and a catch-up before he goes back. Besides I just want a hot bath and an early night. I was happy for him to go."

There was more head shaking from Morag. "And I suppose you'll say no to having dinner with us as well."

"Thanks, really." I tried a placating smile. "But I'm not hungry, not after all that tea and sandwiches. No, you've been a good friend, as always, but …"

"But now you want your precious privacy back, I know." Morag spoke kindly, but I could tell she found my need to be on my own difficult to understand. "In that case," she continued, "I think I'll take Alasdair up on his offer to take me to see the new Bond film. It's on in Portree. And don't be too long outside. You look shattered. After all it's not just been today, you've been looking after your mother for a long time."

"Yeah, I don't know what I'll do with myself now."

"You could try starting to live for yourself a bit more." Morag patted my arm. I flinched at her touch. I couldn't help it.

She appeared not to notice my discomfort. "You've spent your life looking after other people and, with everything that's happened in the last few years, you deserve a bit of happiness." She stretched her arms out towards me. "Oh, come here. You need a damn good hug."

I let her embrace me.

As she let me go she looked at me sadly. "The old Rachel hugged people back."

"The old Rachel!" The force and agony of my raised voice surprised us both.

I closed my eyes, put my head in my hands, pulled at my hair and took a moment to get a grip on my temper. When I could speak again, my voice was strained but quieter. "You've no idea what it's like. Nobody does. Any chance of happiness died two years ago, along with the old Rachel. She's dead and gone to Hell."

Morag looked distraught. I knew she hadn't meant to hurt

me. I was angry because I knew she was right.

"I'm sorry," she said. "I just meant it's time you did stuff for you, got on with your life."

"Right, that's it," I said. "I'm not listening to this. I'm going to check the sheep. Thanks for your help today. You can see yourself out." I hurried out through the doorway that led from the kitchen into the side porch. I shoved my feet into my wellingtons and whistled for Bonnie. My faithful old collie looked at me reproachfully, whether it was for rousing her, or for shouting at my best friend, I don't know. She hauled herself out of her basket by the stove and came to me.

The dark was deep, and sleety rain swirled around us. A screaming northerly blew hard and the rain felt needle-sharp on my face. I didn't hear the sheep's distressed bleating until I approached the bottom of the croft. I swung the torch in the direction of the sound and had to grab the fence to steady myself. The bleating was coming from the burn.

It was one of the Jacob's shearlings, a pregnant ewe. She was submerged to her shoulders in the swirling water and not even trying to climb out. At first I tried grabbing hold of the horns and pulling hard, but to no avail.

It didn't occur to me to get help. I told Bonnie to stay and placed the torch on the ground pointing towards the ewe. Then I slid off the bank into the shockingly cold water. It felt like minutes before the shock passed and I could breathe again. Too late, I realised my mistake. Like the ewe, I was stuck in the mud.

All I could do was try to keep both our heads above the rising water. I knew it was pointless to shout. The wind would swallow the sound and, even if it had been a quiet night, I was too far away from any of my neighbours' houses to be heard. Bonnie barked and darted in and out of the torch's beam. For a while she alternated barking with whimpering. Then she went quiet and the light from the torch disappeared. I could only assume she'd run off, moving the torch as she did so.

In the complete darkness, as the last of the feeling left my body, I felt sleepy. My grip on the ewe loosened. The animal must have felt my hold slacken, and with one huge kick she leapt up the banking and scrabbled to safety.

The force of the kick toppled me over and freed my feet from the mud. I fell backwards and went under. I grabbed at a boulder to prevent myself from being swept away and then I heard a voice. Was it my own? *'Let go. Stop fighting and just let go,'* it said. And I wasn't afraid any more. It would all be over soon and I would find some peace. I loosened my grip and let myself sink. I saw a bright light coming towards me.

Jack

I almost fell over the stupid sheep. It appeared out of nowhere as I followed the barking collie to the water's edge. The beam of my torch picked out the woman's face and her outstretched arm. She let go of the rock and started to slip downstream. I slid down the bank and managed to grab the hood of her jacket. I was surprised by how light she was, even in her sodden clothes. She fought against me as I dragged her from the water.

I put her over my shoulder and half jogged, half stumbled back to the holiday cottage I was renting from Morag. The dog ran by my side and followed us indoors. I set the woman down in a chair at the fireside and threw some more coal into the grate. Then I went to the bathroom and grabbed a towel. I took off my sweater and put it and the towel on the floor in front of her. I told her to get out of her wet things while I made a hot drink.

When I returned with two mugs of tea and a blanket, she was standing, looking into the fire. She rubbed half-heartedly at her hair with the towel. Her wet clothes lay in a pile on the floor. My sweater came down almost to her knees. She turned to look at me. She was slightly built and could only have been about five-foot-three. Her face was pale, her eyes large. She was obviously in shock and she looked exhausted.

I laid down what I was carrying. "Here, let me." I took the towel from her. At first she tensed up, but she allowed me to rub her hair. As it dried I saw that she was a redhead, just a bit of grey here and there. "That'll do," I said, putting down the towel. "Now, get this down you. It's hot and sweet." I handed her a mug. I also gave her the blanket. "And wrap yourself in this."

She took the tea and sat on the sofa. The dog followed her and sat on the floor at her feet.

I remained standing by the fire. I glanced at the woman as I sipped my tea and wondered how she'd come to be in need of rescuing. I guessed she was in her late forties or early fifties, not bad looking, even in her exhausted state. As she drank her tea, she stared into the fire. She'd tucked her legs up under her and covered herself with the blanket. From time to time she ran a hand through her hair, and the more it dried the curlier it became.

She caught me looking at her. "Thanks for the tea," she said. "But now Bonnie and me had better leave you in peace."

I was slightly surprised to hear her voice. She hadn't spoken a word so far.

"No, take your time, there's no rush. Is there someone you'd like me to call? Someone who will be wondering where you are?"

She didn't reply. I saw her jaw tense as she looked at me.

"Maybe I should take you to the hospital, get you checked over."

"That won't be necessary, really, I'm fine." She pushed the blanket aside and laid the mug on the side table. As she stood up, she staggered and grabbed the sofa arm to steady herself.

I went over to her, put my hands on her shoulders, gently sat her back down. "Oh, yes, you're clearly fine. Half drowned, exhausted and probably hypothermic, but apart from that right as rain." I also wondered where she thought she was going, dressed only in my sweater. I sat beside her and, taking her wrist in my hand, felt for her pulse.

She pulled her hand away. "Are you a doctor?"

"No, I'm a policeman, *was* a policeman, retired Detective Inspector, Lothian and Borders. I was trained in first aid in the force. I'm Jack by the way, Jack Baxter."

"Rachel Campbell." She met my gaze, but only briefly, her smile a mere flicker.

The dog stood up, looked from Rachel to me, gave a little bark.

"That's a good dog you've got there, protective and very persistent," I said.

Rachel just nodded.

"It was lucky I'd gone out to get some coal," I went on. "I heard her barking. She was down at Morag and Alasdair's place. I thought she maybe belonged to them, but there was nobody home. I tried to get her to come in here, but she kept running up the track every time I got close, until I got the message and followed her. So I just grabbed my coat and a torch and she led me straight to you."

"Yes, Bonnie's a good dog. I owe her, and you, of course. I owe you both. I'd no strength left." Her voice trembled and she looked away as she finished speaking.

"Look, why don't I get us some more tea and you can tell me how you ended up in the water. And then I'll take you home. I take it you live close by."

"Yes, yes I do, Burnside Cottage. And thanks, more tea would be nice."

"Good, might even throw in some toast." As I stood to go, I took the box of tissues from the coffee table and handed it to her. "Use as many as you like," I said.

Chapter Two

Rachel

Next morning, I was sitting at the kitchen table having breakfast when there was a knock on the porch door and Morag walked in.

"You're up! Mind you, I don't know why I'm surprised. But shouldn't you be resting after last night's ordeal?"

"So, you've heard?" I picked up the teapot. "Tea?"

Morag nodded, took a mug from the dresser and sat down at the table. "Yes, I've heard. We were just getting back last night when we bumped into Jack on his way home from here. He told us what happened. Are you sure you're all right? He said you refused to go to the hospital."

"Yes, yes I'm fine. It was such a stupid thing to do. I don't know what I was thinking of."

"I'm glad you said it. Jack said the ewe saved herself in the end. He was very concerned for you, asked if you made a habit of being reckless."

"I can imagine what you said about that. Who is this Jack anyway?"

"My new tenant, in the holiday let till the end of March. He contacted me a couple of weeks back and moved in a few days ago. I think I mentioned it at the time but with your mum being so ill you probably didn't take it in."

I shook my head.

"Anyway, I simply told him you weren't so much reckless as

stubborn. I told him how fierce you are about your independence, but not to let that put him off."

"What? Morag, you didn't!"

"No I didn't, but I should have... or maybe not." Morag looked uncomfortable.

"What? What is it?" But I knew perfectly well. "Look, I'm sorry about yesterday evening, getting all ratty with you. I know you were just trying to help. You're a true friend. I may be independent but I couldn't have got through all this without you."

Morag leant across the table and squeezed my hand. "I'm sorry too. I do try to let you be. But it just seemed to me it was high time you had some happiness back in your life."

"Yes, well, I don't really know where to start with that one. But I do know I don't need a man."

Morag sat back and shook her head. "You needed someone last night, man or woman. You and your bloody independence. You could have drowned. Thank God Jack was there."

"I'm grateful he was, too. And I know I was stupid."

Morag smiled. "Yes you were."

"So, what's Jack doing here?"

"He's bought Dun Halla Cottage, wants to do it up and use it as a holiday place for himself and his family."

"Dun Halla? That'll need a lot of work, it's been empty for years."

"Yeah, so he's renting the holiday cottage from us for the next wee while. He only has to walk to the end of the track to keep an eye on the renovations. And he'll be doing quite a bit himself as well, apparently."

"Why Skye? Does he have family connections here?"

"Not that I'm aware of. But he hasn't told me that much about himself."

"Wise man," I said, my turn to smile.

"All I really know is he's fifty-six, single, as far as I can tell, newly retired from the police, seems to like Skye. He's a good-looking guy, don't you think?"

"Enough!" I wasn't really annoyed. I knew she couldn't help herself. It was habitual. Ever since I'd come back to Skye five years earlier, Morag had been trying to match-make for me. I began clearing away the breakfast things. "I need to get on. Jonathan will be here for lunch and there are the animals to feed and soup to make before he arrives."

Morag got up too. "Yes, I better get a move on myself. You're sure you're okay?"

"Yes! I'm absolutely fine. I just got very stuck and very cold. I'm sorry I worried you and I'm sorry I'm such a cow sometimes. I don't deserve you." I decided against telling Morag how I'd almost given myself up to the dark, icy water.

"Don't be daft. Come here." Morag hugged me again. And for once I didn't shrug her off. I hugged her back, quite hard.

"Hey, steady!" Morag laughed. "I wasn't expecting that. You're not the real Rachel Campbell, are you?"

"Ha, ha, very funny. I just wanted you to know I do appreciate you, you daft old bag. You're the only person who gives a damn."

"Thanks for the appreciation, but there are plenty of others who care about you. The people here in Halladale, your other friends, Jonathan, Sophie—"

"Yes, I know. Everyone's been very kind. But with everything that's happened, I've become disconnected. As for my brother, he lives halfway across the world. I've seen him—what?—four times in the last ten years. And my daughter didn't even bother to attend her grandmother's funeral. Anyway, I'm fine as I am and I've got you looking out for me. Now go away and let me get on."

The rest of the morning passed quickly as I carried out all the usual crofting tasks and then got on with preparing lunch for my brother and me.

When he'd finished eating, Jonathan pushed his empty soup bowl into the middle of the table and helped himself to more bread. "Great soup, Rache, and this bread is gorgeous. I'd forgotten how tasty homemade lentil soup is."

"I'm glad you liked it," I replied. "The bread's cheese and chilli, my own recipe. And the soup's one of Mum's, her lentil broth..." I paused, recalling all the times I'd seen my mother standing at the stove, cooking.

Jonathan gave a little laugh. "I remember what a tussle she used to have with herself about using ham stock for the soup, but that's what Granny insisted on. No matter how much she may have denied it, her Jewish upbringing never quite left her."

"I just hope she's at peace wherever she is now. She certainly didn't find it here."

"Oh, I think she found a good measure of peace while she was here," said Jonathan. "She made a life for herself, a good life. She and Dad, they were happy. And just look at the number of people who turned out for her funeral. She had lots of friends."

"Yes, but there was a whole part of her, of her past and her heritage, that she just buried."

Jonathan smiled. "Look who's talking." He spoke gently.

"Yeah, yeah," I smiled back. "Look, I've said I'll think about it, about coming to Israel, about exploring my Jewish roots."

"I didn't just mean the Jewish thing. You've buried all of yourself, Rachel, since Peter and the divorce. Then Finlay dying and now Mum. You should be living life to the max, not hiding away here on the croft."

"I'm not hiding away. My marriage ended, my son died. These are facts. I can't hide from them even if I want to. I do have a life here, my work, running the croft—"

"You don't have the most sociable of jobs. Writing and crofting, they're both pretty solitary. How can you be inspired if you're shut away at home all the time? Come to Israel, reconnect, you might get some fresh ideas. Travel broadens the mind and all that."

I shook my head. "I write kids' books and draw the pictures. It's not literature. I don't really think my mind needs broadening to come up with my next animal adventure book."

Jonathan grinned. "So, maybe your next book could be about Camilla the Camel and Gertie the Goat. Come and do some research. I dare you, live a little, get your life back."

I gave a little gasp. "Have you been talking to Morag?" Jonathan looked embarrassed. "You have, haven't you? You two have been talking about me."

"Might have been," Jonathan smiled an uneasy smile. "I met her this morning on my way here. She was walking along the track when I was driving up. I stopped to say hello. Well, actually, she flagged me down."

"Oh, why?"

"She told me about last night, Rache, you in the burn. She thought you probably wouldn't tell me. She was right wasn't she?"

"I'd have got round to it." I glanced at my brother, caught his sceptical look. "Okay, probably not. But there was no harm done. There was no point in telling you."

"Rachel, you could have died. You could have drowned or frozen. If that guy, Morag's tenant hadn't been at home, well..."

Again I suppressed the memory of how I'd been prepared to give in, to let fate take me. "But he *was* at home and I'm fine. It was a stupid thing to do. I should never have gone into the water. I know that. Now can we change the subject?"

But Jonathan wasn't finished.

"Morag's worried about you, and not just after yesterday. She wanted to make sure I'd be here tonight. She says you've been getting more and more distant in the last year, thinks you're a bit depressed and that Mum dying might be the last straw for you."

"Last straw!" I thumped both hands down on the table as I got to my feet. I turned away from Jonathan, went to the sink, gripped its edge, rocking slightly as I looked, unseeing out of the window. I spun round to face my brother. "My son, my Finlay," I stopped, letting the pain come. I stared up at the ceiling, breathing, keeping the anger and emotion under control. "My son being blown to bits, thousands of miles from home, *that* was the last straw. My life was over that day. Mum dying, that was a release for us both. She was tired out, in pain. I—*we* wanted it to end. And now it has and I'm glad. I'm glad. All right? I'm glad." I sank to the floor, my head in my hands, determined not to cry.

Jonathan was instantly beside me, cradling me, soothing me. Sometime later we sat side by side on the sofa, Jonathan with his arm round me and me with my head on his shoulder.

"Rache, I'm so sorry, not just for not being here last night, but not being there for you through it all." He kissed the top of my head.

I took his hand. "Don't be sorry. You've come when it mattered. Scotland isn't your home anymore. And I wanted to be on my own last night. Although I didn't plan the dip in the burn. It was good that you had some time with Alec. He was your best friend once. And as for the divorce, I'm over Peter, the lying, cheating bastard."

Jonathan laughed. "That's my girl."

"And with Mum, like I said, it was time. Her heart was failing. It made her so tired. The doctors thought she'd have longer, that's why I didn't call you. But in the end I think she just decided to go, here at home in her own bed." I blew my nose and then nestled into my brother's side again. "She actually spoke some German that last day, the first time in seventy years. She was very dopey with all the medication. She seemed to be talking to her parents and her sister. Not about them, *to* them. She looked happy."

"That's good, we can be grateful for that at least." Jonathan squeezed my hand.

I sighed. "And, as for losing Finlay, no one could help me with that. There is no help, no peace. It's there all the time, eating away, no matter what I'm doing or who I'm with. People expect me to have moved on. They've stopped talking about him—even Morag. It's like he never existed." I shuddered and Jonathan stroked my hair.

"I'm sure people think they're being kind. They're probably

all too aware of your loss, of the fact Finlay existed. He was a great lad, Rachel. He died doing a job he loved. But you're right, how can a parent ever get over losing a child? I can't imagine it's possible. But you're allowed to live. Finlay would want you to enjoy your life."

I looked up at him. "I'm glad you're here now. I wish you didn't have to leave tomorrow. It's so nice having you to talk to, face to face, to be with family."

"So come to Israel. Spend time with me, with your niece and nephew, get to know Deb. Get to know that other part of yourself."

Chapter Three

The next day, as I stood at the sink, peeling too many potatoes for my evening meal, I felt very alone. It was just after six and it had already been dark for an hour or so. Jonathan was gone. He left first thing for Glasgow airport. I glanced at my watch. He'd be a couple of hours into his flight. The only sounds in the kitchen were the ticking of the clock and Bonnie snoring in her basket by the Aga.

The previous afternoon Jonathan had suggested he help me begin the task of going through some of our mother's belongings, so we'd brought various boxes and bags downstairs to the living-room and set to work. Each object was a marker of our mother's life and each brought a smile, a gasp, or a memory.

There were all the photos documenting her life from primary school in Glasgow to old age in Skye. There were a few pieces of jewellery, her nursing diploma and a bundle of letters. Judging by the addresses on the envelopes, the letters had been exchanged between our parents when Dad was away at sea.

"I don't know what to do with these," I said, cradling the bundle. "It wouldn't be right to throw them away. I so want to read them, but don't know if I should."

Jonathan laid down the pile of photos he was looking through. "We'll read them," he said. "We'll read them right now."

"How can we be brother and sister? You're so decisive, and me, I'm such a ditherer." I untied the faded blue, satin ribbon that had bound the letters together for decades.

And as the already failing afternoon light turned to darkness and the coal burned low and fell through the grate, my brother and I sat side by side on our parents' old sofa and read the letters they'd exchanged before either of us was born. The thin white paper and faded ink added to the feeling of preciousness as I held each one. I ran my fingers along the lines of their writing. I tried to imagine them, my parents, as they would have been. My mother, small and neat, her black hair pinned up, her pretty face smooth and unlined, her expression intense. My dad, his red hair curly and unruly, just like mine, his prickly beard and gentle eyes. The smell of his Old Spice aftershave, his big, capable hands, his quiet voice.

Dad's letters came from all over the world. He described ports from the Arctic to the Mediterranean and from the Atlantic to the Pacific. He described spectacular storms that pulled the bow of the ship so far down that he and his crewmates feared it would never resurface. And he described days of wide, flat blue in the sky and the sea. He told stories of fellow sailors, of being on watch and he asked for news of home and the croft. He finished every letter by telling my mother he missed her and signed off with the words 'your loving husband'.

Mum's letters were quite matter-of-fact. She told Dad about the sheep and about prices at the mart. She told him news of neighbours, friends and relations. There were accounts of her days working at the hospital. The endings to her letters mirrored Dad's exactly.

And when Dad wrote home during his time in Korean waters, when war was raging there, the letters between them were calm and reassuring.

It was that very calmness and understatement that made the letters so special. Their words reflected our parents' personalities. They were quietly loving and underpinned by formidable strength.

"Wow," Jonathan said when we'd finished reading. "These letters, they bring Mum and Dad back to life somehow."

I tied the ribbon around them and stroked the top of the

bundle with my thumb. "I miss their grounded, sensible way of looking at things. I could do with some of their strength. They were always so reassuring."

Jonathan put his hand on mine. "I think you have their strength inside you, Rachel. You're one of the most grounded people I know."

"I'm not so sure," I said.

"It's funny to think of them like they were back then, that they had a life, before we came along."

"Yeah, they were only ever Mum and Dad to us."

We sat in silence for a moment, each of us thinking, remembering.

As I put the letters and other things back in their boxes, Jonathan resumed looking through the photos. A little later he sighed, a long low sigh. "It brings it home to you, what she went through, when you look at these pictures."

"How do you mean?"

"No photos from before the war. No photos of Mum up to the age of eight—not a baby photo, nothing of her parents or sister. She was lucky to escape, I know. But to be the sole survivor..."

Again for a moment or two, we were silenced, contemplating the ghastliness of this miraculous truth.

It was me who spoke first. "I miss her, Jonny. She wasn't easy to live with sometimes, but I miss her already. She was so brave, so resilient. She helped me to stay strong."

"Yes, she was certainly brave, but it could be a bit hard to live up to, all that stoicism. And she was so resolute about having nothing to do with Judaism and Israel. I know she felt I let her down by leaving."

"No, she didn't think that, really she didn't. I think she was very proud of your decision to emigrate, proud of your reasons. She wouldn't—couldn't—go herself, but you only had to hear her telling her friends about you to know how proud she was. She was just too stubborn to admit it to you."

"Really? I wish she'd told me. I know Dad understood, but

Mum... she just wouldn't talk about it and now it's too late." Jonathan wiped away a single tear with the back of his hand.

"I'm sorry," I said. "I didn't mean to set you off."

"Don't be daft." He squeezed my hand. "Right," he said, clearing his throat. "Where were we?" He picked up the photos he'd been looking through. "I've sorted out some pictures I'd like to keep, if that's okay. And if you're sure about Mum's silver bracelet, I know Mari will love it."

"Of course I'm sure. Mari should have something of her grandmother's. I thought I might get her some earrings to go with it, you know, for her bat-mitzvah."

"That's a lovely idea. It would be even lovelier if you delivered them in person." Jonathan pretended to cringe in fear as he spoke.

I swiped him on the arm, but I couldn't help smiling at his persistence. "Stop it, please! Enough pressure."

"Okay, okay!" Jonathan raised his hands in submission. He turned his attention back to Mum's stuff. "Just this left to look at," he said, as he leant over to pick up a small, brown leather case. "Are you up to it? Do it now and then I think we'll both have earned a drink."

"Yes, let's do it. And then mine's a double."

The leather was scratched and tattered. Jonathan ran his fingers over the lid before snapping the catches and opening it. I realised I was holding my breath. We'd always known the case existed—we'd been fascinated by it. Our mother kept it on the top shelf of the cupboard in her bedroom, but we'd never been allowed to see inside it.

And now, we were looking at our mother's seventy-five year old secret hoard. On the top of the pile was a doll. Jonathan handed it to me. I held it as if it was a newborn. It had a china head and a soft body. I stroked its thin and matted blond hair, traced the painted features of its pretty rosy-cheeked, blue-eyed face, examined its beautifully sewn red velvet coat and bonnet, felt the tiny, chipped black shoes. I nestled the doll in one arm while we looked at the other contents of the case.

Jonathan gave a little gasp as he turned over a six inch square piece of card. It bore the number 338. "This must have been her transport number." He stroked it with his thumb and then passed it to me.

"And what's this?" He took an envelope from the case.

I put the card on the coffee table and watched as Jonathan turned the envelope over. He held it up for me to see. It had been opened before—the flap was tucked in. Handwritten on the front of it, in faded ink, was one word—*Miriam*—our mother's name.

"Open it," I said.

The envelope contained a letter and a black and white photo. We looked at it together—silently, reverently.

It showed a man, a woman and two girls. The adults looked solemn and were formally dressed, the man in a suit, the woman in a mid-calf length skirt and high-necked, long-sleeved blouse, her hair pinned up. The older girl wore a flowery, summer dress. She was about fifteen or sixteen and looked shyly to one side. The younger girl, who appeared to be about seven or eight looked directly at the camera and seemed to be giggling. She too wore a summer dress and had a large bow in her hair. I studied it, studied my mother's happy and innocent little girl face. I took the photo from Jonathan and turned it over. On the back someone had written *Die Familie Weitzman 1938*.

"Mum with her parents and Lottie," I said. "Taken the year they sent her away. She had this, only this, to remember them by."

"I wonder if her parents knew by then, when the photo was taken, if they knew what was coming." Jonathan looked grim.

"I hope not. What does the letter say?"

"It seems to be in a mixture of German and Yiddish. It's to Mum from her parents. They tell her how much they love her and that..." Jonathan swallowed. "And that they'll see her soon. There's more, but that's about all I can translate. Here." He gave me the letter.

And now as I recalled the previous afternoon, I sighed. My brother was already hundreds of miles away and I was alone. I looked at my sad and tired face in the dark glass of the kitchen window. I dropped the potato peeler and gave a cry of despair startling Bonnie who hauled herself up and came to my side. I wondered why I was even bothering. It wasn't as if I was hungry.

"How did you keep going, Mum? How did you do it? Your parents and sister dead, murdered in that awful place, and you so young and alone in a foreign country." I spoke to the empty kitchen and tried to stifle yet more tears. I crouched down and put my arms around the dog's neck. "Oh, Bonnie, what am I going to do?"

I considered phoning Morag. But I couldn't face the inevitable tea and sympathy and all that relentless positivity. What I really wanted was to crawl into bed and sleep for a very long time. I'd forgotten what it was like to sleep through the night—to sleep a natural, untroubled sleep. I hadn't done that since Finlay...

I glanced again at my reflection in the window and decided that what I needed was a long, hot soak in the bath, a glass of wine and an early night with the new Kate Atkinson novel, followed by the insomniac's friend—late night radio.

I reached up to close the blind and noticed a dot of light piercing the darkness outside. It was coming steadily closer. Someone was coming up the driveway. The sensor light switched on and I saw Jack Baxter flick off his torch and stride towards the porch door.

Chapter Four

Jack

I looked around Rachel's living-room as I waited for her to return with the tea she'd offered me. It was a small, cluttered, low-ceilinged room and the furniture was old-fashioned and sturdy. I heard a phone ringing somewhere in the house.

The armchair I was sitting in was high-backed and upholstered in a grey, textured fabric that was designed to be hard-wearing and practical. It was also incredibly uncomfortable.

A fire burned in a cast iron fireplace but the coal was almost gone and I wondered if I should add more. Undecided, I got up and went over to look at the photos on the mantelpiece. A black and white wedding photo stood at one end. At the other there was a school photo, its colours faded. In it were two red-haired children, a girl and a boy. The girl had to be Rachel. The red hair was more of an auburn shade now, but those eyes were unmistakeable. Placed at the centre of the mantelpiece was what appeared to be a much more up to date photograph. This was of a young man, a corporal in the Green Berets judging by the Royal Marine uniform. He stood straight-backed, serious and confident. He looked very like Rachel.

There was a scratching at the door as Rachel's dog pushed it open and came in, followed by Rachel carrying a tray.

"Sorry to be so long," she said, placing the tray on the coffee table. "Morag phoned to ask me over for dinner and found it hard to take no thanks for an answer." She smiled, but it didn't quite hide her strained expression.

I was annoyed at myself. I'd clearly come at a bad time. But the truth was I'd wanted to see her again. "Oh no, please, go. I hope you didn't say no because of me. I don't need tea. I'm sorry. I just wanted to check you were all right. That you'd recovered from your dip the other night. I also wanted to give you my condolences. Morag told me about your mother. I'm sorry, I didn't know."

"Why would you know? It wasn't because of you I refused Morag's offer. I seem to have lost my appetite. Anyway, tea's the least I can do." She handed me a mug. "Help yourself to milk and sugar. And I'm fine, thank you, completely recovered." This time there was no smile, strained or otherwise.

I gulped the tea, ignoring its scalding heat. I'd finish it quickly and go. Rachel sat on the sofa, sipping her drink and silently watching me. I glanced around trying to think of something to say. I looked again at the picture in the centre of the mantelpiece. "Your son?"

There was a heartbeat's hesitation before Rachel answered. I flinched inwardly, knowing what she was going to say. "Yes, he was my son. Finlay. He was killed two years ago in Afghanistan."

"Christ, I'm so sorry." There was no turning back now. "Marine commando, I see. What was it? Gun battle?" Rachel looked startled. Nice one, Jack, I thought. Make the poor woman relive it. "Sorry, occupational habit, asking questions. It's none of my business."

She shook her head. "No, no, please don't apologise. You'd be surprised how little I get to talk about him, his life or his death. Yes, he was a commando, like his granddad. Joined at nineteen and loved it. He made it to corporal. He was so proud. He went to Afghanistan on his twenty-fourth birthday, couldn't wait to get out there. Six months later he was blown up by an I.E.D. That's an improvised..."

She frowned, bit her lip swallowed, a small tear ran down her face.

"An improvised explosive device," I said quietly. I found a clean, white cotton handkerchief in my trouser pocket and offered it to her.

She accepted.

"Roadside bomb?"

"Yes, in Helmand. They were on foot patrol, him and four others. Finlay was the leader. Apparently he spotted it just before it detonated. He pushed a couple of the guys clear and then fell on it. Took the full force. The others survived. One of them was very badly hurt. But they survived."

"Brave lad," I said.

I couldn't be sure if she'd heard me. She was looking over at the photo of her son when she whispered, "Stupid, stupid. Why did he have to be the brave one?" She turned to me again. "Why did they survive and not him? Why wasn't it one of them?" She put her head in her hands.

I listened to the dog gently snoring on the hearthrug and heard the embers of the fire shift. I was considering whether to go over to Rachel or to just creep away quietly, when she looked up at me.

"I'm sorry," she said. "What must you think? I've never said that stuff out loud before. It's such a horrible thing to think, never mind say; to wish some other mothers' boys dead so that your own could still be here."

"Don't apologise. You were honest and what you said was completely understandable."

"You just came over to check I was okay and you end up getting my deepest, darkest thoughts." Her face was flushed. "I'm not very good at small talk."

"I asked and you told me. I'm glad you did."

Rachel sat back, quiet again.

Once more I searched for something to say. "Do you have any other children?"

Rachel looked at me. There was more wariness in her expression than when I'd asked about her son. It was something I recognised from when I used to interview victims of crime, the look they gave as they weighed up whether I could be trusted with their story.

She stood up, went over to the bookcase in the corner of the room. There were more framed photos on its top shelf. She took one down and brought it over.

"Sophie." She passed me the picture.

It was a graduation photo. A young woman in academic gown and mortar board smiled out at me. She had long strawberry-blond hair and she looked so much like her mother.

"Pretty girl, and brainy too, judging by this." I got up and gave the picture back to her. She looked up at me, shifted slightly on the sofa. I sat down beside her.

"It's a bit dated. She's thirty-one now." She stared at the image and placed her hand on the glass that enclosed her daughter's face. "Yes, she's clever, got a good job, works for the BBC in Glasgow. We don't—we haven't spoken much in the last year or two—not since Finlay. She blames me—for her brother, for my divorce from her father—everything really. The trouble is I agree with her, so I can't say much in my own defence. It made my mother so angry that Sophie and I couldn't kiss and make up. It really offended her. She said we didn't know how lucky we were to have each other."

Rachel placed the photo face down on the coffee table. "I've made such a mess of things. Everyone that I—that I love—all gone. Sometimes I can't see the point. The other night—in the river—I..." She broke off and looked away.

I reached out an arm towards her, about to squeeze her shoulder. But when I detected the slight tensing of her posture, I withdrew my arm and ran my hand through my hair instead. "Well, all I can say is I'm glad I found you when I did."

She looked at me and there was a smile. Not exactly a broad grin, but it was the warmest yet. "I'm glad too," she said. She tucked her legs up under her and sat back. "You're very easy to talk to, too easy. The things I've told you, I haven't told anyone else. Not Morag, not my brother."

I held her gaze, aware again of the little sounds in the room. I needed to clear my throat before I spoke. "Like I said, I used to interrogate people for a living. Besides, sometimes it's easier to talk to a stranger."

"You don't feel like an interrogator or a stranger. I feel like..." I saw a slight blush creep up her neck. She looked away again before continuing. "My brother says I spend too much time on my own. He could be right."

"What do you do? For work I mean."

"I write and illustrate children's books. And I have the croft too of course, forty sheep and some hens."

"Do you enjoy it?"

"I love what I do. I can't imagine doing anything else. Neither of my jobs will make me rich, but I'm lucky, they don't have to."

"That's a good position to be in, to be able to do what you love."

"I know. It's good that I've no mortgage to pay. When I came back here from Edinburgh five years ago, after my divorce, I planned to buy my own place. But when my father died, it made more sense for me to stay on here. This is the house I grew up in. It's—it *was* my parents' house."

"That explains the furniture," I said and then realised I probably shouldn't have.

"What does? What about the furniture?"

"This is—was—your parents' place. The furniture—it just seemed old, well not old—practical. Bought for its durability rather than comfort—not like something people of our—your age—oh God—beam me up, somebody, please!" I raised my hands in a pleading gesture.

To my relief and surprise, Rachel laughed. "Oh, I know, it's hideous isn't it? I always longed for something more—more John Lewis. But my mother wouldn't hear of it. She couldn't see anything wrong with any of this. She did make one concession after I came back here to live. My work room, at the back of the house, it's all IKEA. I hope you'd approve of that." There was a flicker of a smile.

I decided to get off the subject of furniture. "A writer, don't think I've met one of them before. Not met a sheep farmer either, come to that."

"I'm hardly that. The croft is just subsistence, it's not farming. I have nothing like the number of sheep my father had. After he died I couldn't quite bring myself to get rid of them completely and Alasdair helps me with them when necessary. It wouldn't be a croft without sheep and hens. And Bonnie would be out of a job if there was no stock. Wouldn't you, Bon?" She reached down and stroked the collie's head.

"I've also never met anyone who owns two pairs of wellies before," I said. Rachel looked puzzled. "The other night, you sent me to your house to collect a set of waterproofs and what you called your 'second-best wellies' before I saw you home."

"Oh, yes, well, it pays to have a pair in reserve. That reminds me, I need to give you back your sweater and socks. I haven't had a chance to wash them yet."

"No need, really." The clock on the wall chimed and I glanced at my watch, eight o'clock already. "But now I should go." I stood up. "I didn't mean to stay this long."

Rachel also got to her feet. "Please, don't apologise."

I followed her through to the porch.

Rachel took down my jacket from one of the hooks and handed it to me. It was kind of you to come and check on me this evening and I really am grateful to you for what you did, for saving me.

"It was a pleasure."

"I doubt it was. Hauling a half-drowned woman home to drip all over your furniture and then to be rewarded by having to listen her going on and on about herself. You're a guest and a newcomer to the community. I haven't asked you a thing about yourself or what brings you to Skye. I'm embarrassed at what you must think of me."

"Oh, you're clearly a self-obsessed bore. But I'm prepared to give you a second chance. Come round for dinner one evening and I'll tell you my life story." I stepped outside as Rachel held the door open.

She smiled at me, this one reached her eyes. "Good Night, Jack," she said.

Chapter Five

Rachel

For the next couple of weeks there was no let-up in the bad weather. The usual February, storms continued to scream and rage along the Minch from the Atlantic beyond and Skye was battered by unrelenting rain and sleet.

Outdoors, all loose objects had to be secured if they weren't to become missiles. Just staying upright could be a battle when walking into the gale and it sometimes felt like you were pushing against a solid wall.

Indoors, chilling draughts streamed in through the slightest of gaps. The chimneys roared with the downward rush of air and the roof tiles rattled.

But in spite of the terrible weather, I was glad to have the animals to tend. In the mornings, the hens had to be let out of the coop and fed. Hay and feed had to be taken down the croft to the sheep and they all had to be checked over, especially the pregnant ewes. Then in the late afternoon as the light rapidly faded, the hens had to be shut in and the sheep checked once more. It gave shape to my day, gave me a reason to get up, and helped me to at least try to focus on my writing and illustrating work in the in-between times.

Occasionally, the wind dropped and the sun broke through. I'd linger outside, looking over the loch to the snow-covered Trotternish ridge, the backdrop to our panoramic view and the backbone of the island. I'd look down towards the Cuillin, its jagged granite peaks etched against the sky. Turning westwards, the Outer Hebrides lay hunched on the horizon and sometimes I'd see the Cal-Mac ferries heading across the Minch into Uig from Tarbert or Stornoway. And sometimes there would be hen-harriers skimming the cliff tops in pairs at the bottom of the croft.

But majestic and beautiful as it was, none of it fed my soul like it used to.

From time to time when I was outside, I would find myself looking over to the holiday cottage behind Morag's house. I rarely saw any sign of Jack, and told myself it didn't matter. It wasn't like we really knew each other and he was probably only being polite when he'd invited me for dinner. He would be busy getting on with his plans, getting on with his life.

And I had to try to get on with mine.

But the routine of the croft and the deadlines for the various parts of the new book soon weren't enough. My grief became barely containable.

The loss of my mother had compounded the loss of Finlay. It was over a year since my son was killed but some days it felt like it had just happened, so acute was the sense of bereavement. Some days I didn't know who or what I was grieving for—my mother, my family or myself.

I'd be doing something mundane, something ordinary and it would burst free. I'd fight the tears, terrified to let them come, terrified that if I started I wouldn't be able to stop. I'd cried for the first few weeks after Finlay's death but apart from the recent episode in front of Jack, I'd kept the weeping at bay. But the sobs were becoming harder to control. At times they would come shuddering from deep within me. It was bad enough if they took me when I was tending the sheep or working at my desk. But it had also happened in public places, such as when I was filling the car with diesel, or pushing a trolley round the Co-op. On these occasions all I could do was try to escape to some sort of relative privacy, sit in the car or make a dash for the Ladies and wait for the sobbing to subside.

It took a year for me even to begin to accept my son's death. I could scarcely remember the funeral. The whole thing felt fake, a bad joke. Sometimes, when I was on my own, I'd say it out loud: *'Finlay is dead'*. At other times, I'd be standing in a queue at the bank or the shop and I'd have to fight the urge to say to whoever was there, *'My son is dead'*. It was as if by saying it I'd have a chance to make sense of it.

But now, with my mother gone, I was truly lost and alone. I felt alienated from my own life in a way I'd never been before. The house; Skye. Neither felt like home anymore. I lost interest in life in general, and self-interest in particular. I'd forget to shop, forget to eat, forget to sleep. With nobody else to care for I couldn't be bothered to care for myself. I was displaced, dislocated. I'd no idea where I was heading or even where I wanted to go.

I acknowledged that Jack had indeed saved my life that night in the river—I'd given up. And I knew I needed to do something, something to help myself. I didn't want to get that close to such darkness again.

So, gradually, I made some decisions. And just the act of being decisive made me feel a little better. I looked out the card I'd been given by my GP not long after Finlay died. I called the number, hoping it was still active after the intervening time. It was.

And so in the last week of February I began seeing a grief counsellor. The counsellor, Elsa, was perceptive and skilled and I found I looked forward to our weekly sessions. When I finished the course some weeks later, I wasn't fully recovered, but the tiniest seeds of hope had been sewn. I still experienced the bouts of grief but they were less frightening and a little less overwhelming than before. I had some way to go, but I'd taken the first few steps.

Since Finlay's death, I'd been finding socialising increasingly difficult. When my mother was alive, I'd used her frailty as an excuse for never going out. Eventually my neighbours and friends stopped asking. Now though, with Elsa's help, I realised that one of the things I desperately needed to do was to get out there and mix with people. I needed to start trusting people, start trusting life again.

So when Morag invited me for dinner on a Sunday evening near the end of March I didn't make the usual excuses. After all where better to start seeking out a new situation for myself than at the table of my oldest friend?

When I knocked on their front door and let myself in, it was Alasdair who greeted me. "Hello, stranger," he said, smiling as I stepped into the hallway. "It's great to see you." He kissed me on the cheek. "I'd just about forgotten what you look like. And Morag's thrilled you accepted at long last. You've not even been in for a coffee for goodness knows how long. She worries about you, you know."

"It's good to see you too." I hung up my jacket and placed my torch on the hall table. "I decided it was high time I got out of the house. And yes, I know Morag frets about me. I'm a terrible friend and I don't deserve her."

"How right you are!" Morag appeared in the kitchen door-way at the end of the hall. She beckoned me to join her. "But come in anyway." She turned to her husband. "Alasdair, drinks!"

"Yes, and it's no wonder that he does," Alasdair said, smiling. Morag gave him a look. "Yes ma'am, drinks will be with you very shortly, ma'am."

I found myself grinning as Morag shook her head and rolled her eyes. I felt better already.

The starter was prawns, sweet and fat and fresh, caught in Alasdair's creels that afternoon. And scallops, hand-dived and also fresh out the loch that day. The shellfish needed no other accompaniment than a squirt of lemon and they tasted only of the sea.

"Bloody gorgeous," Alasdair said as he finished the last of them. "Nothing finer, not anywhere in the world."

I agreed. "Reminds me of when we were little and Dad would bring home a pail of prawns on a Saturday night and we'd all sit watching The Generation Game and eat them as if they were popcorn."

"Yeah, I remember that. I came to yours to watch Brucie in colour," Morag said. "Your mum used to say she didn't like prawns and then she'd say 'well, I'll just have one' and she'd eat more than the rest of us."

I laughed. "Yes, but she had a terrible time justifying it. Shell-fish is a banned substance in the Jewish diet, not kosher. In fact, when Jonny was here for the funeral, we were remembering what a tussle she had with herself about using ham stock in her lentil soup. For all she turned her back on her Jewishness, it was deeply ingrained."

Morag smiled. "I remember that too."

And so the conversation, in its usual mixture of English and Gaelic, flowed, as it does between old friends. Although I listened more than I contributed, I enjoyed the reminiscences, the anecdotes and the gentle banter between Alasdair and Morag. The meal itself lived up to expectations. There was a delicious roast chicken cooked with tarragon, rosemary and garlic accompanied by the sweetest roast vegetables. For dessert there was a light and tangy pear tatin.

When we'd finished eating, Alasdair made us coffee. He told Morag and me to go and sit in the living-room. "I'll get this lot cleared up and join you later," he said.

Morag squeezed Alasdair's hand as she stood up to leave the table, and I saw them exchange a look, a look of mutual understanding and appreciation between a close and loving couple. It reminded me of my parents. It reminded me of something I'd lost.

I settled back against a big, squashy, brown velvet cushion in one of the two huge, cream leather armchairs that sat on either side of the fireplace in Morag's living-room. I cradled my coffee cup in both hands and sighed.

Morag, nestled in the other chair, gave a little laugh. "Comfy?" she asked.

"Oh, yes," I said. "I love this room." I looked around at the enormous sofa, at the light, beechwood book shelves and side tables, at the tall ceramic lamps with their jade bases and cream silk shades. "I must get some new furniture. Mum's stuff is well past it." I smiled, remembering.

"What?" Morag said.

"Oh, nothing really. It was just the night Jack was over at the house—he put his foot in it a bit, said the furniture was appalling—just blurted it out. Then got really embarrassed."

"Over at the house? When? You never told me he'd been over."

"It wasn't a big deal. He was just checking I was okay. It was just after he rescued me, just before he disappeared."

"He hasn't disappeared, as you'd know if you hadn't been closeted away from the world. He had to go back down to Edinburgh about a month ago. His daughter's pregnant and she wasn't well. He got an S.O.S. to go and help look after his granddaughter. He phoned yesterday to say he hoped to be back today or tomorrow."

"Oh, right." I was surprised how relieved I felt that Jack was coming back. I tried not to let Morag see my relief. But Morag could read me.

"You're pleased. You are! Trying to play it so cool. What are you like? You like him. I can tell. And I'm certain he's unattached. He never mentions a significant other. So don't be so coy. Go for it, girl." Morag laughed.

"Yeah, yeah, control yourself. I'm not being coy, there's nothing to be coy about. He seems like a nice guy and I'm pleased he's okay." I saw the sceptical merriment on Morag's face. "All right, yes, on the basis of our two meetings, I like him. He'll be a welcome addition to the Halladale community, I'm sure. Now can we change the subject?"

Morag smiled, gave a little shrug. "So, tell me, how are you, really? You look tired and far too thin."

"Thanks! Go easy on the compliments." I laughed, knowing she was just concerned about me.

"Sorry, but it's true. You've obviously not been taking care of yourself. And you've been keeping a very low profile since your mother's funeral. Just the odd text, short and to the point in answer to mine. There's been times when I wanted to come over but Alasdair said to leave you in peace, that you knew where I was if you needed me."

"Alasdair was right. I'm sorry I haven't exactly been communicative, I just needed some timeout, you know?"

Morag nodded. "And now?"

"Now, well, I've been seeing someone, Elsa, a grief counsellor, in Portree. She's been great, helped me to see what I need to do to get some sort of life back."

Morag looked hurt. "You could have talked to me, any time. You know that."

"Yes, I know, and you'd have been sympathetic and kind and tried to make things better for me. But..." I hesitated, not wanting to add to Morag's hurt, but wanting her to understand. "But that's not what I needed. I needed to find my own way out of the mire and this woman—this trained professional—helped me to do that. I found I said things to her that I didn't even realise I'd thought until I said them out loud.

"Okay," Morag said. But she still looked wary, unconvinced.

"Don't look like that. I'd never have got to the point of getting professional help without you. You've kept me going. Not just for the last five years, but since we were at school. Even before the divorce, when we were living three hundred miles apart, you were the first person I called on when I was in trouble. You're my best and oldest friend. Come on, you know that."

"Oh, just ignore me," Morag said, managing a small smile. "You know me. I need to be needed. So, what's the outcome of all this professional help?"

"As you advised, I'm going to begin picking up the threads of my life again."

"Good. Where are you going to start?"

"I'm going to go back to the book group. I phoned Sue, the organiser, to tell her and she sounded pleased. In fact I'm going to have lunch with her and one of the other women in the group next week."

"Wow, that is good news," Morag said. "These are definitely steps in the right direction. I'm sure it won't be long before you're feeling more like your old self."

"They're steps back to some sort of normality. But there's more to it than that. Talking to the counsellor, I realised that I need to really face up to things, let some stuff go and start afresh. I also need to try and work out where my future lies, and where I belong."

"Where you belong?" Morag looked alarmed. "Not necessarily here in Skye then?"

"I don't know. I'm not ruling anything out or in. Everything in my life has shifted and all I know is I need to find my new place in the world."

"What will you do?"

"I need to start to let go of all the anger, about Peter, about Finlay. I know it's been anger that's kept me going, but it's in danger of turning into bitterness. I need to regain the good stuff, the good memories. Elsa suggested that I talk to Peter, bring things to a satisfactory conclusion. I just sort of crept away when he told me it was over, took all the blame. The anger didn't really kick in until after we'd separated."

"And will you? Speak to Peter?" Morag asked.

"I'll have to contact him about Mum's estate. He's the executor of her will."

Morag looked surprised at this.

"I know it must sound a bit strange, but Mum wouldn't change the arrangement after the divorce. In spite of everything she still had a soft spot for Peter. She insisted he was the man for the job. And he was very fond of her. So I'll be getting in touch with him soon."

"Right." Morag looked sceptical. "Pity he couldn't have come to the funeral if he was so fond."

"He offered, but I asked him not to."

"Right," Morag said again.

"And I'm also going to get in touch with Sophie, see if I can build some bridges."

"Oh, that's good!" Morag was much more enthusiastic about this revelation.

"Yeah, I intend to suggest I visit her on my way to Israel, as I'll be flying from Glasgow." I paused as Morag gasped. "Yes, I'm taking up Jonny's challenge. I'm going to see what's so special about the place, get in touch with my Jewish half, see what, if anything, it means to me. And then I'll consider my options after that."

"Blimey, you have been doing a lot of thinking. You're such a brave person, Rachel; a wonderful, warm, strong, brave person. I haven't lost sight of who you are. But you have. So perhaps you're right. You need to take all these steps. Make this journey. Lay all your ghosts."

"Thank you," I swallowed hard. "Thank you for understanding. I was scared you'd think I was mad."

"Just make sure you come back, you hear?"

I could only nod.

Morag stood up and held out her arms to me. "Come here, you," she said. "You're having a hug, like it or not!"

I went to her and when I saw the tears in my friend's eyes, I couldn't hold back my own any longer. We held each other close for some moments.

"Right, a drink is required. Brandies, I think," Morag said, releasing me from our embrace. "Where's that bloody barman?"

At that, the living-room door opened. "You called?" said Alasdair from the doorway.

"How do you do that?" said Morag. "Were you listening at the door?"

"Not at all. Just seemed like you girls had had long enough

to put the world to rights and besides, we have a visitor." He stepped aside. "Jack's back."

Chapter Six

I knew Morag was watching me as Jack stepped into the room, but I didn't look at her. Instead I looked down at the carpet and used the back of my hand to wipe away any remaining tears.

"Jack, welcome back," said Morag, beaming. She'd instantly regained her composure. "We were just talking about you. Rachel was concerned that she hadn't seen you for weeks."

It was all I could do not to gasp out loud at Morag's audacity. I glanced at her—a meaningful glance. She looked back—all innocence.

"Right, come on Alasdair, don't just stand there, let's get these people some drinks—brandy for you, Jack? Rachel and I were about to indulge."

"Yes, please. A brandy sounds good."

"Okay, come and sit down. Make yourself at home. Rachel will look after you while Alasdair and I see to the alcohol." And with that, Morag pushed Alasdair out into the hall and closed the living-room door behind them.

I sat down on the sofa and glanced at Jack. He seemed tired and looked as awkward as I felt. "Please, sit down," I said, pointing to one of the armchairs. "Morag told me about your daughter, is everything all right now?"

"Yes, yes it is, thanks. Maddie thought she was having a miscarriage, but the danger seems to have passed as long as she takes it easy. Her husband Brian's with her, so I stepped in to look after Poppy, my granddaughter."

"I see. I'm glad everything's okay. It must have been very

worrying for you all. How old is your granddaughter?"

"Six, she's a mini dynamo and a great wee character." Jack's apparent fatigue seemed to fade and his face lit up as he spoke about Poppy.

I couldn't help but smile at his obvious delight in her. "It's a lovely age, they're so curious, non-stop questions and exploring everything."

"Exactly, and I don't mind admitting I was struggling to keep up."

"It must have been a great relief for your daughter to be able to call on you." I wondered whether Maddie's mother had been there too.

"We're close, Maddie and me. When her mother and I divorced, back in the nineties, she was still a teenager, but she coped. She lived half the week with me and half the week with her mum. And she still gets on equally well with Ailsa and with me but Ailsa's still working. She's police too, chief superintendent, much more high powered than I was. I wouldn't be surprised if she makes it to chief constable. Anyway, it wouldn't be easy for her to get time off. So Maddie called me. And even though I wouldn't have wished this scare on her, it's nice to think she still needs me."

A sudden longing for my own daughter gripped at my gut. I couldn't help flinching. Would I ever be able to say Sophie needed me? I saw Jack looking at me and hoped he couldn't read my distress on my face. "When is the baby due?" I asked.

"End of August, if all goes to plan." Jack sat forward, looked down at the floor for a moment. "Look, Rachel, about your daughter—"

I immediately tensed. So he had noticed. Part of me wanted to tell this man everything and part of me was utterly terrified at the thought. He'd already proved to be very good at getting me to talk and I felt I'd probably already said too much. I guessed he was just trying to show a polite interest. He was probably wishing Alasdair and Morag would hurry up as much as I did.

"If it would help..." he went on, but he didn't get the chance to finish. At last, Morag and Alasdair were back.

"Here we are. Sorry to be so long. We got the brandy at Christmas and couldn't remember where we'd put it, would you believe?" said Morag, smiling and not looking in the least convincing.

I gave just the slightest shake of my head as I thought, no, I wouldn't believe. I also thought if Morag asked if we'd been getting to know each other, I'd slap her.

Alasdair handed everyone a drink from the tray he was carrying. Morag sat beside me on the sofa. "*Slàinte mhath*," said Alasdair raising his glass. We all echoed his Gaelic toast to good health.

"And here's to your wee baby and no more scares," Morag added, looking over at Jack.

"Yes indeed," Jack replied.

"So, Jack, what's your plan of attack for the work on Dun Halla?" asked Alasdair.

And while the men were deep in conversation about wall demolition and rewiring, Morag and I continued our discussion about the decisions I'd recently made.

"So, you hope to see Sophie on your way to Israel?" Morag asked.

"Yes, as long as she agrees and I don't chicken out."

"I really hope you two do get together, begin to make up. It seems such a waste on top of what you've already lost. I know it isn't easy. I've had fallings out with my four, you know that, but ..." Morag paused.

I knew what she was thinking but was hesitating to say. I knew that she'd never have let things get this bad with any of her children. None of Morag's four grown-up daughters lived on Skye. Two were in England and two in Australia, but she was still very close to all of them. I also knew she didn't want to hurt me. "I know," I said. "I know and you're right. I'm the parent here, it's down to me and I'm lucky Sophie's only as far away as

Glasgow. I'm going to do my best to sort things out."

"I'm glad," said Morag, and I loved her for how genuinely pleased she looked. "And what about Peter, when will you speak to him?"

"Not sure yet. We need to talk about Mum's affairs and I need to tell him I'm going away, so before I go, I expect."

"When are you off?"

"End of May perhaps. Lambing should be over by then. I'd stay until mid to late August. And, I know this is a big ask, and I could probably employ someone, a student home for the holidays maybe, but I was hoping you and Alasdair would see to the animals for me while I'm away."

"Of course we will. I'll just tell Alasdair."

"You mean *ask* him?" I smiled at this typical Morag behaviour.

"I know what I mean!" Morag laughed.

"Alasdair, you'll be okay looking after Rachel's croft when she goes away in May, won't you?"

"Yes, yes of course. It's time you had a break. How long are you going for?"

"I'll be away around three and a half months. I hope that's okay with you?"

"Three months! Blimey, where on earth are you going?"

"To Israel, would you believe? I've finally given in to Jonathan's pleas for me to go and see the place for myself."

"Wow, right, I can see why you'd want to spend a reasonable amount of time if you're travelling that far. It's not exactly a day out in Inverness or a weekend in Glasgow. Will you be safe? Isn't it a bit of a dangerous place? Have you thought this through?"

Even as I smiled at Alasdair's reaction, I was aware of Jack looking at me. I glanced at him, met his gaze. I wasn't sure what his intense expression signified. Most likely he was thinking I was even madder than he'd previously thought.

I turned back to Alasdair. "Yes, it's further afield than I've been in a long time—but I have been abroad before. And, yes, it's probably not the safest place in the world—but I'll be with my brother and he's lived there twenty years and not come to any harm."

"Yes, but—"

"I've put it off long enough. It's certainly not been fear of any of the possible dangers that's held me back from going. Peter was never keen and my mother was against it too. I respected her reasons. But now there's nothing to stop me, as long as you can keep an eye on things here."

"Of course, I will," said Alasdair, smiling at me, "but I reserve the right to worry about you while you're gone."

"Thank you." I smiled back at him.

"I just wish I could go with you," said Morag. "That way I could make sure you'd come back. But I'll be needed here on the croft and for the holiday lets."

Alasdair smiled at Morag. "I think the Middle East's got quite enough problems, without having to cope with you as well. What do you say, Jack?"

Jack raised his hands. "Leave me out of this," he said.

"Yes, yes, Alasdair, very funny." Morag laughed too. And I saw that same look again, the look that passed between Morag and her husband. And again I yearned for what I'd lost, yearned for that kind of closeness.

"Now, can I get anyone anything?" asked Alasdair. "More brandy or coffee?"

I looked at my watch. "Not for me thanks, I've had plenty. It's been lovely, but it's later than I thought. I really must go. Bonnie will have her legs crossed." I stood up.

Jack also got up. "And I must go too. It's been a long day. Thanks for the drink."

Morag and Alasdair stood at their front door and waved as Jack and I went out of the gate and onto the track.

"Sorry," said Jack as we both flicked on our torches. "I didn't mean to interrupt your evening. I just meant to collect the cottage key and go."

"No need to apologise. Alasdair's very hospitable. There's no way he'd just let you go. He makes it sound like you'd be doing him a favour by staying for a drink."

Jack laughed. "Saying no wasn't an option."

"Goodnight then," I said. We were standing at the foot of the track that led behind Morag and Alasdair's place and up the hill to the holiday cottage.

Jack hesitated for a moment before he replied. "Did you say you'd be taking Bonnie out when you get back?"

"Yes, she'll need a bit of a walk. Why do you ask?"

"Oh, it's just—would you like some company? I've been cooped up in the car all day and a bit of fresh air before bed seems like a good idea. Would Bonnie mind if I came too?"

"Not at all. I think Bonnie would like it very much." I smiled in the darkness.

Bonnie, far from minding about Jack's company, seemed overjoyed to see him, and we headed northwards along the single track road that ran from Morag's house to the far end of Halladale.

It was a crisp, clear night. The only light came from our torches and the occasional chink from a cottage window.

"Just look at that!" Jack stopped to look at the sky. I stopped beside him and looked where he pointed. "You forget how dark it really gets when you live in the city," he continued. "Isn't Orion a magnificent sight? And there's Ursa Major and Polaris at the top of Ursa Minor. It's so unbelievably clear, you can even see the Milky Way. And Mars is over there. You can see its polar ice-caps easily this winter. You just need a pair of binoculars. It's not normally possible without a powerful telescope but—"

I laughed as Bonnie barked. The dog circled us as if trying to round us up and move us on.

"Sorry," said Jack as we began walking again. "You know all this stuff. It'll hardly be a novelty to you. I've even bored Bonnie."

My eyes had grown accustomed to the dark so I'd seen Jack's expression of rapt wonder as he viewed the sky. I found his enthusiasm endearing.

I laughed again. "No, I'm ashamed to say that despite the best efforts of my seagoing father, I know very little about the night sky. I know Orion. He's directly overhead in the winter. He's the hunter, right?"

"Yes, that's him. Astronomy's a hobby of mine. It's one of the reasons I find Skye so appealing. No light pollution, but I do tend to bang on a bit."

"It's good to be passionate. I saw it." I glanced up at him and then looked away, suddenly shy. I sensed him looking at me.

"What? You saw what?"

"Passion, I saw it in your face, when you looked at the sky." I squirmed, wishing I hadn't been so direct, so personal. Why couldn't I just have said it was a good hobby and left it at that? I looked down at the ground as we walked.

"Passion, eh? Sounds much better than hobby, less old and boring."

I didn't look at him, but I could hear the smile in his voice. I smiled too.

We walked on in comfortable silence.

When we got to the end of the track Jack swung his torch to shine in the direction of the last house. "My new place," he said.

"Morag told me it was Dun Halla that you'd bought. There'll be a lot to do. It's not been lived in for some time."

"Oh yes, there's loads to do and I really need to get on and do it. I only have Morag's cottage until the beginning of next month when she begins the holiday lettings."

"You're going to have your work cut out," I said. I shone my torch along the track. "Where's Bonnie gone?" I put my fingers in my mouth and whistled. Bonnie appeared instantly.

"Impressive," said Jack as we turned to walk back.

"What—the whistling or Bonnie's speedy return?"

"Both."

It was getting colder and we walked back briskly. When we got to my gate, Jack said, "I haven't forgotten I promised to cook you a meal. I was wondering, would you like to come round tomorrow evening?"

"And I haven't forgotten that you have to tell me your life story. So you're on." Again I smiled in the darkness. "Good night, Jack."

"Good night, sleep well and I'll see you tomorrow—around six?"

"I'll be there," I said.

Chapter Seven

Jack

I wasn't sure where I was when I first woke up. Fleeting images of my Edinburgh flat and then my daughter's place ran through my head. None of these images matched the yellow, flowery wallpaper and dormer window that faced me across the cottage bedroom.

Then I remembered. I recalled the last few weeks, the worry and then the relief. Maddie and the baby were going to be fine. I smiled at the thought of Poppy, her mischief and her amazing power of complete control over me.

And then my thoughts turned to Rachel. There was something about her. I wanted to get to know her, hoped we could be friends. I wasn't sure why I was drawn to her. She wasn't my type. Small, red-haired, unassuming, quiet, troubled. She couldn't be more different from Ailsa, or any of the other women I'd been with. They'd all been tall, confident and extrovert, brunettes mostly. And now—now there was Bridget—tall, blonde and very sexy Bridget. I pushed thoughts of her out of my head and got out of bed. I pulled on my old, work jeans and an ancient, paint-spattered sweatshirt. I planned to work on Dun Halla all morning and then go to Portree in the afternoon for some food shopping.

As I approached the kitchen I realised the flaw in this plan. There was no food in the house. I was still not used to the fact that the nearest shop was twenty-five miles away. I cursed myself for not bringing anything back with me the night before.

I opened the kitchen door. On the table there was a box of eggs, a loaf of bread, a pack of butter and a carton of milk. The note beside these provisions said,

Eggs laid yesterday by my own dear hens, bread made by my own fair hand.

Milk and butter are the Co-op's finest. I guessed you might be in need for breakfast. Enjoy! Morag.

At first, instead of gratitude, I felt bewildered, rattled even. As a recently, city-dwelling policeman, the thought of someone just letting themselves into my house was unsettling to say the least. I was also used to looking after myself. If I messed up by forgetting to buy groceries, then I dealt with it.

Feeling annoyed at Morag was ridiculous. She'd been welcoming from the start. When I'd enquired about the let of the cottage, she'd been very apologetic about the fact that it would revert to its much more lucrative status of holiday let in April. She'd even offered me free tenancy of their aged caravan for as long as I needed it. And Alasdair had been incredibly helpful, putting me in touch with various tradesmen and telling me the best places to get hold of building supplies.

I got a grip on myself and sent a brief thank you text.

After a satisfying breakfast of eggs, toast and coffee, I drove the mile and a half along the track to Dun Halla. I was now a month behind schedule but I was pleased to see the building contractors had finished the re-roofing in my absence. I planned to finish removing and boarding up the old windows.

It was a bright, cold morning. The tide in the loch was running fast, whipped along by a keen north-easterly breeze, but I didn't feel the cold as I worked. I paused occasionally to look out to sea and the mountains of Harris on the western horizon, or down the loch towards the mountains, still snow-topped. At one point I stopped to watch a buzzard flying higher and higher over the water as it was harried by two crows. I inhaled deeply as

I looked out through the empty space of what would eventually be my living-room window. The only sounds I could hear were birdsong, the occasional bleating of my neighbours' sheep and the tidal rush of the loch.

At around twelve-thirty, hunger forced me to down tools. I'd removed all the remaining windows, the glass and the rotten frames. After I'd nailed the last plywood panel in place, I walked through the rooms making mental notes of what I'd need to do next. I was pleased that once the new windows were installed later in the week, the house would be wind and watertight, and work could really get going on the interior. I was impatient to get it all sorted. I wanted to have use of the cottage as soon as possible and I only had the builders and other tradesmen working with me for a limited time.

By mid-afternoon, I was back at the holiday cottage after lunching and shopping in Portree. I'd just finished putting a venison casserole together and was about to have a shower when there was a knock at the door, followed by someone calling hallo. Alasdair appeared in the kitchen.

"Afternoon, Inspector. Busy I see." Alasdair grinned and raised his eyebrows as he surveyed the aftermath of the dinner preparations.

"Alasdair, good afternoon. Yes, I've been getting dinner ready. But I've never quite mastered the art of cooking without making a complete mess."

Alasdair laughed. "I've never mastered the art of cooking full stop—messy or otherwise. That's always been Morag's department. I'd starve without her."

"It's amazing what you can do when you have to—necessity and all that. Mind you I don't always go to this much effort, not when it's just me."

"Having company are you? I thought it looked a lot for one."

"We could have done with your powers of deduction on the force," I said, smiling. "Yes I'm having a dinner guest and I really need to get on. So was there something?"

"Ah, yes. Your new windows, the guy dropped them off this afternoon while you were out. You'd locked the door up by, so we just stacked them outside. But we should probably get them under cover."

"Right, thanks, sorry you were troubled. I didn't know it would be today. They didn't let me know."

Alasdair laughed again. "Don't be daft. It was no bother. Willie probably didn't know it would be today, and he's the van driver. They'd just be waiting until they had a few deliveries this far up. So, you fit? Get it done before it's dark? I've got my truck outside. I'll drive us along." Alasdair was already heading towards the front door.

"Right, yes." I picked up the casserole dish and put it in the oven, closing the door with my knee and twisting the thermostat knob before chasing after Alasdair.

By the time we got back it was almost five thirty. As I got out of the truck, Alasdair said, "Have a good evening with Rachel."

"How do you know it's Rachel?"

Alasdair grinned and winked, "My amazing powers of deduction," he said, before driving off.

Chapter Eight

As soon as I was back, I peeled some potatoes and rinsed the broccoli ready to go in the steamer. Setting the table would have to wait until I'd changed. I had a very quick shower, and as I came out of the bathroom and headed down the hall with only a towel round my waist, there was a knock at the door. Before I could do anything the door opened and Rachel stepped in, carrying a small holdall.

"Oops, sorry," she said, looking me up and down.

I gripped the towel. "Does nobody on this island ever wait to be asked in?"

"Not that I know of. I'm sorry, am I early or was it supposed to be informal dress?" She put down her bag and slipped off her coat and hat as she spoke.

Now it was me who did the looking up and down. It was quite a transformation from her usual jeans, thick sweater and scraped back hair. She was wearing a short, v-necked, green dress and her hair was loose. As she leant forward to remove her wellies, I had a glimpse of cleavage. I forced myself to shift my gaze. She produced a pair of black, high-heeled shoes from the holdall.

"I wasn't risking these on the muddy track," she said, pushing her feet into them. She ran her hands through her hair as she did so.

"What?" she said.

I realised I was staring. "Sorry, it's just, well, you look different. You look nice." I cringed—nice—was that the best I could do?

"Whereas normally..." Rachel gave a little laugh. "I do occasionally, very occasionally, forego the jeans and wellies. It was good to have an excuse to get dressed up."

"You could have dressed up last night, for Morag's."

"Oh, that was just Morag's. This is ..."

"Different?"

"Yes." Rachel looked me up and down again. "Different." She glanced at the towel as she spoke. Then she reached into the holdall and took out my sweater, socks and handkerchief. "You might need these."

"Yeah, right—well—go on through to the living-room. Make yourself at home. I'll get some clothes on."

As I scrabbled around in the wardrobe for a clean pair of jeans, I was surprised at how nervous I now felt. Why now? Why be nervous now? Why did it matter? It was only a meal, a gesture of friendship.

On the basket chair in the corner, among the mountain of waiting-to-be-ironed garments, I found a clean white tee-shirt and a reasonably uncreased, checked shirt. I smiled as I did up the shirt. It was one Poppy liked, my 'soft shirt' she called it. Thinking of Poppy calmed me down.

I went through to the kitchen, put the potatoes on to boil and opened a bottle of wine.

"Nice shirt." Rachel was standing in the kitchen doorway.

"Thank you," I said. "You share my granddaughter's taste. She likes the feel of it." Why didn't I just stop at thank you? I didn't have to say she had the tastes of a six-year-old or imply that she should feel my shirt. Jesus!

But Rachel didn't seem to notice me squirming. She smiled, that semi-serious, fleeting smile of hers, and said, "I can't comment on how it feels. But it suits you and it's nice to know I share Poppy's good taste."

"Wine," I said. I held up the bottle of red, trying to ignore the fact that my voice suddenly sounded like a frog with tonsillitis. But I was also strangely pleased that she remembered my granddaughter's name.

"Yes please."

I cleared my throat and poured us each a glass. "Please, sit down," I said, indicating one of the chairs at the kitchen table. "That is unless you want a comfy seat through in the other room. But dinner won't be long. I just have a couple of things to do."

Rachel pulled out a chair and sat down. "Here's fine. *Slàinte*," she said, raising her glass.

"Cheers," I said and took a large gulp of Merlot. I had my iPad set up on one of the worktops. I opened up the music library and tapped play.

"Ah, Runrig, the local boys," said Rachel.

"Yes, indeed, they've been favourites of mine for a long time."

I was very aware of her as I put our smoked salmon starter together and then set the table. But I didn't feel uncomfortable. In fact I felt myself relax. It must have been a combination of the effects of the wine, I'd downed the glass alarmingly quickly, and Rachel's own calm, quiet presence. I poured myself another.

Soon we were tucking in to the salmon and salad along with some fine, crusty bread from the Portree bakery. "Sorry I wasn't ready for you arriving. The new windows were delivered to Dun Halla while I was out this afternoon and me and Alasdair had to go and shift them."

Rachel took a sip of her wine. "No need to apologise. I enjoyed the floorshow when I arrived." And it was there again, that half serious, almost shy smile.

"That wasn't exactly part of the plan."

Rachel took a last forkful of salmon and laid down her cutlery. "That was very nice, thank you," she said, as I removed our plates. "So, how are you getting on with the renovations?"

"Good, it's going well. Like I said, the new windows are here. The roof's finished. It shouldn't be long before we can get going on the inside." As I spoke, I mashed the potatoes and put them and the broccoli into serving dishes. "There's a wall to come down, rewiring, re-plumbing, re-flooring and re-plastering and then the kitchen and bathroom to be fitted. After that it's just decorating and carpeting."

"Not a lot to do then."

I laughed. "Alasdair asked me why I didn't just do a new build. He reckons it would have been quicker to demolish the old place and put up a kit house." I took the casserole out of the oven and put it and the vegetables in the middle of the table. I handed Rachel a plate and a serving spoon. "Please, help yourself."

"Thank you, it smells wonderful."

"It's venison, I hope that's okay."

"It certainly is." Rachel took a small helping of everything while I topped up our wine glasses.

"Morag gave me half a deer for the freezer when I arrived," I said. "She even brought me stuff for my breakfast this morning," I added, as I filled up my plate. "I get the feeling she thinks I need looking after. Not something I'm used to—being looked after."

"That's Morag, always clucking round, organising, making sure everyone's okay. You won't be surprised to hear she was a teacher before she took early retirement last year."

"Oh, really?"

"She was a maths teacher and Alasdair taught geography, at the high school in Portree. Alasdair's a bit older than Morag and when he retired she decided to go too."

"But she's also very kind, in spite of the bossiness."

"She's a good person, my oldest friend. We've known each other all our lives, same class at school, everything. But sometimes all that kindness and fussing, it can get a bit overwhelming."

At first we ate in silence, an easy silence.

It was Rachel who spoke first. "Mmm, this is very good. Is that chestnuts I'm tasting—and beer?"

"Yep, chestnuts and one of Skye Brewery's best real ales."

"I'm impressed. It's delicious."

"Thanks." I felt ridiculously pleased with myself. We both cleared our plates. Rachel refused a second helping and when I suggested dessert she asked for a bit of a pause.

"Between Morag's last night and this tonight, I think I've eaten more than I usually do in a week. I need a timeout." She pushed her chair back slightly and put her hands on her stomach.

"Fair enough," I said. "But I'm going to have a bit more. All this fresh air and the labouring on the house, I seem to be permanently hungry. But I'm really enjoying it, doing something real, creating something."

"And a new build definitely didn't appeal?"

"Not at all. I like the old stone and the thick walls, the traditional design. The structure was basically sound. It just needed restoring and some TLC. As soon as I walked in I liked how it felt. It had soul, I suppose."

"And why Skye? Why now?"

"Why Skye? That's easy. What's not to love? I've been here a few times over the years and it always impresses me. It's got everything—sea, mountains, and wilderness. I always unwind here, get back in touch with what matters—you know?"

Rachel's expression was serious, thoughtful.

"I can pursue all my hobbies here. I like to walk, climb hills, trek across country and, as you saw last night, I like to stargaze. I also want to get into photography a bit more. I've dabbled a bit, taken some classes, and I got a digital SLR camera as my retirement present from my colleagues. What better place to take pictures than beautiful Skye?"

"True," Rachel said. "And how do you feel about being retired?"

"Good question. I'm getting used to it. It's a big adjustment. I'm fifty-six and I've done more than the required thirty years. But I hadn't planned to quit just yet. Then, last year, I failed the routine medical. Long story short—it turned out that the pains I'd been ignoring were caused by a blocked heart artery."

"Oh no," Rachel said. "Have you had treatment?"

"I've had surgery. It was all very straightforward. I now have a couple of stents keeping the blood flowing and a load of tablets to take, but I feel better and fitter than I have in long time."

"Couldn't you have gone back to work afterwards? If you were fit again?"

"I could have. Nobody forced me to retire. But a scare like that, it's the proverbial wake-up call. It wasn't an easy decision to quit, but I realised there was more to life than being a cop— more I wanted to do before the twilight home and the graveyard. The heart thing, it brought it home to me I'm not immortal. It was time to go."

"Sounds like a wise decision. Brave, too. But what about your daughter and her family? If you're here in Skye, you're not going to see much of them."

"I won't be here all the time. I still have my flat in Edinburgh. I'll split my time between here and there. And Dun Halla is for them to use too. But I was also aware that with all this time on my hands, I didn't want to be just living through them. They need their own space, have their own lives to lead, and so do I. I need some time and space to think about what's next, life after retiring. And I need to decide—about some other stuff." I stopped speaking and cleared my throat, aware that I'd strayed into territory I didn't really want to discuss and that Rachel probably wasn't interested in hearing.

"I hope Skye lives up to your expectations." Rachel raised her glass in a toast. "Now, where's that pudding?"

I smiled, grateful to her for changing the subject, for seeing I'd had enough of talking about me. She seemed so understanding that I wondered for a moment if I should have been more honest, told her everything. Then I realised she was looking at me expectantly, dessert spoon in her hand. "Right," I said. "Don't get too excited. It's just ice cream. I'm no good at making puddings, I'm afraid."

"Bring it on. I love ice cream."

And she meant it. She didn't speak as she ate. She just nodded and muttered the occasional sound of appreciation. At one point she closed her eyes and tipped her head back as she let the caramel and vanilla slide down her throat. I put my spoon down and just watched her. I was aware I was smiling. It was sexy, charming, beguiling. But I'm certain she had no idea how it looked. She seemed to be completely wrapped up in the moment and in her own enjoyment.

When she opened her eyes, she saw me watching her. "What?" She laughed as she spoke and looked slightly embarrassed, as if she suddenly realised how she must have looked. However, she continued spooning in the ice cream.

"Nothing, I was just enjoying watching you. You really do love it, don't you?"

She raised her free hand, shook her head to indicate the impossibility of speech, then she then raised one finger to indicate the last spoonful. "God, that was good," she said, licking the spoon and then her lips. "It's just the best thing." She beamed at me.

"Would you like some more?" I asked.

"Hmm, too much of a good thing?" She looked at me, raised an eyebrow and then said, "Oh what the hell—of course I want more." She looked at the carton on the worktop and made a beckoning gesture. I got up and got it for her.

She tilted the carton in my direction and gave me a questioning look. I shook my head

"Right answer." She grinned, just like the proverbial cat.

I would have been happy to sit and watch her finish it. Her lack of inhibition had me mesmerised, but I thought I'd probably done enough staring. "So, will you want coffee after you've licked the carton clean?"

She gave a little laugh. "Yes please."

We took our coffees through to the living-room. The fire was burning low and the coals glowed in the grate. I switched on the two little table lamps. Rachel sat at the end of the sofa. I noticed she tucked her legs up under her like she had before. I sat in the armchair nearest the fire. At first we sipped our coffee in silence.

I was pleased to see that Rachel looked so relaxed. I found her to be very easy company. I suspected that with Rachel what you saw was what you got. I liked her openness, her directness, but there was also a stillness, a tranquillity about her that I wasn't used to in those around me. Again I hoped we would become friends.

I remembered what Morag had said the previous evening about Rachel going away and I must admit I was a bit disappointed that she was going to be leaving. I wondered what the trip was all about, but I sensed that was a conversation for another day. Tonight was pleasant, easy. I wanted to keep it that way.

I think I was probably too much at ease because I put my head back and closed my eyes for a moment. The combination of the wine, the big meal, the warmth of the fire and my labours outdoors was having an effect.

When I opened my eyes again, Rachel was gone. I wasn't sure how long I'd been asleep. I cursed myself. What a great host. Ten out of ten for after dinner conversation. Rachel must have found me to be fascinating company and would certainly be eager to repeat the experience. Yeah, right.

Then I heard sounds coming from the kitchen; one sound in particular—singing. I went to the kitchen and stood in the doorway and watched as Rachel finished stacking the dishwasher and began to wipe the worktops. I listened to her singing along with Runrig. She had a lovely voice and she matched Donnie Munro's plaintive, sorrowful tone—singing, like him, in Gaelic. It was a beautiful sound.

She turned and saw me. She jumped. "God, Jack! What a fright. How long have you been standing there? Please tell me you didn't hear me singing."

"I heard. I enjoyed it. But, please, stop with the clearing up. You shouldn't have done all this. I'm so sorry for falling asleep."

"Don't be daft. You've had a very busy day. This is the least I could do after that lovely meal." She went to wipe the table.

"Please, stop. I feel bad." I went over to her and took the cloth out of her hand. I was standing very close, facing her, looking down at the top of her head. The flowery scent of her shampoo, the slight gape in the v at the neck of her dress, the sheen on the pale skin of her arms. It was heady. "I don't know what you must think."

She looked up at me. "I think you're a very nice man and I've had a lovely evening. But now I'm going to go home and let you get some much deserved rest." She walked around me and out into the hall.

I followed her and watched her put on her boots.

"Thanks for the lovely meal, Jack. I'll return the favour some time. But first I'm going to take you on a bit of a walk, get you started on getting to know this island a bit better. I'll call you at the end of the week, okay?"

"Okay," I said, smiling.

Chapter Nine

Rachel

Next morning, I was up early as usual. The mornings were definitely getting lighter but it was still bitterly cold. I made sure I was well wrapped up before venturing outside.

As Bonnie bustled the hens out of the coop, I paused to watch the sun come up over the ridge. The earlier wash of turquoise and purple, that had streaked the eastern sky when I first got out of bed, was now replaced by colours from the red end of the spectrum and the sun was a huge golden disc. While I fed and checked the sheep, I thought about how much I'd enjoyed the meal at Jack's, how much I'd enjoyed Jack's company. It felt good to be starting a new friendship; at least I hoped that's what it would turn out to be. I realised that the fact I was going away for three months might stop it in its tracks.

But I had no doubts that I'd made the right decision to go to Israel. I smiled as I recalled the phone call I'd made to Jonathan a couple of days earlier.

"Say that again please, I heard you, but I just want to hear you say it again." I could hear the smile in his voice.

"I'm coming to Israel at the beginning of May, if that's all right with you."

"All right? Of course it's all right! What made you decide?"

I told him about how I was feeling after the counselling, how I wasn't recovered but that going to Israel would help the healing process, that it would give me a different perspective.

"How long will you come for?" he asked.

"Until about the middle of August, if you can stand it."

"I think I'll cope," he said. "And Deb will to be so excited. So will the kids. And you'll be here for Mari's bat-mitzvah. I'll see if I can get some time off."

I listened, enjoying his excitement, as he continued thinking aloud and making plans for my visit.

And now, on this cold March morning, as I checked the last of the pregnant ewes, I could hardly believe that in a month-and-a-half's time I would be in the Middle East. I began to think about all the things I'd have to do before I left. Lambing would be underway in around three weeks and could last at least a couple of weeks. So I really needed to get organised before that. As I walked back up to the house I began making a mental checklist of preparations.

A car horn sounded just as I reached the porch door. I looked towards the track and saw Jack drive past, waving. I waved back and then went indoors for a hot bath and breakfast.

By lunchtime I'd booked my flights, checked my passport and made a list of the new clothes and other things I'd need for my trip. I'd also phoned Lana, my longsuffering editor, down in Glasgow. The call was prompted by shame. I hadn't responded to any of her recent emails.

"Rachel, long time no hear!" she said. "How are you?"

"Getting better. Sorry not to have been in touch before now. You've been very patient."

"Not really." Lana laughed. "It took all my self-control not to call or text you and demand a response, but I knew you'd be needing some quiet time. I didn't want to pressure you."

"Thanks for understanding, but I'm ready to get back to work."

"If you're sure, that's great. I've got production breathing down my neck, wanting to know how *Seamus the Sheep to the Rescue* is coming along. They're keen to have the illustrations and text in the next couple of weeks."

"Ah—yes—well—it's not quite finished—but it will be—very soon."

"Uh huh, so not nearly done then?"

I laughed, an embarrassed laugh. "You know me too well."

"I know writers well—procrastinators all! How 'not quite finished' is it?"

"I'd finished the text, made the tweaks you suggested, just before Mum passed away. And I'd got the go ahead on the pencil drawings I sent in. Jan inevitably wanted a couple of changes."

"Of course, art directors never sign things off first time. So it's just finishing the artwork then?"

"Yes," I said weakly. "Just that."

"Will you be able to meet the original deadline? I might be able to get you a bit of extra time, under the circumstances."

I considered Lana's offer. But I'd resolved to move my life on and getting an extension on the deadline felt like falling at the first hurdle. I did a quick mental calculation. Colouring the final artwork usually took a couple of months. But, if I worked flat out for the time before I left for the Middle East, and if lambing went smoothly, I should be able to complete for the original end of April deadline.

"Thanks, but no, I'll get it all done on time. I have to complete on time because I'm going away."

"Oh really? Where might you be going?"

I told Lana about my planned journey and how I'd reached the decision to go. She asked lots of questions and finished up by saying she could see writing possibilities arising out of the trip.

"I could certainly help you with contacts for pitching a travel feature or whatever," she said.

"I'm not actually planning on doing any writing, but I'll bear it in mind." I laughed. "It's supposed to be a holiday, an alien concept to you, I know."

"Ah, that's where you're wrong. I've a new man in my life so I've been having lots more leisure time. If you get my drift." She told me a few details about Matt including that he was a wine merchant and that they'd met at a friend's dinner party. "And that's all you're getting for now. It's early days. I don't want to jinx anything, get carried away too soon. Come and see me before you fly out and I'll tell you all. In fact come and stay."

"Oh, that's very kind but—"

"Are you flying from Glasgow?"

"Yes, but I—"

"But nothing. You can leave the car here and I'll drive you to the airport."

"Well—if you're sure—that would be great." I didn't suppose Sophie would be offering to put me up or run me to the airport.

"Good," Lana said. "I'm looking forward to it already." We chatted on. It was good to catch up.

I'd known Lana for around twenty years. We first met in Edinburgh when I went freelance as a children's book illustrator and she worked at one of the publishers I did commissions for. I liaised with her on several projects and despite being very different we got on well. But we didn't really get to know each other until ten years later, when I got the publishing deal for my series of 'Henrietta the Highland Cow' picture books. By then Lana was senior editor of children's books at the Glasgow company who'd signed me up. She'd been my editor ever since.

I'd almost forgotten how good Lana was for me. She always made me laugh with her anecdotes and asides. Her Glaswegian humour and take on life were entertaining and refreshing. She didn't know me as Peter's ex-wife, or as a mother—bereaved or otherwise—or, as I was mostly known on Skye, Donald Macpherson's daughter. She knew me as a fellow professional. She knew the facts of the divorce, of Finlay's death and of my troubled relationship with my daughter, but she'd never met Peter or the children and she'd never been to Skye. I suppose with Lana I felt the weight of my emotional baggage a bit less. I was pleased I'd be staying with her when I was in Glasgow.

That afternoon I was back at my drawing board for the first

time in almost two months. I began the job of transferring my line drawings onto the textured paper that I liked to work on when using pastels. Some book artists find this part of the illustration process to be tiresome and boring, but for me it was therapeutic. I enjoyed the level of concentration required as I traced my pictures and prepared them for colouring. My mind emptied of everything else as I focussed on Seamus and his mission to rescue a stranded lamb. It was only the stiffness in my back that forced me to stop. I was surprised to discover it was after five o'clock.

Later, after I'd shut the hens up for the night and done a last check of the sheep, I dined on a boiled egg and some toast. It was all I felt like after the two big dinners I'd had on the last couple of evenings. Not that I had much choice, eggs and bread were virtually all the food I had in the house.

As I ate, I psyched myself up for the two phone calls I'd promised myself I'd make that evening. I dreaded them both for different reasons.

I rarely spoke to Peter. His infidelity, the things he'd said when I found out about it, and the fact that at the time of the split I still loved him, all continued to hurt. So unless it was absolutely necessary, I didn't get in touch. But now it was absolutely necessary.

I poured myself a glass of red wine and selected Peter's home number on my phone. As I pushed the call button I prayed that it wouldn't be Carla who answered.

Carla answered. "Rachel, how lovely to hear from you." Her tone conveyed sentiments that were quite the opposite. "How are you? Sophie was just saying to us that she hadn't spoken to you for ages."

"I'm fine." God that woman knew what buttons to press. So Sophie had been in touch with her father and Carla. I tried to swallow the jealousy that rose like bile in my throat. "How are you?"

"Oh, I'm very excited. Peter and I fly to St Lucia on Saturday. We're going on a cruise from there, all round the Caribbean. It will be wonderful."

"Right—well—have a lovely time. I'd like to speak to Peter. Is he there?"

"Yes, he's right here. I'll put him on."

"Hello, Rachel, good to hear from you. What can I do for you?"

I felt a spasm of annoyance at Peter's assumption that I needed something, made worse by the realisation that I *did* need something from him. I kept my voice even.

"I'm sorry to bother you, but I wondered how you're getting on with completing all my mother's affairs. I'm keen to have everything tidied up."

"Not like you to want things tidy." Peter laughed.

When we were married, my untidiness was one of the things which Peter regularly mentioned as one of my many shortcomings. I didn't reply.

"Sorry, that was flippant. Right, your mother's estate. It's like I said when she died, these things take around three to six months. But your mother's case is fairly straightforward. You should hear about the re-assignation of the croft very soon. Everything else should be completed by the middle to end of May. I'll chase things up when I get back from holiday but I don't envisage any problems."

"Right—good—thanks."

"So, how are you, Rachel?" His voice sounded surprisingly soft now, like he actually cared. This was harder to bear than his sarcasm. Even now, even after... I could still recall how it was once. How he made me feel before...

I was in danger of being swept away. I caught hold, remembered what I was doing.

"Oh, I'm good—fine—really."

"Really?"

"Yes, it's still difficult at times of course—Mum, Finlay—you know..." I swallowed and breathed, swallowed and breathed, clutching on hard, determined not to break down.

"Yes, I do know. I miss—I sometimes—well it doesn't get any easier—I miss him too—wish he'd not gone..." Peter paused, cleared his throat.

This was dangerous territory. Peter was the only person who could really share the loss of Finlay. He was also the person it was hardest to talk to about it.

"I've had some counselling—professional counselling—about Finlay and—everything. It helped."

"Oh, right, good."

"Yes, it is. It's another reason I called you."

"Is it? Why?"

"Because, I'm tired of being angry. Angry at you—at everything. The counselling made me realise that I need to let it go."

"So, what are you saying?"

"Just that, I suppose. I'm letting go—of you, of the bitter feelings about the divorce and what you did. We'll always be the parents of our children. We'll always have that in common. I want to be able to talk to you about them and I want to be able to look back at the time we did have together and not be filled with bitterness and regret."

Again I heard Peter clear his throat before he replied. And when he spoke his voice was husky with emotion. "That's—that's good news, Rache. I'm pleased. I'd like to be able to talk—about Finlay—and about Sophie."

Peter's evident relief and his gentle tone brought me close to tears, but I knew I had to press on. "I'm going to get in touch with Sophie. My relationship with her is another thing I have to deal with. Carla said you'd seen her recently."

"Yes, she was here."

"How was she?"

"She was well, busy at work, but that's not unusual."

"Did she mention me?"

"Not really—no—I'm sorry. Would you like me to have a word with her? Open up the lines of communication?"

"No—thanks—but no. I'm going to do this myself. I'm going

to call her and arrange to see her."

"Right, well I hope it works out. I really do. For what it's worth, I think she's in the wrong. She has been completely unfair towards you. I've tried telling her, tried discussing it, but it's a no-go area. But I don't want to push it and have her withdraw from me as well."

"Thank you for trying and you're right, it's better that she's talking to one of us at least."

"So when will you see her?"

"In May, I hope. I'll be down in Glasgow anyway. So it makes sense."

"What brings you down to Glasgow?"

"I'll be flying out of Glasgow airport. I'm going to Israel."

"You're what?"

"I'm going to Israel at the beginning of May for three months."

"But—"

"But what?" I said, defensive, but prepared.

"It's not the safest of places, is it? And why go anyway, why now?"

"Why? Why do you think? To visit Jonathan and his family, to do something new and different, to explore my—my Jewish half—"

"Your Jewish half? Oh, come on, Rachel. Your mother certainly wouldn't approve would she? She made her feelings very clear. She turned her back on all that. And it's not something you should concern yourself with either. It's—it's irrelevant. Just because your daft brother did it, doesn't mean you have to."

I was determined not to get angry, not to rise to the familiar baits. I kept my voice level. "Jonathan isn't daft and neither am I. I'm not blindly following him. I'm going for good reasons, just as he did. As for Mum's disapproval, it's no longer relevant. I'm free to do as I please, go where I please and live where I please."

"Live where you please? You're not thinking of emigrating? I thought you said three months."

"Yes, this trip will just be for three months, but if I wanted to

I could settle there."

"You'd actually leave your precious island? There was a time when that was all you wanted. You couldn't wait to run away back there."

This was another familiar taunt, but again I kept myself calm. "If you mean my homesickness for Skye when we were married—then yes, I've never denied how much I missed it when I lived in Edinburgh. But it wasn't ever *all* I wanted. And I didn't run away. I simply didn't want to stay in Edinburgh, not after what happened. It was natural I'd come home."

"Yes, okay, fair enough, so why leave?"

"I'm not leaving. I'm visiting my brother. I'm exploring another part of my heritage. I'm putting a bit of distance between me and everything that's happened and I'm hoping to find a bit of peace and perspective along the way. Can you not just wish me well?"

"Of course I wish you well. It's just—well couldn't you just go—I don't know—"

"On a Caribbean cruise?"

Peter laughed at this suggestion. "Yes, although I know that's not your thing. But there are plenty other places, places that aren't war zones. Take time out by all means, find yourself some peace of mind. Just not in the Middle East. Please, Rachel."

I could hear the concern in his voice as he finished. And, as at the start of our conversation, it was harder to bear than any taunts. "It will be fine. I'll be fine. Jonathan knows the country. He'll advise me, keep me safe."

"But you don't *have* to go to Israel. So why take the risk?"

"But that's just it. I do have to go to Israel. It's a risk worth taking."

There was silence at the other end of the line. Then I heard Peter exhale. "It scares me, Rachel. I don't want what happened to Finlay to happen to you. I do still care about you, you know, no matter what happened between us."

Now it was me who was momentarily silenced.

"Rachel?"

"Look, Peter, I'm going. I appreciate your concern. But I'm going to Israel."

"Okay, okay—just for goodness sake keep safe. And I hope you find what you're looking for. Take care of yourself."

"I will—and thanks."

"For what?"

"For listening. It helped."

"It helped me too. I'm glad you called."

As I hung up, I felt drained. The little bit of resolution and resilience that I'd so painstakingly gathered recently had all but leaked away.

But I was determined to hold on to the few remaining drops and to phone Sophie. It was almost two months since we'd spoken and that had been when I phoned to tell her that her grandmother had died. On the couple of occasions I'd called her since then, her phone had gone straight to voicemail and she hadn't responded to the messages I'd left. I was far from confident that she would pick up this time. However, the phone was answered, but not by my daughter.

"Hello Sophie's mum," said a male voice.

"Oh—hello—is Sophie there? It's her—"

"Mum—yes—you came up on the caller display," said the voice. "I'll give her a shout."

I had no idea who this man was, or what he was to Sophie. I got a bit of a clue when he came back on.

"Soph's on her way. She's just out of the bath but she won't be long. I'm Steven by the way."

"Right—Rachel—I'm Rachel," I said. "You're a friend of Sophie's?"

"Yes I am. Has she not—oh, here she is now. Nice talking to you, Rachel."

I heard some muffled talk and then Sophie came on.

"Mum, what's up?" All the usual prickly wariness that Sophie adopted when talking to me was there in those three words. It was what I'd expected, but it was still disappointing. It still hurt.

"Nothing's up. I just—I just wanted to talk to you." I struggled to keep my voice normal and not to betray my churning emotions. Going by past experience, if I came across as pleading or even worse, began to cry, then she'd accuse me of being manipulative and hang up. "How are you?"

"I'm fine."

"Good—that's good. I'm fine too—better than I was—than I've been since... I'm getting counselling to—you know—help me with—with Finlay and—and everything."

"Good for you. So you'll be able to get over him then—get over the fact you sent him away to—"

"Please, Sophie—please don't—I didn't phone for this. I—"

"Then why did you phone?"

"I want to see you, Sophie. I want to come and see you. I want us to try and—"

"Now's not a good time. I'm really busy at the moment, hardly have any time off."

"No—not now—I didn't mean now. I'm going to Israel at the beginning of May and I thought—I hoped I could come and see you on my way out there. I'm flying from Glasgow so it seemed like a good opportunity." I closed my eyes, held my breath.

"Oh—right. Israel—to stay with Uncle Jonathan?"

"Yes, I've finally decided to go. It's something I need to do and it feels like the right time."

"Does Dad know you're going?"

"Yes, I phoned him earlier."

"And what does he think about it?"

"He wasn't exactly keen. He was worried about my safety, but I think he understood."

"But you'd go anyway, wouldn't you, no matter what Dad thought?"

"Yes, I would." I suppressed the urge to remind her that what I did was no business of Peter's, that I had told him out of courtesy. I fought back the desire to say never mind him, I'm talking about me.

"Right, so how long are you going for?"

"Three months."

There was the briefest of pauses before she said, "Oh, three months, right." Another pause before she continued, "I hope you enjoy it and—and find what you're looking for."

"Thank you. So, can I visit you in May, on my way?"

"If you really want to—yes, okay. Call me nearer the time. Now I have to go. Steven and I—we're going out."

"Oh, right—well—have a good time—you and Steven."

"We will." She hung up.

I put down the phone, curled up on the sofa, and fought not to give in to a rush of overwhelming sorrow.

Chapter Ten

Jack

Although I still wasn't sure what to make of Rachel, I was increasingly drawn to her and I continued to hope we'd become friends. I wasn't looking for more than that. I couldn't have more than that, not least because I was already in a relationship. But if I was going to spend a lot of time in Skye I would need friends. I wanted to be part of the Halladale community. Getting to know my neighbours was important.

I'd enjoyed Rachel's company when she came for dinner. I smiled every time I recalled her delight in the ice-cream. She'd seemed at ease, but it was an ease overlaid with reserve. She'd spoken very little about herself. I knew she'd said the point of the evening was so that I could tell my life story. Yes, she'd opened up to me on the night we met, but that was shock and adrenaline. That and the fact I was a stranger.

She hadn't talked about her plan to visit the Middle East when she'd been round. All I knew about it was from Morag's announcement the evening I got back from Edinburgh. It was clearly no ordinary trip and I was curious to know why Israel and why now. But I sensed it was something I should wait for her to tell me about.

I was thinking about all of this a few days after the meal. It was a Saturday morning, the last weekend in March. I'd been working on Dun Halla all week and felt like a break. It was a fine, bright day. The sky was mainly blue with only scattered high cloud and the strong wind of the last few days seemed to have dropped to a stiff breeze. I decided a walk was just what I needed.

A few minutes later, I was sitting in the living room looking at my copy of *Walks on the Isle of Skye,* when there was a knock at the front door followed by a voice calling, "Hallo."

Before I could get up, Rachel appeared in the doorway. At least this time I was dressed.

"Good Morning," she said. "I hope I'm not disturbing you, but Bonnie and I wondered if you'd like to join us for a walk."

I held up the book. "Great minds!"

She smiled a big smile. "I've even got a picnic in the boot."

"I'm all yours," I said.

We headed south to pick up the main single track road, but instead of turning towards Portree we swung north.

I wasn't used to being driven. Being a passenger usually made me twitchy, but Rachel seemed a more than competent driver. She swung the 4x4 round the bends with ease and after about ten minutes I sat back and decided to enjoy the ride. Rachel gave a little laugh.

"I passed then," she said glancing at me.

"Yes—I mean—I wasn't checking—"

"Yes, you were, sitting on the edge of your seat, checking the road. At least you didn't step on a phantom brake or make a grab for the wheel."

"Sorry," I said. "I can't help myself—part policeman, part control freak."

"A total bloke," she said, giving me another sideways look and what can only be described as a snigger.

"Shut up and drive," I answered, smiling at the road ahead. I loved the gasp and slightly startled chuckle that greeted my remark.

We drove along the west coast of the Waternish peninsula to where the road ends high above Ardmore point and parked up in a lay-by opposite a ruined church. While Rachel changed into her walking boots, I wandered over to look at the ruins, which, according to the notice board, were all that remained of Trumpan Church. One grey stone gable still stood but the other three walls were only a few feet high. Outside the walls there was a little graveyard. As I looked across at the headstones, a movement to my left made me turn. A weasel—or was it a stoat?—ran along the top of one of the walls. It stood up for a moment, revealing a white chest. Its sharply pointed ears pricked, its long, black-tipped tail standing straight up. And then it was gone, disappearing among the boulders.

"Stoat," Rachel said, nodding at where the animal had been as she walked up behind me with Bonnie on the lead. She put down the rucksack she was carrying and zipped up her jacket.

"Ah, I couldn't decide, stoat or weasel, lovely sleek little beast."

"Hmm, not so lovely when they take one of your hens, but yes they're smart wee creatures. Sophie used to say they looked like furry pencil cases."

I detected some sadness as she mentioned her daughter and I wondered again what had gone wrong there.

"They have a black tip on their tail and they're a bit bigger than a weasel," she added.

"Right," I said. "I was never sure of the difference."

"I remember a really bad joke that my dad told Finlay when he was a wee boy, about the difference between the two animals. It really tickled him."

"Oh?"

"A weasel is weasily recognised and a stoat is stoatally different."

I grinned at her. "That is truly awful, but I'll save it for Poppy. She'll love that in a couple of years."

Rachel looked away, ran the back of her hand across her face.

I reached over to her, put my hand on her arm. "Look, Rachel, I—"

She moved out of my reach, pulled her arm back. "No, I'm

fine. I'm fine."

I wished I knew her better, wished I could reach her. But for now I realised it would be best to change the subject. "So," I said, gesturing at the ruins around us. "The parishioners have fairly let this place go."

"Ah, well," she said, her shoulders relaxing a bit as she moved on to less personal ground. "Thereby hangs a gruesome tale. The church was set on fire in 1578. The Macdonalds, from the island of Eigg were avenging a massacre committed on them by the Macleods of Skye. They sailed in one Sunday morning, crept ashore and set this place alight. The church had a thatched roof and the fire would have taken hold quickly. The Macleods, singing their Gaelic psalms inside, all died. Then the Macdonalds found their boats stranded by the tide and were killed by the remaining, non-church going Macleods. It's said their bodies were piled up under a stone dyke and covered only by the stones. It was named the Blar Milleadh Garaidh—the battle of the Spoiling of the Dyke."

I watched her as she told the tale of the ruination of this little church. She was so engaged and engaging, a true storyteller. I guessed I was getting a glimpse of the undamaged and unguarded Rachel. I enjoyed the glimpse.

Bonnie, who'd been sitting patiently up until then, let out a little whine and looked from Rachel to me.

I picked up the rucksack and swung it onto my shoulder. "I think Bonnie's trying to tell us something," I said. "Let's get walking."

At first we walked in silence. We followed a rough track that led across the heather moor. A herd of Highland cattle raised their heads from grazing to watch us pass. Once we were clear of the cows, Rachel let Bonnie off the lead, but kept her close with a flick of her hand. I was surprised to find that Rachel was outpacing me. And, unlike me, she wasn't in the least breathless. However, I was delighted to discover that my breathlessness was only slight and there was none of the pain this sort of activity would have caused before my heart operation.

A little later, Rachel nodded in the direction of a small hill to our left. "Last one to the top's an unfit townie." She scrambled over a low fence and was off up the slope, with Bonnie still close by her side, before I'd even realised what she'd said.

I chased after her, relieved to be able to catch up fairly quickly. As I overtook her near the top, I grabbed her arm and momentarily pulled her backwards. Bonnie barked and raced in circles around us. Rachel shouted something, but her words were snatched away by the brisk breeze. I think I got the gist of what she said from her tone. I sprinted to the summit, arriving at least two seconds before her. I collapsed on my back. She sat down beside me and smacked me on the arm. She told Bonnie to sit and I was pleased to note Rachel was now out of breath.

"Cheat!" she said, grinning at me, but trying to look serious.

"Shh," I said, propping myself up on one elbow and squinting up at her. "Get that breathing under control."

She smacked my arm again, still smiling.

I looked around. "What's that?" I stood up and pointed at a beehive-shaped cairn over to our left.

Rachel scrambled to her feet too. "Come and see," she said. We walked over to the cairn. There was a plaque on the front. It said the memorial was to Roderick Macleod of Unish 'who fell in the second battle of Waternish which was fought on this moor against the Macdonalds of Trotternish about 1530'.

"They really didn't get on did they, those two clans?"

"We haven't exactly moved on have we? The human race, in our tribes, we still fight, still slaughter each other..." Rachel turned away, called Bonnie, and marched off down the hill. I followed her and we resumed our walk northwards along the track.

The day remained bright and the north-easterly breeze whitened the tops of the waves that ran along the surface of the Little Minch. Cormorant and shag circled above us, squawking their croak-like call, then dropped down out of sight to their colonies on the cliffs below.

"Is that a broch?" I asked, pointing out a partially ruined, curved, stone structure that stood above the track.

"It's called a dun in these parts. As in your cottage, Dun Halla, which gets its name from the Iron Age fort that once stood behind it on the Ben." She smiled. "But you knew all about that, right?" She raised a sceptical eyebrow, the smile now holding a hint of mockery.

"Yeah, I knew that, sort of..." I had a vague memory of the estate agent saying something along those lines, but I hadn't really paid that much attention.

"Uh huh," She nodded. "Anyway, this one here's Dun Borrafiach and there's another one further up—Dun Gearymore. This is the better preserved of the two, over two thousand years old and the dry stone wall is more or less intact on one side. The ground's a bit boggy but we could take a closer look if you like?"

"Sounds like it's worth the effort."

We crossed the damp, peaty ground and climbed to the ancient homestead. I ran my hand along the curve of the wall. "Impressive," I said. "Not a bit of cement and still standing, after more than two thousand Skye winters."

"There are remains like this all over the island, all at defensive viewpoints of course and all within sight of the next and the one before. So when a warning beacon was lit at one of them, it would quickly be transmitted to all the others."

"And this is some viewpoint," I said. We'd been able to see the Western Isles from the track, but the view was even more amazing from this lookout position. It was a clear enough day to see not only the mountains on Harris, but to pick out a row of white houses and a ribbon of road running in front of them. We paused for a few moments and watched the ferry making its way across the Minch from Lochmaddy. Little birds chirped and flitted above us and rabbits popped their heads out of burrows all around our feet. They soon ducked back down as Bonnie scampered from hole to hole.

"This was one of my father's favourite walks," Rachel said,

still looking out to sea. "We used to come here on Sunday afternoons when I was growing up."

"Were you close, you and your father?"

"Very." She sighed. "I don't think anyone's understood me quite as well as my father did."

"When did he pass away?"

"Four years ago, just a few months after I moved back. He was eighty-three and died in his sleep after a day spent doing what he loved, working outdoors on the croft."

"That's the way to go."

"Yes. But, of course, Mum missed him terribly, not least because he'd been looking after her as her health failed. So I put my plans to get a place of my own on hold and stayed on at Burnside to take care of her." Rachel looked down at her feet and kicked at a stone, lost in her thoughts for a moment. Then she pushed her hands into her pockets and turned to look at me. "Shall we head on out to the point? We could have the picnic at the lighthouse."

"Sounds good to me," I said.

As we continued on our way, we got occasional glimpses of the lighthouse. It wasn't long before the track curved north-east and we came to the ruined settlement of Unish. The foundations of several croft houses were still visible and one large, rather stark and imposing ruin remained standing on the exposed and deserted site. We paused so I could look round.

"This place gives me the creeps," Rachel said. "Too quiet. It always feels so sad."

"Was it the clearances?" I asked.

"Yes, the residents were all forced to leave, roundabout 1880 I think it was. They were either thrown out or burned out, to make way for sheep."

"Yeah, more money for the landowners in sheep-farming than in their human tenants."

We walked on until we reached the tip of the headland at Waternish Point. The white and rather stubby lighthouse sat on a low cliff and the panorama was even more stunning than earlier. Now we could see not only the Outer Hebrides, but also the small and rocky Ascrib islands crouching to the north-east of us, with the impressive Trotternish ridge rising behind. I wished I'd brought my camera and promised myself that I'd return to take some pictures.

The wind was stronger at this exposed position and the screeching seabirds stalled in mid-air as they approached the cliff below. Depending on the way she was facing, Rachel's hair either blew straight out behind her, having escaped from under the little fleece hat she was wearing, or plastered itself across her face. She gathered it in one hand and removed her hat with the other.

"Here, let me," I said, as she struggled to try and tuck it up and replace her hat. She turned her back and I took hold of her hair. It felt thick and soft and I caught a faint scent of shampoo. I noticed the slick of sweat that glistened on the back of her neck as I coiled the long auburn ponytail onto the top of her head. "Right, hat," I said. She passed it to me. I pulled it down over the twist of hair. "There." I rested my hands lightly on her shoulders.

"Thanks," she said, turning to look at me. For a few moments we stood, looking into each other's faces. Without thinking I ran one of my thumbs along her jaw line. In her eyes I saw—what? Pleasure, pain, fear. She gently took hold of my hand and removed it from her face.

My stomach chose that moment to let out the loudest rumble.

Rachel laughed, really laughed, the heartiest I'd heard from her so far. "Okay, I can take a hint. Let's eat."

Chapter Eleven

Rachel

After putting the groundsheet down in the lee of the lighthouse, I gave Bonnie some water and unpacked the picnic.

I was glad I'd brought plenty. Jack devoured twice as many cheese sandwiches as I did, pronouncing them to be proper sandwiches because of the thickness of the bread and the maturity of the cheddar. He also commended the coffee as suitably strong.

"This bread's got a bit of a kick," he said as he took another bite.

"I put chilli in the mix. It's my speciality, cheese and chilli loaf."

"You made it?" He raised his coffee cup. "Respect!"

I was surprised by the surge of pleasure I felt at his enjoyment of the bread. I couldn't help grinning. Jack just grinned back and kept on eating.

After he'd polished off a slab of homemade fruit cake, washed down with more coffee, he said, "That's got to be the best picnic ever."

"I'm glad you enjoyed it." I experienced a further bubble of pleasure.

Jack lay back using his jacket as a pillow. He sighed and closed his eyes. Bonnie lay down beside him. The spring sunshine felt quite warm now that we were out of the wind. I leaned back a little, turned my face up to the sun and I found myself remembering Finlay, how he'd enjoyed his food, how much pleasure I'd got just watching him eat. The tears started. They ran down my face and onto my neck. Not now, I thought. Please, God, not now. Too late, I tried to stifle the sob that grabbed at my throat. I turned away from Jack, praying he hadn't heard. But he had.

"Rachel?" He put his hand on my shoulder just as another sob tore through me.

I stumbled to my feet, started to walk away. I heard Jack get up, knew he was about to follow me. I shook my head and put my hand out behind me to show him and Bonnie to stay where they were. Bonnie obeyed.

"Rachel, stop. Wait, what is it?" He overtook me in about three strides and stood in front of me.

I looked at him, unable to speak.

"God, Rachel." His expression was a mixture of horror and pity.

I put my hands up to cover my face and felt my knees buckle.

Then he pulled me to him, trapping my arms between his chest and mine. One of his hands pressed firmly into the small of my back, the other stroked my hair as grief engulfed me.

I had no choice but to lean on him. It felt strange at first to be held in this way. It was a long time since I'd been in the arms of a man. But the strangeness was fleeting. Having Jack's arms around me, sensing his strength and his kindness made me feel cared for and protected. I rested my head against his chest, felt the soft wool of his sweater as I soaked it with my tears. I breathed in the smell of him—that unmistakeable masculine scent—and was comforted. I knew I could trust this man.

And, as Jack held me and stroked my back and muttered reassurances in that wonderfully rich voice of his, with its gentle east-coast burr, my distress ebbed away and the crying stopped.

When he released his grip, I realised that I didn't want him to let go of me. I realised that it wasn't just comfort that I felt in his embrace but something altogether stronger and much more dangerous. I had to resist the urge to grab hold of him.

"Here," he said. And for the second time since we'd met he offered me a clean, white, cotton handkerchief.

"Thanks," I mumbled, taking the hankie from him. I was aware of him looking at me. At first I was too embarrassed to meet his gaze—and not just because of the crying. But as I wiped my tears, I glanced at him.

His eyes looked into mine. "Finlay?" he said softly.

"Sorry," I whispered.

Jack reached for my hand. "Come on," he said, pulling me along with him. "Come back over."

We sat side by side on the groundsheet, looking out to sea. I drew up my knees, hugged them to my chest and twisted the hankie in my hands. My intense feelings of grief had passed, for the moment at least, but my emotions remained in turmoil. I was surprised and shaken that I'd broken down so completely, but I was even more surprised by the feelings that had been stirred up when Jack held me. These were feelings I hadn't experienced since Peter, feelings I hadn't believed I could still experience. But Jack, this kind, honest, straightforward man, this man who I already regarded as a good friend, he'd reawakened something in me. Something I was both afraid of and exhilarated by. Something I couldn't afford to feel and was determined not to give into. Besides I was sure the last thing Jack would want would be to have me behaving like a schoolgirl with a crush. I took a deep breath, tried to regain my composure.

"Does it happen a lot?" Jack asked. "The crying?"

I shook my head, continued to stare at the horizon. "No, I've hardly cried at all. I've been too scared to let go. The counsellor I saw, she said it would happen, it needed to happen, and it would when I was ready."

"And you were ready just now?"

"You reminded me of Finlay with your hearty appetite and your obvious enjoyment of the food. The tears just started..."

"Sorry," Jack said.

I allowed myself to look at him, a sideways glance. "You keep doing this to me. I seem to lower my guard more with you than with anyone else. But I'm glad to be letting go at long last. And I'm glad you were with me when I did."

He turned to look at me. "Oh right, good."

We both stared out to sea again. Neither of us spoke but the silence between us was comfortable.

After a little while we were no longer sitting in the sun and the chilly breeze had swung round and found us. I shivered.

"We should get moving," Jack said, standing up.

"Yes." I started to pack up the picnic things while Jack rolled up the groundsheet. I was still holding his handkerchief. "I'll get this washed and return it to you," I said, as I put it in my pocket.

Jack smiled. "Keep it," he said. "You never seem to have one of your own."

"I do actually. My jacket pocket's full of them, if you count disintegrating and disgusting paper ones."

"No, I don't count them. Like I said, keep it. You can't beat a heavy duty, cotton job."

"For the heavy duty crying?"

"Exactly."

We followed the line of the coast around the point and took the cliff-top path down the peninsula's eastern side. At first we walked in silence, concentrating our energy on striding out. Jack set a brisk pace and I soon felt warm again.

We paused above Creag-an-Fhithich. "Raven's Crag," I said. "That's what the Gaelic name means."

"I can see why," Jack said, indicating the ravens flying above us.

"And along there is Biod a'Choltraiche—or Razorbill Crag."

"So-called because of the..?" Jack frowned and stroked his chin.

"Razorbills—yes." I laughed. "I hope you're not accusing us of a lack of imagination."

Jack grinned at me. "No, they're an inspired choice of names."

A short distance beyond Razorbill Crag, a tall sea stack came into view.

"Go on then, surprise me. What's that called?" Jack asked.

"Ah, that's Caisteal-an-Fhithich—or Raven's Castle. You must agree it's quite stirring and dramatic."

"Mmm, yes, I suppose so, still rather literal though."

"Oh it is, is it?" I knew he was teasing me. I liked that he felt he could. "The literal can be dramatic—poetic even."

"Now, you've lost me. That's way too deep for my plodding policeman's brain."

"Yeah, yeah," I said. And, as I laughed at Jack, I realised how much I was enjoying showing him this place. This place that meant so much. I felt a rush of affection for the land around me, for its beauty, its history, its permanence. I felt a humbling gratitude.

"But I like the frown lines you get when you're trying to be serious. Just there." He stroked his thumb along the middle of my forehead. And for a second or two his fingers rested on my cheek and he looked into my eyes. I wondered what he saw there. I didn't lift his hand away as I'd done earlier. A little muscle twitched at the corner of his mouth. He looked thoughtful.

Standing so close, feeling Jack's hand on my face, picking up the scent of his after-shave, the scent of him, it was too heady, too perilous. I felt flustered. I tried to steer us back onto safer ground, to get back to the banter of a few moments before. "Frown lines? The Botox hasn't worked then. I guess it'll have to be cosmetic surgery."

"You're fine as you are," he said, putting his hands in his pockets. "So, where do we go from here?"

All sorts of possible responses floated into my brain. Most of them would have sent Jack running in the opposite direction. I fought the urge to say something ridiculous like, 'Why don't we go to bed together?' I turned away from him and stepped off the path. "We need to head inland again," I said. "We have to go back over to the west and pick up the track we walked out on."

The moor consisted mainly of peat bog so the going was fairly tough. Once again we needed all our breath for walking. I was glad not to have to talk. Glad too of the familiar landscape, of being calmed by it, of having the reassurance of its timeless steadfastness. And with each footstep, each connection with the ancient land beneath my feet, I regained some sense of perspective.

There was no path to follow so, as always, I used the two hills ahead of us as navigation points. After we crossed the saddle between Beinn a'Ghobhainn and Ben Geary, it wasn't long before we were back on the track and approaching Trumpan.

When we got to the last part of the walk, where the cattle still grazed, I stopped to put Bonnie on the lead. Jack waited while I did so and, once again, I sensed him watching me. I wondered what he saw, what he made of me, why he even bothered.

"Here," he said, as we continued on our way. His gesture making it obvious what he wanted me to do.

I only hesitated for a split second. We walked back to the car arm-in-arm.

Chapter Twelve

Jack

Something changed that day on the walk, something about the way I felt about her. Or maybe nothing changed. Maybe it was how it had been since I pulled her out of the river.

Rachel was private, vulnerable, damaged, complicated. She didn't want anything more than to be friends. I could see that. I was involved with Bridget. I didn't need another woman in my life, but...

I wanted her. On our walk together, I hadn't been able to stop myself from touching her face a couple of times. I didn't want the afternoon to end. As we drove home, I had to remind myself of all the reasons why I'd be bad for her, why she'd want nothing other than friendship with me. It was going to take all my self-control not to act on how I felt.

But I reckoned there was nothing to stop us spending the evening together. We could go to the pub, have a bar meal. Friends did that, didn't they? So, just before she dropped me off at the foot of Morag's driveway, I made the suggestion.

"Do you fancy going down to the inn later? Get a drink and a bite to eat. I'll drive."

"Mmm, let me see," she said, pulling in close to the verge. "I have a lot on. Don't know if I can fit in any more social commitments." She looked straight ahead as she spoke.

"Oh, that's fine. Don't worry." I tried to keep my voice neutral, told myself it didn't matter. I opened the car door.

"Jack, wait!" She was looking at me now, smiling that smile, the open and unreserved one, the transforming one. "I was being sarcastic. Bonnie has a better social life than I do. I'd love to go out this evening."

"You know what they say about sarcasm," I said as I stepped out of the car. Then, before closing the door, I bent down and said, "I'll pick you up about seven."

My phone rang as I let myself into the cottage. It was my daughter.

"Maddie, how are you? Everything okay?"

"Everything's fine." She laughed. "You'd think I only phone when something's wrong. I just wanted a chat."

"Sorry, it's just with the pregnancy and everything."

"Yeah, well, don't worry on that score. The midwife popped in yesterday and she's quite happy with everything. Me and the baby are thriving. Mind you Poppy is wearing me out. Brian has taken her out for the afternoon so I've been able to get a bit of a rest and peace to call you."

"Good, that's good. I was thinking of coming down the week after next for a few days. I want to see you. And Poppy'll be on Easter holidays, won't she?"

"Yes she will and we'd love to see you. But can you spare the time? How's the house coming along?"

"I can always make time for you, Maddie. I've done a lot on the house this week. Beginning to feel like I'm getting somewhere. Took a bit of a break today. Went for a walk with a neighbour all the way out to Waternish point. Stunning views. My neighbour's a native, so she's very knowledgeable about all the landmarks along the way. I really enjoyed getting out and exploring."

"And which neighbour is this?"

"Rachel, the woman I—"

"The one you rescued? Was she not a bit weird and crazy?"

"She's not weird—or crazy! She's just, I don't know, sad, I suppose. I told you she lost her son. But she's amazingly strong, a very private, dignified person. She's also funny and interesting and kind. I think we'll be good friends. I need to make friends up here, become part of things."

"Yes, sorry. I'm sure she's very nice and yes, of course losing a child, it's unthinkable."

"Indeed."

"And what about Bridget?"

"What about her?

"Is she any happier about you spending so much time away?"

"We haven't spoken since I came back up, just a couple of texts."

"Oh dear."

"Quite." I wasn't comfortable talking about Bridget.

"You need to speak to her, Dad."

"I know. I know I do. She wants me to give up the Skye idea. I don't think she believed I'd go through with it. But Skye's not negotiable, so..." I decided to change the subject. "Anyway, don't you be worrying about the intricacies of my love life. It will all get resolved, one way or another. Now, tell me, how's Poppy? Is she missing her granddad?"

Our conversation moved onto easier ground, and it ended with us firming up arrangements for my Easter visit.

But later, as I showered and changed for my evening with Rachel, it was Bridget I was thinking about.

Chapter Thirteen

The Acarsaid Inn was popular with residents and tourists. It had been an inn since the eighteenth century and was in a tiny hamlet a few miles south of Halladale. Good food and good beer ensured its appeal, as did its location beside a pier and moorings for small boats. When we arrived, it was already busy and we were lucky to get a table. We sat at a small one in the corner close to the log fire and the bar.

Thoughts of Bridget receded as I watched Rachel enjoying her evening meal. Her hair was loose and she'd pulled it back and round onto one shoulder while she ate. Her face was slightly flushed, probably from the heat of the fire. She wore a dark orange sweater, its neckline cut straight across so that her collar bone and the beginning of her shoulders were visible. Round her neck she was wearing an amber pendant.

The colour of the sweater, the pendant, her hair, they all suited the creaminess of her skin perfectly. I was tantalised. So much so that I'd stopped eating.

"Are you not enjoying your steak?" she asked.

"What? No, I mean, yes. Yes I am." I cut into the meat on my plate. "You certainly seem to be enjoying your meal."

"Mmm, yes, beer-battered Mallaig haddock, I can recommend it. The walk has given me quite an appetite."

"Me too," I said, glad she couldn't read my thoughts.

When we'd both finished and pushed our plates away, Rachel stretched and sighed. She looked into the fire for a moment before turning to me and smiling.

"It was a good idea to come down here. I haven't been for ages."

"It's a great wee place. And the beer's good too." I drained the last of my half pint. "Pity it's too far to walk," I said, as I laid down my glass. "You're not a regular then?"

Rachel shook her head. "Not exactly, no. Days or nights out were impossible while I was looking after Mum."

"It must be strange for you not having her to look after anymore," I said.

"Yeah, the house is too quiet. She wasn't exactly noisy, but she was there. There were things I had to do for her. She needed me and we got along." She smiled. "Most of the time."

"I'm sorry I didn't meet her. What was she like?"

"Strong, clever, brave, uncompromising, stubborn, infuriating..." Rachel gave a little shrug. "She was my mum."

"Was she born in Skye?"

"No, she wasn't." Rachel took a sip of her wine before she continued. "She was born in Berlin in 1930. Miriam Weizmann was her name and her father was a rabbi."

"Right." Now I was beginning to see what the connection with Israel might be. I also realised the fuller implications of what she'd just said. "So, she must have grown up in very dangerous times."

"She was one of the lucky ones, if lucky's the right word. Her parents got her out of Germany in 1938—three weeks after Kristallnacht. Have you heard of that?"

"Yes, the night of the broken glass, the anti-Jewish riots."

Rachel nodded. "My grandfather's synagogue was burned down. He must have known how much danger he and his family were in. He got my mother out of Germany on the Kindertransport. She and others in her group ended up in Edinburgh. She was only eight years old, but she was well cared for and she was eventually adopted by an elderly Jewish couple."

"And what happened to her family?"

"It wasn't until after the end of the war that my mother found out what became of them. My grandfather was arrested just after my mother got away. He died in Dachau in 1940. My grandmother and my mother's older sister were sent to Auschwitz after war was declared in 1939. They died in the gas chambers there in 1942. My aunt was only nineteen years old when she died." Rachel sighed.

At first I didn't know what to say. The silence was broken only by a log cracking in the fireplace. After a minute I said, "God, what an appalling story. I'm so sorry for what happened to your family and for making you relive it. Let me get you another drink?"

"Appalling, yes. But it's a story that should be told. And no, no drink. I've got a better idea. Why don't we go home? I have a bottle of Talisker malt, Mum's bottle. Come and drink a toast to her with me."

"That sounds good," I said.

A little while later I stood beside the fireplace in Rachel's living-room while she organised our drinks. The fire had burned low but still gave off a good heat. Bonnie, who'd got over her euphoria at our return, was snoozing at my feet. I looked again at the photos on the mantelpiece, at the pictures of Rachel's children and of her parents' wedding. There was another photo there that hadn't been there the first time I'd been in this room. I picked it up. It was a picture of a white-haired, elderly woman. She was sitting looking directly at the camera, her brown-eyed gaze very similar to that of her daughter. Her chin jutted forward slightly, almost as if she was offering some sort of challenge and there was a slight smile on her face. Her bearing and expression combined to suggest strength and intelligence.

"The woman in question," said Rachel, as she came into the room and saw the photograph in my hand.

"I guessed it must be," I said, replacing it on the mantelpiece. "Even in a photograph it's obvious she was a formidable lady."

Rachel handed me my drink. "Indomitable, definitely," she said, raising her own.

I touched my glass to hers. "To Miriam," I said, before savouring the acrid, golden liquid.

"To Mum," said Rachel. She took a sip of the malt and gave a little cough. "God, that's strong stuff. Mum swore by it, had it as a nightcap every evening. But I'm not really a whisky drinker and I've just remembered why." She sat down on the sofa.

"Philistine," I said, smiling, as I sat down beside her. "It's wonderful stuff. That full on, fruity start and then the chilli type kick at the back of the throat. Magic. Is that the twenty-five year old?"

"Blimey, yes, you're right," said Rachel. "You're a connoisseur. You and Mum would have got on great." She took another sip and made a face.

"Don't drink it if you dislike it so much," I said, laughing.

"I'll drink it in Mum's honour. Strangely it gets better the more you drink." She smiled at me.

"True," I said, smiling back. "So, were you brought up in the Jewish faith?"

"No, no I wasn't. My mother turned her back on all things Jewish after she met my dad. She rebelled against her adoptive parents and their orthodox views and left home at the earliest opportunity. I also think she equated being Jewish with being vulnerable."

"But Jonathan, that's your brother, right, he lives in Israel?"

Rachel took another sip. "Jonathan was always fascinated by Judaism and our Jewish heritage. It was sort of inevitable that's where he'd end up. Mum wasn't happy about it but I think she understood."

"And now you're going for a visit?"

"Yes. It won't upset my mother now. And I'm hoping to get a fresh perspective on my life, I suppose. Explore this unknown part of my DNA."

"I hope you find what you're looking for," I said.

Rachel shrugged. I sensed she didn't want to go into any more detail.

"So," I said, "how did your mother meet your father?"

"She came up to Skye on a cycling holiday with a friend. It was the summer of 1950. They'd just finished their nursing training. They went to a ceilidh one evening in Dunvegan. Dad was home on leave and was playing the fiddle in the ceilidh band. He was wearing his Royal Marine uniform and, according to Mum, he was the most handsome man she'd ever seen. They married within a year of meeting." Rachel paused and took a couple more sips of her drink before continuing. "They were very close. I think meeting my father was a sort of homecoming for Mum. She loved Skye, went native. She learned Gaelic, which she mixed with Yiddish and English, and spoke with a slight German accent. She even joined the church. The Presbyterian mindset suited her perfectly."

Rachel paused again and looked into the fire for a few moments. Then she looked directly at me. "Sorry," she said.

"What for?"

"Going on so much. It's not like me, but you did it again. Got me talking."

"Don't apologise. As I said, I was a professional interrogator and it's a pretty amazing story." I thought I could listen to her all night. I also thought I should go, leave her in peace. She'd probably had enough of my company for one day. I drained the last of my whisky and stood up.

Rachel stood up too. I assumed she was going to see me out. But then she held out her glass to me. "Here," she said. "Have the rest of this and I'll make us some coffee. Then after that you can come with Bonnie and me for her bedtime walk. If you want to that is."

I took the glass from her, put it to my lips and took a sip. She was standing very close, looking up at me. The scent of her perfume overlaid the aroma of whisky and wood smoke and the firelight gave a sheen to her hair and the skin on her neck. I could see little freckles on her cheeks and flecks of green in the amber irises of her eyes. She put her hand across the front of her neck. I noticed the dry, reddened skin on her knuckles, imagined the slight roughness there'd be if I touched or was touched by... She inclined her head slightly, leant in even closer. The wide neck of her sweater gaped a little and I caught a glimpse, a little strap.

"Jack," she said.

I thought how I loved hearing my name spoken in her soft Skye accent. The softness of the 'J', the flattening of the vowel at the back of the throat and the little click on the 'ck'.

"Jack?" she said again.

"Sorry. Must be the whisky. Got me into a bit of a trance there. I think coffee and a walk would be a very good idea, thank you."

While I waited for Rachel to come back with the coffee, I tried to suppress the thoughts of Bridget that crowded into my mind. Bonnie came over and put her head on my knee. I scratched behind her ears and said, "Oh, Bonnie, what am I going to do?"

A little while later we were out in the cold night air. The sky was clear. There was enough moonlight for us not to need our torches. And, just as it had been on our first night walk together, the display of stars was spectacular.

As we looked up at them, Rachel said, "You better make the most of the next couple of weeks for your stargazing. With the clocks going forward tonight, it won't be long before the nights are too light to see them."

"Yes, Alasdair was saying that by June, this far north, it's only dark for a couple of hours and even then it's more of a twilight."

Bonnie scampered off ahead of us but kept coming back to shepherd us along. We talked a bit more about the night sky and then just walked in easy silence. As we turned to head back, Rachel said, "I've really enjoyed today. And it was so nice to eat out. Thanks for suggesting it." She smiled up at me.

I smiled back. "I enjoyed it too."

"I hadn't realised how much I missed doing that sort of thing. Not that my ex was ever much of a one for pub food."

Before I had a chance to think, I said, "Why did your marriage end?"

If Rachel was surprised, she didn't show it. "My ex-husband was unfaithful, more than once, but I loved him. I made compromises. But in the end it was..."

"Unforgivable?"

Rachel laughed, a bitter laugh. "It didn't matter whether it was unforgivable or not. Peter only told me about his final infidelity because he wanted a divorce. He'd met the love of his life. Turned out he'd been compromising too, making do with short-term affairs, but this time it was love."

"Were you... was it ever happy, your marriage?"

"Deep down, no. We were very young when we married, still students. I was only nineteen. I was pregnant and our parents insisted it was our only option. Different times back then. But we did love each other at first, the way you do at that age. But I wasn't, couldn't be, the type of wife Peter wanted. He wanted tidiness, meals on time, a regime. And he wanted me to host amazing dinner parties and to entertain his circle of Edinburgh's finest middle-class professionals. I, on the other hand, was wrapped up in the children and in my artwork. Haute cuisine and socialising really weren't my thing. But, even when things changed between us, I was determined to make the best of it. I wanted my children to have a secure, happy home. So, like I said, I compromised." Rachel sighed.

"And there's been nobody else for you, no new partner?"

"Nobody. I'm not looking. I'm done with all of that."

"Sorry," I said. "I shouldn't have asked. I really need to stop doing this. Forcing you to dredge up the past—"

"It's okay. If we're going to be friends we need to share these things."

Then she surprised me by laughing. She stepped in front of me, pushed me gently on the chest and then raised her hand. "But now it's your turn. I've shared, now you. What brought your marriage to an end and have you had any other significant others since?"

This was it. "Fair enough," I said. And, as we continued on

our walk, I told Rachel everything.

"Like you and your ex, Ailsa and I met and married young. We met at police college, in our early twenties, love at first sight. Nowadays, we'd probably have lived together for a short time and then moved on once we'd grown up a bit. But within a year we had Maddie. I've no regrets there. For a few years we were happy enough. Ailsa stayed at home with Maddie until she started school. I was the breadwinner. Then Ailsa relaunched her police career and she did well, better than me."

"Was that a problem for you?"

"Ailsa reckons it was, but I don't think so."

"So, what was the problem?"

"I was unfaithful and then I left."

"Ah."

"Yes, ah." I was well aware this conversation could be a turning point in our fledgling friendship. Despite what she'd said about sharing, Rachel might well now see me as someone who couldn't be trusted, as someone like her ex-husband.

After a short silence, she said, "Why were you unfaithful?"

"I could make lots of excuses. Ailsa seemed to me to be totally caught up in Maddie and her career. She seemed not to need me. I missed being the main thing in her life. I wanted attention, got bored, wanted something new, wanted to be wanted. I don't know. It all sounds pathetic now. Anyway I met someone, someone who made it clear she wanted me and I went for the thrill and excitement on offer. Even more pathetic, I threw away my marriage on a whim, on a relationship that was never going to last. Ailsa was devastated. What I'd taken for loss of interest on her part was simply the fatigue of a hard-working wife and mother. A loving wife who thought her husband would understand her exhaustion, pull his weight and appreciate her a bit more. Instead she got me, a self-centred bastard. And there you have it."

"Right," Rachel said. Her head was down.

"Things worked out for Ailsa. She met someone else, remarried, happily. She's a chief superintendent now, could well end up chief constable."

"It sounds like you're proud of her,"

"I suppose I am. We're good friends again. It's all quite amicable nowadays."

"And you? Have you met anyone else?"

"I've had a few relationships since the divorce, but none of them were ever likely to last. They were fun, some of them, but nothing deep and meaningful."

"And now?"

"Now, yes, there's someone. That is I've been seeing someone, Bridget's her name. It's a bit... things are a bit difficult between us at the moment. She's not happy about me getting the house up here."

"She's not keen on Skye? Or on you being away?"

"Both. She's a city person and she's not up for a long distance relationship, even if it's just for relatively short spells."

"And you won't give up Skye?"

"Definitely not."

We'd arrived back at Rachel's. We stopped at the gate. Bonnie sat looking up at us both. I felt apprehensive, almost certain Rachel would say something final. Something that would politely, but firmly, let me know she didn't want to proceed with our friendship. Something that would indicate that the last thing she needed in her life, even on a platonic basis, was someone as fickle and unreliable as I was. And I couldn't blame her.

But all she said was, "I appreciate your honesty, Jack, and I hope things work out between you and Bridget."

Chapter Fourteen

Rachel

I'd been surprised when Jack suggested going to the inn. I wouldn't have blamed him if my emotional outburst during the walk had put him right off. But I was glad it hadn't.

I'd really enjoyed our evening together and I was touched that he asked about my mother. Of course I cringed at how much I'd gone on about her. Even someone as nice as Jack would have had difficulty not switching off. I was even more surprised that he later agreed to the late night walk with me and Bonnie. The poor guy then had to listen to me off-loading all that stuff about Peter.

Jack seemed to have a knack of getting me to talk. With Peter I'd learned to keep my own counsel. Even with Jonathan or Morag I was always a bit guarded. Opening up during my sessions with Elsa had been incredibly difficult. But Jack had breached my defences. He was so easy to talk to, a very good listener, and I'd found that liberating.

I was also touched by his honesty when speaking about the breakdown of his marriage, and by his willingness to accept responsibility for it, and I appreciated his openness in telling me about his subsequent relationships.

He was so straightforward that I guessed he'd probably not want to spend too much time with someone like me, someone who was such an emotional mess. But at least I hadn't told him the feelings I'd had when he held me in his arms. I was still a bit mystified where all that had come from. It was presumably an emotional backlash from all the crying and an over-reaction to Jack's kindness. After all he was the first man in a very long time that I'd got that close to.

I so wanted us to remain friends, but was so wary of scaring him off that I decided to suppress any sexual feelings. I was done with all that, of course I was, hadn't had such thoughts in years, was never going to be vulnerable in that way again. And apart from anything else, Jack was in a relationship.

No, I'd decided. Jack and I could be good friends. That was what I wanted and, after all the recent emotional intimacy, it would be best that I give him some space.

That's what I told myself.

Anyway, I'd plenty to occupy me in the remaining fortnight before lambing was due to start. The days were lengthening and I took full advantage of the extra daylight as I pressed on with my drawings.

In the evenings, I worked on a long overdue clean-up and clear-out of the house. This had been another of Elsa's suggestions. When I'd admitted to her that my home was cluttered and crammed with stuff that I hadn't even begun to sort through, she helped me see that organising my physical environment could help me cleanse my emotional state.

Tidiness had never been one of my strengths, but I did have to admit that the house had gone past mere untidiness. The only room that had been touched in recent years was my father's old office, the little room at the back of the ground floor that was now my work room.

My mother hadn't got rid of any of my father's belongings and there was still stuff of hers that I needed to sort through. There were also all sorts of furniture and household paraphernalia long past its best. And then there were all the boxes of stuff I'd brought from Edinburgh after I'd split from Peter. I'd left them piled up at one end of my work room and the rest were in Jonathan's old bedroom. I hadn't touched them since I'd brought them in from the car almost five years before.

So, each evening, I put on some music, poured myself a glass of wine and then tackled a cupboard or a shelf or a chest of drawers. I boxed and bagged items for the charity shop and for the tip, and set aside stuff I wanted to keep. I pulled the furniture away from the walls and hoovered behind and underneath. I washed windows and changed curtains. I dusted and I polished. It took a couple of weeks, but I hardly recognised the house at the end of it.

The only boxes I didn't tackle during that time were the ones containing Finlay's belongings. I wasn't ready for that.

It was Good Friday, at the end of my manic two weeks, when I decided to move into my parents' former bedroom. I'd been using my childhood bedroom up until now, but my parents' room was bigger. It took up half of the upper storey. It was a light and airy room with a window at the front that looked out over the loch and a window at the back that caught the breeze coming down from Ben Halla.

That evening, while I was putting away my clothes in my new bedroom, Morag came round. I heard her calling me from the foot of the stairs.

"Pour yourself a glass of wine and come up," I shouted.

"My word, someone's been busy," she said when she joined me in my new bedroom. "I thought I'd come into the wrong house. Everything's so tidy downstairs, and now this."

"Yeah, once I got started, I couldn't stop." I continued hanging things in the wardrobe as I spoke. "It was high time for a clear out and it's been therapeutic."

"I'll bet it has," Morag said. "Good idea moving in here." She plonked herself down on the bed and stroked the bedcover. "More room?" She raised her eyebrows, gave me a meaningful look. I just shook my head and began to fill up the drawers in the dressing table. "*Slàinte*, by the way, and Happy Easter," she said, raising her glass and taking a sip. "What have you done with that big tallboy thing that was in here?"

"I dragged it through to the other bedroom. I want to get rid of it but I'll need help to get it down the stairs."

"I could lend you Alasdair, but couldn't you get Jack to help you?" There was another look, one that indicated this was a far from innocent question.

I laughed. "You have no shame. I know what you're trying to get out of me, and the answer's no."

"I don't know what you mean," she said, trying to look puzzled. But her slightly embarrassed giggle gave her away.

"Yeah, right," I said, shaking my head.

"It's just you and Jack seemed to be getting very friendly. There was dinner and then your day out. I thought you'd be comfortable asking him to help with the manly chores by now."

"I'm sorry, 'manly chores'? Have we slipped back to the fifties?"

"No, but it's one of the things we have men for, the heavy work. And now you have a man—"

"Stop! Stop right there. I do *not* have a man. As you clearly already know, Jack and I have spent some time together socially, and I hope we'll establish a good friendship. But that's it. I won't be asking him to help out with the household chores. I haven't seen him for almost a fortnight, at least not to speak to." I decided against telling Morag that Jack was in a relationship. It felt like I would be betraying a confidence.

Morag raised her hands in submission. "Okay, okay, whatever you say. But I did mention to him last weekend, when he was moving into the caravan, that I was surprised you weren't lending a hand."

"What? Oh, Morag, you didn't!"

She laughed. "I did. But don't worry, he was as pathetic as you. He said there was no reason why you should, sounded quite cross actually. I think I hit a nerve and that he secretly hoped you would be there."

"God, you're impossible," I said, but I couldn't help smiling. "It's more likely to have been your feeble and unsubtle attempts to read more into our friendship than actually exists that got him cross." I picked up my empty glass. "I need another drink. Come on, let's go downstairs."

I refilled my glass and joined Morag on the sofa in the living-room. "So, have you got folk in the cottage, now that Jack's moved out?"

"Yes, from tomorrow. It's booked for a week. The bookings in general are looking pretty good for the whole season. I do feel bad about Jack having to move out, but he was very understanding about it. He says he's comfortable enough in the caravan."

"I suppose it suits him to be close to his house and there's nowhere else he could stay locally."

"Yeah, and at least the van's got electricity and a loo and running water. It's not too spartan. I told him he can have a bath at ours any time he wants, but he says it won't be long before he has a functioning shower at his place."

"Oh, right. He must be making good progress then."

"Alasdair's very impressed with how it's looking. He's been lending a hand when he can." Morag looked around the room. "And I must say I'm impressed with your progress too. This room's looking great."

"It is, isn't it? It's amazing what a bit of de-cluttering can do."

"But it's not just that. It's the throws and the cushions, and these lamps. What a difference!"

"They all came from the house in Edinburgh. They've been in boxes for the last few years."

"A bit of paint and some new furniture and you'll have transformed the place."

"We'll see. It's not long now till I go away. After that I don't know what I'll do. I might not even stay here."

"Oh, so you're still seriously considering moving away?"

"I don't know. I don't know what I want or where I should be. I feel like—displaced, forced out of my old life."

"But this is your home. Skye is your home. It's where you came back to." Morag looked so sad, I was touched.

"Don't worry. We'll always be friends, no matter what, no matter where I end up. I'd never have got through the last few years without you. You've been great, you and Alasdair."

Morag managed a wan smile. "Yes, well, I'll always be here for you. Don't you ever forget that, no matter where you are."

"Of course I won't."

"I hope not," Morag said. "So, have you got any plans for the Easter weekend?"

"Nothing special. I need to keep working on the pictures for the book and lambing is getting close. So no, it'll be business as usual. If it's nice on Sunday I might take time out for a walk. What about you?"

"I'll go to church as usual, and I'll do us a nice Sunday roast, but other than that nothing special. You're very welcome to join us."

"That's very kind of you but I won't, thanks. Like I said, I've got a lot to do."

"I thought you might say that," Morag said, smiling. "I invited Jack too, but he's gone down to his daughter's for Easter. He left this morning. He was really looking forward to seeing his granddaughter."

"That's nice," I said. I took a gulp of wine and tried to ignore the pinch of disappointment. Disappointment that, if I did get out for that walk, there'd be no chance of Jack joining me.

Chapter Fifteen

In the end, I didn't get my walk on Easter Sunday. The weather turned cold over the weekend. A sharp north wind brought sleety showers and the occasional flurry of snow. Of course I had to go outdoors to check the sheep, but the rest of the time I was content to stay inside.

By Easter Monday I'd finished sorting out the house. After breakfast, I wandered from room to room and felt very satisfied with the lighter atmosphere throughout the place.

I'd already spent a couple of nights in my new bedroom. It was good to be in a double bed again, even if it was on my own. The bed itself was hardly used. My mother had bought it just before she became too ill to continue sleeping upstairs. I'd bought a new duvet cover from the Skye Batik shop in Portree. Its blue and white tie-dye pattern made a dramatic splash in the white-walled, wooden-floored room. I'd also been to the Halladale sheepskin shop and bought a big rug, made from the fleeces of Jacob sheep. This now lay at the side of the bed. And, as the house wasn't overlooked, I'd decided to dispense with my mother's heavy curtains, preferring instead to have only a white voile panel hanging at each of the two windows. The finishing touch was a blue ceramic jug filled with daffodils from the garden.

My old room was now set up as a spare bedroom. I'd found a patchwork bedspread in the linen cupboard. It had been made by my mother just after she got married. It was a bit worn in places but its colours were still bright. It suited the room and its single bed perfectly. I also unearthed some of my childhood books from a box in the loft. They included my Winnie-the-Pooh collection, as well a beautifully illustrated book of fairy-tales that I'd been given on my sixth birthday. I placed them on the bookshelves my father had put up many years before.

I also came across Jonathan's old Beano annuals and put them on the shelves in his former bedroom. I'd even got new bedding and linen for his old bed. Although I doubted I'd need one spare room, let alone two, it looked much cheerier to have both rooms made up.

I was pleased with the living-room as well. It had always been very much my mother's room; it had been functional, practical and very old-fashioned. But now I'd been able to put a bit of me into it.

I smiled to myself when I remembered Jack's comments on the furniture. He'd been right of course. I hadn't replaced the armchairs, but I'd unearthed some cushions from one of my boxes. I'd made the covers years before. They were bright green cotton with little mirrors and beads sewn into the fabric. Along with a pair of green and white striped throws they made the chairs look better, even if the comfort wasn't greatly improved. The sofa, though ancient, was at least comfortable, and it felt lovely and luxurious with my jade cashmere blanket draped along the back of it.

Having completed my tour of inspection, I spent the rest of the morning getting the lambing pens set up in the barn, spread-ing straw and checking the shelves for feeding bottles, old towels and all the other bits and pieces that might be needed. Most of the ewes would probably give birth without any problems, but it paid to be ready for any that might need extra help.

After lunch I fetched my dad's beautiful old wooden crook with its softly worn, ram's horn handle, and Bonnie and I set about gathering the thirty two mums-to-be from the common grazing and bringing them into the field by the barn.

It was a cold and grey afternoon. Squalls of icy rain blew in over the loch and I was glad of my warm jacket.

Bonnie and I worked well together. She responded instantly to my whistled and verbal commands as we guided the ewes down the hill and over the track to the field. The sheep trail from the hill-grazing led down onto a gravel path at the side of Morag's place. As we came out onto the road, I heard a car approaching from the left. I glanced at the slowing vehicle and turned to raise my hand in thanks and apology. Jack waved back.

Once I'd finished seeing to the sheep I headed home. But after I'd given Bonnie some biscuits and she'd settled in her basket by the Aga, I found myself pulling on my wellies and jacket again and striding up Morag's drive towards the caravan.

I caught a glimpse of a face at one of the windows as I got close, and then the caravan door opened.

"Hello," Jack said, smiling down at me as I stood at the step. "You were spotted approaching."

"Hello," I replied. "I just wanted—"

"Is it the sheep lady, Grandpa?" A little girl appeared at Jack's side.

"Yes, it is," Jack said. "Would the sheep lady like to come in? It's marginally warmer in here than out there."

"I won't stay long," I said, stepping inside.

"Rachel, this is Poppy," Jack said, closing the door behind me.

"It's lovely to meet you, Poppy," I said. I smiled at the pretty, golden-haired child. She caught hold of Jack's hand and pressed her face into his arm.

"Say hello to Rachel," Jack said, looking down at his granddaughter.

She peeped at me and gave me a shy smile, then whispered hallo.

Jack laughed. "You go back to your picture, Poppy" he said. We both watched her as she slid along the bench seat at the little Formica-topped dining table and resumed her drawing. Jack turned to me. "She's not always this shy or quiet."

"I'm sure she's not. I'm sorry to have disturbed you both. I just came to say hi and welcome back and to see if you were okay here in the van."

"That's nice of you. I'll be fine here." He glanced at Poppy and then lowered his voice. "I hadn't planned on Poppy coming to stay but she's on holiday from school and Maddie's been advised to get complete rest. Her blood pressure is way up again. If they can't get it down they'll hospitalise her. And with my son-in-law being a police officer, it's difficult for him to get time off at short notice. So I said I'd have the wee one for a while. We're going to go to a B&B in Portree. I don't mind roughing it here, but it's not really suitable for us to share. We only came to the caravan so I could get some clothes."

"Oh, right, I see." Although I was disappointed that Jack was leaving again, I did understand. The caravan wasn't exactly cosy and it was showing its age. Even the shearers, for whom it had originally been purchased, had preferred to stay in their camper vans during their most recent stints. "I'll not keep you. As I said, I just wanted to say hello."

As I turned to go, Poppy said, "Grandpa, I'm cold and I'm really hungry." She looked quite miserable.

"I know, sweetheart. I'm sorry. We'll be on our way soon. Come here." Jack held out his arms to her. She clambered down from the table and went to him. He picked her up and turned to me. "She wasn't very hungry when we stopped for lunch, so it's not surprising she's hungry now." He looked at his granddaughter and kissed her cheek. "Oh, you are cold! We better get on our way." Poppy leant her head on his shoulder.

"It'll be another forty minutes before you're in Portree, even if you leave now," I said. "Look, why don't you come over to my house. I'll make you both a hot drink and you can have something to eat and get warmed up."

Jack hesitated, glanced at his watch and then looked at me. "It's very kind and very tempting—"

"So, give in to temptation," I said, smiling at him.

He smiled back and nudged Poppy's head with his shoulder. "What do you say, Poppy? Would you like to go to Rachel's house for something to eat?"

Poppy raised her head and looked at him. She nodded.

"Good," I said. "I'll go on ahead. Come over when you're ready."

The heat from the Aga meant the kitchen was wonderfully warm. Bonnie opened one eye when I came in and she did a feeble stretch before settling back into her stupor. I went through to the living-room and lit the fire that was ready in the grate. I also flicked on the central-heating for the rest of the house. Back in the kitchen, I began to prepare some afternoon tea. I put the kettle on the hotplate and dropped a couple of slices of bread in the toaster. I boiled some milk and made a jug of hot chocolate. Fortunately, I had done some baking a few days before and still had some marmalade cake left so I put that on the table along with plates, mugs, butter and jam. Jack and Poppy arrived as I spread butter on the toast. Jack knocked on the porch door and I shouted to him to come in.

Bonnie got out of her basket for Jack. She yelped with excitement, her tail wagging wildly. Poppy hid behind Jack as the two of them stood in the doorway.

"Sit, Bonnie," I said. Bonnie did as she was told, but didn't take her eyes off Jack. Her tail swept the floor. "Don't worry, Poppy," I said. "Bonnie likes your Grandpa and she gets very excited when she sees him. She won't hurt you."

Jack scooped Poppy up in his arms and bent to pat Bonnie's head. "Bonnie's a good dog," he said. "Would you like to pat her?" Poppy shook her head. "Maybe later," he said, smiling and turning to me. "It's lovely and warm in here."

"Please sit down, both of you. Help yourselves to toast. I buttered it while it was warm and there's more about to pop."

"Wow, this looks so good!" Jack said. He put Poppy down on one of the chairs and then sat next to her.

"There's tea in the pot and hot chocolate in the jug." I sat at the end of the table and buttered the rest of the toast. I handed Jack a little Peter Rabbit mug. "For Poppy," I said. "Would you like some hot chocolate?" I asked, smiling at the little girl.

She shook her head. "I don't know."

"I don't think she's ever had it before," Jack said. "Give it a try, Popps. It's yummy." He poured a small amount into the mug and took a sip. "Mmm," he said, handing it to her. "Delicious and it's not too hot."

She took a sip.

"Well?" he asked. She nodded her head. Jack filled up the mug. "It's a nice cup too. You like Peter Rabbit, don't you?" Poppy nodded again.

Jack watched Poppy tucking into the toast and sipping her drink then he turned to me. "Thank you, it's just what she needed."

He looked strained and exhausted. I wanted to reach over, put my hand on his, soothe him in some way, but I knew I mustn't.

"It's a pleasure," I said. "Really it is. It's a long time since there was a child in this house—and it's good to see you again too."

He looked at me. I was unsure what the expression that crossed his face meant. At first he looked happy, as if he was about to say something. Then there was doubt, maybe even sadness.

But then he smiled and poured himself a mug of hot chocolate. "I've not had this for years." He took a couple of sips. "I'd forgotten how much I liked it."

"Good," I said. "Help yourself to some cake to go with it."

I chatted to Poppy as we ate. She told me about school and about her friend Amy. I looked over at Jack a couple of times as Poppy and I talked. He seemed slightly less strained and was tucking into a second slice of cake. It was then that I had the idea. I didn't give myself time to think about it. It would just be one friend helping out another.

"I don't know how you'll feel about this, but you could stay here—while Poppy's with you."

As before, he looked pleased at first, then doubtful. "That's very kind of you but I couldn't impose—"

"You wouldn't be imposing. I've been having a bit of a tidy up and clear out. There's now two proper spare rooms upstairs. It would be simpler for you here, with Poppy to look after, rather than in a B&B. And it would easier for you to keep an eye on things at your place. And besides, I'd enjoy the company."

"I don't know, Rachel. Don't get me wrong, it's tempting. I didn't really think things through before I suggested bringing Poppy back. I was just keen to give Maddie the rest she needs. But, you're right, there are a couple of things I have to see to at the house..."

"Look, you're obviously tired, too tired to be driving back into Portree and looking for somewhere to stay. At least stay tonight and if you're still unsure, you could move on in the morning. Come and relax in the living-room. I've got a fire going in there. I'll make us all some supper later and then you can get an early night."

Jack smiled. I could see him wavering. "What do you think, Poppy? Would you like to stay here at Rachel's tonight?"

Poppy looked at me and then at her grandfather. "Yes," she said, before turning back to me. "Can I see my room?"

I laughed. "Of course you can. Come on. I'll show you." I stood up and held out my hand to her. She took it and slid off her chair.

"Right, that's that decided then!" Jack smiled at us both. "I'll go and get our bags in from the car."

Chapter Sixteen

Jack

As I walked out to the car to fetch our bags, I acknowledged to myself that I wasn't at all sure about staying at Rachel's. On the one hand I was really pleased that she felt able to make the offer. After all it was a sign of trust and friendship. But I knew I'd have to be careful not to get too relaxed. I knew I mustn't overstep. I couldn't be more than a friend to her, no matter how much I wanted to. I wouldn't risk hurting her, not like I'd hurt Bridget.

I'd made a point of seeing Bridget when I was in Edinburgh. She'd been pleased to hear from me and clearly still hoped that I'd give up on Skye. I tried to tell her how I felt—again. I tried to make it clear I'd be splitting my time between Halladale and the capital. But she hadn't been receptive. She'd accused me again of selfishness and betrayal. I didn't defend myself as I was guilty on both counts. The meeting hadn't ended well. I'd already received texts from her and there'd been one missed call while I was driving north. I knew there'd be a message and I knew I'd have to listen to it. I thumped the boot lid down. But not now. I couldn't listen to Bridget now. I snatched up the bags and returned to the house.

I went straight up the stairs and followed the sound of Rachel's voice to the doorway of a small bedroom at the back of the house. I stopped on the threshold and my breath caught as I looked at the scene before me.

Rachel and Poppy were sitting side-by-side on the brightly-covered bed, backlit by the soft glow of a little bedside lamp. Rachel was reading to Poppy, a Winnie-the-Pooh story. They were both engrossed and didn't notice me. Poppy was sucking her thumb and leaning against Rachel.

I first told my little granddaughter I loved her when she was a few hours old and my son-in-law handed her to me in the maternity ward of Edinburgh's Royal Infirmary. I hadn't been prepared for the onrush of emotion her arrival produced in me, neither its immediacy nor its intensity. It felt stronger even than the feelings I'd experienced when Maddie was born, perhaps because I didn't feel the same weight of responsibility that goes with becoming a parent. My love for Poppy was unconditional, uncomplicated and unbounded. Seeing her sitting there on the bed was simply one of those moments of realisation of what she meant to me.

Seeing Rachel sitting on the bed on that late April afternoon also induced strong feelings, but they were far from uncomplicated.

I tapped on the open door. "Your bag, ma'am," I said, giving a small bow.

Poppy giggled. "Thank you, Baxter," she said.

Rachel laughed at Poppy's reply.

"It's a running joke between Poppy and me. She's always known that I'm her devoted servant. I just decided to formalise the arrangement by teaching her the correct form of address."

"Right," Rachel said.

"I know, I've created a monster!" I laughed.

"Grandpa, Rachel was reading me a story. It's really good, about a bear and his friends," Poppy said.

"Yes, I saw. You looked like you were enjoying it."

"Maybe Grandpa can finish reading it to you at bedtime," Rachel said, looking from Poppy to me.

I nodded.

Rachel handed the book to Poppy. "Why don't you have a

look through the rest of it while I show your Grandpa his bedroom."

"Okay." Poppy sat back against the pillows and was immediately engrossed.

Rachel showed me to the bedroom at the other end of the landing. It was at the front of the house and about the same size as the one Poppy had. There was an incredible panoramic view from the window, and Rachel was telling me about the various peaks and ridges we could see, when my phone rang. I took it from my pocket. My heart sank. The display showed it was Bridget. I selected voicemail and shoved the phone back in my pocket.

"Sorry," I said.

Rachel shrugged. "You could have taken it."

"It was nothing important." I hoped she couldn't detect my annoyance or my guilt.

She turned away from the window. "This was my brother's room," she said. "And Poppy has my old room."

I put my bag on the bed. "This is really good of you. Thank you."

"It's a pleasure." She glanced at her watch. "I need to go and check on the sheep now, but please, you and Poppy, take your time and get settled in. The bathroom's next door and there are towels in the cupboard in the hall. I shouldn't be very long."

After Rachel left, I went back through to Poppy. She was still sitting on the bed looking at the book. And just for a moment, before she noticed I was there, I enjoyed watching her studious little face. When she did look up from the book she said, "Hello, Grandpa, you look happy. What are you thinking about?"

"You, sweetheart, I was thinking about you and what a lucky Grandpa I am."

She put down the book and held out her arms. "Cuddle," she said.

I bundled her up in my arms and kissed her blond curls. She looked up at me and then gave an enormous yawn. I laughed.

"Somebody's tired. How about a bath and then a bit of supper and bed?"

She nodded.

I carried Poppy downstairs after her bath. In the kitchen, the tea things had all been tidied away and there was a pot of soup simmering on the Aga. I set Poppy down at the table. Her little face was flushed with the heat from the bath and her eyes were heavy. She sat there in her fleecy, red dressing-gown and matching slippers, her legs dangling and her head resting on her hands. She watched me as I called Maddie on my mobile.

I wanted to let my daughter know where we were staying and to let Poppy say goodnight to her mother.

"So you're at Rachel's. That'll be your 'just good friend' Rachel, will it?" I could hear the smile in Maddie's voice.

"Maddie—"

"I'm just teasing. It's very kind of her. I must admit it sounds like a much more comfortable option than the caravan and easier than a B&B. Say thank you to her from me."

"I will."

"And thanks to you too, Dad. I really appreciate this. So does Brian. Like he said he knows you understand how difficult it would have been for him to get time off."

"No need to thank me. Just make sure you do as the doctor said and get that bed rest."

"I will. But God, it's boring, and I'm already missing Poppy. Put her on, please."

As I handed the phone to Poppy, the kitchen door opened and Rachel and Bonnie came in from the porch.

"Everything okay?" I said, patting Bonnie who'd immediately came up to me wagging her tail.

"Yes, I was just checking the ewes. I don't think it'll be long now till lambing starts. That's why I moved them into the field, to keep them close by and near the barn." She washed her hands at the sink as she spoke.

"I was impressed this afternoon, watching you and Bonnie

guiding the sheep down."

"You were watching? I thought you'd just arrived when I got down to the road."

"Ah, no, Poppy caught sight of you as we drove along the track. She insisted we stop to watch the lady and the dog chasing the sheep." Rachel raised her eyebrows. "Don't worry, I explained about sheepdogs. And, like I say, I was fascinated watching you at work."

"Right. I didn't realise I was engaged in anything fascinating. I was brought up with it. My dad showed me how it's done." She reached for a towel. "But without a good dog, it wouldn't work. Bonnie's one of the best."

"I'll bet she is," I said, stroking the dog's back. I didn't add how I'd been so pleased to see Rachel that I could have watched her all afternoon.

Poppy appeared at my side as I spoke. She handed me my phone. "Mummy said to say goodnight to you—and Rachel."

"How is Mummy?" Rachel smiled at Poppy.

"She said she's fine and she's going to bed early." Poppy looked at Bonnie all the time she was speaking.

"Would you like to stroke Bonnie?" Rachel asked.

Poppy nodded.

Rachel held out her hand to her. Poppy took it. Rachel crouched beside Poppy and called Bonnie over to them. She told the dog to sit. "Bonnie, this is Poppy," she said. Rachel stroked the dog's head with her free hand. "Now you," she said to Poppy. Poppy solemnly did exactly what Rachel had done. "Try scratching behind her ears," said Rachel. Poppy tried it. Bonnie wagged her tail.

"Does she like it?" Poppy whispered, still holding onto Rachel.

I was transfixed at the sight of my granddaughter's little hand held in Rachel's. It looked—right.

"She likes it very much," Rachel said. "That's why she's wagging her tail."

Poppy nodded and then turned and smiled at Rachel. Rachel smiled back and squeezed Poppy's hand.

Poppy turned to me. "Look, Grandpa, Bonnie likes me."

"Indeed she does," I said.

Poppy let go of Rachel's hand and began to stroke Bonnie's back. "It's okay," she said to Rachel. "We're friends now." Then she gave a big yawn.

Rachel laughed and stood up. "Somebody needs their bed," she said, looking at me.

"I was going to get her a bedtime snack if that's okay," I said.

"Of course."

While Poppy had some milk and biscuits, Rachel went to put more coal on the living-room fire. When she came back to the kitchen, she filled a hot water bottle and handed it to Poppy.

"A pink sheep," Poppy said, cuddling the bottle in its fleecy cover, a cover which did indeed look like a sheep. "It's lovely," she said.

"I'm glad you like it," Rachel said. "The cover used to belong to my girl, to my Sophie, and so did the Peter Rabbit cup."

"Doesn't she want her sheep and her cup?" Poppy asked.

"She's grown up now. She lives in her own house and she didn't take all her stuff with her."

"Does she use the cup when she comes to see you?"

"I don't see that much of her. She lives far away. But if she came, yes, she might use her cup."

Poppy nodded.

"Right, young lady," I said. "Time for bed. Say goodnight to Rachel."

Poppy stood up and went to Rachel. She put her arms round Rachel's waist. "Goodnight Rachel," she said.

Rachel was obviously surprised by the fierce hug and staggered slightly. She gave a little laugh and bent down to Poppy. Poppy reached up and kissed Rachel on the cheek. "I like you," she said.

Rachel smiled and stroked Poppy's hair. "And I like you too," she said, kissing Poppy back. "Sleep well."

I took Poppy's hand and wished I could be as open about my feelings towards Rachel.

Chapter Seventeen

When I returned to the kitchen, Rachel was setting the table. The mouth-watering smell of mushroom soup made my stomach rumble.

"How's Poppy?" Rachel asked.

"Very tired. She fell asleep before I'd even read half a page of Winnie the Pooh."

Rachel smiled. "Hungry?"

"I am. I shouldn't be, but I am." And then my phone rang again. Bridget. I jabbed the off button and forced a smile as Rachel turned to me. She didn't comment on the call and I was grateful for her lack of curiosity.

"Have a seat." She ladled thick, creamy soup into two bowls.

A few moments later we were seated opposite each other. Rachel sliced the bread. Once more I watched her slender hands.

"Help yourself," she said.

I took a slice and as I bit into it I smiled. She was watching me. "Ah, chef's speciality, cheese and chilli," I said. She grinned. I took a sip of soup. The mushroom flavour was intense, the feel velvety. Still she watched me. "Wow!" I said.

The grin never left her face.

We ate in easy silence. I hadn't imagined that my evening would be anything like this when I'd set out in the morning. I could have stayed there, in Rachel's warm, aroma-filled kitchen, eating supper opposite this lovely, quiet, unassuming woman, forever.

When we'd finished our soup, Rachel took a dish out of the

Aga and brought it to the table. "Apple crumble," she said. "And …" She went to the freezer. "Ice cream. Sorry there's no custard. I wasn't expecting company. Fortunately I had the crumble already made."

"No custard," I said. "What sort of establishment is this?"

"I know. I'll lose my four-star rating if you report me." She smiled at me, an unguarded, open smile, and for a moment I was lost.

"Seriously, Rachel," I said, "It's so good of you to take us in. I didn't expect it and I certainly don't expect you to be cooking and cleaning up after us."

"I'm doing it because I want to. It's nice to have company." Her voice faltered slightly but she quickly recovered. "So you won't be wanting any pudding then—since there's no custard."

"Well, it won't be perfect but I'll make do with the ice cream accompaniment."

Rachel laughed and served us both a generous helping. Again we ate in silence. Once more I savoured the easy atmosphere. I also savoured the dessert—the apples, the cinnamon—the sweet, crunchy crumble.

"That was gorgeous, thank you," I said, dropping my spoon into the bowl when I finished.

"You know, when I first made the crumble, I couldn't be bothered eating it. That's why I froze it. I needed someone to share it with. Eating on your own is no fun."

I insisted that Rachel go through and have a seat while I cleared up and made us coffee. When I joined her in the living-room, she was sitting at the end of the sofa, legs tucked up, staring into the fire. The transformation in the look of the room was amazing but I tried not to make my surprise too obvious. I didn't want to repeat any of my clumsy remarks about the furniture. So when I commented on the difference, I did my best to keep my tone casual.

But she saw through me. "I'm sorry I haven't replaced the uncomfortable chairs," she said, smiling. "But I'm pleased with the changes."

I sat down beside her on the sofa and we sipped our coffee. Bonnie twitched in her sleep as she lay stretched out on the hearthrug. The clock ticked and the coals shifted. I couldn't remember the last time I'd felt this relaxed—probably the last time I'd been with Rachel. I could feel my eyes getting heavy and the next thing I felt was a hand on mine. I opened my eyes to find Rachel sitting very close. She had one hand on my coffee mug and the other on my wrist.

"Sorry," she said. "I tried not to wake you, but your cup was at a precarious angle. I thought I better take it away."

"God, I've done it again, fallen asleep in your company. Sorry."

She laughed. "At least this time you did the clearing up first. I'm obviously scintillating company."

"No, you're not. I mean, yes, you are—I mean..." My brain and my mouth seemed to have parted company.

"Okay, here, take your coffee. I think you need it." She handed me my mug but her other hand still rested on my wrist.

I took a gulp of coffee. "I meant you're relaxing company, easy to be with. I felt at home and I just drifted off. Sorry."

She squeezed my wrist. "Don't be. That was a lovely thing to say." She spoke quietly in her beautiful soft accent.

I could feel her breath on my face, smell the scent of her. The firelight gave sheen to her skin and her hair. I so wanted to put my arms around her. I so wanted—her. I struggled to remind myself why that was a bad idea. I looked into her eyes.

She was staring at me. She released her grip on my wrist and stroked the back of my hand with her thumb a couple of times. She gave a small sigh as she stood up. "I need to do a last check of the ewes. Like I said, I don't think it'll be long before lambing. Feel free to put the TV on or whatever."

"Thanks, but I think I'll just check on Poppy, then get an early night."

Rachel looked at me for a moment, frowning slightly. I wondered what she was thinking, but all she said was, "Okay, sleep well and I'll see you in the morning." Then she called to Bonnie and was gone.

Poppy was sound asleep, her thumb in her mouth, her teddy held close. I straightened the covers and stroked her hair. She didn't stir.

I slept soundly too. I heard nothing until Poppy came to wake me around seven. I told her that we should try to be quiet in case Rachel was still asleep. I gave her one of the old Beano books that I'd noticed on the shelf the night before and sent her back to bed with it while I had a quick shower.

The house was still very quiet when I went to Poppy's room to help her get dressed, not that she needed much help. We crept downstairs and into the kitchen. The central-heating had only just clicked on, but the Aga had kept the kitchen warm. Bonnie got out of her basket to greet us. Poppy was perfectly relaxed with her and even told her to be quiet and go back to her bed. Bonnie obeyed. I put the kettle on, got some toast on the go and found some cereal for Poppy. While she was eating, I went through to the living-room to put the TV on for her.

And there was Rachel asleep on the sofa. The room was cold. She was wearing blue pyjamas. Her jeans, sweater, socks and a mug of cold tea lay on the floor. I took the blanket that lay along the back of the sofa and covered her with it. She moved but didn't waken. I looked down at her for a few moments and it felt like my heart hurt—a mixture of want and need pressing in on it.

I went back to the kitchen and explained to Poppy why she wouldn't be watching TV. Then I nipped upstairs for my laptop and the DVDs Maddie had given me. Poppy chose '*Sleeping Beauty*' and I set it up for her on the kitchen table. She was soon engrossed.

I left her to it and took a tray of tea and toast through to the living-room. As I poured the tea, Rachel opened her eyes. I smiled at her. "Good morning," I said.

"Good morning," she replied as she sat up. "You?" she asked, indicating the blanket as she pulled it round her.

"Yes, I found you in here when Poppy and I came down."

"Where is Poppy?"

"Munching toast and watching *Sleeping Beauty* on my laptop in the kitchen." I handed her a mug of tea.

"Oh, lovely," she said, as she sipped it.

I sat at the other end of the sofa and put the plate of toast between us. "I hope you don't mind me helping myself."

"No, no, not at all," Rachel said, taking a piece of toast. "This is great—breakfast in bed—sort of. I can't remember the last time someone did that for me." Again there was that hint of a frown and again I wondered what she was thinking.

"So, how did you end up sleeping here?" I said.

"I didn't mean to. I was just going to drink my tea and then go back to bed, but I must have fallen asleep almost straight away." She licked marmalade off her fingers and I tried not to stare at this unselfconsciously provocative action.

She pushed the blanket aside and got up to pour herself more tea. Before she lifted the teapot, she swept her hair back and over one shoulder. As she did so her pyjama jacket rode up slightly. I made myself look away. When she leant forward to pour the tea and the jacket gaped at the top, I gave up trying not to look. She seemed unaware of the effect she was having on me.

"Would you like some?" she asked.

Oh, God, yes, I thought, in the split second before I realised it was tea she was offering. My mouth had gone dry. I felt light-headed. There was that heart pain again.

"Jack—tea?"

"Please," I managed to rasp. "So, did you spend any part of the night in bed?" I asked as she refilled my mug.

"Yes, I don't normally wear pyjamas under my clothes." She smiled at me and pushed her hair back again. "I went to bed for the first bit of the night. But I was fairly sure a couple of the pregnant ewes were about to start when I saw them last thing, so

I set the alarm for two a.m. and went out to check on them. Sure enough, one had had her lamb, but the other one was in labour and struggling. The lamb was stuck and the ewe was exhausted. I had to give her a bit of help, but we got there in the end. By the time I got mother and baby bedded down in the barn it was nearly four."

"No wonder you were tired."

"Yeah, and now I better get going. I should check on the sheep and then get on with my artwork." She drank the last of her tea and stood up. "What are you going to do today? Do you have to be at Dun Halla at all?"

"I'll probably look in tomorrow, but today I thought I might take Poppy to the toy museum and then maybe have a walk at the coral beach."

"Sounds good," she said. "Just let yourselves in when you get back. The door won't be locked even if I'm over at the field."

And it was good. My granddaughter and I had a fine day out. Poppy loved the toy museum and she bewitched me into buying her a kite at the museum shop. We had lunch at a little cafe across from the museum.

The pink sand and crystal clear water at the coral beach also proved to be a hit. We paddled in the icy water and, because it was low tide, we were able to walk out to the little island off the shore. Poppy thought this was very exciting and said she wished the tide would come in and cut us off. We investigated rockpools and watched the seabirds and the fishing boats in their pursuit of fish.

On the way home, I bought some groceries in the Dunvegan store. I'd been feeling guilty about eating Rachel's food and wanted to make a contribution. I was also somehow persuaded to buy Poppy's favourite biscuits.

We got back to Halladale in the late afternoon. Rachel wasn't in when we arrived. I made myself a coffee and poured Poppy a glass of milk.

We were still sitting at the kitchen table munching Poppy's biscuits, drinking and chatting, when Rachel and Bonnie got back.

"Hello, you two," Rachel said. Her smile was warm but she looked tired. "Did you have a nice day?"

"Yes, we saw all the toys and Grandpa got me a kite and we paddled and the water was freezing. And we walked to this place where if the sea came we wouldn't have been able to get back, and I wanted to stay there and get trapped, but Grandpa said he wasn't good at fishing and we'd have no food so we better come back." Poppy jumped down from the table as she finished speaking and ran to Bonnie. She flung her arms round the dog's neck. "Hello, Bonnie," she said. "Did you miss me?" Bonnie wagged her tail and seemed to enjoy the attention.

Rachel laughed and looked at me. "My goodness, sounds like you had a great time."

"We did," I said, standing up. "Coffee?"

"Oh yes, please, I'd love one." She turned to Poppy. "Would you like to give Bonnie some of her biscuits?"

Poppy nodded. Rachel took some dog treats from a box under the sink and handed them to Poppy. "Tell her to sit and then hold out your hand like this." Poppy copied Rachel exactly and fed Bonnie three biscuits.

"Look, Grandpa, I'm feeding Bonnie." Poppy was so delighted, I felt a lump in my throat.

"Yes, you are, sweetheart. Yes, you are." Poppy didn't seem to notice the catch in my voice, but Rachel glanced over at me. She came and took her coffee from me. She patted my arm as she did so, and her smile told me she understood.

"Can I watch TV?" Poppy asked.

"If it's all right with Rachel," I replied.

"Of course it is. Do you want me to switch it on for you?" Rachel said.

"No, thank you," Poppy said. I watched Grandpa doing it this morning before we went out. I know which button to press." She walked to the kitchen door. "Come on, Bonnie. Come and watch TV." Bonnie followed her out of the room.

"I think you've been dumped," Rachel said, smiling as she sat down at the table with her coffee. "Bonnie has found a new human to worship."

"I think you may well be right." I sat down at the other side of the table with my second cup of coffee. "How did you get on today?"

"I got a bit more done on the illustrations this morning and then this afternoon four more of the ewes gave birth—all singles. One had a bit of a hard time and it seems like she might reject her lamb. I've got her in the barn along with her baby and I'll need to keep an eye on them. The tricky birth from last night seems to be doing all right though." She yawned as she finished speaking.

"You must be exhausted," I said. "Will you have to go out again?"

"Yep, that's lambing I'm afraid—sleep deprivation and lots of checking of mums and babies, but it should all be over in a week or so."

"And the book, you've got to work on that too, at the same time?"

"Yes—the timing could have been better—but with Mum getting ill and—and everything—I got behind with the book and then my decision to go to Israel at the end of the month meant the deadline was even more pressing."

I'd been trying not to think about Rachel's imminent departure, about the fact that she was going to be away for the whole summer. I realised I'd been hoping she'd change her mind. "Ah, yes, Israel, not long now. Your brother must be looking forward to seeing you. How long has he lived there?"

"Jonathan emigrated nearly twenty years ago."

"You still think now's a good time to go, no second thoughts?"

"No second thoughts. It seems like the perfect time. Jonathan has asked me several times over the last twenty years, but..."

"But you didn't feel you could go until now?"

"No. When I was with Peter, he was dead against it. He thought Jonathan's decision to live there was ridiculous and that his embracing of all things Jewish was an affectation. He said there would be nothing for me there."

"And you felt you couldn't go without Peter's approval?"

"I know, it's pathetic, but it's—it's how it was. Peter was... still is... a high profile Q.C. Everyone in Edinburgh's legal community knows everyone else. His reputation and social standing were important to him. He expected me to behave in a way that wouldn't damage either of these."

"And you going to Israel would have damaged him?"

"Apparently. Edinburgh's a small city and the legal community is a close one. It would have raised eyebrows at the golf club, the church and the dinner tables of the capital's middle-classes if Peter Campbell's wife was discovered not only to be half-Jewish, but also crazy enough to want to visit Israel."

"Peter Campbell Q.C.?" I thought I knew the guy. His reputation as far as I was concerned was that of an arrogant tosser and womaniser.

"You know him?"

"Our paths crossed—when I was in the force. I had to give evidence at a couple of cases he was involved in."

"Oh, yes, of course—small city—like I said."

"So, why didn't you go when your marriage ended?"

"Several reasons. Most recently, after Finlay died, I simply didn't have the energy to make a decision, let alone travel anywhere. But the main reason was I'd come back to live on Skye. At the time it was where I wanted to be. Edinburgh had always felt alien. I never felt accepted—not for me, for who *I* was. I was always Peter's wife or the children's mother. Then after Dad died, it made sense that I stay on here in this house and look after Mum, but she was also against me going to Israel. For her it was complicated. I think she was secretly proud of Jonathan, of his conversion and of him taking Israeli citizenship but it also scared her. To her, being Jewish meant being vulnerable. And I think she feared that if I went, I wouldn't come back either. So I respected her wishes." Rachel sighed, looked away. "God, you must think I'm so weak, always doing as I was told, scared of disapproval, not wanting to upset anyone."

"No, not weak, not at all," I said.

Rachel didn't seem to notice I'd spoken. "But now there's nothing to stop me. It's something I need to do. It's something I'm ready to do. I'm hoping it will help me—I don't know—reposition myself."

"How do you mean?"

"I've lost my way. I don't know where I should be. I don't know where I belong anymore."

"You don't feel you belong here?"

"I don't know." She sighed again, tipped her head back for a moment then looked directly at me. "Do we—do people belong to a particular place? What does that mean? My mother was born in Germany but she didn't belong there. Edinburgh was only ever my home while the people I loved were there and I think now the same is true of Skye."

"But it's where you grew up. You still have friends here, memories, heritage..."

"But there's no solace in it. I'm no longer affected by it, stirred by it, embraced by it. I'm no longer rooted. Sorry, I know I'm rambling. It's you, you're doing it to me again. The only other person I speak to like this is my counsellor."

"Well, if it helps, I'm happy to listen, and I don't charge counselling fees." I smiled at her.

"It does help. I've bottled things up for far too long. I see now that being stoical is an over-rated virtue. And that's something my mother would definitely have disagreed with. She took stoicism to a whole new level."

"So, you think you might find some answers in Israel—about where you fit?"

"Maybe. A bit of distance from all this, from the past, it could help." She gave a grim little smile. "Jonathan thinks I should emigrate, make a fresh start—"

"Is that a possibility?" I asked, a bit more sharply than I meant to.

She frowned. "Why's that so surprising? It's like it is for you. You've decided to spend a lot of time here. You said that Skye could give you something that Edinburgh couldn't."

Yes—you, I wanted to say. Skye has *you*—never mind any other reasons I may have had. And now you might leave. But I didn't say it. Instead I said, "Yes, but it's not a full-time move and I haven't left the country. I imagine Israel is very different from Scotland."

"Undoubtedly. All the more reason for me to investigate its possibilities. For Jonathan, going to Israel was a kind of homecoming."

"How long will you be away?"

"Three months or so, I'll be back in August."

I forced a smile and pushed down the urge to beg her not to go. "I really hope you find what you're looking for, Rachel."

"Thanks," she said. There was a slight smile but she looked very tired.

I stood up. "I'm going to check on Poppy and you should go and put your feet up. It's pasta for dinner this evening and I'm cooking."

Now her smile was bigger. "That is so kind of you. I'm not going to argue. In fact I think I'll go for a bath." She put her hand on my arm as she passed me on her way out of the kitchen. "You're not going to a B&B then?"

"Doesn't look like it."

"Good, I'm glad. See you at dinner."

And it was at that moment I realised that this was the life I wanted—to have the opportunity to cook for Rachel while she soaked in the bath and then to share our evening meal, to share all the daily routines with her. I wanted that and more...

Chapter Eighteen

Rachel

Sitting round the kitchen table with Jack and Poppy that Tuesday evening, I realised I was experiencing a kind of contentment that I hadn't felt for a very long time. It had been lovely relaxing in the bath and hearing Jack and Poppy downstairs. And then to come down to the cosy kitchen where the table was set, ready for us to eat, and to be handed a glass of chilled white wine, told to sit down and that there was nothing for me to do, was blissful. I didn't let myself think about it too much. I didn't examine any underlying feelings about Jack. I didn't dare to.

Poppy came through soon after I'd come down with Bonnie at her heels.

"When does Bonnie get her dinner?" Poppy asked me.

"Not until after we've eaten," I said. "Tell her to go to her bed just now and then you and me will feed her later."

Poppy ordered Bonnie to her basket and told her when she could expect to be fed.

The roast tomato pasta Jack cooked for us was wonderfully warming and filling, true comfort food. Olive oil, pine nuts, cherry tomatoes, cheese and fresh basil all combined with pasta quills to make a colourful and aromatic dish. And the flavour…

"This is gorgeous," I said, after my first couple of forkfuls. "I'm impressed, and not just with the cooking. You must have shopped specially for these ingredients."

"Yes, there was some forward planning," Jack said, smiling. "Some of us men are capable of such feats you know."

"I do now." I picked up my glass of wine. "*Slàinte mhath*," I said.

"*Slàinte mhath*." Jack touched his glass to mine.

"What's slan jay va?" Poppy asked.

"It's a toast—you know—like when you say cheers to someone before you take a sip of your drink," Jack explained.

Poppy nodded.

"What I said was in Gaelic. That's a different language. It has different words from English, which is what you speak," I said.

Poppy thought for a moment. "Is it like Polish or, what is it again? Urdu—Simon and Sanjay, in my class, that's what they speak with their mummies and a special teacher sometimes comes to help them learn our words."

"Yes, exactly like that," I said, smiling at this bright wee girl. "People in Skye speak Gaelic and English and what I said to Grandpa was in Gaelic. It means 'good health' and when you say it to somebody, you're telling them you hope they stay well."

Poppy nodded again. She picked up her glass of orange juice and held it out towards me. I raised my wine glass.

"*Slàinte mhath*," I said.

"*Slàinte mhath*," Poppy repeated, as she chinked her glass against mine. "*Slàinte mhath*, Grandpa."

The contentment I felt that evening persisted throughout the remaining few days that Jack and Poppy stayed with me. I knew it would only be for a short time but it meant I savoured it all the more. I savoured the present, savoured being with Jack.

And in spite of being sleep-deprived and under pressure to finish the book illustrations, I relished the feeling of normality that my two guests brought to my life. It was lovely to have a child in the house and Poppy was such an adorable wee girl. I loved her inquisitiveness and her serious expression when she listened to the answers to her many questions. I envied the deep bond that Jack and his granddaughter shared. But I also enjoyed watching the interactions between them. He was so in tune with her needs and so proud of her. And she obviously adored him.

On the Wednesday morning, Jack's phone rang while the three of us were having breakfast. I'd noticed that he often didn't take calls, preferring to let them go to voicemail. On these occasions he would usually look annoyed, almost agitated and mumble something to me about it not being an important call. It crossed my mind that it might be Bridget trying to reach him, but I didn't ask. It was none of my business and I didn't want to know. However, that morning, he took the call. It turned out to be from Mac, the local joiner, to say that Jack's kitchen units and worktops would be delivered in the next hour or so.

I guessed he'd want to be at the house for the delivery and offered to look after Poppy.

"I can't ask you to do that. You had another broken night last night. You must want to rest."

"There won't be any rest until all the lambs have arrived. Besides, I'll need to check on last night's arrivals and I suspect I've got one that's going to need bottle feeding. Then there's the book."

"Exactly, you've got enough to do."

"Please, I'd like to have Poppy's company for the day. She can help me with the lambs. What do you say, Poppy?"

"Please, Grandpa. I'd like to help Rachel. She's tired and so she needs me to help and you don't. You had a good sleep. I heard you snoring."

I gave a little laugh at that.

"I wasn't, I didn't." He smiled at me and raised his hands in a gesture of denial.

"Yes, you were," said Poppy. "And I don't know how to help you with your kitchen, but I think I can look after lambs."

Jack laughed. "I've got no chance of winning this, have I?"

"No," said Poppy and I together.

So Jack made himself a packed lunch and went off to spend the day working on the house.

"I'll make this up to you," he said before he left. I'd walked out with him to collect Poppy's wellies from his car.

"There's nothing to make up for. I'm delighted to be able to borrow Poppy for a day. She's a very sweet girl."

"Yes, she is," he said, his voice tender. He put his hand on my arm then covered my hand with both of his. "Rachel, I…" He studied my face for a moment.

"What?" I said.

"Thank you," he said, and turned to walk down the drive. His phone rang as he strode away. His voice sounded impatient, almost angry as he answered it, but I couldn't hear what he said.

As Poppy and I cleared away the breakfast things, I noticed she was good at stacking the dishwasher.

"Grandpa showed me. He says most ladies make a mess of doing it because they don't have a—a system," she said.

"Oh he does, does he?" I smiled.

"That's what Mummy said when I told her!" Poppy said.

It was a bright day but there was a brisk wind blowing, pushing the high cloud southwards towards the Cuillin and whipping up the surface of the loch. Poppy and I put on our fleeces, scarves and wellies and walked over to the barn with Bonnie.

I gave Poppy a small bucket to carry and I put my own pail and a couple of sacks of feed in the wheelbarrow. As we made our way to the field I said, "The sheep are usually well-behaved, but they do have horns and sometimes they can be a bit grumpy. There's nothing to be scared of, but you must stay close to me."

"Okay," she said, her little face solemn.

We fed the ewes that weren't pregnant first. They were penned separately in the furthest corner of the main field. I explained to Poppy as I filled her bucket, that these sheep were too young to have babies. Then I showed her how to rattle the bucket to get the sheep to come to her and how and where to scatter the feed. She followed my instructions precisely. She also came to the burn with me and I filled our pails with water for the drinking trough. She was determined that I fill her pail right up and insisted she could carry it. And even although she needed both hands and staggered with the weight, she did indeed carry the full pail of water to the trough.

Next we went to the large pen and fed the pregnant ewes. There were ten of them. I checked them over.

"Why do you feel their tummies?" asked Poppy.

"I do it to see if I can feel the lamb inside and to see if it's about to be born. Do you want to feel?"

She nodded.

I took her hand in mine and guided it along the belly of one of the ewes.

"You might feel the lamb move," I said.

She frowned in concentration. "Is it like when I feel Mummy's tummy and I can feel my baby brother or sister kicking?" she asked.

"Yes, just like that," I said.

Her eyes widened. "I can feel it. I can feel the lamb. It's moving!"

"That's because it's just about ready to be born." I was fairly sure this one and several of the others would be in labour sometime in the next twenty four hours. I reckoned it was probably wise to get all the remaining pregnant ewes indoors. "We'll get Bonnie to help us take her, and all these others who are going to have their lambs soon, back to the barn."

Poppy stroked the ewe's back. "Why has it got brown spots? I thought sheep were white. And these ones over there are black."

"These are much more interesting than white sheep," I said. This one here, and the other ones with the spots, they're Jacob sheep. And the black ones are Hebrideans."

Poppy nodded, her brow furrowed again in concentration.

"Right," I said. "Let's go and feed the tups."

"What are tups?"

"They're the daddy sheep. We'll need to go out of this field and climb up that slope at the back. The boys have a field to themselves."

At the gate to the field I refilled Poppy's bucket with feed. I stood behind her, to steady her just in case the two rams were over exuberant when they came running up. "Right, give it a good shake," I said.

Jason, my four-horned Jacob tup was first to arrive with Hector the Hebridean following at a more sedate pace. Poppy scattered the food and we watched them tucking in. We patted their backs and I told her their names and ages. She worked out for herself which was the Jacob and which was the Hebridean.

Back in the main field, I whistled to Bonnie and we got started on moving the remaining mothers-to-be into the lambing pens in the barn. The process went smoothly and I was aware of Poppy watching my every move.

I already had fresh straw down and the basket feeders were full of hay. I got the ewes settled in while Poppy scampered round looking at the newborns.

"They're so cute," she said. "Oh, look, this one's wagging its tail and that one's sleeping and its mum is licking its head."

I laughed, enjoying her enthusiasm. "Yes, they're very sweet."

In the post natal pens all but one of my new mother and baby sets were doing well and were ready to be put back to grass. Poppy climbed up onto the middle crossbar of the pen to watch while I checked the lamb I was concerned about. It had been a long labour and it was this ewe's first time. The lamb seemed weak and listless. It didn't seem to be suckling. There wasn't a problem with the ewe's milk and she seemed to be taking an interest in her baby but to no avail. I decided to check back later and to defrost some of the colostrum I'd collected from one of my experienced girls, who was a prolific milk producer. I suspected I'd have to tube feed.

"I don't think this one's very well," I said to Poppy, holding up the lamb so she could stroke it.

"Aw, poor wee thing," she said rubbing its head. "What's wrong? Does it have a sore tummy?"

"Not sore, just empty. She needs to drink milk from her

mummy but she doesn't seem to want to." I laid the lamb down close to the ewe's udder but the little one showed no interest. "We'll come back and see her later."

I climbed out of the pen. "Right, last job for the morning. Let's get the other lambs and their mums out into the field. Go and call Bonnie. She should be sitting outside where we left her."

It was lovely to see the lambs relishing the space and freedom of the field. They scampered over the grass, bleating and chasing each other. The ewes immediately got down to eating the grass.

Once we were back at the house, we hosed down our wellies at the outside tap and then I showed her how to thoroughly wash her hands with the antiseptic soap. As I knew to expect by now, Poppy listened intently to my explanation about the need for good hygiene when looking after the animals.

By the time we got indoors, Poppy and I were ready for our lunch. When I looked into the fridge and cupboards, I realised I'd need to fit in a trip to Portree somehow, as supplies were running low. However, there was enough soup left from a couple of days before to do us for our lunch. So we had that along with the end of the wholemeal loaf from breakfast time. Our second course was apples and some of the cheese Jack had bought the previous day.

As we ate, Poppy told me a bit about her school. Her best friend was Coral who had really long hair and had lost both her front teeth—both things that Poppy envied. She liked her teacher, Miss Maxwell, who apparently wore nice clothes and had really cool earrings and never shouted. She hoped that the baby her mummy was expecting was going to be a girl, although she thought it would be nice for her daddy if it was a boy.

It was, of course, Poppy who stacked the dishwasher. Then she fetched a pad of drawing paper and some coloured pencils from her bedroom and was quite happy to sit at the table and draw while I compiled a shopping list. I glanced at Poppy's drawings when I'd finished and was waiting for the kettle to boil.

"That's me and you and Bonnie and there's Jason and Hector."

"Wow, that's really good, Poppy," I said.

"You can have it if you want," she said.

"I'd like that very much." I was surprised how touched I was by her offer. She wrote along the bottom of the picture before she handed it to me. "Thank you," I said, as I read what she'd written. It said *'to Rachel I love you from Poppy xxx'*. Then my mind did one of those unexpected flashbacks and I saw a very young Sophie and Finlay sitting painting pictures at the table in our Edinburgh house. I was horrified to find my eyes filled with tears.

"Are you crying?" Poppy asked. She sounded alarmed.

"No, no, I'm fine. I'll just see if I can find a pin to put your picture up." I turned away from her and rummaged around in a drawer in the dresser. "Why don't you go through to the living-room, see if there's anything you want to watch on the television."

"Okay," she said and she took her pad and left with Bonnie following her.

I grabbed some kitchen roll and blew my nose and wiped my eyes. I couldn't give in to the longing, to the sadness. I mustn't break down in front of Poppy. Instead I looked at the drawing and concentrated on the present, on the little girl who'd done this drawing here and now. It *was* good. She had the makings of a good artist. I pinned the drawing up on the wall to the right of the window.

I made myself a strong coffee and went through to join Poppy. She was watching a cartoon about a boy who appeared to be called Ben Ten. I was trying to work out how I could fit in going to Portree, checking the sheep, clearing out the fireplace and cooking the dinner when the phone rang. It was Jack.

After he'd checked that Poppy was fine he said that he was going into Portree to get some stuff at the builders' merchant and he wondered if I needed anything from the shops.

"You are the answer to my prayers," I said.

"I am?"

"Oh yes, you will be my hero if you go to the Co-op for me. Can I give you a list?"

"Hero, eh? I like the sound of that. Fire away."

I dictated my requirements. When I finished I asked how he'd got on at the house.

"Everything for the kitchen was delivered as expected and we've made a good start on the installation. I reckon I can leave the guys to it for the next few days. And, Rachel, I really appreciate you having Poppy."

"It really is a pleasure and besides, we're friends, aren't we? We help each other out. I appreciate you doing the shopping. We make a good team."

There was silence on the other end of the line. "Jack? Hello? Are you still there?"

I heard him clear his throat. "Yes. Friends... a team. Yes, absolutely. Right, I'd better get on. I'll see you later."

I was a little surprised by the abrupt end to the conversation. I hoped I hadn't overstepped the mark, embarrassed him by saying we were a team. I hoped he didn't think I was hinting at something more—although of course that *was* what I was doing, what I wanted, what I couldn't have.

But I didn't have time to dwell on it. I drank the rest of my coffee and then cleaned out and re-set the fire. The wind whistled and roared in the chimney. The room felt chilly and when I looked out of the window, the sky was completely grey. I could see a wall of rain out over the Minch. It was only a matter of time before it swept up the loch. I guessed we had about an hour before the downpour hit.

"Are you ready to get back out to the sheep?" I asked Poppy.

"Yes!" She jumped to her feet. "Let's go! Come on, Bonnie!"

I laughed at this display of enthusiasm. "Yes, let's!" I said.

We added hats and gloves to our outdoor attire this time. I felt better outside. The air was fresh and full of the smell of the sea. A buzzard mewed overhead and curlews called from the cliff top moor. The ewes and their lambs held a bleating conversation.

The wind had gone from brisk to strong and I took Poppy's hand as we made our way to the barn.

A quick check showed that I had another ewe in labour and things seemed to be moving along quickly and well for her. I told Poppy to sit on the top rail of the ewe's pen and watch her for me while I checked the sickly lamb from earlier. It still wasn't suckling so I fetched a feeding tube and a bag of colostrum and then I set about getting some nourishment into the poor little creature. Poppy clambered down off the railing and came to watch. I showed her how to hold the bag and it was a delight to watch her eager little face as the lamb, at last, got on with feeding.

Next I went back to check on the ewe that was in labour. The lamb's head was now crowning. I took Poppy into the pen to watch the birth. She was enchanted and almost speechless. Her hands went to her mouth and she said, "Oh," as I cleaned the new arrival with some straw and put it to the ewe's udder.

"It's so sweet," she said. "And it's drinking from its mummy. That's good, isn't it?"

"Yes, it is," I said smiling at her.

When we got back to the house, I left Poppy at the kitchen table drinking a glass of juice and doing more drawings. I lit the fire in the living-room and then went through to my workroom to check emails and catch up on some paperwork.

A little while later, Poppy came to find me. She stood in the doorway looking around the room.

"Come in," I said.

"What is this room?" she asked, looking at the drawing board and the shelves of art materials.

"This is where I work. I write stories and draw pictures for children's books." I beckoned her over to the drawing board. "This is what I'm doing at the moment." As she stood on tiptoe to look at my drawing, I reached over to the shelves and took down a copy of *Seamus the Sheep*, and handed it to her.

"It's Seamus!" She looked at the cover and put her finger under my name. "Rachel Campbell," she said and looked at me. "Is that you? You're Rachel Campbell?"

"Yes, I am," I said. "Have you seen the book before?"

"I've got it at home and I took it to school and my teacher read it to the class. Did you really make it?"

"Yes, I did." I laughed. "Don't you believe me?"

"Yes, but I didn't know. I thought you were a sheep lady. I didn't know you made books as well."

"Well I do. I'm a shepherd and I'm an author and illustrator."

"Cool!" she said.

"Would you like to have a go at colouring in some Seamus pictures?"

She nodded.

"Come and sit at the drawing board," I said. I helped her up onto the high stool and took my work off the board. "Here are some of the sketches I did when I was doing the first Seamus book." I laid them out in front of her and flicked on the overhead lamp. "And here are the crayons I used."

"Can I have the book, so I can see which colours to use?" she asked.

I handed it to her. She frowned in concentration as she began to colour in—slowly and carefully. After a quick check on the living-room fire, I went back to my desk and continued with my paperwork.

For a while we both worked in silence. Then Poppy asked, "Is this the right red for Shona's jumper?" She held up a crayon.

I got up to take a closer look. "Yes, that's the right red. Oh my, sweetheart! You're doing a really good job." I put my arm round her and squeezed her shoulder.

"Am I?" Poppy beamed at me.

"If Rachel says you are, then you are. She should know." Jack was standing in the doorway and his warm smile encompassed us both.

Chapter Nineteen

Jack

At first I was speechless. I just stood in the doorway watching Poppy and Rachel. Seeing them together and so comfortable with each other was a heart-lifting experience. Poppy sat in the lamp's spotlight, completely focussed on what she was doing. Rachel, too, was engrossed in her own work. Then Poppy spoke to Rachel and it was what happened next that really got to me. Rachel—she called Poppy sweetheart—and I loved the fact that she did.

"Grandpa!" squealed Poppy, clambering down off the high stool. She ran to me and put her arms round my waist. I picked her up and hugged her. "Have you had a good day?" I glanced over at Rachel as I spoke. She was smiling at me and Poppy.

"Yes. We fed all the sheep. The boy sheep are in their own field. There's Hector he's a Heb…" Poppy looked at Rachel.

"A Hebridean," Rachel said.

"Yes, a Hebridean—they're the black ones and he has two horns. And Jason is a Jacob and he has four horns. I got to hold the bucket of food and rattle it so the sheep came and we had to feed one of the lambs with a tube into its tummy because it won't suck from its mummy and I watched one of the ewes have her lamb and that was amazing!"

I laughed. "My goodness, you have been busy!"

"And that's not all, Grandpa. Did you know Rachel is Rachel

Campbell? She's not just a shepherd. She made the story Seamus the Sheep and did all the pictures and now she's doing a new Seamus book."

I smiled at Rachel. "Well, no, I didn't know that. I knew she did books but I didn't know she was *the* Rachel Campbell."

"Right, put me down, Grandpa. I need to finish my picture."

"Yes, ma'am," I said, returning her to the stool. "I'll go and get the shopping in from the car."

A little while later, as she shoved packets and tins into the kitchen cupboards, Rachel said, "Thanks for getting all this stuff."

"I think I got the better end of the deal," I said. "You had a lot to do too and you had Poppy. It sounds as if she had a great time with you."

"I hope so. I certainly enjoyed being with her. She's been a real tonic. I'd forgotten how much children live in the moment."

"Yes, no chance to dwell on anything, not when Poppy's around."

I took two pizzas out of one of the bags I'd brought in. "Dinner," I said. "I thought we could do with something easy."

"Great idea." She smiled. "Very thoughtful."

"Coffee?" I asked, picking up the kettle.

"Even more thoughtful." She sat down at the table and picked up the newspaper I'd brought in with me. "I haven't read the Scotsman since I lived in Edinburgh," she said. "Peter used to get it delivered. He liked reading the court reports, especially about cases he was involved in." She laughed. "If it was about a case he'd won, he made sure me and the kids read it too."

"Modesty not one of his attributes, then?" I said.

Rachel frowned slightly. "No, I suppose not, but he just wanted us to be proud of him. He enjoys winning, goes with the territory. It must have been the same for you whenever you got your man."

"Yeah, I suppose so." I didn't enjoy being likened to her ex-husband. I didn't like that she defended him even in this small way. Nor did I like feeling so ridiculously jealous.

I turned away, looked around the kitchen, willed the kettle to boil. It was then I spotted the drawing and the inscription Poppy had written on it.

"It's lovely, isn't it? The drawing and the message."

"Yes—yes it is," I eventually managed to mumble. And once again I wished I could be as uninhibited as my granddaughter. I also wished Rachel wasn't going away for three months, wished life wasn't so bloody complicated.

At last the kettle whistled. I snatched it up and spilled boiling water on my free hand. I let out a howl of pain.

Rachel jumped up and went to the sink. She turned on the cold tap. "Here," she said, "Get it under here." As I held my scalded hand under the icy water, she took a towel out of a drawer and stood holding it until I felt the heat leave my skin.

When I turned off the tap she came to me and gently wrapped the towel around my hand. She stood so close as she dabbed it dry, I could smell the lemony scent of her shampoo. I could have reached out and stroked her hair. The pain of the scald was nothing compared to the torture of not being able to touch her.

"How does it feel?" Rachel looked up at me as she unwrapped the towel.

"I'll live." The skin was only slightly reddened and the pain was all but gone.

Rachel continued to support my hand in both of hers as she inspected it for herself. She looked up at me again and said, "Doesn't look like it's going to blister."

I was so aware of her cool hands on mine, so aware of *her*, that I gave into impulse. "Rachel," I said, in no more than a whisper, my eyes looking into hers.

"Yes?" she whispered, holding my gaze.

"Grandpa! I've finished my Seamus picture. Look." Poppy burst into the kitchen.

For the next few minutes Rachel and I devoted our attention to Poppy's impressive efforts. My relief at being prevented from saying something stupid and jeopardising my friendship with Rachel, only just outweighed my frustration at not being able to take the risk. Rachel seemed unaware of any turmoil on my part and the moment passed.

That evening we ate pizza in front of the fire and then watched Poppy's *'Toy Story'* DVD. Poppy insisted we all sit on the sofa together to watch the film. She curled up between Rachel and me and gasped and giggled as she watched.

Her enjoyment was infectious. At one point I laughed at her laughing. "She's only seen it two hundred times already, so it's still funny," I said to Rachel who was also laughing.

"Shush, Grandpa," Poppy said.

"Yeah, shush, Grandpa," Rachel said. And her smile rendered me speechless.

I didn't see much of Rachel over the next week. She was busy with the sheep and finishing her illustrations. She did, however, find time for Poppy, letting her draw alongside her in her study in the late afternoons, or go with her to see the lambs. She even let Poppy be in charge of letting the hens out and feeding them in the morning as well as carrying on her role as chief egg collector. It was made clear to me by both Poppy and Rachel that I could accompany Poppy as she carried out her duties, but only as her assistant.

The weather improved and settled bright and fair, so Poppy and I were able to go for several walks. We took Bonnie along when she wasn't needed as a sheepdog. We climbed Ben Halla and went rock-pooling on the beach at Torrin. I also looked in at Dun Halla each day to check on the progress of the kitchen.

It was in the late afternoons that we got together with Rachel. Rachel and I shared the cooking and we ate together. After dinner the three of us either watched one of Poppy's DVDs, or Rachel and Poppy drew pictures together, sitting side by side on the sofa while I sat in the armchair by the fire and read the paper. After Poppy went off to bed, Rachel would return to her drawing board for an hour or so and then go out to do her last check on the sheep.

I loved the days spent with my granddaughter. But those evenings with both her and Rachel were the best part. During our time at Rachel's, I made a conscious effort not to examine my feelings for her, and settled for a sort of tormented contentment.

On the Friday morning of our second week, Maddie phoned to say she was officially off bed-rest and desperate for the return of her daughter. I agreed to take Poppy home the next day as it meant she'd be home in time for the first day of the summer term. As soon as the call ended I went and knocked on the door of Rachel's workroom.

"That's good," she said when I told her Maddie's news. She sat back on the high stool and smiled at me.

"It is. I must say I'll be glad when this baby's safely here. It can't come soon enough. I wish there was more I could do to ease Maddie's path, to make the pregnancy safe, make her safe, you know? I didn't get this anxious when I was facing the hardest of criminals. But when your child's wellbeing is threatened..." I realised what I'd said. "Christ, Rachel, sorry—that was insensitive—I just meant... sorry."

She leaned towards me, put her hand on my arm. "Don't apologise." She spoke softly. "Of course I know what you mean and you're right. We would lay down our lives for our kids. But that's not how it works. It's the price we pay for having them in the first place." Her customary solemn expression had returned, but there were no tears, there was no self-pity and I realised she wasn't thinking of herself. She was only concerned with how I was feeling.

"Yes," was all I could say. I looked into her face, into her beautiful, serious face. I thought about stroking her cheek, or taking hold of her hand as it rested on my arm. She looked straight back at me for a moment. Then she took her hand away and stood up.

"Coffee?" she said.

"Good idea," I replied.

Poppy took a break from watching cartoons and came to join us for elevenses. As we sat at the kitchen table, I glanced out of the window. It was a bright day. High, white cloud moved briskly across a clear sky. An idea came to me, a way of making the most of our last afternoon together. "There's a good breeze blowing out there. Do either of you fancy a kite-flying trip this afternoon?"

Rachel and Poppy looked at each other, nodded and grinned.

"Yeah!" Poppy said. "At last. I thought we were never going to fly it."

"Sounds like fun," Rachel said.

"I'll go and get it!" Poppy scrambled down from the table and ran off upstairs.

I laughed. "You'd think it was months she'd been waiting. We only got it last week!"

"Yeah, well, time goes much slower at that age." Rachel smiled.

"Sorry, I probably shouldn't have asked you in front of Poppy. I know you're under pressure—"

"It's fine. I need a break from the desk. It's a great idea. I'll go and finish off now, then we can have an early lunch and head out."

We climbed Ben Halla in warm sunshine and it wasn't long into the climb that we all removed our jackets and tied them round our waists. Poppy had insisted on carrying the kite to begin with, but she soon handed it to me saying it was my turn.

The wind was really blowing at the top of the hill and I hoped it wasn't too strong. It was years since I'd flown a kite and I was aware as I threw it into the air and let the line unwind, that I didn't want to fail to get the thing airborne in front of Poppy— but even more so in front of Rachel. I needn't have worried. The force of the breeze caught the kite immediately. Its red and white fabric whipped and snapped and I felt a hard pull on the line winder. Rachel and Poppy clapped, and Poppy ran along to get ahead of the kite's trajectory.

Rachel stood beside me, her hands clasped in front of her smiling face, her gaze fixed on the kite. "Isn't it grand?" she said, turning to me.

And, as I looked at her in that instant, she appeared the most carefree and enthusiastic I'd seen her. "Here," I gave her the winder. "Try letting the line out a bit more."

"Oh, wow!" she cried, as the kite rose higher and traced curves and loops in the air. She staggered a little under the kite's pull. I moved behind her, put my hands on her shoulders to steady her. Her hair blew against my face, the scent of it filled my nostrils and the wool of her sweater was soft below my palms. I looked down at the pale, freckled skin on the side of her neck and cheek and wondered what it would be like to kiss it.

"I want a shot!" Poppy came running back to us. She pulled on my arm.

"Okay," I said. "But I'll have to hold onto you. Rachel was nearly swept off her feet."

Rachel glanced at me, looked momentarily thoughtful and then gave a little smile. "Only nearly," she said. I did wonder for a moment if it was the kite she was talking about.

Rachel produced her phone from her jacket pocket and photographed Poppy and me as Poppy grasped the string and I grasped Poppy. Poppy giggled and shrieked as the kite twisted and turned, but her arms soon got tired. She passed the kite back to me and ran over to Rachel.

"Take a picture of Grandpa," she said.

"Oh no," I protested.

"Yes, yes," Poppy urged.

Rachel laughed. "Yes, yes," she said, raising the phone.

But Poppy wasn't finished yet. "Now you, Rachel, you take the kite and I'll get a picture of you with Grandpa's phone. Grandpa give me your phone." I had no choice but to do as I was told.

I heard the phone's camera click as Poppy took a couple more pictures. I stood behind Rachel, prepared to steady her if necessary. I'd no idea how capable Poppy was with a camera phone but she certainly appeared confident. In fact she was rather reluctant to give it back and darted about snapping goodness knows what.

When we got back, Poppy wanted to draw kite pictures so I left her to it and went upstairs to pack. I'd finished putting Poppy's stuff into her little case and was in the front bedroom, packing the last of my own things when Rachel tapped on the open door.

"Anything I can do?" she asked.

"No, thank you, that's all I can really do just now. The rest is stuff we'll need tonight and in the morning."

"So, do you plan to leave early?"

"Yeah, I said to Maddie we'd be on the road by about nine. She's really missing Poppy."

"I'm sure she is. How is she? Has she managed to rest?"

"She says she's feeling fine and is bored stiff, wants her daughter back. I'll probably stay for a couple of days, make sure she's coping."

"Right," Rachel nodded. "Is there anything I can do for you at the cottage while you're away?"

"Paint and tile the kitchen if you like." I grinned at her.

"Yeah, sure!" She laughed. "I meant things like letting in deliveries or checking on how the guys were getting on."

"No, it's fine, but thanks. The lads are almost finished in the kitchen. There's just the decorating, and I'll get on with that when I get back."

Rachel glanced at my holdall. "You—you don't have to move back to the caravan—you know—when you come back. You're very welcome to stay on here—if you want to that is..."

Yes, I thought. Yes, I'd like that very much. But what I heard myself saying was, "Thank you, but the cottage is nearly ready for me to move into—well, to camp in at least. It'll be good to have my own space." But, what I meant, what I really wanted to say was, I can't stay. I can't take the acute and wonderful torture of this proximity any longer.

"Right," Rachel said.

I hoped I hadn't hurt her feelings by not accepting her invitation. "Not that it hasn't been good to stay here," I said. "You've been so kind to Poppy and to me. I didn't mean to sound ungrateful, sorry."

"No, no, it's fine. It's good that you're nearly finished at the house. I completely understand about you needing your own space."

She sounded neither disappointed nor upset at my rejection of her offer. Probably only made it out of good manners. Probably relieved.

She gave that semi-smile of hers and turned away from me to look out of the window.

Chapter Twenty

Rachel

I had a lovely farewell dinner with Morag and Alasdair on the eve of my departure. Before the meal, I'd walked around the croft with Alasdair and done a full handover of all the details he'd need to keep the place ticking over in my absence. I was surprised at how difficult I found it to be leaving the land and the animals.

"Not having second thoughts, are you?" asked Alasdair, as we walked back to his house. "Only you seemed a bit flat as we were taking the tour."

"No... yes... I don't know. It's only now starting to feel real. I'm just beginning to realise how much I'm going to miss the croft and you and Morag and Bonnie of course." I glanced down at my dog as she walked beside us. "It seemed so right when I made the decision but now..."

"But now it's scary?"

"Very."

"That's natural. But you're doing the right thing. You need this trip, Rachel. You need to get away from here, explore all your options, kick-start your life again. It's a healthy thing that you're doing. It's brave and it's good." Alasdair put his arm round my shoulders and gave me a squeeze.

"Hmm, I don't know that Morag would agree with you. She's not all that keen on me going, not at all sure it's a good thing."

"Don't worry what Morag thinks. She loves you and she'll miss you terribly but she knows it's something you need to do. Now come on, cheer up. It's time to get excited about this trip of a lifetime."

I smiled at him. "You're right. Thanks, Alasdair."

"Good, glad that's sorted," he said.

As we made our way up the track, I thought of how different my goodbye to Jack had been. I'd seen him briefly, earlier that day. He'd driven past me when I'd been coming back from checking the sheep. I signalled to him to pull over and I'd asked him over for a goodbye coffee.

"Ah," he said. "I don't know. I've got a lot on today at the house."

I couldn't really read his expression. Was it reluctance? He seemed a bit irritated and distracted—worried even. And although I felt disappointed, I said, "Oh, it's okay. Don't worry if you're busy."

"No... sorry... I'm sorry." He smiled and looked at me for a moment. "I'd like that—to come for a coffee—say goodbye properly. See you in half an hour?"

But when he arrived he had the distracted and irritated expression again.

As we sat down at the kitchen table with our coffee and biscuits, I said, "Are you okay, Jack? You seem worried, maybe a bit annoyed. Have I upset you?"

"What? No!" he said. "You haven't upset me. It's just stuff, stuff I need to sort out—a lot on my mind." He smiled, but it seemed a bit of an effort. He looked around the kitchen, at Bonnie in her basket and then directly at me, and when he spoke, his voice sounded a bit hoarse. "I wish you well, Rachel." He cleared his throat. "I hope this trip is everything you want it to be and that you find what you're looking for." He raised his coffee mug. "To new beginnings," he said. And his smile this time was softer, more genuine.

"New beginnings," I replied, raising my own mug, smiling

back at him.

"And I'll help Alasdair in any way I can around here—around the croft—and I hope I can have Bonnie's company on some of my walks," he said.

"I'm sure Alasdair would be grateful for any help you can give and I know Bonnie would love to come with you on your walks."

"Good," he said. "That's good." And that was it. He drained the last of his coffee and stood up, smile gone. "Now, I really must get on."

"Oh, right," I said, surprised at this abrupt change. But then I supposed that my departure was probably not that much of a big deal for him and he was probably just being polite. I stood up too.

"Goodbye then," I said.

"Goodbye Rachel," he said. He reached out his arms towards me. I thought he might be about to hug me. I both hoped and feared he would. But then he just shook me by the hand and was gone.

I watched him from the kitchen window as he headed along the path. I wondered if it was Bridget that was on his mind. And I realised that I didn't really know Jack at all. I also realised how much I was going to miss him. But I'd be leaving soon and I was excited at the prospect. Not going wasn't an option. Now was not the time to examine how I felt about Jack and what, if anything, I was going to do about it.

On Friday the thirtieth of April, I drove down to Glasgow to stay with Lana for the weekend prior to me leaving for Israel.

I'd arranged to see Sophie the next day. I'd had to insist on meeting at her flat. She wasn't keen. She'd have preferred a café or a walk in the Botanics—but not because that's the pleasant sort of thing a mother and daughter might do on a pretty spring morning in Glasgow's West End. How I wished we had that sort of relationship. I longed to share a relaxing stroll, followed by a frothy coffee and a gossip with my daughter. But I knew Sophie's reasons for wanting to meet in the safety of a public place. In public, the talk would remain neutral and polite, the surroundings would distract from the inevitable strain between us. I, on the other hand, didn't intend on making polite conversation. I was on a mission. I didn't want any distractions or inhibitions on what I'd come to say.

Lana's Kelvinside villa wasn't far from Sophie's flat, so I walked the couple of miles. I walked past gardens with cherry trees in blossom, pink against the deepest of blue sky. Birds flitted and trilled. Lawnmowers whined and the traffic on Great Western Road rumbled in the background. I walked briskly, concentrating on the sights and sounds around me, keen to arrive, but trying to keep my nervousness under control. My head ached in spite of the painkillers I'd taken. I hadn't slept well. I took deep breaths of morning air as I walked, hoping it would help disperse the fog in my brain and the dread in my stomach.

At the appointed time of ten-thirty, I arrived at the tenement block where Sophie lived. I pressed the intercom buzzer.

"Yes?" Sophie inquired, even although she must have known it was me.

"It's Mum," I said to the grille, as brightly as I could. The buzzer sounded and the door yielded to my push. I climbed the two flights of stairs to her flat. With every leaden step my fragile optimism about the outcome of this meeting evaporated a little bit more.

She met me, unsmiling, and showed me into the living-room. I took off my jacket and looked around while Sophie disappeared into the adjoining kitchen to make coffee. It was generously sized. The carpet was cream, as were the walls. The furniture was made of a light wood. A widescreen TV took up one corner of the room and a desk with a laptop and printer filled the opposite corner. There was a table and four chairs in the bay-window area that overlooked the street. I gazed out, watching a young mother walking along the road, pushing a baby in a buggy and holding the hand of a toddler.

Reminiscence.

"Here." Sophie held a mug in her hand. I turned and stepped forward to take it from her. But she wasn't looking at or approaching me. She placed it on the coffee table and sat down on the armchair facing the window. She tucked her legs under her, folded her arms and looked at the floor.

"Thanks," I said, picking up my coffee and perching on the edge of the sofa. I could see my reflection in the widescreen. "You not having one?"

She shook her head.

I sipped silently. I struggled to retrieve my rehearsed speech—the one with no small talk—just heartfelt pleas. But it was lost in the fog.

"Nice flat," I said.

Sophie looked round the room, nodded.

"Six months—is it—that you've been here?" I asked.

"Nine—nine months."

"Is it handy for work?"

"Yes."

"And, how is work?"

A small sigh, a flicker of the eyes. She looked pale and tired. She leant forward. Her long red hair shone in the sunlight from the window and curtained her face.

"It's fine. Work is fine."

We went on like this for several minutes. However, it must have been a combination of the caffeine and the Paracetamol taking effect, because I suddenly regained some clarity and resolve. I put down my cup and moved along the sofa to be nearer to her chair. I leaned towards her.

"Sophie, I want us to talk—to really talk. This—this has gone on long enough. You're all I've got, I miss you. I want—I need to be close to you—like we used to be."

She put her hand out, warding me off. Still she didn't look at me. She shook her head. I thought she was about to ask me to leave. Then she looked up, looked right at me. Her eyes bright with fury, she leant back in her chair, her hands gripping its arms.

She gave a horrible little laugh. "Oh really? Like we used to be? When was that? Ah, yes—that would be before you divorced Dad, before you persuaded Fin that joining up was a good idea. Before you wrecked everyone's lives."

I wasn't shocked. I'd heard all this before. But I was sad. Sad she was still angry, sad she still blamed me.

I understood how Sophie viewed things. I didn't agree with her view, but knowing how she worshipped Peter, I did see where she was coming from. She felt that I'd given in too easily when Peter and I separated. She'd even said that her father probably had affairs because I couldn't be the wife he wanted. She needed the divorce to be my fault as this protected Peter's position on the pedestal where she'd placed him. And she blamed me for Finlay's death because when he decided he wanted to follow his grandfather into the Royal Marines, I did nothing to stop him. Peter on the other hand had been against it and had tried very hard to stop Finlay joining up. He wanted Finlay to follow him into law—something Finlay would have hated.

"I had to leave your father, Sophie. There was nothing to stay for. He met someone else. He asked me for a divorce. There was no point in fighting it. Look how happy he is now—how happy he is with Carla." It felt like my daughter was thirteen rather than thirty-three, but then I suppose we all revert to being children when we're with our parents.

"Yes, but you could've made him happy too—if you'd wanted to—but you couldn't wait to get back to your precious Skye. Did you even try to forgive him? He made one mistake—one mistake and you had to punish him."

"No—no that's not how it was. There were..." I stopped short—stopped short of the whole truth of Peter's several infidelities. I wasn't out to destroy my daughter. "There was nothing left—not for me. You and Fin were grown up. I couldn't stay."

"It suited you, didn't it, that Finlay left when he did—cleared the way for you to go too. No wonder you couldn't wait to see the back the back of him."

That one hurt. I fought not to recoil—to double up with the pain of that well-aimed blow. I sat back, looked at the ceiling—wondered what I was doing there—struggled to stay focussed and see this thing through.

"No—no that's not how it was. Come on, Sophie—you know it isn't. Finlay left home two years before I did. I'd no intention of leaving your father at that time. It's ridiculous to suggest I sent Finlay away. Yes, I gave him my blessing. I was very proud of him. But don't you think I'd do anything—anything—to turn back the clock and persuade him not to go."

She shrugged, pushed her hair back behind her ears, folded her arms, looked away. I was reminded of a much younger and just as stubborn Sophie. I was reminded of myself.

I moved nearer to her again, put my hand out to touch her, thought better of it and clasped my hands together. "We need to put this behind us. I miss you, Sophie. Can't you forgive me? I didn't plan for things to turn out this way."

"Okay, I know you didn't plan it but—but..." She jumped to her feet and strode over to the table before rounding on me and shouting, "You could have stopped it all from happening." She was crying now—angry tears. She swiped at her eyes with her fist. "I'll never forgive you." She turned her back.

I went to her, put my hands on her shoulders. She stiffened as soon as I touched her. "Look at me—please, look at me." I stroked her hair, let my arm fall along her shoulders. She didn't push me away, but she didn't look at me either. "Dad's happy—and you have the same strong relationship you always had with him. Our divorce doesn't change that. Losing Fin was terrible—for all of us—it nearly broke me. I can't bear to lose you too. If you had a child you'd know—you'd know—"

"Shut up! Shut the fuck up!" She spun round so fast that her shoulder caught me under the chin like a punch. I staggered backwards. It was only the end of the sofa that stopped me falling.

I put my hand to my jaw, fighting back tears, unable to speak, even if I'd wanted to.

Sophie's face was red and blotchy, twisted with anger as she looked at me. Then she laughed—a horrid, empty, mocking laugh. "Well, that's not going to happen."

I tried to swallow but my mouth was parched. My face ached. I managed to mumble. "What isn't?"

She leant against the table, looked suddenly calm. "Me having a child. It's not going to happen. I've made up my mind on that."

Again I struggled to speak. She put up her hand to stop me from even trying to respond.

"It's all right," she said. "I know what you're thinking. You think I'll change my mind, that I'll get pregnant and be happy about it—but I won't. How could I be happy about bringing a baby into the world knowing I couldn't protect it from..." She paused, raised her arms in a helpless gesture, before continuing. "From all this shit—its parents hating each other, getting killed in a pointless war."

I felt weak, shaken, had to sit down. "Stop it—please just stop. I need a minute and then I'll go. Do you think I could have a glass of water?"

Sophie went into the kitchen. I sat back, closed my eyes. I felt homesick already.

"Your water."

I opened my eyes. Sophie was bending over me, looking at me. She handed me the glass and straightened up, still watching me.

"Is your face okay? There's a bit of a bruise. I didn't mean to bump you like that."

"It's fine—it just hurt at first—and I got a fright."

"Right." Her face was no longer red—in fact she was quite pale again.

I took a few sips of the water and then reached for my jacket and handbag. I stood up. "I'm sorry," I said. "Sorry you still feel so angry, sorry I came. But you're my daughter and I love you. I always will—no matter what you may think of me. I hope in time you'll get over—everything."

"Like you have, you mean? All over Fin—and now gallivanting half way across the world."

I put on my jacket and swung my bag onto my shoulder. "I need to make this trip. And I'll never be over Fin. You lost your brother, Sophie—but he was my son. You can't possibly understand what it feels like to lose a child—and God forbid you ever have to." Sophie flinched. Had I actually got through to her? Was she beginning to empathise? I almost took my jacket off, was prepared to sit down and try again. What a bloody idiot I was! It wasn't empathy on Sophie's part. I'd hit a nerve and her retaliation was vicious.

So vicious that I don't remember leaving Sophie's flat. I do know I bumped into a young guy in the passageway at the foot of the stairs—almost knocked him over as I ran past. I also remember just making it outside before throwing up in the gutter. I've no recollection of walking back to Lana's. She was out when I got back. She wasn't expecting me to return so soon and so had arranged to meet a friend for lunch.

I curled up on the couch, still wearing my jacket and I cried until I was empty. I awoke when I heard Lana's key in the door. I sat up and made a futile attempt to look normal.

"Hi," she said, as she came into the room. "I thought you'd still be at Sophie's..." She stopped speaking when she saw the state I was in. "Oh, Rachel, no." She sat down beside me and rubbed my arm. "I'm guessing it went badly?"

I couldn't speak.

Lana ran me a bath while I drank the peppermint tea she'd made me. She helped me out of my clothes and into the bath. She sat on the loo while I soaked my aching body. She didn't ask questions.

When I was ready she wrapped me in a big soft towel and guided me back to the bedroom. "Right, come through when you're ready. If you want to talk about it, I'll listen, but if not there's a couple of DVDs we could watch—accompanied by a good bottle of red."

A little while later I joined her in the living-room.

"Better?" she asked.

"Yes," I said, trying to sound as if I meant it. "Sorry, I don't know what you must think."

"Don't be daft." She smiled. "Come and sit down."

I sat beside her on the sofa.

"So it was worse than you'd expected?" she asked.

"Much worse. I didn't expect it to be easy. but I took it as a good sign that she'd at least agreed to see me. And I hoped we'd talk and maybe we'd meet again when I get back. I hoped that slowly we'd make our way back to each other. But then—as I was about to leave, she—Sophie said..."

"Said what?"

A sob caught in my throat, I closed my eyes for a moment, struggled to form the words.

"Rachel? What? What did Sophie say?" Lana spoke softly and put her hand on mine.

"She told me she's pregnant—that she's ten weeks pregnant - and she's going to have an abortion."

"Oh—right. But if she—"

"Don't get me wrong. It's not my principles that have been upset. And it's not the regret of the lost prospect of a grand-child—although that would be difficult enough. I wish it was as simple as that. But it was what Sophie said about her reasons and the vehemence with which she said it. That's what made it so unbearable." I couldn't hold back my tears any longer. "It's all such a mess."

"Oh, Rachel," Lana squeezed my hand and then stood up. She disappeared into the kitchen for a moment and came back with a whole kitchen roll. "Here," she said handing me the roll as she sat down beside me again.

An image of Jack and his white cotton hankies popped into

my head. For a moment I wished I was at home, wished I could talk to him about Sophie.

"So, what are her reasons—for the termination?"

"Me—I'm the reason."

Lana shook her head and frowned. "You? Why?"

"Peter and I—we had to get married—we were only twenty—not even finished uni—when I got pregnant with Sophie."

"Did you want to get married? Did you want a baby?"

"Oh, yes I wanted both—eventually—but not right at that moment—and not necessarily with Peter. Getting pregnant was an accident. Peter and I had known each other less than a year. I'm not sure we'd even have gone out together for much longer—if there'd been no baby."

"So, why go ahead? Why get married?"

"Don't you remember what it was like in the seventies?"

"Yes—abortion was legal—and single mothers weren't unheard of."

"That's true, but they were unusual and I had a very conventional upbringing. The way things were—the way I was—it didn't seem like I had a choice. My parents were shocked—marriage was the only option as far as they were concerned and Peter's parents were the same. The four of them got together and worked it all out—a registry office ceremony and the rent on a tiny flat in Edinburgh paid for by Peter's parents. We were both to finish our studies and Peter's mother would take care of the baby until I graduated."

"And you and Peter really had no say?"

"No, not really. I think we were in shock. It all felt quite exciting—quite—grown up. In some ways our parents made it very easy for us."

"Hmm, and you didn't think of just going off quietly and ending the pregnancy, of not telling your parents."

"No—Peter suggested an abortion when I first told him, but I couldn't contemplate it. I wanted my baby. So I had to tell my parents."

"Right—so you married the baby's father and had the baby—Sophie. So what's her problem? Why are you the reason she wants to end her pregnancy?"

"Because, according to Sophie, having her ruined my life and Peter's life and she doesn't want her child to have the guilt she feels at having been born." I put my face in my hands and let my tears fall.

I scarcely noticed Lana getting up and going into the kitchen. When she came back she said, "Drink this." She handed me a brandy and sat down beside me once more. "Do you want to know what I think?"

I nodded, took a sip of the brandy.

"I think that's an excuse on Sophie's part—a way to hurt you. I don't know Sophie very well but, from what I do know, she's not crippled with guilt about being born. Up until the divorce and Finlay's death, you two had a good relationship. No, this is anger talking. I'm no psychologist, but I reckon she's angry at life *and* she doesn't want this baby for reasons that are nothing to do with you."

"But why, why wouldn't she want her baby?"

"Not maternal? Not in love with the father? Not ready?"

I shrugged. "She always used to say she wanted children—in fact she talked about having lots of them. I don't know anything about the father—and, it seems, I don't know anything about my daughter." This time I took a gulp of the brandy. "I think maybe I should cancel this trip. I should go back to Sophie—try to get this mess sorted out—get her to—to..."

"Kiss and make up? Keep the baby?" Lana shook her head. "It's your decision, of course, but—"

"But you think that would be the wrong thing to do?"

"Yes, I do. Sophie's an adult, Rachel. The decision about the pregnancy is hers to make. Yes, the reasons she's given you are probably designed to hurt you, but if she really wanted the baby, she'd keep it. And now is not the time to try and mend your relationship."

"So, I should just walk away—abandon her and my—my grandchild to their fate."

"Yes, you should. This is for Sophie to handle. You've made a move. She knows the door's open. It's for her to come to you when she's ready. And you need to make this trip—go on your own journey."

"But it's—you don't—"

"I don't have children—so I can't know what it feels like for you—as Sophie's mother?"

"No! Well—yes, actually."

"You're right, I'm not a mother. And maybe I'm completely wrong, but you said you wanted to know what I think and I've told you. But, like Sophie, you have to make your own mind up."

I knew she was right. I knew there really was nothing I could do. But it took all my willpower to get on the plane a couple of days later.

Chapter Twenty One

"Rachel!" Jonathan bounded across the concourse of Tel Aviv airport towards me. I only just had time to put down my bags before he gathered me up and spun me round. "It's so good to see you," he said, kissing me. Then he released me and held me at arm's length. Because I loved my brother, I tolerated all the hugging and kissing, but I was glad when it was over. I tried not to let my relief show.

Jonathan smiled as he stroked my cheek. "Ah, Rachel still the little hedgehog, rolling into a ball when anyone gets too close."

"Sorry, I am working on getting better at the cuddly thing," I said, returning his smile. "It's lovely to see you."

A little while later, as Jonathan drove us through the darkness to Jerusalem, he said, "I can't believe you're really here."

"I'm having difficulty believing it myself." I glanced sideways at my brother. I felt suddenly shy and I was glad he had to keep his eyes on the road.

"Twenty years it's taken—twenty years to persuade you to visit. You were always adamant that you'd no desire to come here—so bloody stubborn—just like Mum. I'd given up hope."

"Yes, well, a lot has changed."

Jonathan reached for my hand and squeezed it. "I know, sis, I know. But now you *are* here, I'm going to make sure you enjoy it. I want you to love this infuriating country as much as I do."

As it was dark, the first thing I noticed about Jerusalem was the smell. The air on this May evening was warm and still and laden with the rich, resin scent of the city's pine trees.

I inhaled deeply as Jonathan got my bags out of the boot. "Smells like Christmas."

"Yeah, Christmas and Caledonian forest. I told you you'd feel at home."

I laughed "You don't give up, do you?"

My brother's apartment was in a modern, five-storey block at the top of a steep, winding street. As I followed Jonathan from the car park, I glanced back down the hill towards the centre of the ancient city. All I could see were its distant lights.

"Rachel, dearest Rachel—at last—you are here. I am so happy to see you. Welcome, welcome." Deb hugged and kissed me on the threshold of the apartment.

Jonathan edged past me with the bags. He winked at me over his wife's shoulder as I accepted the embrace. "I'll take your bags through," he said, disappearing through a doorway on the left.

"Come," Deb said, smiling warmly as she closed the front door. There was no hallway, just two, long, shallow steps leading down into a large square living area. "I'll check on the supper. You sit, rest, relax. Help yourself to coffee and cake." Deb indicated the low table and seating in the centre of the room. I'll be in the kitchen." She pointed at a doorway, at the foot of the steps. "I won't be long."

I sat on one of a pair of low-backed, metal-framed sofas, poured myself some coffee, sank into the pale grey upholstery and tried to relax. It was only three days since I'd left Skye, but it seemed much longer. I felt very tired. But, as I sipped the incredibly strong, black, Turkish coffee and ate some sweet honey cake, I began to feel less weary.

The sofas were placed at right angles to each other along the edges of a beautiful rug, intricately patterned in red and gold. The rug was the only covering on the pale tiled floor. There was a black leather armchair facing me. It had a matching footstool and I guessed it was probably Jonathan's. Also facing me, was a big flat-screen television. Beyond that the far wall was largely taken up with glass doors, presumably leading onto a balcony.

On the wall to my right there were floor to ceiling bookshelves running the whole length of the room. And just along from the kitchen doorway there was a dining table with six chairs.

But what really caught my eye, in this otherwise minimalist room, was the painting hanging on the wall to my left. I got up to take a proper look.

Dominating the picture, was what appeared to be a huge escarpment, floodlit scarlet against a black background. The line near the top of the picture, where red rock met the black darkness, was picked out in whitish gold. When I looked closely, I saw that this golden line was composed of buildings along the cliff-top. It was an impressive piece of work.

"The kids will be here in time for dinner," said Jonathan, as he came back into the room. "They both had stuff on after school."

I turned from the painting. "Oh, that's good. I was wondering where they were."

"You like it?" Jonathan nodded at the painting.

"I do, very much."

"It was a present from a good friend of mine. Eitan Barak, a good artist and good bloke. You'll get to meet him while you're here. Now, let me show you to your room, you're probably desperate to freshen up."

After a quick and cooling shower, I felt quite revived. As I got dressed, I could smell supper and it wasn't long before Jonathan was knocking on the door to let me know the meal was almost ready.

My niece and nephew had returned by the time I went back through to the living-room. "Auntie Rachel, it's so nice to have you here," Mari said. She smiled warmly. Fifteen-year-old Gideon was shyer and more awkward than his sister and had to be coaxed by Jonathan to shake hands.

Once everyone was seated round the table, Jonathan said, "Before we start eating, I'd like to propose a toast."

"Dad! Can the toast not wait till later?" Gideon looked at me. "Sorry, I'm very hungry."

"Yes, Father, save us the speeches—please." Mari groaned as she spoke. Then she looked at her mother. "Ema, tell him."

Deb laughed and reached over to pat Jonathan's arm. "Let's eat the food while it's hot."

"Yes!" Gideon said.

"Looks like I'm outnumbered!" Jonathan raised his hands in submission. "Okay everyone tuck in."

"Rachel, please help yourself—before Gideon." Deb smacked her son's hand away from the serving dish as she spoke. "Guests first!" She raised her eyebrows at Gideon before turning back to me. "Here is moussaka and here's salad, and this is sesame bread, freshly baked. I hope you will like them."

"Of course she will," Jonathan said. "Deb's moussaka is outstanding, Rache. It's her mum's original Turkish recipe."

The food was delicious. And as well as enjoying the food, I was pleasantly surprised to find how much I enjoyed sitting with my brother's family. I'd thought it might be difficult, that it would serve only to highlight what I'd lost. I couldn't remember the last time I'd shared a happy family meal. But it felt good being part of a family again—eating, chatting, sharing.

The children talked about their day at school. At least Mari did. Gideon, like most boys of his age, didn't have much to say on the subject. He had to have some maths test results dragged out of him by his mother and he was not at all comfortable with the praise he received for his good marks.

"Ema, you always sound so like a teacher. You're off duty now. Anyway, you probably already knew my score. I bet you followed my teacher round the staffroom until she told you."

"I most certainly did not! At school I'm a teacher and at home I'm a mother—your mother—your proud mother." As she spoke, Deb ruffled her son's hair.

"Ema!" Gideon batted his mother's hand away. "Get off! Aba, help me," Gideon laughed.

"Leave me out of this," Jonathan said, raising his hands.

"Your father wanted to know your grades as much as I did.

He is as pleased as I am. Why do you criticise only me?"

"Because, Mother, you over-parent." Gideon sat back, grinning, obviously aware that he was winding his mother up.

"What?" Deb gasped, attempted to look outraged and pretended to take a swipe at the back of Gideon's head. "Jonathan, help me out here. You must back me. He's doing that good parent bad parent thing he does."

"Uh, right—yes, Gideon—stop giving your mother a hard time. Rachel—tell us please, how was your flight?"

Deb narrowed her eyes at Jonathan. "That was a pathetic and blatant attempt to change the subject. But, yes, Rachel how was your journey? It's a long way from your island of Skye to here."

"Yes, a very long way, but I broke the journey, stayed with a friend in Glasgow for a couple of nights." I didn't mention seeing Sophie. I felt a tightening in my stomach just thinking about her. "I flew to London this morning and onwards from there. It all went smoothly and everything was on time."

"So, what do you think of your niece and nephew?" Jonathan said. "Mari is thirteen already. Can you believe that?"

"No, I can't. She was only eight the last time I saw her—when you all came to Scotland—and Gideon was ten. You've both changed so much." I looked across the table at my brother's children. They were both very good looking. They'd inherited their mother's dark colouring, her glossy black hair and the darkest of brown eyes. Mari was petite and fine-boned like her mother. Gideon was at that gangly stage and looked as if he'd end up even taller than his father—just like Fin did. They seemed such fine young people; intelligent, funny, loving. "You must be very proud of them," I said. And as I spoke I thought, *so cherish them and keep them close.*

I struggled to keep such thoughts down, to keep them in the box in which I'd placed them when I decided to make this trip. I caught Jonathan's eye and I could tell from his expression he knew what I was thinking, that he sensed my desperation. He came to my rescue, moved things on.

Glancing at my empty plate, he said, "You obviously enjoyed that!" He began to pile up the dishes. Deb also began to clear the table. "You stay where you are," Jonathan said. Me and the kids will tidy up this lot and get the washer stacked. Then we'll bring dessert." Jonathan ignored his children's protests and they didn't put up much resistance before following him to the kitchen.

"Deb, that was wonderful, thank you," I said. "It was the best moussaka, I've ever tasted, great flavour."

"I'm glad you liked it. There was cumin and allspice in it and the best lamb. It was the proper Turkish recipe—handed down through my mother's family."

"How are your parents? Jonathan said you'd recently been to London to visit them."

"My mother is well, but my father he is frail. I hoped they might be able to come here for Mari's bat-mitzvah, but my dad could not cope with the journey and my mum won't leave him. But it was good to see them both and good to get back home to London for a while."

"You still think of London as home? Not Turkey? Not here?"

"Hmm—a difficult question. I left Turkey when I was ten—but it was my birthplace, we are a Turkish family and I do feel a connection. But it's hard to think of it as home. We Jews, we weren't exactly welcome and, as you know, with my father's politics, we couldn't stay. It was London that took us in, made us welcome. I was happy growing up there. It was home until I was twenty-five and it will always have a part of my heart. But now—yes—now, Israel is my home. It's where I am truly me, I suppose." Deb smiled and gave a little shrug.

"I envy you that certainty. I used to think I knew where I belonged—where home was. But now..."

Deb put her hand on mine. "I know. You've been through so much in the last few years. But this trip—it's about trying to find out where you belong now, isn't it?"

I could only nod.

"Okay, I hope you've made room for this amazing pudding,

ladies." Jonathan returned followed by the children. He was carrying a large plate which he placed at the centre of the table.

"Oh, wow, Deb, that looks gorgeous," I said.

"Ahem, excuse me, I made it," Jonathan said. "It's my speciality. Honoured guest, I give you—baklava." He bowed and sat down. The children shook their heads. Jonathan sliced and served. "Enjoy!" he said, handing me a bowl.

For a few minutes nobody spoke as we all feasted on the wonderful confection of honey and almond pastry suffused with cinnamon and cloves.

"Well?" Jonathan asked.

"Scrumptious," I said.

Later, after the children had retreated to their bedrooms, Jonathan, Deb and I sat sipping glasses of lemon tea.

"Are the arrangements for Mari's bat-mitzvah all in place?" I asked.

"Sort of. There's plenty time yet to finalise everything. It'll be just after her birthday in August. We're keeping it fairly low key. It'll be a secular affair, a lunch followed by various celebrations. Mari's already started working on her presentation and Deb's going to make a speech." Jonathan grinned at his wife as he said this last part.

"Is that traditional—the mother making a speech?" I asked.

"Yes and no—for sure, it wouldn't happen in an orthodox synagogue." Deb laughed. "But although we're not having a religious ceremony, Jewishness passes through the maternal line, so it seemed appropriate for me to do my daughter's address. Besides, Jonathan did it for Gideon at his bar-mitzvah."

"I think it's a lovely idea—not just the speech, but having a bat-mitzvah."

"Glad you think so," Jonathan said." It could be seen as hypocritical, but the way we see it, it's about the Jewish culture and tradition. You don't have to a believer to value those things. It's a basic human need, isn't it—to have rites of passage—markers along the way."

I nodded and then failed to hold back a yawn.

Deb put her hand on my arm. "We're so glad you're here and that you'll be at Mari's party. We'd like you to have a part in it, but we can discuss that another day. Right now you're exhausted and should go to bed."

I didn't need persuading. We said our goodnights and Jonathan told me to have a lie in the next day. "We'll all be away early to work and school. Take your time to recover from the journey. Help yourself to breakfast. There is a garden at the back of the apartments if you want to go outside. Call my cell if there's anything you need. Leave a message if I'm in theatre."

I shook my head. "I won't disturb you at the hospital. I'll be fine."

"I have some time off organised, so we can plan a bit of an itinerary for you and me, but now go—sleep."

Chapter Twenty Two

By the Friday of my first week in Israel and after a couple of days resting, reading and unwinding, I was ready to go exploring. Jonathan wasn't too keen on me going out on my own, but I'd assured him I'd keep my wits about me and that I wouldn't go far.

As on the first two mornings, the bedroom was already warm when I awoke. It was nearly nine o'clock. I'd fallen asleep almost immediately the night before and, for the first time in a long time, slept right through. I hadn't even heard the family leaving.

I got out of bed and the floor tiles were beautifully cool beneath my feet. I opened the blinds, and pushed the window open. Sunlight filtered through the mesh of the fly-screen and the scent of pine drifted in. I unhooked the screen and folded it back.

The view was beginning to become familiar, but it was still new enough for me to spend a minute taking it in. My room was at the front of the building and faced another apartment block across the street. On its flat roof, and on all the roofs that I could glimpse looking down the hill, there were solar collectors and water cisterns in amongst the forests of satellite dishes.

After I'd showered, I got dressed in what was now my customary attire—cotton trousers and a tee-shirt. Then I went in search of breakfast. As on previous mornings, there was fresh bread wrapped in foil on the worktop, and a selection of other breakfast food in the fridge. Indeed there was a whole platter of things for me to choose from—cheeses, olives, salad, fruit. There was also the usual jug of freshly squeezed orange juice. I poured myself a glass and sipped it as I waited for the coffee to percolate. Then I took my breakfast of coffee, bread and fruit out to the table on the balcony.

Shaded by the overhang of the balcony above, it was a cool and pleasant place to sit at this time of day. The bread was soft and yeasty and the fresh melon and mango were luscious, perfectly ripe and intensely flavoured—so much better than the poor, pale and insipid specimens that suffered the long journey to the U.K. I fetched my book and spent a comfortable hour or so reading and watching the life of the street below.

Then I couldn't put it off any longer. I wanted to go out. So, fully armoured with sunscreen, hat and sunglasses, I left the apartment and stepped out onto the dazzling white pavement of Kobobi Street. The heat was tolerable—but only just.

I paused to get my bearings. To my left, the steep slope of the road levelled off and seemed to come to a dead end just past the next block of flats. So I turned right and headed downhill. A small flatbed truck laboured up the narrow street towards me. I glanced at the elderly, sweating, baseball-capped driver, his arm trailing out of the open window. He looked back at me and had plenty time to watch me as I passed. He called out something and I looked away quickly. No translation was needed. I got the gist from the tone of the laughter that followed. I was fairly sure I'd just been propositioned in Hebrew.

The main road ran past the bottom of the street and I'd not gone far along it when I came to a short row of shops. The first one in the row was a cafe—*Shalom Kafe* it said above the door, and on the pavement there was a battered and faded sign advertising 'ice-cold coca'. After the cafe was a small supermarket, a pharmacy and then what appeared to be a book shop and art gallery on the end of the row. I walked on for ten minutes or so and arrived at the gates of the Ramat Dania Park.

I decided a walk through the park would be perfect for my first solo venture. The path from the gates rose gradually uphill.

It was lined by olive and fig trees and I was enchanted to see jewel-bright humming birds flitting around the nectar-laden bougainvillea. I took my camera from my bag and managed to get a few reasonable shots of the beautiful little birds. I wished now that I'd brought some drawing materials with me and resolved to return for a morning's sketching.

At the top of the hill, I sat for a while on a bench under the shade of the trees. As I sat, I was aware of a delicious smell wafting towards me. It was the smell of food cooking. I realised I was hungry and a glance at my watch confirmed it was lunch time. I decided to track down the source of the aroma. I hadn't gone far down the other half of the sloping path when I arrived at a food van. The smell was even nicer close up. Falafels sizzled on a hot plate. A short while later I'd bought my lunch and had returned to my bench to eat it. I felt quite proud of myself for having managed to communicate what I wanted to the elderly woman in the van and for having managed to figure out the right amount of cash to pay for it.

The falafels lived up to the promise of their smell. They were gorgeous, all nestled inside warm pitta bread and smothered in the best hummus I've ever tasted. As I ate this wonderful middle-eastern feast, I felt very relaxed. I turned my face to the sun. It was hard to believe I was in a very foreign and potentially dangerous environment because at that moment, I felt at home.

By the time I got back to the flat, I was hot and pleasantly tired. I stripped down to my underwear and lay down on my bed intending to have a short nap. A couple of hours later I awoke to the sound of voices– children's voices drifting up from the street below. I pulled on a silk bathrobe and padded barefoot through to the living-room.

I stepped out onto the balcony. In the street, several boys— they looked about nine years old—were playing football. I watched them for a while. One of the boys reminded me of Finlay—slight and nimble—similar in his movements.

I became lost in thought and recollection. Finlay had loved

football. His passion for it had survived both his father's and his school's attempts to convert him to rugby. He too had played it in the street, as a small boy with his friends, and later in city parks and playing fields. I'd watched him from the sidelines as he grew from skinny wee boy to wiry young man—cheering him on—celebrating and commiserating—always proud. I remembered the photo of him taken in the camp in Afghanistan—wearing shorts and boots, his ID tags glinting against his bare chest. He stood, arms raised in a triumphant gesture, a football placed under one foot. He was laughing, enjoying the moment, full of life. It was taken the day before he died. One of his comrades had sent it to me, hoping it would be of comfort. But although I carried it around in a pocket at the back of my writing notebook, I could rarely bear to look at it.

The boys began to argue, their raised voices broke into my thoughts. I realised I was crying, but I was smiling too. Smiling at the life and passion so evident in the boys' football dispute, smiling because, for the first time since his death, Finlay seemed close by.

I stepped back into the living-room, looking around for my bag. It was on the sofa where I'd dropped it on my return to the apartment. I snatched it up and pulled out my notebook. I tugged the folded photo of Finlay free from the plastic pocket. It was just a paper printout of the emailed j-peg, but to me, at that moment, it was the most beautiful photo in the world. I wasn't sure why, but I knew as I gazed at Fin's smiling face that something inside me had changed.

The sound of a key in the front door made me jump. I stood up as Jonathan stepped into the room.

"Hi, Rache—just up?" He bounded towards me, arms outstretched, not even bothering to close the door.

"No, no," I said, as he hugged me. "I've been out. I had a bit of a siesta when I got back. I was just going to get a shower."

He released me, but kept his hands on my shoulders.

"If you say so."

171

"Honestly, I was up about nine and I was out by about eleven—"

"Relax, it doesn't matter, you're on holiday. You're allowed to slob around in your dressing gown all day."

Before I could answer a voice said, "Are you going to stop teasing your sister and introduce me?"

I stepped aside and looked past Jonathan. A man stood leaning on the frame of the open door.

Jonathan laughed as he turned round. "Come in, come in," he said.

I pulled my robe more tightly around me, suddenly aware of its shortness and of my bare legs and feet. I pushed my hair back as the man approached me. He was tall and broad with lots of curly black and grey hair. I guessed he was in his fifties. He wore jeans and the sleeves of his blue cotton shirt were rolled up. His forearms and his hands were deeply tanned, as was his face.

"Rachel, meet Eitan Barak. Eitan, my sister Rachel, Rachel Campbell."

"Pleased to meet you," I said, holding out my right hand, still clutching the robe with my left.

Two large hands enclosed mine and my arm was vigorously shaken. "Good to meet you too, Rachel Campbell. Welcome to Israel." Eitan smiled, a warm, crinkly-eyed smile and he kept hold of my hand.

"Thank you." I smiled back and I couldn't help but return his direct gaze.

"I didn't believe Jonathan had a sister. I still don't. You don't look like him. You are much more pretty."

I felt myself blush. I glanced at the floor and then back at Eitan. He was grinning.

"Let her go." Jonathan laughed. "Take no notice, Rachel. He's a smooth-talking sod—always flirting."

Eitan released my hand and inclined his head towards me, still smiling.

"Please excuse me," I said. "I need to get changed."

As I showered, I realised that the lightness of feeling I'd experienced earlier was still with me. I decided to put on my green dress and my new brown sandals, bought specially for this trip. I twisted my hair up and caught it in a large amber clip. Not bad, I thought when I checked myself in the mirror.

By the time I returned to the living-room, Deb and the children were also home. Gideon sat at the table tapping away on a laptop and I could hear Deb and Jonathan's voices coming from the kitchen. Mari and Eitan sat side by side on one of the sofas. Mari seemed to be showing something to Eitan, something on a piece of paper, and Eitan pointed at and commented on what he was seeing. He spoke in Hebrew so I'd no idea what he was saying. Mari blushed and smiled as she nodded at Eitan. Neither of them noticed me standing watching them.

"Hi, Aunt Rachel," Gideon said, glancing up from the computer.

"Hi, Gideon," I replied.

"Ah, you are back," Eitan said. He stood up and stretched out an arm towards me as he looked me up and down. "Very nice, that colour. It suits you." Again his gaze was direct and intense.

I glanced down at my dress, ran my hands down its side seams, felt myself blush again, knew he was still looking at me. It had been a long time since I'd been spoken to or looked at in that way.

"Come, see what you think of—of—how do you say it—your brother's daughter?"

"Niece—my niece," I replied.

"Niece." He nodded as he tried out the word. "Come and see your niece's work. She's a talented girl." He indicated the other sofa and handed me the paper as he sat down beside me.

I glanced over at Mari who had her hands on her face and was shaking her head.

"No—don't look, Aunt Rachel. It's not very good." She covered her eyes and turned away.

"Don't listen to her," Eitan said laughing. "She's going to be a fine artist one day."

I looked at the sketch. It was a pencil drawing of a landscape, hills in the background and cypress trees and flat-roofed houses in the foreground. The lines were clear and confident and the proportions and perspective, though not perfect, were surprisingly competent for such a young artist. The shading was especially good. "This is very good, Mari," I said.

Mari turned and peeped out from behind her hands. "Really?" she said.

"Really," I replied. "Eitan," I paused, feeling slightly awkward as I said his name—and again very conscious of him watching me. "Eitan's right. You have talent."

"I told you so. If you don't believe me, you must believe your aunt." Eitan smiled at Mari and then at me.

Mari gave a little shrug and then a big smile. "I guess."

"Rachel is an artist—like me. She knows what is good."

"Oh, no, I'm an illustrator. I just do children's books. I'm not like you at all. It's been years since I did any painting. I could never do something like that." I looked to the painting on the wall.

Eitan shook his head. "What's with the women in this family? Is it a Scottish thing? You are afraid to say you are good."

"No! Well that is yes, it is a bit of a Scottish trait. But what I do, it's not on the same scale as you." I felt flustered. I directed my attention at Mari. "Where is this, in the drawing?"

"Upper Galilee. It was a school trip, that is Rosh Pina." Mari pointed at her picture.

"You've done a good job of showing the hills in the distance and I like how you've put in the shadows. It brings it to life." I held out the picture to Mari.

"Thank you," Mari said. She stood up and came and took her drawing from me. "Now I must go and get changed."

Gideon continued to tap away on his laptop, engrossed in whatever he was doing.

"I will take you there, to the Galilee. We will draw and paint together. And to Masada too," Eitan said, indicating his painting.

"Oh, no I—"

"Don't let him boss you about," Jonathan said, as he appeared from the kitchen. "Here." He handed one of the two bottles of beer he was carrying to Eitan. "We haven't had a chance to discuss where Rachel might visit yet. Besides, I might want to take her to the Galilee, or wherever." He sat down on the leather armchair and took a gulp of his beer.

"Yes, but you cannot take a lot of time off from the hospital and I can be free when I need to be. I can—"

I laughed. "Please—don't argue about me."

"Oh, these two, they have to have something to argue about. If it wasn't you, it would be something else, politics most likely." Deb had emerged from the kitchen. She had a glass of white wine in each hand. "I thought you might like a drink," she said, offering me one.

"Thank you, I'd love one," I replied.

"Dinner will be in about an hour," Deb said. "Gideon, can you please put the laptop away and set the table, the white table cloth and the menorah, the full works for Shabbat. And, Jonathan, can you keep an eye on the chicken? Rachel and I are going to sit on the balcony for a while." She beckoned to me.

"Don't mind Eitan," Deb said, as we sat side by side at the little, white, wrought iron table, looking out at the city skyline. "He's—"

"Opinionated, over-confident and over-familiar?" I said.

Deb laughed. "Yes, he's all these things. But what I was going to say was, he's full-on but he's also a very interesting man. And he's kind-hearted and totally honest."

"And a control freak?"

"Yes, that too."

As I sipped my drink and relaxed, I inhaled the warm, pine-scented air and listened to the Imam's voice, drifting from one of Jerusalem's mosques, calling the faithful to prayer.

"I love Fridays. School stops at lunch time and then at sunset the weekend begins," Deb said. "I'm not religious, but I love the tradition, the idea of stopping it all for a while, all the busyness, taking time out each week to reflect. Shabbat gives you permission to rest."

"And do you manage to do that—rest for the whole of Shabbat?"

"Not the whole time. You know what it's like when you're a working mother. I spend some of Saturday doing chores—that's when I wish I was more orthodox."

"And what about Sunday—do you get some time then?"

"Oh, no, it's back to work. Sundays are only for the Christians."

"I didn't realise you just have one and half days off. That makes me feel very spoiled. Mind you, as a crofter, there aren't really any days off."

"Ah yes, that must be true. Who's taking care of all your animals while you're here?"

"A couple of good friends. Alasdair, a neighbouring crofter and his wife Morag—and then there's Jack."

"Jack? He sounds interesting."

"How can he sound interesting? All I said was his name."

"Yes, but it was the way you said it." Deb smiled.

"What? I didn't say it in any particular way. It's his name—Jack."

Deb raised her eyebrows, obviously waiting for more.

"He's a neighbour, a new neighbour and, yes, he's become a friend. He—"

"Oh, wait a minute. It's the guy who pulled you out the river, isn't it? Jonathan told me. This Jack, he saved your life, didn't he?"

"Well, yes he—"

"How romantic! He saved your life and now you're—"

"Friends—we're friends. He's already in a relationship. What we have, Jack and I, it's in no way romantic." I hoped Deb couldn't see what I was really thinking as I said this, that she couldn't detect the feelings I was trying so hard to suppress.

"If you say so. Tell me about him anyway. What do you two friends do together? What do you share?"

But it was no good. I could see there was no way Deb was going to be put off. And I wanted to talk, to tell someone how I really felt. So I told sister-in-law all about Jack Baxter. I told her I was in love with him, but that it was one-sided. I told her I'd settled for friendship and I asked her to stop when she tried to persuade me that I should at least tell Jack how I felt.

Chapter Twenty Three

It was half way through the main course of that first Shabbat meal that I felt it. It was a stronger version of what I'd felt on my first evening at my brother's table. It was a feeling that I would come to recognise as the dominant one throughout my time in Israel. We'd said our 'Shabbat Shalom' toasts and finished our tomato salad starters. It was a bittersweet feeling.

I was still aware of the underlying depth of my bereavement but I also felt a connection, a strong sense of belonging. These people were my family.

As we ate, Jonathan and I reminisced about our childhood on Skye. He recalled some funny moments, largely at the expense of our parents. And we both recounted stories of summers helping at the sheep fank, or hauling creels up the makeshift steps cut into the cliff that took us from the shore to the croft. Deb and the children, and even Eitan, seemed to enjoy hearing our anecdotes. Revisiting these shared episodes also felt like a sort of homecoming.

Whilst eating the delicious paprika chicken and the crunchy green pepper and rice salad that accompanied it, I paused for a moment and took a sip of wine. Jonathan caught my eye and smiled. I knew that he understood how I felt and I smiled back at him.

"Do they still have ceilidhs in the Halladale hall?" Jonathan asked. "We had some great nights there, didn't we?"

"We did, and yes, they still happen, but I haven't been to one, not since—not since I went back to Skye."

"What is a cay—what did you call it a cay...?" Eitan asked.

"Gideon can tell you, and so can Mari. Tell Eitan what a ceilidh is, kids," Jonathan said.

"It's a sort of party, everybody does something, plays music, or sings, or tells a story and there's dancing too." It was Mari who answered. Gideon appeared to be texting. Deb noticed and grabbed the phone out of his hand.

"Ema!" Gideon gasped, scowling at his mother.

"Not at the table and not in company." Deb raised a hand to silence any further protest.

Jonathan seemed oblivious to the exchange, caught up in a sudden thought. "You know what we should do?" he said. "We should make Mari's bat-mitzvah a bit of a ceilidh, mix the traditions, a Highland-Hebrew hootenanny sort of thing. Don't know why I didn't think of it before."

"Yeah," Deb said. "That's a great idea."

"You could sing something, Rache," Jonathan said.

"Oh, no I—"

"Don't worry, we'll sort you out with an accompanist—Gideon could play guitar for you," Jonathan said, ignoring my panic.

"It's not that—"

"And you too Eitan, you must do something too."

"I will if Rachel will," Eitan replied, smiling directly at me.

"Good—that's sorted then," Jonathan said. "Right, where's dessert?"

At the end of the meal I insisted that I did the clearing up. Eitan said he'd help me and drafted the children in as well. Jonathan and Deb were ordered to go and relax.

"They work hard, your brother and his wife," said Eitan, as we cleared the table. "He does many more hours than he is paid for at Hadassah, and Deb is a very committed teacher."

"I work hard too," Gideon said, pausing on his way from table to kitchen.

Eitan laughed. "I'm not sure you do. Not when I see you take only two plates on each trip to the kitchen. And if you are trying to get out of helping us clean up because your life has exhausted you then it won't work." As Gideon made a face and continued on his way to the kitchen, Eitan smiled and said, "Teenagers."

"Don't include me in your disapproval," Mari said, as she cleared the last of the crockery. "Gideon is very lazy. I am not!" Mari turned and strode off through the kitchen doorway.

"You are right," Eitan called after her. "It is just teenage boys who are afflicted in this way. Do you not think so, Rachel?"

For a moment I was thrown. Images of a fifteen year-old Finlay played in my mind. Finlay lying in his bed till noon, or later at the weekends, his bedroom a maelstrom of discarded clothes, dishes and general detritus; Peter getting angry, shouting at Fin and not listening as I tried to get him to leave it. Then, Fin sitting up in bed, squinting at the sudden light as I opened his bedroom curtains. His strong, young, boy-man body, bare-chested and propped against his pillows as he accepted the lunchtime bacon roll and mug of tea that I'd smuggled to him. "Thanks, Mum," he'd say and he'd smile. He always got round me with that gentle, lazy smile...

"Rachel?" Eitan was staring at me. "Are you all right?"

"What? Oh, yes sorry. I'm fine. It was... I was..."

"No, it is I who am sorry. You thought of your son. I asked a stupid question. It upset you. I am sorry. I—"

I raised my hand, shook my head, "Please, don't apologise. It's good—to think of him—of my son and all the memories."

"And the memories—the ones you just had—they were happy ones?"

"Yes, yes they were."

"Good." Eitan inclined his head slightly as he spoke. "And now we better join the young people in the kitchen or Gideon will be calling *us* lazy."

A little while later Eitan and I joined Jonathan and Deb on the balcony. The four of us sat, sipping our coffee and staring down at the lights of the city.

"Tomorrow," Jonathan said, turning to me, "I have the afternoon off, so I'll take you on your first tour of Jerusalem."

"I'd like that," I said.

"It's a beautiful city," said Eitan. "Best in the world. You'll love it. It's just a pity we can't have it to ourselves."

"Eitan!" Jonathan spoke sharply and raised his hand as if to stop his friend from speaking.

"Yes, yes, but I'm not sure how much Rachel knows about the politics of our country and it's important—"

"Not now!" Jonathan's voice was slightly raised. I was surprised at how agitated he seemed.

"Why not now?" Eitan said, shrugging. "Your sister needs to understand what—"

"You always do this!" Jonathan looked really rattled now.

"What? What do I always do?"

"Boys," said Deb, leaning forward and putting her arms out as if she was refereeing. Neither of the men even looked at her.

"You always grab any chance to preach your gospel," Jonathan said. "Eitan's solution to the problems of the Middle East. Rachel is still—it's too complex—"

"Yes, it's complex so the sooner she starts—"

"Please," I said, putting my hand on Jonathan's arm. "I am still sitting here you know. I think I can cope with a bit of political debate. And," I turned to look at Eitan, "I do actually know a bit about Israel's situation and I'm perfectly capable of following a complex issue. It shouldn't take me too long to get my head round what you have to say."

Eitan laughed. "Good!" he said. "So, do you agree, we would be better off having our capital city to ourselves—to say nothing of the rest of our country?"

"Here we go," Jonathan said, looking at Deb.

Deb smiled at her husband and reached her hand out to him. "I think we should leave these two to it."

Jonathan smiled too. "Yeah, good idea. I'm sure Rache can fight her corner and I do have an early start tomorrow." He and Deb stood up and said their goodnights.

"So," Eitan said, once he and I were alone, "What is it that you know about our situation here in Israel?"

"I know it's complicated. I know it's difficult for everyone, whatever side they're on, and I know there's no easy answer."

Eitan tilted his head in a slight nod. "Mmm," he said. "A typical British, liberal and passionless response."

There was also a glint in his eye and a twitch at the corner of his mouth. I recognised the good-natured provocation for what it was and found I relished the challenge of a good-going debate with this man.

"Fair enough," I said. "I'll try to be more passionate." I took a deep breath. "I think the pro-Zionists of the far-right are wrong. I think that Israelis should be more generous towards the Palestinians and should treat them as fellow citizens. I think the wall is outrageous and I'm appalled at the blind nationalism displayed by this country."

"That's better!" Eitan smiled even more broadly. "I don't agree with a word of what you say, and it's still British liberal nonsense, but at least there's some feeling there."

"Nonsense—in what way?" I sat forward.

"First—it's not blind nationalism to want to protect your country, to want to keep out undesirables and those who would harm you. You Brits control your borders tightly, do you not?"

"Yes, but—"

"And second," Eitan continued, "Why would we be generous to the Palestinians? They will not be generous to us. They won't be happy until all of Israel is dead and they can establish their own state."

"Yes, of course Israel—any country, Britain included, has to police its borders. That's not what I'm saying. I'm talking about the divisions within this country. The way the Palestinians are herded behind that wall, the conditions they endure. And then there's the actions of the settlers, the provocation, that can't be right. When I say generous, I mean show humanity, show respect to people who should be your fellow citizens. Surely then this country would be better for everybody."

Eitan shook his head. "I can see Jonathan has persuaded you to his pro-Palestinian views. He's—"

I raised my hand. "No," I said, feeling my face flushing. "No, he hasn't. I reached my conclusions myself. I know Jonathan loves this country, but we've never really discussed its politics. And besides, I form my own views. I read the papers, watch the news—"

"Ha, the British press and the great BBC, not at all biased and knowing all things, especially what's good for everyone else."

"Okay, I know my knowledge is limited and comes from biased sources, but you can't deny the wall exists, you can't deny how badly the Palestinians are treated, and you can't deny the bloodshed should stop."

"No, you are right. I can't deny any of those things. But what I do deny is that any of it is simple and that there aren't big risks if Israel gives in. I don't trust our enemies, and make no mistake, that is what they are. This isn't some pointless war like the one Britain is involved in, in Afghanistan. This is our war, our fight for our survival. The bloodshed is regrettable of course—" Eitan stopped. He'd obviously heard my small gasp, probably seen the pain on my face when he mentioned Afghanistan.

"Rachel—I am sorry, again. That was bad. I was enjoying our discussion. I forgot..."

"No, it's all right. I was—I am—enjoying the discussion too. What you said is right. I'm afraid the Afghanistan thing probably is pointless, but I still hope it isn't—if you see what I mean."

"Of course I do. If that war is pointless, then your son's death will also have been pointless."

"Yes, exactly and that would be even more unbearable. Finlay—my son—he believed he was doing some good—that our forces were bringing about real change for the better. But I'm afraid I do doubt that. Is there really such a thing as a just war?"

Eitan leant towards me. He reached out and took one of my hands in both of his. "Yes, I believe there is. World War Two was certainly just. Hitler had to be stopped. And I believe our war here is justified also. It's our survival that's at stake. I think what I meant was that Afghanistan isn't about the U.K.'s survival as a nation. But that is a discussion for another day. And whatever history decides about the politicians, your son believed in what he was doing and did it willingly. Yes, his loss is an unbearable sadness for you, but be proud, Rachel, proud of your brave soldier son." Eitan squeezed my hand, before releasing it. He looked into my face.

I looked back at him, looked into his eyes and what I saw there made me momentarily cover my mouth with my hand. "Oh," I said. "Oh, you've lost someone too, haven't you? Someone close has been killed—died—fighting?"

Eitan looked away for a moment and then he said, "Yes. My brother, Amnon. He was nineteen, doing his national service. It was the Yom Kippur war, 1973. He was killed in the Golan Heights, on the nineteenth day of a nineteen day war."

"Nineteen," I whispered. "The same age as Fin was. I am so sorry."

"As am I. It is because of Amnon, because of what he, and others like him, sacrificed, that I am determined that we will not give up what we have fought so hard for." Eitan reached across once more. "Your face," he said. "It is very white. Come, we should go inside. Get ourselves a drink."

As I stood to follow him indoors, he raised his hand and stroked my hair. His hand slid down my cheek and his thumb traced along my jaw.

I could only nod. Part of me wanted to let my head fall onto his chest, to let him embrace me, to give me some of his obvious strength. But I couldn't, or wouldn't, give in to the impulse. I took a small step back from Eitan. He immediately drew back his hand. He gave a small smile and bowed his head slightly as if to let me know he got the message. He indicated that I should lead the way inside.

"Now, where does Jonathan hide the good stuff?" Eitan said,

going over to the wall cabinet and looking inside. "Aha, right, first time." He brought out a bottle and two glasses.

He came over to the sofa where I was sitting. He placed the glasses on the coffee table and poured a good measure of malt into both. He handed one to me.

"*L'chaim!*" he said, raising his glass."

"To life, *l'chaim*," I replied. I took a sip. Immediately I was reminded of Jack, of that night at home, drinking—or rather not drinking—whisky with him. I glanced at the label on the bottle. Yes, it was Talisker, as it had been on that other occasion. It reminded me of home. I felt quite strange, not exactly homesick, but a kind of yearning. I took a gulp of malt and almost choked on its acrid taste. But then its warmth kicked in and I sat back, enjoying the sensation. It was then that I became aware that Eitan was watching me—watching me closely.

He smiled as I returned his look. "You are enjoying that," he said, nodding at my glass. "It took you to another place—a happy place. You look much better."

I nodded. "It reminded me of home. It reminded me of a friend—somebody I shared a drink with—a drink of this very same whisky."

"A good friend, judging by the look it brought to your face."

I felt the reddening on my neck and face. "Well, yes a reminder of home and a good friend."

Eitan just nodded.

We drank the rest of our whisky in silence—companionable, comfortable silence. Eitan stood up as he took his last swallow. "I should go. It's quite a long walk home."

I went with him to the door.

"Goodnight, Rachel," Eitan said. "I have enjoyed your company—and your—your passion. I look forward to more discussions with you, and if Jonathan will let me, to showing you more of this crazy country. We should go to Masada soon—before the weather gets too hot."

"I'd like that," I said "Thank you." I held the door open for him and waved to him as he walked away.

As I prepared for bed a little while later, I reflected on the evening. It had left me invigorated, tired, sad and happy all at once. But the main thing I seemed to feel was alive. I felt alive.

Chapter Twenty Four

I fell instantly in love with Jerusalem. From that first Saturday afternoon, when Jonathan took me on a drive around the city, pointing out places I'd heard of since childhood times at Sunday school, I was smitten.

It was a beautiful city, but it wasn't just its good looks that hooked me. It was a beguiling mix of familiar and exotic. Mosques, synagogues and churches all jostled for position on its slopes. In some ways it reminded me of Edinburgh with its hilltop vistas, rich history and its compact layout, but in other ways it felt completely foreign.

The warm, pine-scented air and the smoky aroma of food cooked at the street stalls filled my nostrils as we walked around. The golden limestone, the whitewashed buildings, the blue sky and the full spectrum of Mediterranean light imprinted themselves on my eyes, used as they were to the soft greys, violets and greens of more northerly light.

As my weeks in the city passed, I came to especially love late Friday afternoons when Muslims hurried through the streets, heeding the haunting calls to prayer from the Muezzins, and Jews bustled homeward for their post sunset Shabbat supper.

On my second Friday in Jerusalem, I took a taxi to the Hadassah hospital at Ein Kerem. I was going to meet Jonathan when he finished his shift at four in the afternoon. We'd arranged to meet there so that Jonathan could show me round his place of work. He was waiting at the hospital gate when I arrived.

"Impressive," I said as I got out of the cab and looked around.

"It is, isn't it?" Jonathan slid his arm across my shoulders and we both stood for a moment, looking at all the dazzling buildings that stood before us.

I guessed I'd probably have to see it from the air to get a true impression of its size. One tower block looked to be about twenty storeys high. I told Jonathan I hadn't imagined it would be so huge.

He laughed. "What were you expecting, a third world field hospital?"

"No, but it's much larger and, yes, more modern than I thought it would be."

"This place set the standard for Israel's healthcare—first heart transplant, first robotic surgery—lots of firsts. It's probably more state-of-the-art than any of your UK hospitals. And it treats everyone—regardless of race, religion or ethnicity."

I smiled at my brother. "I can see how proud you are. So, are you going to show me round?" I took his arm as the automatic doors slid open in front of us.

Jonathan guided me through many departments—A&E, oncology, cardiology, orthopaedics, to name but a few. He introduced me to several of his colleagues. We passed labs, lecture theatres and clinics.

He took me into the hospital synagogue. "Wait till you see this," he said, as he opened the door.

I was speechless. There were the twelve stained glass windows. I recognised them immediately. They were created by Chagall—one window for each of the twelve tribes. Chagall was one of my artistic heroes. I loved his use of colour and had, of course, seen pictures of the windows, but nothing could have prepared me for the vibrancy and genius displayed in the real thing. I sat in awe for some minutes before managing to utter, "Wow! I'd forgotten they'd be here. It's been a long time. I was a student when I first read about them."

"Thought you'd be impressed," Jonathan said.

And finally, he showed me round his own department—paediatrics. I was moved by his obvious pride in his work and found myself envying his passion.

"Are you okay?" Jonathan asked as we stood in the children's surgical ward. He'd been in the middle of telling me about an operation he'd recently carried out. "You're not squeamish are you? You look awfully serious."

"No, not squeamish, just jealous."

"Jealous? What of me?"

"Yes—well—no, not exactly, jealous of your enthusiasm, of your commitment. You do such great work and you so obviously love it. Me, I don't do anything as important and I certainly don't derive anything like your level of satisfaction or joy."

"I'm sorry. I shouldn't bang on. I know I get carried away. And there are bad days—days when I could quite cheerfully walk away."

I looked at him. "Hmm," I said.

"No, really there are times—"

"Okay, I believe you!"

"Anyway, you used to love your job, or should I say jobs. You used to be really into your drawing and your books—to say nothing of the sheep."

"Yeah, well..." I looked away, my laughter of only a moment ago well and truly gone.

"Rache? What's wrong?" Jonathan took hold of my arm, tried to get me to look at him.

I glanced at my brother, felt a tear escape. I blinked hard.

But Jonathan wasn't fooled. "Right, that's it. Come on," he said, putting his arm around me. "Time to show you the hospital's excellent cafeteria, and you can tell me what's upset you while we have a cup of coffee."

I wasn't sure that I wanted to talk. "No, it's—"

"Don't even think of arguing. I know you, how you bottle things up. I've touched a nerve of some sort and you're going to tell me all about it."

We were soon settled at a table by one of the café's large windows, overlooking the hospital grounds. "So," Jonathan said, stirring the froth on his cappuccino. "Why is work such a touchy subject?"

I sighed and gave a little shrug. "I don't know exactly. With the books, it took a while to get back into them after Fin, and then after Mum's death I lost momentum again. Drawing pictures and writing silly wee stories just seemed pointless after— after everything." I swallowed. The tears were back.

Jonathan checked his pockets then grabbed his paper napkin and handed it to me. "Here," he said. "Sorry I haven't got a tissue."

I took the napkin. "Thanks. I really should carry a packet with me." Of course I was reminded once more of Jack and I realised just how much I missed him. The realisation didn't help my lack of composure.

"It's not surprising," Jonathan said, as I wiped my eyes. "I'm not particularly creative, but I imagine that if your emotions are in turmoil then it's bound to interfere with your output. It's another children's book you're working on at the moment, isn't it?"

"Yes, my second *Seamus the Sheep* story. I got it to where it needed to be for the publishers before I left to come here. But it was hard to motivate myself. In fact, it was having Poppy around that helped."

"Poppy?"

"Jack's grandchild—my neighbour—Jack."

"Oh, yes, Jack. Your lifesaver."

"Yeah—my lifesaver." Now I couldn't help smiling.

"Ah, so the mention of his name makes you smile?" Jonathan raised his eyebrows. "Oh, and blush!"

"Don't be daft!" I said. "You're as bad as Morag. Anyway, it was Poppy I was talking about. She'd make anyone smile. I was looking after her one day and I showed her some of my pictures and she knew my books. Her enthusiasm was infectious. It helped."

"And what about the real sheep? No joy there anymore?"

"It just seems a bit pointless. I kept the flock going after Dad died—as a sort of memorial to him. And Mum liked that there were still sheep on the croft. But now they've become a bit of a chore." I paused and gave a little laugh.

"What?" Jonathan said.

"Poppy again. I showed her the sheep and the lambs. All her questions did sort of rekindle my interest. Seeing something through a child's eyes can be very refreshing."

"I guess. It seems like Jack's granddaughter has been spending a lot of time with you. How come?"

"Oh, they came to stay—Jack and Poppy. I put them up for a while."

"Really? Interesting!" Jonathan only just ducked in time to miss a swipe from me. He leaned back in his chair laughing. "What?" he said.

I tried to explain how it had come about that Jack had come to stay with me and I also mentioned that Jack had a girlfriend, but Jonathan was enjoying the teasing far too much to just accept my explanation.

"Just good friends. If you say so," he said. He laughed again. "Okay, I'll come clean. I've been pulling your leg about Jack. Deb told me what you told her about your feelings for the guy."

"What?" I gasped. "It's not funny. You knew how I really feel about him and you still teased me. "

"Sorry. It was unfair of me and yes, unkind. But I wondered if you'd tell me the truth if I pushed it."

"It's hard for me to talk about."

"Are you sure there's no chance that you and he—"

"No! There's no chance. He has a girlfriend. And I'm way too screwed up for him, far too much baggage. Now, can we change the subject."

"Okay. But whatever, it's good that Poppy revived some of your enthusiasm, well done her. Though it's not surprising that you've been feeling flat. You've been through a hell of a lot. I don't know how you've kept going at all. Maybe you need a new project."

"Yeah, I've been doing some sketching since I've been here and I did have some discussions with Lana. She thought I could do something about this trip."

"There you are then." He reached across the table and took my hand. "Coming here's already having a positive effect. I think this country will really get under your skin and, who knows, you might decide to settle here."

"You don't give up! I like what I've seen so far, very much, but settling here—"

"Why not? You could do your writing and illustrating just as easily here and pursue new projects. You could even farm some sheep—or goats. A fresh start, a new perspective, it's what you need."

"Yes, but not necessarily here in Israel. Look, it's early days. There's still lots for me to see and this is a holiday. I'm going home at the end of it, whatever happens."

"Of course, but then, after some reflection, you could come back to stay, maybe, possibly..." Jonathan looked at me, saw my exasperation. "Okay, okay, enough said. Come on, drink up. I'm going to take you to the Mount of Olives to see the sun set over this magnificent city."

But Jonathan was right. Over the next few weeks I did indeed find Israel getting under my skin—or Jerusalem, at any rate. I visited many places, including all the key religious sites, the two beautiful silver and golden domed mosques, the Church of the Holy Sepulchre and the Wailing Wall.

Sometimes Jonathan came with me, sometimes Deb or one of the children. And sometimes I went alone. I found being on my own particularly exhilarating. I went to a couple of art exhibitions and this prompted me to get my sketchbooks out. I did several sketches of city scenes from a selection of high vantage points, including some at the park I'd visited on my first day. I went to cafes and people-watched or wrote in the travel journal that I'd been inspired to start.

The two places that made the deepest impression on me during my stay in Jerusalem were the Holocaust Museum and the huge barrier wall that cut off East Jerusalem from the rest of the city.

It was an unusually overcast day, at the beginning of June, and the atmosphere was aptly oppressive when Deb and I visited the Yad Vashem museum. The ghastly photographic and documentary record of the holocaust was repellent, horrific and fascinating.

"All those lives—millions of lives—how could it have happened? How was it allowed to happen?" I said, as Deb and I sat on a low wall outside the museum and slowly regained the power of speech after all that we'd just seen.

Deb shook her head. "I don't know. I've visited this place a few times now. I don't think it sets out to provide answers. It simply and brutally states 'It happened'. I suppose all a person can take away from here is a conviction that it can't be allowed to happen again."

"But it has and it does. It doesn't matter what we think—what any individual visitors to this place think. We haven't learned—as a group—as a race," I said.

"The Jewish race, you mean?" asked Deb.

"No, I mean the human race. We haven't learned compassion and tolerance. After what we saw in there—after what happened to my mother's family, to your family. I look at that wall and I think..." I shrugged, not sure what I thought.

"I take it you don't mean the Wailing Wall," Deb said.

"No, I mean the wall that cuts off the east of this city, the wall that separates the West Bank."

"You may see it as making a ghetto, so do I. But plenty of people see it as protection, as keeping out those who would do us harm."

"But isn't that doing the very thing that was done to us? The demonising, the corralling?"

"Interesting you used the word *us*," Deb smiled. But you won't get an argument from me about the wall or from Jonathan. It's Eitan you need to speak to. He seems to be able to make sense of it in his ever so reasonable way."

"Hmm, I'll bet he can, but I just don't get it."

"Look, let's take a break for now. I think we could both do with a good lunch, somewhere pleasant, get rid of the taste of this place." Deb stood up.

"Good idea," I replied.

"You know, if you're interested, I could arrange a trip for you, a visit to the other side of the wall," Deb said, as we sat in a small courtyard cafe waiting for our lunch.

"Really? Is that possible?"

"Yes, very possible. There are several local tour operators who can organise visits. You stay in the home of a local person or in a guesthouse and there are local guides."

"Have you been?"

"Yes, yes I have. I've been a couple of times."

"How was it?"

"Like everything else in this bloody country—a mass of contradictions. In places it was beautiful, vibrant, rich in culture and, oddly, peaceful. There was a film festival on in Ramallah one of the times I was there. But then you go to Hebron and the tension is everywhere. There are the refugee camps and the deserted shops and empty schools. And for the schools that remain open there's daily violence from the settlers towards the pupils on their walk to school."

"But that—the tension, the threat of violence—it hasn't put you off going?"

"Not at all. There's so much propaganda on both sides, from the extremists and the fundamentalists. I wanted to see the territories for myself. Jonathan wasn't keen and I'll probably be in trouble with him for suggesting that you go."

I thought of Peter and his objections to me visiting any part of Israel. I smiled wryly as I made up my mind. "Jonathan can object all he likes. It sounds like a very worthwhile visit. I'd appreciate your help in getting it organised. I'm going to Masada with Eitan next week so maybe the week after that?"

Deb nodded. "I'll see if I can get a couple of days leave and come with you."

"So, I take it Jonathan hasn't been over?" I said.

"No, he hasn't. Don't misunderstand me. He'd never stop me from going, and he's been very interested to hear what I've seen and thought when I've returned. It's just actually going there, it makes him uncomfortable."

"And so evil succeeds—isn't that the saying? If good men look away..."

"Don't be too hard on him," Deb said. "He has his reasons and he certainly wouldn't willingly let evil succeed. I'll get in touch with the tour operator, get something arranged and you can tell your brother."

Chapter Twenty Five

Jonathan was very quiet when I told him of my plans to visit East Jerusalem and the West Bank. We were sitting on the balcony one evening after dinner, drinking coffee, just the two of us. Deb was busy inside marking schoolwork and the children had gone to their rooms immediately after eating.

"I'm planning to go at the end of the month with Deb. We'll be away for two nights."

Jonathan nodded, staring down into his coffee cup.

"Jonny?"

"What?"

"What do you think?"

He looked up at me. I knew that look. "I don't think anything," he said. "They're your plans. You should go where you want to."

"Oh, come on. You're not normally this quiet and I know that face. You're struggling not to say something."

Jonathan sighed. "It's difficult, complicated. No doubt Deb told you I wasn't that keen on her going when she's been in the past."

"Mmm." I nodded.

"I hate the wall. I hate what it stands for—all that's bad about our country. It symbolises our ignorance, our unwillingness to learn, our blind nationalism." Jonathan almost spat out the last word. "The wall embarrasses and offends me."

"I understand that. I agree with you. But why not cross over, see for yourself how the Palestinians live. Talk to the locals. Let them see not all Israelis approve of their situation."

"I see plenty of Palestinians at work, talk to them every day. Remember the Hadassah treats all comers. I know from Deb that it's not all misery in the territories but it's so shameful, *I'm* ashamed. We're prisoners turned captors, victims turned bullies." Jonathan leaned forwards, his head in his hands. He sighed again. "At work, I can make changes for the better, I can heal, I can do something for my fellow humans, but over there—I'd just feel helpless and angry and I—"

"What—and what? What aren't you telling me, Jonny?" And as I looked him in the eye, I saw fear, disgust, anger.

"When I was in the army, doing my National Service, not long after I first arrived in Israel, I was stationed in Gaza. I was out on patrol. I was with my unit, six of us. Things were very tense in the region. A young Israeli conscript had been killed by the PLO a few days before—a grenade." Jonathan paused, swallowed, looked into the distance. "Sorry, this is hard for me." Then he looked back at me. "It can't be easy for you either to revisit this kind of stuff."

I shook my head. "Go on," I said. "I want to know. What happened?"

"We were moving down a street. It was past curfew, late evening. We heard footsteps around the next corner. We had our guns ready. It was a split-second decision, Rachel. We saw it coming towards us, some sort of missile. The order came to fire. I saw him too late. I shouted a warning, fired in the air. But one of our guys...he... it was too late, he fired. It was—he was just a child—twelve years old. He'd thrown a stone at us. I tried to help him but it was already too late. I was led away by my comrades. We had to get out fast. We only just made it to the armoured vehicle before a mob caught up with us. He died—the boy died—just a kid—a stupid kid." Jonathan rubbed his palms roughly across his cheeks. "Sorry," he said. "It's pointless, I know, insulting even, shedding bloody tears."

"I don't believe it's pointless. I'd like to think that the people who blew Finlay up felt some sort of remorse. But what were you doing in an armed patrol—you were a medic, weren't you?"

"Yes, I was—but I volunteered to go on patrol and take my turn. I'll never forgive myself."

"Why? There's nothing to forgive. You tried to help the boy, tried to prevent him being shot. It was tragic but—"

"Yes, it was fucking tragic! Senseless, pointless and tragic. And that's why I can't visit the territories. I can't face them—ordinary Palestinians, ordinary family people like us—who love their children."

I was crying now too. Jonathan stood up, turned away from me and leant on the balcony rail. I went to him, put my hand on his shoulder. He turned and we hugged each other tightly.

After a few moments, I looked up at my brother and said, "But you do face them. You tend to their children's health every day at the hospital. You must have saved many lives."

"Yes, but they come to me. I don't invade their space. It's bad enough that we've erected that wall. But visiting the territories would be—I don't know—like adding insult to injury... patronising, unbearable."

"God, it's a mess. We're a mess, life is a mess." I rubbed his arm, turned to look out over the city. Together we gazed up at the night sky, at the new moon and the many stars. "We're so small, so insignificant compared to that great big universe. We have such a short time here. Why can't we get along? Why do we have to resort to violence? Why do mothers have to bury their sons?" Two long tears ran down my face.

"Hey," said Jonathan. He put his arm round me. "Hey, now," he whispered. "I think we could both do with a drink. Sit down and I'll be back in a moment."

By the time Jonathan returned with a brandy for each of us, I was even more certain that I had to visit the West Bank.

"I'm going, Jonny. I need to see for myself, to understand how it is on both sides."

He sipped his drink. "Yes, I understand. I admire your courage, especially after everything—after Finlay. Nobody could blame you for wanting to stay well clear of any conflict area."

"But that's just it. It's because of Finlay. I never really understood the conflict in Afghanistan, why we were involved in the first place. Oh, I know, on the face of it, it was all about the aftermath of 9/11 and about weeding out the Taleban. But it was also portrayed as some kind of liberation mission. Who were we fighting for exactly? Finlay was absolutely convinced that there was a job to be done, that he was helping to protect and free an oppressed people. He never doubted the value of what he was doing."

"And going to the other side of the wall—that'll help you? How?" asked Jonathan.

"I'm not sure how to explain it," I said.

"Try."

"I think I want to see both sides of the story. I want to understand what's so important about territory and tribalism that we humans will fight to the death for it—even within our own country. Is our Jewish heritage so important that it's worth doing what's being done here? How can we square being the agents of all this displacement and suffering with our own experience of persecution?"

"We square it by perceiving all on the other side as terrorists. Terrorists who won't rest until the state of Israel no longer exists. Or, in the case of the Taleban, until the whole of the infidel western world is brought down."

"Exactly—we demonise, dehumanise, deliberately misunderstand and the cost is terrible. We should be talking, accepting, respecting, not killing each other's children. That's why I must visit."

"Yes, I think you must," Jonathan said. He took a mouthful of brandy and sighed. "But first you're off to Masada in a couple of days." He managed a smile.

"Yes I am," I said, glad to be changing the subject. "I just hope I can cope with the climb in the desert heat."

"I'm sure you'll manage. You're in good shape, what with all those sheep to look after."

I gave a little laugh. "That may be so. But I'm used to freezing, driving rain and a wild south-westerly."

"You'll be fine. I just hope you can put up with Eitan. He's more of a force of nature than the desert when he gets started."

"Oh, I think I can handle him," I said. "I can stand up for myself, you know."

"Yes, I know you can. From what he said after your first meeting he seemed well impressed by your feistiness."

"Did he?" I said, feeling rather pleased by this piece of information. I couldn't help smiling as I spoke.

"It matters to you, doesn't it? It matters what Eitan thinks of you."

"Yes," I said, looking at my brother. "Oh, here we go again! It matters, but not for the reasons you're thinking."

"Hmm. Eitan is charismatic—charming—I can see why you—"

"Stop! Stop with the matchmaking! Eitan's your best friend so it matters to me that I made a good impression for your sake. And, yes, I enjoyed his company, enjoyed our discussion. I'm really not looking for romance. I'm done with all that. Really, I am."

But when Jonathan replied, it was as if I hadn't just spoken, "Be careful, Rache. Eitan's charismatic but he hasn't exactly got a good track record with women."

Chapter Twenty Six

Masada loomed above us as we toiled up Snake Path. We'd set off from the hostel before dawn, but the sun was now up and, even although it was still early, the heat was intense. I wished we'd taken the easier route up the Roman ramp on the west side. But Eitan had insisted on approaching by the only path that would have existed when Herod built his pleasure palace on the summit.

"Stop, please, can we please stop just for a minute?" I ran the back of my hand along my forehead, in a vain attempt to stop the stinging combination of sweat and sun cream running down into my eyes.

Eitan glanced back at me and smiled. "Here," he said, swinging his backpack off his shoulder and taking a small towel out of it. In a few steps he was beside me. He removed my sunhat and dropped it at my feet. He tilted my head up and back with one hand and towelled my damp face and neck with the other. It reminded me of drying the children's faces when they were little. But, I was surprised to realise that, standing this close to Eitan, I felt anything but childlike.

"Thank you," I said, pulling the towel out of his hand. "I can do it." I stepped back from him and wiped the back of my neck, fresh sweat already seeping from my hairline.

Eitan shrugged, still smiling, and took a long drink of water. He looked impossibly cool. He held out the bottle. "You should drink."

I took off my rucksack and put it on the ground. I got my

own bottle of water out. Eitan shrugged and returned his to his bag.

I gulped the lukewarm water, aware of Eitan staring at me as I drank. I looked back at him as I wiped my mouth with the back of my hand and then replaced the cap on the bottle.

Eitan gave a slight shake of his head. "Come, we're nearly there," he said, turning and leading the way once more.

Nothing, not even Eitan's painting, could have prepared me for my first sight of that flat, rugged hilltop. Once we arrived at the massive fortress wall, we entered through the Snake Path Gate. Substantial parts of Herod's palaces and the Roman fortifications survived intact. I gasped at the sheer scale of the place.

After Eitan had led, and talked me through the palace complexes with their remains of bathhouses, reception halls, kitchens, living areas and garden terraces, he took me up to the centre of the summit, to what remained of a Byzantine church.

"Wow," I said. "This is all so incredible. I thought the UK, and especially Scotland, couldn't be beaten for palaces and castles, but this is strong competition."

Eitan beamed. "Yes, indeed. This is a remarkable place and not only because of the ancient architecture, of course."

"No, of course not. I must admit there is an atmosphere, a melancholy about the place."

"Not surprising, nine hundred and sixty Zealots took their own lives here rather than submit to the Romans. It's a sacred place, a symbol of Jewish resistance to oppression."

"Indeed," I said.

And for a quiet moment, we both stood, looking around us.

"Now, come and see the view." Eitan, grabbed me by the hand. He led me first to the western edge of the crag's flat summit. There below was the Judean Desert with its terraced golden hills. Then we looked east out to the Dead Sea and I was surprised at the water's colourful beauty. To the south, Eitan pointed out how the crag's tail led eventually to the Syrian edge of the African rift valley.

"Enough!" I said, laughing. "I can't take in any more. This place is amazing!"

"Better than home?"

"Hmm, I don't know about that. We have some ancient and very bloody sites too, even just in my tiny patch."

"Ah, yes your island—Skye?"

"Yes, Skye." I was caught by a sudden twinge of emotion. Was it homesickness? But homesickness for what exactly? I wasn't sure. I pushed it away.

We took the cable car down from the visitor centre and walked back to Eitan's jeep. As he drove away from the fortress site, Eitan said, "We should go check in at the hotel. We can shower, get some lunch and then later we will swim."

"Okay," I said, feeling slightly irritated. Eitan's plans did sound good, but I couldn't quite get used to having someone else planning my day for me. I reminded myself that I was on holiday and that I was trying to reconnect with my fellow human beings. And so I made a conscious effort to just go with the flow as Eitan went on to tell me about other sites we could visit in the Judean desert and around the shores of the Dead Sea.

Our hotel was one of several on the sea's western shore and I had to admit to myself that Eitan had chosen well. He hadn't gone for one of the more modern, high-rise establishments. Instead, our accommodation was small and homely, a low, white-washed building with a central courtyard shaded by olive trees and decorated with terracotta pots of red geraniums. Its dim interior, with its marble floors, shutters and excellent air-conditioning was beautifully cool.

After showering, I sat on my white-covered bed and towelled my hair dry. I was hungry and looking forward to lunch. I also realised I was looking forward to spending the next couple of days seeing all the places Eitan had just told me about. I smiled at myself in the mirror, acknowledging that I was in serious danger of relaxing.

And, as I got dressed in fresh green cotton trousers and a

cream-coloured, short sleeved blouse, I was aware of a feeling of wellbeing and of peace. I felt I was where I was meant to be. My earlier pangs of possible homesickness were gone. Israel was definitely getting under my skin.

We sat in the courtyard to eat lunch—a delicious salad of goat's cheese, olives and huge sweet tomatoes accompanied by thick slices of rye bread. We also shared a jug of freshly-pressed apple juice. I continued to feel relaxed and at home, happy to listen to all that Eitan had to tell me about the history, geography and geology of the region. His love for his country was very apparent and I envied him his sense of certainty about his place in the world.

We finished off the meal with coffee. While we were drinking it, I reached into my bag for a hairclip and sat back, twisting my hair into a knot and fixing it in place at the back of my head.

As I did so, I was aware that Eitan was watching me closely. "What is it?" I asked.

"I prefer it—your hair—I like it down on your shoulders." Eitan sipped his coffee and continued to stare at me over his cup.

"Oh," I said, unsure how to react. "It's just—it's cooler—up off my neck." I felt flustered, embarrassed by this sudden intimacy. I picked up my own cup and looked down into it.

I jumped at Eitan's sudden laughter. "What's funny?" I said.

"You—you have no idea do you? No idea of the effect you have on men, on me."

Now I felt a blush flood my neck and face. I really hadn't been prepared for his answer.

"You are beautiful, Rachel. Don't you know that? Your face—with its many—many what do you call it—how you look like you think?"

"Expressions?"

"Yes, your many expressions. So much is there on your face—and it is beautiful. You are beautiful."

"Oh," I said again. I gulped some coffee.

"Your husband—he must have told you this?"

"Peter? No, I don't believe he did. Oh, he said nice things—of course he did—in the early days at least—but never that."

"And since your husband—surely—there is someone— someone in Scotland who tells you this—someone special?"

I now managed to laugh. "Eh—no—not in the whole of Scotland—there's no one who has told me I'm beautiful and there's no one special—if by that you mean a man."

"Then I am not impressed by Scottish men."

"Now you come to mention it, neither am I," I laughed again.

Eitan laughed too and put down his coffee cup. "Now we should rest. And later we will swim."

I couldn't think of any reason to disagree and after arranging to meet again in a couple of hours, we went to our rooms.

I lay on the bed, enjoying the wafts of cool air from the ceiling fan, and thought about what Eitan had said. Even although I remembered Jonathan's warning about Eitan and his relationships with women and even although my head told me it was probably just Eitan's charm talking, I was flattered. Who wouldn't be? It was lovely to be complimented and, more than that, to be treated as an attractive woman. After so long it was actually quite exhilarating and there was something so open and uncomplicated about Eitan, nothing bottled up, no need for guesswork. It was refreshing to be in his company. I decided to enjoy it for what it was—a harmless flirtation.

I was awakened an hour or so later by my phone ringing. It was Morag. She was calling for a catch up. The first thing she asked me about was how I'd got on with Sophie. I hesitated before answering but I decided to tell her everything. I hadn't shared what had happened with anyone. Every time Jonathan had asked about my daughter I'd changed the subject. And who better to tell than my best friend.

I could sense Morag's shock at what I told. It was in her voice when she said, "I don't know what to say."

"There's not much you or anyone can say, but thanks for listening. I don't know why exactly but I've felt too ashamed and embarrassed to tell anybody about it." I replied.

"You've nothing to be ashamed of but I do understand why you wouldn't find it easy to talk about. I'm just so sorry, Rachel. Sorry for you, sorry for Sophie. Will you see her again on your way home?"

"We parted on such bad terms, I honestly don't know."

"Well whatever, I hope it doesn't spoil your time away."

"I'm trying very hard not to let it. Now let's change the subject. How are things on Skye?"

So Morag filled me in on how the lambs and the ewes were doing and brought me up to date on all the local gossip. And then I told her about the trip I was on.

"It sounds amazing," she said. I can't really imagine what it's like in the desert."

"Yeah," I laughed. "It's quite different from Skye! But it's just as beautiful, only in a different way. We're going for a swim later in the Dead Sea. I can't imagine what that'll be like either."

"Oh, swimming together, you and this friend of your brother's—Eitan, was it?" I could hear the smile—the mischievous smile in Morag's voice.

"Yes—Eitan," I said, smiling too. "Yes, swimming together. What of it?"

"I don't know. It just sounds sort of intimate. You're not just on holiday together, but you're also—"

"Swimming. Scandalous, I know! But as long as Queen Victoria doesn't find out it should be fine."

"Yeah, yeah," Morag said. "Okay it's not scandalous. Of course it isn't, but—but you haven't, you don't—you wouldn't normally—"

"What—I wouldn't normally what? Dare to have a life—to enjoy myself. I'm sorry if you don't approve." I spoke a bit more sharply than I'd meant to.

"Sorry," Morag said. "I'm not criticising. It's great that you're enjoying yourself, great that you're with a, that you've made a—a friend."

"No, it's me who's sorry," I said. "I've no idea why I was being so prickly—or rather I do know why."

"Why?"

"Because you're right. I have made a friend. I've made a friend who's a man. A man who has told me I'm beautiful. A lovely, passionate, charming man who I'm enjoying spending time with."

"Well, it's about time!" Morag said. "I don't know. What are you like? You hide away from men for years and then it's one after the other. First Jack and now Eitan."

I gasped, then laughed. "No, what are *you* like? They're both new friends of mine who just happen to be male. Don't go getting carried away. How is Jack by the way? Have you seen much of him recently?"

"I have as it happens and he's well. He asked me if I'd heard from you, said to say he was asking after you if we were in touch."

"Really?"

"Yes, really. But if you're such good friends, why don't you call him, find out for yourself how he is."

"Yes, okay, maybe I will," I said. "It would be good to talk to him." I realised as I said this that I really did want to speak to Jack; that I wanted to share my experiences in Israel with him.

"Yes, go on, I dare you—call Jack—let him know you're missing him."

I gasped again. "I never said I was missing him. I simply asked how he was."

"Uh huh," said Morag. "You can say what you like but I know you. I can tell by your voice it's more than polite interest. And there's nothing wrong with that, nothing wrong with getting closer to Jack and—."

"I'll call him! As soon as I'm back in Jerusalem I'll call him." I knew Morag had my best interests at heart but she was pushing it now. I was also very glad that she didn't know the true extent of my feelings for Jack.

"And," said Morag, not in the least put off, "I dare you to let that guard of yours down in Israel too. Let yourself go under the desert sky with Eitan, the lovely, passionate charmer."

"Okay, I need to go now, but it's been good to talk to you."

"Yes, okay. Sorry to go on, Rache. It's because I care."

"I know it is. I know."

Walking to meet Eitan, I smiled to myself as I reflected on Morag's advice. She was right. It was time to let myself go, at least a bit. Why not let a man get close to me? I was free of responsibilities. I was on holiday. I was on an adventure and, for now, I'd flirt right back with Eitan.

As I swam, my mood matched the incredibly buoyant waters of the Dead Sea. I felt light in body and heart. And my carefree frame of mind persisted after our swim and meant that I was comfortable enough to smooth the sea's black, therapeutic mud onto Eitan's back and chest as we sat at the water's edge.

"You have a very soothing touch," Eitan said, as I spread and rubbed the thick, dark gloop on his back and shoulders. He was sitting and I knelt behind him. He caught hold of my wrist and turned to face me. He stroked the back of my hand with his thumb.

I pulled my hand away, stood up and laughed to cover the embarrassment I felt. Flirting was all very well, but I wasn't sure I was ready for anything more intimate. "It's nothing to do with me. It'll be the sea's special powers." I walked away. "I'm going in for one more dip. No need to wait for me. I'll see you at dinner."

"It has been a long time, I think," Eitan said. We were finishing dinner in the hotel restaurant with a cup of Turkish coffee. We'd enjoyed a delicious meal of stuffed aubergines and fragrant rice, followed by a wonderful orange cheesecake. Eitan had been his usual relaxed self. Helped by a large glass of red wine, I also felt relaxed. We were talking about our work, about our art training and influences and the kind of stuff we did now. I complimented

Eitan again on his painting of Masada. He said how he'd like to see some of my work. I'd even managed a flirtatious reply along the lines of 'Well come to Scotland and I'll show you my samples'. We both laughed. Eitan put his hand on mine. I let him hold it for a moment, looked at him across the table, then pulled away.

And that's when he remarked that it had been a long time. "How long, Rachel? How long has it been?" he persisted.

"What do you mean? What's been a long time?"

"Since you've been with a man."

"What?" I couldn't keep the annoyance out of my voice.

"Sorry, sorry!" Eitan raised his hands in submission. "It's none of my business. I'm just a typical rude Israeli. Sorry."

"It's okay, but, yes, it is none of your business and yes it's been a long time. There's been no one since my divorce five years ago." I stood up. "I'm tired. I think I'll go to bed."

Eitan stood up too. "I'll see you to your room."

We walked along the corridor in silence and stopped at my door. We stood facing each other. Eitan raised his hand and stroked my cheek. This time I held his gaze. He leant forward, tipped up my chin with the tip of his finger, and kissed me on the mouth. I didn't resist. I enjoyed it and I kissed him back. He put his arms around me and I let him. My level of surprise at myself was considerable, but I savoured the wonderful feeling of being held for quite a few moments before gently extricating myself from his arms.

"Goodnight Eitan," I said. "Thanks for today and for this evening. I've enjoyed it." I smiled, turned away and let myself into my room, closing the door gently but firmly behind me.

Next morning, we met at breakfast. Eitan was already seated at a table when I walked out into the courtyard. He stood up as I approached.

"*Boker tov*," I said.

Eitan laughed. "Hebrew! I'm impressed. Good morning." He leaned across the table and kissed me on both cheeks.

"You slept well?" he asked as we sat down.

"Very well and I had a lovely day yesterday."

"Me too—a perfect day and a perfect ending." Eitan smiled even more broadly.

"Yes, Masada is an amazing place, a dramatic setting and an even more dramatic history. And as for the Dead Sea, I don't know what I expected exactly, but it goes way beyond anything I could have imagined. I certainly didn't expect it or the desert to be so beautiful. Thanks, Eitan—for bringing me here and for—for everything."

"You're welcome. I love my country. I love showing it off. And I'm very much enjoying your company—as I hope you know."

"Yes," my voice was no more than a whisper, but my gaze didn't waver from Eitan's face.

"Now, let's eat. The breakfast buffet looks good."

"Yes, let's," I replied, and my gratitude to Eitan for not referring directly to last night's kiss made me feel all the more warmly towards him.

As we ate eggs, yogurt and oranges and drank large cups of milky coffee, Eitan explained where we would be going on the last day of our desert trip. But even Eitan's detailed descriptions didn't prepare me for the outstanding beauty and sheer contrasts of the landscapes I was about to see.

Qumran, with its two thousand-year-old ruins was breathtaking. It was situated on the edge of the Judean wilderness and I stood in silence surveying the crumbled, pale limestone buildings. They were all that remained of the settlement where the scribes of the Dead Sea Scrolls wrote their parts of the Christian bible.

It was already very warm, but not as intensely hot as it had been at Masada. There was also an occasional cooling breeze.

I walked quietly along a pavement that two millennia before would have led to the baths, potteries and refectories of the ancient sect who had lived there striving for spiritual purity. I touched the stonework and for a moment felt a connection—a deep wordless connection with life, with Earth, with eternity. I thought of home, of Sophie and of Finlay and for a moment I felt hope. It was only a moment but again it was as if something had shifted, fallen back into place. I looked around for Eitan.

He'd left me to my contemplation and busied himself taking photographs. Again I felt grateful to him for his sensitivity. I took some photographs too and then I went over to him.

"What an incredible place," I said.

"It is," Eitan said. "The desert and the wilderness, people think they are barren places, that they are ugly and not welcoming. But when you get to know a place like this—Judea or the Negev—then you see such richness. It is where I come to—to fill up—you know what I mean?

"Like a well—you refill. You come to here to be inspired."

"That's it, yes. For an artist, the colours, the light, the feeling around..." Eitan gestured around him.

"The atmosphere?" I suggested.

"Yes, the atmosphere. You feel it too, as an artist?"

"Definitely, and more than that, I sense a connection, something ancient but also timeless. I already felt it a little in Jerusalem. It's that kind of city. But out here it's more than history. It's, oh, I don't know how to describe it..."

"I haven't seen you look like that before," Eitan said.

"Like what?"

"Your eyes, they shine, you are more—more alive. You really are inspired by all this. The land, it moves us. We don't just look at a place. The place it looks back, it changes us, tells us truths. You say you can't put it into words, but you could paint what you're feeling, couldn't you?"

"I don't know, perhaps. Like I said before, it's been so long since I painted anything. I mean I do my book illustrations and some sketching, but it's been years since I did anything on canvas."

"But from what you and your brother have said your island is a beautiful place. You have mountains and wilderness and sea.

And yet you do not paint."

"Skye is beautiful, wild and beautiful and full of contrasts, but I think I've just stopped seeing it. I feel like I've been sleep-walking for a very long time."

"And now, I think something has changed for you?"

"It's beginning to, yes."

Eitan put his arm around my shoulders. "Come," he said. "We should move on, get to Ein Gedi before it gets much hotter."

Much as I'd been unprepared for the tragic majesty of Masada and its desert setting, for the weirdness of the Dead Sea, and for the spiritual connection I'd experienced at Qumran, they all became rather milder surprises when I saw Ein Gedi.

I'd known beforehand that it was an oasis and therefore knew to expect vegetation and some water. But the sights that greeted me were utterly stunning.

On arrival, Eitan pulled into the car park at one of the wadis. "First we will walk and later we will swim," he said.

And, as we walked in the cool shelter of the tall Ha'etekim cliff and breathed the bromide-laden air, I struggled to take in the full intensity of the colours. The predominant greens and blues were daubed here and there with vibrant reds, pinks, oranges and yellows.

Ein Gedi was not so much an oasis as the Garden of Eden. It was lush with trees and flowers. Even the cacti were in flower. There were rivers and waterfalls that crashed into crystal pools, spas with hot springs and mud baths.

I gasped and exclaimed at each new sight. I took lots of photos. I took panoramic shots of the cliffs and close-ups of the sparkling water and the trees and flowers.

"I can see you are impressed," Eitan said.

"I am. It's yet another inspiring place."

We walked on a bit further before turning back to the car.

"What now?" I asked as Eitan drove out of the car park. I took off my hat and pushed my sunglasses up onto the top of my head as I relaxed back into my seat.

"We are going to Kibbutz Ein Gedi where we will stay tonight. I think you will like it."

A little later I could indeed confirm that I liked the kibbutz. It sat on the top of a hill with beautiful views all around. Eitan had ordered a picnic lunch from the guesthouse and we ate it sitting on a bench in the kibbutz's botanical garden surrounded by yet more gorgeous flowers and trees. Lunch was followed by a siesta and then a swim and massage at the spa.

So I was very relaxed when I showered and dressed for dinner that evening. I decided on the green dress again. Checking myself in the mirror, I noticed my normally very pale skin was taking on a slight tan and my freckles were out in force over my nose and cheeks. I put in my amber drop earrings, applied some lipstick and a quick spray of perfume and I was ready.

The guesthouse restaurant was small and intimate. The outside wall was almost entirely made up of sliding doors which stood open and led out onto a veranda. It was there that I found Eitan, sitting at a small bamboo table. A bottle of champagne in an ice-bucket sat in the middle of the table along with two glasses.

Eitan stood up to greet me. "You look lovely as always," he said, looking me up and down before kissing me on both cheeks.

"Thank you," I replied. I no longer felt embarrassed by his obvious appreciation, in fact I quite enjoyed it. I smiled at him as I sat down.

"Champagne?" he said, lifting the bottle out of the bucket.

"Yes, please. But what are we celebrating?"

"Many things. Being here, being alive, being together," replied Eitan, passing me a glass and looking into my eyes. "L'chaim," he said.

I laughed as we chinked glasses. "Yes, to life," I said.

As we drank our champagne we chatted about the things we'd seen on the trip. As before, Eitan was very knowledgeable about the flora and fauna as well as the history of the area and I enjoyed listening to him.

"This is such a beautiful place," I said. "Thanks again for bringing me."

"It has been a pleasure," he said, smiling. "So, which part of our lovely country will you visit next?"

"Ah, I'm not sure you'll approve," I said.

"Oh, why not?"

"I'm going to the West Bank with Deb. We're going for a couple of nights at the end of next week."

"Why would I not approve? It is good that you go. You should see for yourself, reach your own judgement. Too many people comment without knowing what they are talking about. I look forward to hearing what you think on your return."

"I look forward to telling you," I said. We looked at each other, acknowledging that a challenge had been set down and accepted.

We'd just ordered our meals and moved through to our restaurant table when my phone rang. I wasn't going to answer it, but Eitan said he didn't mind.

"Hello, Jack," I said. I was conscious of the flush creeping up my neck and face. I was also conscious of Eitan watching me.

"Hi, I hope you don't mind me calling," Jack said.

It was so good to hear his voice. "I don't mind at all," I said.

"How are you? Are you enjoying Israel?"

"I'm well, thanks and enjoying my time here very much. Israel's an amazing country. How are you?"

"Oh, I'm fine. The house is finished and even though I say so myself, it's looking pretty good." There was a pause than he went on, "So, I hope I haven't disturbed you. Are you at your brother's this evening?"

"I'm not actually. I've been away on a trip for the last few days down in the desert in the south of the country. I go back to Jerusalem tomorrow. I'm in a restaurant at the moment. We're just waiting for our starters."

"Oh, sorry. Are you with Jonathan and the family?"

"No—no I'm not." I felt uncomfortable "I'm with Eitan. He's a friend of Jonathan's. He was keen to show me this part of the country. He's—he's a very knowledgeable guide."

"Ah, sorry, I'd no idea. I just assumed you'd be with your family, not with a—a friend."

"No need to apologise. It's good to hear from you."

"Is it? I'm sure you'd rather not be interrupted in the middle of an intimate meal." I probably imagined it but he sounded irritated.

"It's not intimate and we haven't started eating yet. And, yes, yes it is good to hear from you. I was just saying to Morag yesterday that I would be phoning you when I got back to the city." I rubbed the back of my neck. It felt clammy.

"Oh, were you?"

"Yes, yes I was." I swallowed. My cheeks were burning. I glanced at Eitan who was still watching me, a slightly amused expression on his face.

"Okay then. I look forward to hearing from you soon."

"I'll call in the next couple of days. I promise."

"Okay." Jack's voice sounded different, softer.

"Okay. Bye." I dropped my phone back into my bag.

Eitan sat back, still smiling, still watching me.

"Sorry. That was Jack—from home—the friend I told you about."

Eitan leant in towards me. "I think he is more than a friend to you, Rachel."

"What? No he isn't. I told you before—there's nobody—no one—who's—Jack's a friend. I haven't known him very long—but we...we get along.

Eitan shrugged and refilled my champagne glass.

The hummus and falafel starter was superb. It was followed by an equally delicious main course of fish, caught that day and barbecued within sight of our table, served with couscous and vine tomatoes. Our conversation throughout the meal was

mostly light-hearted and amusing. We talked more about painting and Eitan urged me to take it up again when I got home.

As I drained the last of my champagne, I was infused with
a feeling of wellbeing. And I don't believe this was entirely due
to the alcohol I'd consumed. It was as we had our coffee that I
acknowledged to myself just how fond I'd become of Eitan in
a relatively short time. I hadn't met anyone quite so open, so
transparent and so honest. He was very easy to be with.

So, when he suggested a walk after dinner I said I'd like that
very much. We walked out onto the beach. I carried my sandals and walked barefoot on the now cool sand. And when Eitan
took my hand, it felt natural to let him.

I glanced up at the moon and thought briefly of home, of
how the moon would also be looking down on Skye—and on
Jack. It had been good to talk to him, even if it was only briefly. But I suppressed the yearning I felt at the thought of him. I
couldn't have him. I had to get over it. I'd spent long enough on
'if only'. What mattered was what was possible, what was happening now.

"What are you thinking?" Eitan asked, stopping and also
glancing at the moon.

I turned to face him. "I was thinking of home—of Skye."

"Homesick?" he looked deep into my eyes.

"Not homesick exactly. I'm enjoying my time in Israel very
much." I held his gaze.

Eitan lifted his hand to my face. When he spoke it was very
softly. "I hope that you come to love—Israel." Then he kissed me
and I put my arms around him and kissed him back.

When we stopped kissing, Eitan whispered, "Come." He took
my hand once more. I allowed myself to be led back to my room
and this time when we got to my door, I realised that I didn't
want to part from this man—not yet.

"Would you like to come in for a—for a while?" I asked.

Eitan looked at me. He stroked my hair. "Yes, Rachel, I would like very much to come in."

Making love with Eitan felt like the most natural thing in the world. As we undressed, Eitan said, "You are sure about this?"

"I'm sure," I said, as I lay down on the bed.

Eitan's lovemaking was skilled and generous and I gave myself up to the sensations that swept my body. And in my turn, I explored and pleasured Eitan until we rolled apart exhausted and satisfied. For some moments neither of us spoke. Then Eitan turned onto his side and pulled me close in beside him. He covered us both with the sheet.

"I think your awakening is complete," he said, smiling at me.

I smiled back. "Mmm, I believe it is."

We were up early the next morning. Or rather Eitan was. It was the sound of him singing in the shower that woke me. I stretched and smiled to myself as I listened to him and thought back over the last few days and the previous evening in particular. When Eitan emerged from the shower wearing only a towel, I was still in bed, lying back on a pile of pillows.

"Good morning," he said, coming over to sit on the edge of the bed. He took my hand. "You are okay?"

"Yes, I'm more than okay. I feel good—very good."

"So, no regrets about last night?"

"No, no regrets. I owe you, Eitan."

He looked at me, puzzled.

"I mean it," I said. "I've enjoyed the journey, your company, the—the sex."

"You don't owe me a thing. I have enjoyed it too, being with you wasn't a favour. I wanted it. I wanted you." He leant over and kissed me lightly on the forehead and then more passionately on the lips. As he did so, I lifted the sheet that covered me and we made love again. It was unhurried and deeply satisfying.

And afterwards, when Eitan had gone to his own room for a second shower and to get some fresh clothes, I recognised that it was just that. Deeply satisfying and wonderful sex. I knew that a long suppressed need had been satisfied and a very important part of me had been revived by this lovely, interested and interesting man. And I was glad. It is what it is, I thought, and I'm going to enjoy it while it lasts.

After a lazy breakfast together accompanied by relaxed conversation, we packed up the car and set off back to Jerusalem.

Eitan dropped me off at Jonathan's. He couldn't come up to the flat as he had to go and prepare for a work trip to Tel Aviv where he was meeting with a couple of gallery owners. He put my bags down on the pavement and then took me in his arms. He kissed me and stroked my face and hair. "I look forward to seeing you when you return from the West Bank," he said.

Nobody was at home when I let myself into the apartment. I was glad to have a bit of time on my own. There was a lot for me to reflect on. As I unpacked and showered I thought back over the trip—the places, the stories, Eitan. I was now certain I'd done the right thing coming on this journey. I felt like a very different person to the one Jack had pulled out of the burn.

I'd just finished eating my lunch when Morag phoned. At first I was surprised she was calling again so soon. Of course I shouldn't have been surprised. I quickly realised what had motivated her.

"You want the gossip, don't you?" I said. "You want to know if anything happened between Eitan and me." I couldn't help smiling.

"No! That is, yes. I do. I'm sorry. I'm a nosy cow, I know."

"This is like when we were teenagers!" I was laughing now.

"So, tell me. Did anything happen?"

"Yes, if you must know. Yes it did. We slept together and—and it was great."

There was a gasp followed by a pause. I could imagine Morag's surprised expression.

"There," I said. "You didn't expect that, did you?"

"No. I thought you'd go all private and evasive on me. And I didn't expect—"

"And you didn't expect an answer in the affirmative!" I laughed again.

"Well good for you! It's about time. But you're not going to marry him and settle in Israel are you?"

"Right, that's enough. You're incorrigible. Marriage has not been discussed, strange I know, after one whole night together!" We chatted on a bit more, me trying to change the subject and Morag trying to get every last detail of how I felt about Eitan. It was fun and it really did feel as if we were back at school discussing boys.

When Deb got home in the late afternoon, I was sitting out on the balcony reading. "It's good to have you back," she said, hugging me. "It was a good trip?"

"It was - wonderful, thanks," I replied.

Deb looked at me. "I can see that. You look—you look different. Something—something in your eyes is different. Right, this calls for a large glass of wine and a long girly chat." She went off into the kitchen and soon returned with a glass of white wine in each hand. And once we were both settled at the balcony table, Deb said, "Right, tell me everything."

I recounted my impressions of Masada, Ein Gedi and the other places we'd visited. I enthused about Qumran and the deep connection I'd felt there. "It was such a good trip. This country is amazing. I do love it here."

"And?" Deb raised an eyebrow.

"And?" I said, unable to stop myself smiling or blushing.

"And what else? What of Eitan? How did you two get along?"

I felt my neck and face become even hotter. It was one thing telling Morag what had happened with Eitan. She was my oldest friend and she was thousands of miles away. But Deb was much closer to the situation, in every sense, and I felt more exposed. "Fine, we got along just fine," I said.

"Oh my—you didn't! You did! You and Eitan—you." Deb put

her hands to her face.

I realised there was no point in being evasive. "Don't look so shocked."

"I'm not shocked. I'm just surprised—not at Eitan—but—but—"

"At me. At dull old Rachel who never has sex!"

"No! Well—yes—not dull—but sensible. I was only teasing when I asked how you got along. I didn't expect... Look, I don't doubt you have sex, but with Eitan, he's so... I'm sorry Rachel. I don't mean to offend you." Deb looked stricken.

I smiled. "I'm not offended. And I don't—I haven't been with a man since Peter." Deb tried unsuccessfully to hide her surprise. "No, really I haven't," I continued. "The truth is I've been in a very long limbo since the divorce."

"And now you've come out of that limbo?"

"It seems I have. Coming here, it's changed my perspective on so many things. I feel connected again to life, to myself. There's colour, intensity, passion. I'm so glad I came. And Eitan, I suppose, is some sort of embodiment of all that."

"Hmm," Deb said, "I suppose you could describe him like that, and it's cool that you and Eitan get along so well. But be careful, Rachel. Don't give him your heart."

"I don't intend to."

Deb looked sceptical.

"It's true! Now, any chance of a change of subject and a re-fill?" I raised my empty glass.

Deb laughed. "You got it."

Chapter Twenty Seven

As my time in Israel passed, Skye seemed further and further away. I wasn't homesick, but there were things I missed—the view from the croft, Bonnie, hearing Gaelic, local gossip, Morag, the soft rain and yes, Jack. I often found myself wanting to tell him what I'd been up to, to tell him of my impressions, to share how I was feeling.

I called him, as I'd said I would, on my return from the desert. It was good to speak to him. The first part of our conversation was taken up almost entirely by me. I described Masada and its eerie sense of tragedy. I talked about the history and vibrancy of Qumran. I spoke of how it felt to swim in the Dead Sea and of Ein Gedi's amazing lushness. I mentioned Eitan in passing, saying he'd been an excellent guide and describing some of the meals we'd shared. "But that's enough about me," I said, realising that Jack was very quiet on the other end of the line. "I'm sorry for going on and on. How are you?"

"I'm fine. And no need to apologise. I enjoyed hearing all about the places you've been. It seems like quite a country."

"It's a very special place. I feel quite restored, brought back to life in a way, I suppose. I know that probably sounds a bit daft."

"Not daft at all. It sounds understandable and it seems like you and Eitan have struck up a friendship as well."

"Yes—yes we have. He's been kind to me and we—we get along."

"Right. So, what's next on your itinerary?"

"I'm off to the West Bank for a long weekend at the end of this week—"

"With Eitan?"

"No, with Deb, my sister-in-law."

"Ah right. Isn't that area a bit dangerous?"

"Yes and no, probably not any more so than anywhere else here, as long as you're careful. We're going on an organised tour with a local guide. The people there welcome tourists."

"And you're keen to visit?"

"Definitely. I've only seen Israel from the Jewish perspective so far. There are two and a half million Palestinians living behind that wall. I want to get the whole picture. After all if I decide to settle here, I need to know—to understand more about the politics."

"Oh? That's still a possibility, is it? That you might settle there—leave Skye?"

There was a strange tone to Jack's voice. He seemed irritated. I guessed he was probably just a bit baffled.

"I don't know—not yet—but it's more of a possibility now than it was before I came. I've fallen in love with the place and my family's here after all."

"But you have family in Scotland, your daughter, and other people who—who love you. Wouldn't you miss them, miss your Scottish life?"

I gave a mirthless, little laugh. "I wouldn't see any less of my daughter than I do now. Of course I'd miss my friends, but I don't really have a life anymore in Scotland. Recently, I've just been existing, not living. It's high time for a fresh start." I swallowed hard. I needed to change the subject. "Anyway, like I said, enough about me." Jack didn't speak. I began to wonder if we still had a connection. "Are you still there, Jack? Jack, hello?"

"I'm still here."

"Ah, good. I thought we'd lost each other. So, how's the house? How are Poppy and your daughter?"

"Poppy's great and Maddie's pregnancy is progressing okay now, thanks. And I'm very pleased with how the house has turned out."

"That's good."

"I've actually got a guest at the house at the moment."

"Oh?"

"Bonnie has come to stay."

"Bonnie? Bonnie's with you? Why?"

"She sort of adopted me. She kept turning up on my doorstep. She would scratch on the door to be let in and if I was out, she'd be on the step waiting for me when I got back. Poor Morag kept having to come looking for her. So I said it would be easier if Bonnie just lodged with me."

"I see. Well, thanks. I'll reimburse you for food and stuff when I get back."

"No need. It's a pleasure to have her around. She's good company and we walk down to the croft every day and help with the sheep. According to Morag, I'm becoming a not bad shepherd."

"Praise indeed!" I said.

"Yes, though I don't think Alasdair's all that impressed. Those ewes of yours know how to give me the runaround. Even the lambs get the better of me a lot of the time."

I laughed. "How are the lambs doing?"

"I'm no expert, but Morag and Alasdair seem quite happy with them. There's been a fox around, got a couple of Alasdair's lambs, and some from other crofts in the township, but yours haven't been touched so far."

"Oh, right."

"And one of the ewes, number twenty-seven I think it is, she keeps getting out of the field. Alasdair swears she knows which fencepost is the dodgy one and she head butts it till it gives way."

"Number twenty-seven? That's the ewe that ended up in the burn that night—the night we met."

"Oh, is it? They all look the same to me. Well she's obviously still a bit of a renegade—but not all bad."

"No?"

"No, she brought us together. Or not together exactly, but you know..." There was a pause. Jack cleared his throat.

I thought he was probably kicking himself, saying something unintentionally intimate and daft. I helped him out. "Made sure we met?" I offered.

"Yes—and I'm glad she did."

There was another pause. Then I said, "Me too." And for a moment I had the strongest urge to see Jack, to be with him. I struggled to push the feeling away. Struggled with the pointlessness.

This time it was Jack who moved the conversation on. "I took a walk with Bonnie the other day, out to the point, the walk you and I did together. It was a beautiful day. There were a couple of sea eagles flying out over the water. An adult and a young one, I think. They were a magnificent sight. And there were dolphins—or maybe it was porpoises—it's the stoat-weasel thing again. I'm not sure of the difference to be honest. Anyway they appeared while I was eating my sandwiches."

I pictured the coastal path, the moor and the cliffs, and the view over the Minch. I imagined Bonnie running and chasing the gannets, heard the ewes calling to their lambs. I pictured the landscape and Jack as part of it. The yearning took my breath away and, for a moment, I didn't trust myself to speak.

Now it seemed it was Jack's turn to wonder about the phone connection. "Rachel? Rachel, hallo, are you still there?"

I took a deep breath. "Yes, yes I'm still here. It was just what you said about your walk. I felt a bit homesick."

"Ah, there's hope then."

"Hope?"

"Yes, hope that you'll come back, that Skye will still be home."

"I'll definitely be back, in the short term at the very least. After that I'll see."

I thought I heard Jack sigh then he said, "Okay, well keep in touch and call me when you get back from the West Bank."

I promised I would. Talking with him had been bittersweet. I'd enjoyed it but the yearning it had set off persisted for some time.

Chapter Twenty Eight

Deb and I boarded the tour operator's mini-bus in the late afternoon. It was the end of June and I'd been away from home for eight weeks.

Besides us, our group consisted of two young women back-packers travelling together, and a woman of about my age, on her own, plus our guide. The bus headed south through the city.

Although the hottest part of the day had passed, it was still very warm. I could feel the perspiration on my back forming a damp patch on my t-shirt and my legs felt as if they were stuck to the seat even through my cotton trousers. The air-conditioning on the bus wasn't exactly efficient and blew out stale, warm air. Sitting at the checkpoint, waiting to cross through the wall was even more uncomfortable as the engine and air-conditioning had to be turned off.

It wasn't much better when we got out of the bus to have our papers checked. The air inside the control point was still and stagnant, the atmosphere oppressive. The young Israeli soldier who checked my passport and visa smelled of sweat. I watched a line of perspiration trickle down his neck and round his Adam's apple as he read my details. An automatic rifle hung from his shoulder. He was probably a conscript doing his national service. He looked both innocent and threatening. He looked like a boy doing a man's job. He was very young, younger even than Finlay would have been. The thought of my son made me catch my breath, I felt light-headed. I thought of this soldier's mother, thought of how she must fear for her son. I swayed, desperate to sit.

The young man looked at me sharply. "You are okay?" he asked, his expression not unkind, but still serious.

"I'm okay, yes," I replied. I glanced over at Deb, but she wasn't looking at me. She looked as if she was explaining her travel documents to the soldier inspecting them. I turned back to my own inquisitor. "It's just the heat," I said.

The young man nodded and returned my papers. "Go," he said.

I stepped out of the checkpoint shed into the white light and heat of the day and rejoined the other members of the group at the dusty roadside.

At last we were on our way again. The bus continued south for another hour or so before pulling over close to some fields. Our little group had chosen to walk the last kilometre or so to the guesthouse rather than be driven. I'd thought this was a great idea when it was suggested by the guide. And it certainly proved to be so.

Walking in meant we saw things close up. We walked on the paths the local farmers walked. We passed one farmer who was out harvesting herbs. We passed some sheep grazing under olive trees and I stopped to watch and listen as the shepherd played panpipes to his flock of ewes and lambs. I smiled as I watched him and he nodded and smiled back. He looked at least seventy and his face was lined and weathered. He wore traditional Arab dress and could have stepped out of a picture in a bible storybook.

I turned to the guide, who'd stopped beside me. "I have sheep at home. I've never thought of playing live music to them!"

"I'll tell him," the guide replied. She called over to the shepherd and pointed at me as she translated what I'd said. He nodded and smiled again as he replied. "He says that the music keeps the mothers calm and makes them produce more milk. He also says that the lambs grow fatter because of the music."

"I'll give it a try when I get home," I said, looking over at the elderly man. The guide passed this on and he smiled more broadly.

All the way along our route the local people stopped what they were doing and welcomed us with smiles. Their children ran alongside us laughing and shouting. We stopped to talk to a group of women who were hand-milking their goats. The guide told us that the local women wanted to know if any of our group had children.

Deb said she had two, a boy and a girl, and this was met with smiling approval. But when the other middle-aged woman in our group said she had four sons, the response was rapturous and she was told she was a rich woman. The two young back-packers, who reported that they were childless, were told that they should hurry up and have lots of babies. I was last to reply and Deb squeezed my arm as I did so. I let the pain rise and pass. "I have a daughter," I said. "A grown-up daughter."

This brought lots of smiles and the guide reported that the women said that it would not be long before I was a grand-mother. I forced down the sarcasm and bitterness that rose to my lips and managed a tight smile. Thinking about Sophie and the abortion was only slightly less painful than thinking about Finlay. I was relieved to hear the guide say that we'd better be moving on to the guesthouse. Deb gave my arm another squeeze as we moved off, waving to the women.

"You okay?" Deb asked, as we returned to the dusty path.

"I'm fine, honestly," I said. I was determined not to let thoughts of Sophie, or of Finlay, encroach on my enjoyment of this trip, or on my impressions of the territory. Such thoughts were for another time and another place.

The Arab Women's Guesthouse was in the small town of Beit Sahour, near Bethlehem. The town itself seemed quiet and pleasant and the guesthouse shared the street with a few shops and a restaurant.

Our group was welcomed by a small, elderly, traditional-ly-dressed and softly-spoken Palestinian woman. She intro-duced herself as Hana Aker and told us that she ran the guest-house. She shook each of us by the hand and repeated our names back to us as we introduced ourselves to her. After she'd indicated where the dining-room and lounge were, she showed us to our rooms.

On the little, round, wooden table in the room that Deb and I would be sharing, two glasses of lemon tea awaited us along with a teapot, a plate of flatbread, a pot of honey and a bowl of figs, dates and Turkish delight. The twin-bedded room was simply furnished and was very clean and comfortable. It had air-conditioning and its own bathroom. It also had a long wide balcony with pots of geraniums all along its length as well as a table and chairs in the centre.

"I don't know what I was expecting exactly, but this wasn't it," I said, as Deb and I sipped our tea. We were standing on the balcony looking down at the street below.

"I know what you mean," Deb said. "The first time I was here, I thought it would be more primitive, less civilised somehow. It seems a terrible thing to say, but we're fed so much negative stuff about the Palestinians and the Arabs in general that to come to this pretty house in this normal, middle-eastern town is a surprise."

"And the people, the farmers and the families we met on the walk in, they were so lovely, so welcoming. They seemed genuinely pleased to see us."

Deb nodded. "It's quite humbling." We stood for a few more moments, taking in the sights and sounds of the street, and then Deb said, "Those goodies on the table inside are beckoning to me. Shall we go and sit indoors, get out of the heat for a while?"

"Sure," I said.

Once indoors, we topped up our tea and helped ourselves to some bread and honey. We sat in the low basket chairs in the cool shaded room, and for a while we ate in silence, apart from the occasional appreciative sound. The food was simple but delightful.

When we'd finished eating, Deb said, "You were very strong back there, when the women were asking us all about our families."

"I had to be. I didn't want to put a damper on everything by mentioning Finlay. And it's also sort of private."

"Mmm, I can see that, but I still think you're very brave."

"No, not brave. It's just easier, in certain situations, not to mention it. It helps sometimes just to let it lie, for a little while at least. Doing that sort of allows an illusion of normality."

"And Sophie, what about her? You've hardly mentioned her since you arrived. Jonathan says you change the subject any time he mentions her."

"Yes—yes, I know. It's difficult. It's such a mess. I don't know where to start."

"I know from Jonathan that she distanced herself from you after the divorce and that she blames you in some way for Finlay's death. But you visited her on your way to Israel. Did something happen then?"

I nodded.

"What, Rachel? What happened?"

I told Deb the whole sorry story. When it was told, I said, "So there you have it. My daughter is so unhappy she can't contemplate having her baby."

Before an obviously shocked Deb could say anything, I stood up, walked over to the balcony door and stepped out. I went over to the rail and looked down at the street. I wrapped my arms tightly around myself.

Deb came out and stood behind me. She put her hand on my shoulder. " Rachel," she said. "I'm so sorry."

"Yeah, well..." I turned back to face Deb.

"Come here," she said. She put her arms round me and hugged me. There were no words.

After a few moments, I said, "I'm glad you know, but let's leave it for now. Come on, let's have a bit of a walk before dinner, see a bit more of the town."

"Good idea," Deb said.

Later that night, after a tasty meal of lamb and rice in the guesthouse's pretty dining-room, I lay in bed thinking. Deb had fallen asleep quickly, but my mind wasn't ready for sleep, even if my body was.

The words of the farmer women, the things they'd said about grandchildren, repeated in my head. And of course, there was all the stuff I'd told Deb about Sophie. I picked over the details of that last meeting with my daughter. I should have fought harder, tried harder, reasoned harder. I should have offered her support. I shouldn't have got angry. I shouldn't have blamed and criticised my daughter. I shouldn't be thousands of miles away.

I sighed as I lay there watching the ceiling fan ticking away the moments of the night and tears slid down my face and neck and onto the pillow. I felt worthless. I'd lost everyone: husband, son, daughter...

Right, that's enough, I told myself. I didn't want to revert to being the person Jack had hauled out of the burn, the person who was just about ready to give up on life.

I got up, pushed my feet into my flip-flops, picked up my Kindle, and crept across the room. Thoughts of Jack stayed with me as I went downstairs and I realised that actually, right now, he was the person I'd most like to talk to. I wanted to tell him how I was feeling and to have him hold me close. This thought was followed very quickly by me telling myself to get a grip.

I'd intended to sit in the guest lounge for a while and read. But I noticed the kitchen door was ajar and there was a light on. Curiosity led me to the doorway. Hana stood at the wooden table in the centre of the room. She was kneading dough and singing softly to herself. I decided against disturbing her and turned to go. But the creak of the floorboards must have alerted her to my presence.

"Hello? Rachel, isn't it? You cannot sleep?"

"No, I can't. I thought I would read in the lounge. I'm sorry, I didn't mean to disturb you."

"Tea," Hana said. "I will make you tea. Come in. Sit down." She nodded at a chair at the head of the table where she was working. She rubbed the flour from her hands and then wiped them on her apron.

I hesitated in the doorway.

"Come, come, sit." Hana beckoned as she turned to fill the kettle.

I went in and sat down at the table. Hana returned to kneading the dough as the kettle sang its own little song. I watched Hana work. Neither of us spoke and by the time the kettle boiled, Hana had put the dough into a covered bowl and set it to prove on a shelf above the stove. I felt very soothed just sitting there, watching.

Hana tidied and wiped the table and then spooned tealeaves into a blue china teapot, before filling it with the hot water. She put two large blue teacups and their saucers on the table alongside the teapot. As I observed the small elderly woman, I was struck by her neatness and grace. She wore a white apron over her long robe-like dress, but she'd removed the headscarf she'd been wearing when she greeted us on our arrival. Her grey hair was swept back and pinned up in a bun. Her eyes were dark brown and deep-set, and the skin on her face and hands was weathered to a very deep tan. Her movements were deft without being rushed and she gave off an aura of stillness and of peace.

It wasn't until after she'd poured us both a cup of fragrant camomile tea that Hana spoke again.

"You are troubled," she said.

I took a sip of tea before I replied. "I had too many thoughts going round in my head. They were stopping me sleeping."

"Perhaps if you share your thoughts they will lose their power to keep you awake." Hana smiled kindly.

"Your English is very good. Have you lived in the UK?"

"Yes, in Oxford, many years ago. My ex-husband is an academic. I fear my English is not as good as it was. But I know enough to be able to listen if you want to talk."

I was reminded of my mother. The cup of tea, the kindness and the interest. Perhaps it was that which weakened my resolve not to tell Hana the true content of the stuff which had robbed me of sleep. Whatever it was, my normal reticence seemed to melt away.

"I don't know where to start. I thought coming to Israel—to Palestine—might help."

"But it hasn't?"

"Not really."

"Why did you come?"

"I've never been before, even though I'm half Jewish, but my brother has lived in Jerusalem for many years. I wanted to visit him and his family and to see this country for myself at long last."

"And why now?"

"So much has gone wrong lately. I feel out of place in my own life. I thought perhaps if I came to Israel, explored my Jewish side, tried to understand why my brother feels so at home here, I might be able to start afresh—discover where I'm meant to be."

"But it hasn't helped?"

"Not really. I love being with my brother and his wife and children. It's lovely to spend time with them, but I'm not sure I could settle here. It's an amazing country, but complex, difficult—you must know what I mean."

"Indeed. And it's true what people say, you can't run away from trouble, it will just come with you. And I think Israel-Palestine is a country of questions rather than answers."

I nodded. "Yes, it's as messed up as I am."

"In what way are you messed up?"

"In every way. I wasn't a good wife and I'm not a good mother. My son—he—he died when I could have tried harder to keep him safe and my daughter—well—my daughter wants nothing to do with me. I'm a bit of a useless human being really."

"I see," said Hana. "I see how you would not be able to sleep if that was what you were listening to. But they are only thoughts. They might not be correct thoughts."

I frowned. "It's correct that my son is dead. It's correct that my daughter and I don't talk to each other. It's correct that I'm divorced."

Hana smiled and looked directly into my eyes. She leaned across the table and put her hand on mine. "It is awful that your son is dead. No worse thing can happen to a mother. But why do you think it is your fault? Was he a child when he died?"

"No, no he wasn't. He was an adult, a soldier. He was killed in Afghanistan."

"How? How did he die, Rachel?"

"He died," I paused, struggling to keep my composure. "He died trying to protect his comrades from an explosive device. It went off and he was killed."

"That is awful. But why would you blame yourself?"

"Because I let him go." I was on the point of tears. "I did nothing to stop him becoming a soldier. I let him go. I let him put his life in danger. I let him be killed."

"No, no," Hana said. She now had both my hands in hers. "No, you did not. No mother allows her son to be killed. He was an adult. He decided to be a soldier, no?"

"Yes, he decided. He wanted to go into the same regiment— the same part of the army his grandfather, my father had been in. But I did nothing to stop him."

"And what could you have done? Nothing, Rachel. You could have done nothing. And did he, did—what was his name?"

"Finlay. His name was Finlay."

"Did Finlay believe that it was right to fight for his country and for what he believed in?"

"Yes," I said. "He loved being a soldier. He was committed to the army and its mission in Afghanistan. He really believed that he and his comrades were changing things for the better."

"So you raised a brave young man who wanted to make the world a better place."

"Yes, but—"

"Yes, and you could not have stopped him. Indeed you should not have stopped him."

"Maybe not. But I can't get away from feeling responsible and—and I just want him back. I just want him back." I bit my lip, fought the urge to cry.

Hana stroked my arm. "Finlay followed his heart and it cost him his life. It is terrible. You will always miss him. But you are not to blame that he died. You must let that bit go."

I sighed. "Even if I could believe that, it's still a fact that I messed up my marriage and—"

"Your husband, he was perfect?"

I couldn't help smiling at that notion. "No, of course not but—"

"So it was both of you who were responsible?"

"It was me, me who didn't fit, not with him, with his lifestyle, his hopes and dreams. I couldn't make him happy, so he found someone else who could. Even my own mother was disappointed in me. She said I knew what he was like when I fell in love with him and let him get me pregnant. As far as she was concerned I should have tried much harder to adapt. She said it was what she and my father did."

"And what about what you needed? It seems you and your ex-husband were very different people who didn't fit. It wasn't anybody's fault. I guess your mother and father had a happy relationship, that they became a good fit. It seems your mother was very fortunate and wanted the same thing for you."

"My mother wasn't always fortunate. She was a child in Nazi Germany, a Jewish child. She escaped to the UK, but her family didn't survive. She was very strong, very stoical—you know?"

Hana nodded. "I know."

"She was amazing. I looked after her when she was dying. And through all the pain and the indignity she never once expressed any self-pity or any complaint."

"She sounds like a formidable woman. And to be a victim of that evil regime, to lose so much... home and family... I know something of how that is. But you have your own life. It's not for anyone, mother, husband or child to control your life or how you feel about it."

"I know. I know, you're right."

"It seems to me you need to get back in charge of your own life. There is nothing worse than to feel powerless. You still have your daughter and you must fix it with her. I find it hard to believe she wouldn't want to be on good terms with you."

I shrugged. "She can't forgive me for separating her from her father and she blames me for Finlay."

"I think that is her problem, not yours."

"But—"

"She is also an adult, yes?"

I nodded.

"Then, just as you do, she needs to see Finlay was responsible for his own decisions. And as for you and your husband divorcing, she must see that life is not always perfect. She knows that adults, even parents, make mistakes. She must stop blaming you."

"I think she probably knows that deep down. She got pregnant. She viewed that as a mistake and so she got rid of it, ended the pregnancy. She told me just before I came to Israel. She was about to have the—the abortion."

This information seemed to affect Hana more than any of my other revelations.

"But why? Why would she not keep her baby? Life is so precious? Why would she do this?"

"Because of me. Because her father and I got married when I became pregnant with her. She decided that me having her led to all the unhappiness that the family went on to experience."

"Forgive me, but it seems she is only thinking of herself and is blaming you for her mistakes. She needs to grow up I think. And you need to stop taking the blame. Life is what it is, Rachel. We can't control it. All we can do is live it."

"You're right, again," I said quietly.

"And there are other people who care about you? Family, friends, no?"

"Yes, they're very kind, but—"

Hana raised her hand. "No, no buts. There are people here who care about you. And the people at home, you care for them, you miss them?"

"Yes."

"And they miss you? They call you? Keep in touch?"

"Yes."

"And your family here? You might want to settle close to them?"

"Yes I might. It's what my brother wants."

"So there are people who care about you here and in the UK. You can't be completely messed up. It seems to me you've lost sight of yourself and that you live your life for other people. It's time you live it for yourself, no?"

I thought about what Hana was saying. "Yes, maybe."

"And once you do that, then you will find your place in the world. You'll know who and where is home for you."

I smiled at her. "Are you some kind of therapist? I mean, as well as running this place, do you do counselling as well?"

"No," Hana laughed. "I'm not a therapist. But I have lived a long time. And I had to get to know myself, assert myself, find my own place in the world. It's not usual or easy for a Muslim woman to be apart from her husband. But I could no longer live with Ali. He wanted us to live permanently in the UK and for me to be a university wife. I knew I couldn't. I love Palestine, especially after..." Hana shook her head. "That's another story. I wanted to work to bring understanding of what it is like to live here, to be a Palestinian woman on the West Bank. This house, this work that I do, this for me is home, and this is who I am. And so I left the UK and I left Ali."

"You had no children?"

"No, we... I couldn't have any." Hana paused. "But you, you had a son. He existed. He lived and he delighted you. Be glad. And you still have a daughter."

I nodded, pondering what Hana had said. "And you, Hana,

what about you? Why have you been up most of the night?"

"The bread has to be baked."

"Maybe so, but that doesn't take all night. You're as much of an insomniac as I am."

Hana gave a little nod. "You take the tour tomorrow, to Hebron and the hills?"

"Yes."

"When you visit they will tell you of the demolished houses, the confiscated land, the stolen water. That is my story, the story of my family. We were farmers, some goats and sheep and an olive grove. Then it was all taken from us. The Israeli Defence Force came one day and took it all away. My brother and my nephew and his wife and his small children were left sitting at the side of the road. They had half an hour to get out before the bulldozers came in. They watched, and they cried as they lost everything. I was in the UK at the time. And that is why I had to come home. This town, Beit Sahour, it's a special place. Here we work for justice. We work to bring the injustices faced by the Palestinian people to the notice of the world. And this house, it too is a special place. Ali, he gave me the money to buy it."

"Really! Even although you left him?"

"He is an exceptional man. He loves me. I love him. He works for change at an academic level. He recognises that I have my job to do and that my job is here. People come from all over the world and stay here. From here they visit more of the West Bank, meet the people, learn the truth."

"That's an amazing story. I admire your courage."

Hana shook her head. "No, it's not courage. It's conviction. I'm true to myself and I know my place in the world. And I have the dream that one day my work and Ali's work will be done and we'll be together, here, at home in a free Palestinian state. But until then the bread has to be baked."

Chapter Twenty Nine

I went back to bed at around four o'clock in the morning after my talk with Hana. I was up again a couple of hours later. Our group had to be on the bus by seven thirty if we wanted to avoid being out during the hottest part of the day.

During our visit to the South Hebron hills, we heard testimony from one of the former Israeli soldiers who'd founded a group called 'Breaking the Silence'. Sweating profusely, and probably not just because of the thirty degree heat, he spoke of some of the objectionable tasks he and his comrades had been required to undertake whilst serving in the Israeli army. These included the harassment, bullying and intimidation of Palestinian civilians, people who were just trying to get on with their lives in difficult circumstances. He struggled to maintain his composure as he spoke of firing over the head of a little girl and of how frightened she'd been. As a father now himself, this incident appeared to haunt him the most. This honest and brave man spoke of many other incidents, incidents similar to the ones experienced by Hana's family.

We also heard from some of Hebron's residents about how difficult life was under occupation, of the daily disruption and humiliation.

I felt very humbled by their stories but also strangely comforted. Their bravery and dignity were both reassuring and inspiring. I was also reminded of Finlay's stories of the Afghan people and of how he admired them and wanted to help them. I began to understand why he felt that what he'd been doing was right.

That evening our group had dinner together at the guesthouse. Hana sat with us. She listened as we talked about what we'd heard. She answered our questions and shared her own experiences of living on the West Bank.

After breakfast the following day, we left the guesthouse. As well as sharing in the group's farewells to Hana, I said my own private goodbye to her and thanked her again for listening to me and for sharing her wisdom. We exchanged email addresses and vowed to keep in touch.

After our farewell hug, Hana said, "Always remember, live in the present and make plans for the future. Keep moving, take risks, be exhilarated."

"I'll try," I replied.

"And promise me that you will start living again, that you will forgive yourself and be happy."

Confronted by this wonderful, brave and strong woman, how could I not agree? "I promise," I said, and I meant it.

The next stop on our tour was a surprisingly cool Bedouin tent, in the Judean desert east of Jerusalem. There, a very elderly man, speaking through an interpreter, told us how life had changed for his tribe since the formation of the Israeli state. He spoke of how their tents and animal shelters were regularly bulldozed, of expulsions from their land, of forced resettlement, of water diverted to the properties of Israeli settlers, of children cowering at the sight of the soldiers and no longer able to get to their schools, and of his son, shot and killed for standing up to the soldiers, for trying to defend his home by throwing stones. But although the old man's sadness and his sense of loss had an almost physical presence, his dignity was immense.

Again I was humbled and again I acknowledged the integrity of my son's mission to improve the lives of disenfranchised people. The more I listened, the more I understood and admired my son's ability to look beyond the complexities of the politics and to see the value of the individual human lives caught up in the power struggles of their states.

After the mini-bus dropped us in the centre of Jerusalem, Deb and I took a taxi home. During the drive, I put my head back and closed my eyes. I reflected on how I'd visited the Dead Sea resort and had had no inkling of what it was like for the Palestinian people living nearby. I wondered what Eitan knew—really knew—of the plight of the Palestinians. I wondered how Deb and Jonathan could live so close to all this suffering and tolerate what was being done in their name.

Recalling the words of the Israeli soldier made me think of Finlay and about what states ask of their military forces. I thought of all the dead sons. I thought of all the grieving mothers. I thought of all the displaced people. Why did we never learn? I sighed.

"You're awake then?" Deb said. "You've been so quiet I thought you must have dropped off."

"I was thinking, not sleeping."

"Oh? Thinking about what?"

"Everything, everything we've seen and heard these last few days and about war and fighting and people's lives being torn apart. And I was wondering what it's all for."

"Yes, this bloody country can get to you like that."

"How do you do it, Deb? How do you and Jonathan live with all that's going on? I know you don't approve."

"You're right. We most certainly don't approve. And we both try in our own ways, small ways, to work for understanding and change. Jonathan does his work at the Hadassah and I teach in a multi-cultural school where we have Jewish and Arab pupils. We've also brought our children up to question what's being done. And of course we'll soon have to face the question of Gideon's national service."

"It can't be easy," I said.

"It certainly isn't, especially the thought of Gideon and then

Mari in the military, as I'm sure you can understand."

"Yes, indeed." I sighed again.

Deb patted my arm. "It will be nice to be home," she said. "It's been a full-on few days. Lunch, shower and a sleep, I think."

When I awoke from my afternoon rest, I could hear voices coming from the living-room. I was surprised to see that it was almost five o'clock. I dressed and went through to join Deb, Jonathan and the children. But it wasn't Mari and Gideon who were with my brother and sister-in-law. It was Eitan.

"Rachel!" Eitan stepped forward and embraced me. He looked down at me while I was in his arms and kissed me on the forehead. "It's good to see you," he said, more softly.

For a moment I was thrown, disconcerted by the feel and the scent of Eitan, by his closeness. I was acutely aware of Jonathan and Deb watching us. "Hello Eitan," I said, trying to sound cool.

Eitan stared intently at me and gave a little bow of his head as he released me.

"Hello, sis," said Jonathan. "We were about to have some iced coffee. Would you like some?"

"I'd love some," I said. "What are you doing home so early?"

"I took a half day. I'm cooking dinner to welcome you and Deb home. I invited Eitan to join us. He's a fan of my roast chicken."

"I see. That's nice," I said. "Where are the children?"

"Both are out for the evening, staying over at the homes of friends. We'll have peace," Jonathan said.

"So, Rachel, what did you think of what you saw on your trip?" Eitan asked.

"Give her a chance!" Jonathan said. "She's only just home. Let her relax for a while before she reports back."

I looked at my brother. I wouldn't have minded speaking about the trip there and then. But I detected the anxiety in his tone. I remembered how Jonathan had found the whole idea of the trip uncomfortable. I smiled at Eitan. "Later," I said.

So the conversation was light and easy as the four of us sipped our iced coffees. Jonathan and I spoke about our planned trip to the upper Galilee. And Deb and Jonathan told us about their plans for Mari's bat-mitzvah.

The air-conditioning thrummed cool air around the room and I relaxed. Eitan was charming as always and I sensed no tension between us. He remained very easy to be with.

Dinner was enjoyable too. Jonathan's roast rosemary chicken with roast potatoes and fresh peas was delicious.

"That was as good as Mum's," I said, as I pushed my empty plate away and raised my wine glass towards my brother. "To the chef."

The other two also raised their glasses.

"Thanks," Jonathan said. "I was hoping you'd think it was up to Mum's standard. But I'm afraid dessert is just a shop bought lemon cheesecake."

"So not a complete cooking god, then?" Deb said, smiling at Jonathan.

"God-like enough for me. The chicken was excellent," Eitan said. "Now bring on the pudding."

It was after dessert that the mood turned more serious.

As the four of us drank our small cups of Turkish coffee, Eitan leaned across the table and looked at me. "So, the West Bank, it was worth visiting?"

"Most definitely."

"Good. And did you learn anything about the Israel-Palestine relationship?" Eitan glanced at Deb and Jonathan before returning his gaze to me, a slight smile on his face.

"I learned quite a bit."

"Such as?"

I took a breath before I spoke. "I learned that Israel's treatment of the Palestinian people is cruel, inhuman and immoral." The smile vanished from Eitan's face. He looked as if he was about to speak but I didn't hesitate before continuing. "But even more than that, it's irrational and incomprehensible."

Eitan shook his head. "These people really did a job on you. I credited you with more intelligence, more powers of discernment."

In the heartbeat before I responded, I was aware of Deb watching me. I glanced at her. Her expression seemed to be one of admiration. I was also aware of Jonathan. He was sitting forward but his head was in his hands and he was looking down at the floor.

"I don't really know where to start replying to that." I raised my arms and shook my head. "Could you be any more patronising? How dare you?"

"I dare very easily, and if I was patronising, too bad. When it comes to defending my country, I'll do what it takes. Surely you must see it was propaganda that you were subjected too, leftist liberal nonsense, dangerous leftish liberal nonsense."

"Look, I don't pretend to grasp all the political implications and complexities of what we saw, but I did grasp that here were displaced, disenfranchised, disrespected people. I did grasp that the Israeli state is treating the Palestinian people appallingly. Corralling people in ghettoes and camps, trying to drive out a whole ethnic group. Have we Jews learned nothing? Us of all people!"

Eitan hit his hand down on the table. "Yes, we of all people, we should never forget what our enemies tried to do to us and what they will do again if we're not very careful. The Palestinians must be corralled, must be kept securely behind the barrier. It's a fact that since the wall the incidence of suicide bombings has dropped to almost nothing. Remember, Rachel, those people you met, they hate us."

"I sensed no hatred, only despair. And that wall is an abomination."

"Have you any idea what a suicide bomber can do? Have you ever witnessed the aftermath of such an attack? If you had you'd call the wall a blessing."

Jonathan bristled and I heard Deb gasp. I forced down images of Finlay's death. I raised my hand in my brother and sister-in-law's direction to assure them I was up to replying for myself.

"I haven't personally witnessed such an attack, no. However, I do know that terrorism achieves nothing, but talking just might—"

"Israel will never negotiate with terrorists." Eitan thumped his hand down on the table again. "And I say again, Rachel, if you saw—"

"My son was killed by an explosive device, a device planted in misunderstanding, ignorance and hatred. And I know that nothing positive was achieved by it."

Eitan's expression softened. "Of course. I'm sorry. It was clumsy, unforgiveable of me to recall the death of your son, but that's my point, if we contain the terrorists, then we save lives."

"No, no, I hear what you say about the wall being a barrier to attacks, attacks of the nature you describe at any rate. But it has done nothing to defuse the tension and hatred. You can't possibly believe that with the wall all the militants just faded away."

"Of course not, and we will fight them wherever we encounter them. Our military is strong. The defence forces are good at what they do."

"What? Young conscripts, brainwashed into behaving like thugs? Oh yes, they're good at what they do, terrorising women and children, robbing men of all hope and dignity. They stand in attendance while their country steals and destroys the lives and livelihoods of ordinary, peaceful people."

"Young conscripts, yes, brainwashed, no. I think it is you who are being patronising now. Our young men and women, they grow up knowing they must do military service, as their parents did. They go in with their eyes open. They know their country needs them, needs to be defended."

"Okay, yes, all countries have a right to defend themselves from their enemies. But the people I met, they are part of this country. They've lived here for generations, longer than most of the Jews. They don't present a threat. They're just ordinary people, farmers with families, people with hopes and dreams for their children. They don't wish anyone dead. They just want to work their land and to be treated fairly and humanely in their own country."

"I wish that was true. I really do. I wish it was possible. I know a lot of the world views us as bullies, including many of you Brits. But remember it was Britain that way back in 1917 gave the Jews the right to live here, established a national home for Jewish people, established the boundary, put the Palestinians in their place."

It was Jonathan who responded to this. "Yes and I think you'll find that it was also stated in the Mandate that nothing should be done which might prejudice the civil and religious rights of existing non-Jewish residents."

"Jonathan, how many times have you and I had this discussion? We could go on all night and we would not agree. I know you love this country as much as I do, and it is home, perfect or not."

"On that relatively harmonious note," Deb said, getting up from the table, "I think we should call it a night." She smiled at Eitan.

"Ah, Deb, always the diplomat," Eitan said. "And you are right, time to go." Eitan said good night to Deb, kissing her lightly on the cheek. And then he turned to Jonathan. "My old friend," he said. "Good cook and good man."

"Come here, you argumentative bastard," Jonathan said. The two men hugged and slapped each other loudly on the back.

"Right," Deb said. "We'll leave the clearing up till morning." She took Jonathan's hand. "Let's make the most of the kids being away. Get an early night." She smiled at Eitan and me. "Good night, you two."

"Rachel," Eitan said, once we were alone. He smiled and looked into my eyes. "My new intellectual opponent." He took me in his arms and I looked up at him. "Your passion is admirable," he said. "Even if I don't agree with a word you say about Israel."

I couldn't help laughing. Then I kissed him on the mouth as much to my own surprise as his. We spent the next couple of hours making love. He was misguided, opinionated, patronising but, I had to admit, he was also very likeable and very, very sexy.

Chapter Thirty

It would be over a month before I saw Eitan again.

In the intervening time, I had a week walking in the beautiful Upper Galilee with Jonathan. We based ourselves in Rosh Pina, a delightful town on the slopes of Mount Canaan. With its pretty stone-walled and pan-tiled houses and its panoramic views to the Sea of Galilee in the south and the Golan Heights in the north, it was the perfect spot. Our hotel was the wonderfully and aptly named Serenity Lodge. Rosh Pina had several art and craft shops and I visited them all.

We also visited the old city of Sfat. We strolled along its narrow, cobbled alleys, past its many synagogues, and we agreed it lived up to its reputation as a mystical place. I wasn't surprised to learn it was a popular destination for artists with its lovely views and inspiring atmosphere and here too there were galleries and craft shops. I took many pictures and did several sketches around the town.

My favourite part of the Galilee was the Hula Valley. Jonathan and I walked its trails and watched the many birds and animals that lived there.

Some of the birds were exotic variations of species familiar to me from Scotland, species such as the short-toed eagle which circled overhead as we ascended a mountain trail. There were short-winged plovers and purple herons by the edge of one of the ponds. I also spotted a kingfisher preparing to dive. But the most spectacular birds were ones I'd never seen before. The vibrant red, yellow, orange and turquoise plumage of a bee-eater in flight had me reaching for my camera, as did the rather weird looking hoopoe. The hoopoe is the national bird of Israel and it's certainly memorable with its long beak and amazing tall feathered headdress.

The animals were worthy of lots of photos too. There were water buffalo, donkeys, coypu and, the highlight for me, Caspian turtles basking on rocks in the middle of a lake.

The Upper Galilee reminded me of Scotland and of Skye in particular, with its mountains, valleys and lakes. The colours weren't quite as they were at home but the landscape and its contours almost felt like home. Almost.

Going away together gave Jonathan and me lots of opportunities to talk. It was a special time, being with my brother like that. We hadn't spent as much time together since we were children. We talked a lot about the past, about our parents and about our childhood in Skye. It was on our last evening in the Galilee that our conversation turned to the future. We'd eaten dinner and were relaxing with a brandy in the hotel's cool and comfortable lounge.

"You've been amazing, Rache, coming here," Jonathan said. "I never thought you would. And all you've done and seen and learned while you've been here. I'm proud of you. Has it helped? Has it been worth it?"

"Definitely worth it. I had to get away, had to widen my horizons and move my life on. It's been good to explore the Jewish thing, get to know this homeland, if that's what it is."

"And how do you feel about it, now that you have? Do you have any sense of your Jewishness? Could you settle here? Could this be your home?"

"I don't know about a sense of Jewishness. I certainly know a lot more about what being Jewish means, in the sense of race, if not religion. But as for settling here, I'm not at all sure. It's a beautiful country, fascinating, infuriating, exciting. It's been lovely to be here with you and with Deb and the children. You're the only family I've got, apart from Sophie. But—"

"But Scotland's still home? You'll be going back as planned?"

"I'll be going back, yes. I have to, at least in the short term. And I do miss it. I miss Skye, the croft, and my friends. And I—I want to have another try at patching things up with Sophie."

"Sophie, yes, Deb told me what you told her about Sophie, the abortion and everything. I'm so sorry, Rachel." Jonathan leant over and put his hand on mine. I felt the pain of unshed tears, struggled to hold them back. But it was no use, a couple escaped. I wiped them with the back of my hand. "Oh, Rache," he said. "I'm sorry for bringing it up. I've not been sure whether to mention it. I didn't want to upset you."

"It's okay. Really it is. I didn't mean it to be secret or a no-go area. It's just it hurts, you know?"

"Of course. It sounds as if she's pretty messed up."

"Yes, she is and so all the more reason for me to go back and have another try at a reconciliation."

"And if you do put things right with Sophie would you consider coming back here, back here to stay, to settle?"

"I don't know. I—"

"What about Eitan? Would you consider settling here to be with him?"

"Eitan? Why would I? What do you mean?"

"Oh, come on, sis. I know you two have had a bit of a thing, been—together. I'm not daft. It's obvious. And, anyway, Deb confirmed it."

"Obvious is it?" I smiled. "Yes, we have been together, as you put it. But it's not a serious relationship. We're very different. You've seen how we argue."

"Exactly. You two have a powerful chemistry."

"That's as maybe. Anyway I thought you wouldn't approve. You warned me about him. Remember?"

"Yes, I know I did. But you look like you can handle him and if your relationship with Eitan means you'll stay here, well then, I'd happily approve."

"There's no relationship, not in the way you mean. As to me

staying here long term, I'm—I'm on a path and I'm finding my way again, but where the path is leading me, I don't know yet."

After our return from the north, I went on several more outings on my own into the centre of Jerusalem. I took yet more photos and did more drawing. I was now determined to take my painting seriously again when I got back to Skye and I wanted to begin with some landscapes of Israel. One day when I was walking on the Mount of Olives and wanted to photograph the view, I found I'd forgotten my camera and had to use my phone instead. As I flicked through and checked the pictures I'd just taken, I came across the photos Poppy had taken the day we flew the kites. There was one of Jack and me. He was standing behind me, steadying me as the wind pulled on the kite. I realised that's what he did. Jack steadied me, and the extent of my longing for him was almost unbearable. But in that moment, standing in that ancient beautiful city, thousands of miles from home, thousands of miles from Jack, I also felt a reconnection; a reconnection with life and a deep conviction that however things turned out, I was going to be okay. I felt—hope.

During my last few weeks in Israel, I also got involved in helping Deb and Jonathan prepare for the bat-mitzvah. It would take place in the middle of August, just a couple of days before I was to return home. There was the menu to think about for one thing. I offered to bake. I planned to make a couple of Scottish things, tablet, a very sweet Scottish fudge, and cranachan, a raspberry, cream and meringue dessert. And then, one evening, when Jonathan was drawing up a draft programme of events for the celebration, he asked me again if I'd sing at the party.

"You know we want to make it a bit of a ceilidh, so we want everyone to do something. And you have such a lovely voice."

"Oh, I don't know about that," I said. "I haven't sung in public for ages."

"Well that's a waste and should be put right immediately!" Jonathan said. "Don't you sing in the Gaelic choir anymore?"

"Not since Finlay. Haven't had the heart."

"Ah, I see, sorry, I—"

"I'd love it if you sang at my party, Auntie Rachel." We hadn't noticed Mari coming into the room. "Wouldn't Finlay be sad if he knew you no longer sang?" Mari walked up to me as she spoke.

I hugged my niece. "Okay," I said. "Okay, I'll do it for you, and for Finlay. I'll sing at your bat-mitzvah. But I must warn you I'm very rusty."

"You can practise," Mari said. "Gideon will play for you. He is very good on his guitar. Will you sing some Scottish songs?"

I laughed. "Yes, probably. I'll have a think and I'll speak to Gideon."

"Cool! Thanks Auntie Rachel." Mari danced out the room.

"Yes, thanks, Rachel. I hadn't realised how you felt about singing these days," Jonathan said.

"It's fine. Mari's right, Finlay would approve."

I decided to sing two of my favourite Robert Burns songs 'Ae Fond Kiss', and 'The Silver Tassie' at Mari's party. Gideon found the words and music online and the two of us spent some time in the evenings practising. He was an accomplished guitarist and his confidence seemed to rub off on me. Although it had been a while since I'd sung, especially solo as opposed to as part of a choir, my voice sounded all right. At least I hoped so.

"Not bad, you two," Jonathan said one evening, after he'd loitered in the doorway of Gideon's room while my nephew and I practised.

"It's better than not bad," Gideon said. "Aunt Rachel is a good singer. Much better than you. She must have got all the musical ability, none left for you." Gideon grinned at his father.

"Thanks very much," Jonathan said. "But Gideon's right, Rachel. The songs sound really good."

"I enjoy singing these old, traditional songs. 'Ae Fond Kiss' is such a romantic song. I've sung it since school. And the 'Silver Tassie', just seemed appropriate. The haunting tune, and its story of a soldier going off to battle. I don't know, it seemed like a way of bringing Mum, Dad and Finlay to the celebration."

Jonathan smiled. "They're both perfect."

While Gideon and I practised our musical contribution, Jonathan worked on putting together a slideshow tribute to his daughter.

Mari was also working on a presentation. It was traditional for the young person whose celebration it was to give a talk on their family, or on their role models or heroes. She planned to give a talk on the lives of her two grandmothers. She came to me and Jonathan with lots of questions about our mother. It was good to be able to talk about Mum and we told Mari about the doll and the photograph we'd found from her grandmother's childhood.

Deb had organised the venue. It was the hall at the school where she taught. She also saw to all the invitations and then, during the final few days before the Saturday party, she and I cooked and baked for the celebratory lunch. We made various salads and breads to go with the chicken and cheeses we'd bought. I did my baking and Deb baked baklava and a honey cake.

I got so much pleasure from being part of the preparations for this big family occasion that I realised just how much I missed this sort of thing. The rituals and celebrations of my own family life seemed a very long time ago.

I was glad that I'd thought to bring a smart dress with me to wear for the occasion. It was a cream silk shift dress that I'd bought years before, while I was still married to Peter. It was expertly cut and sewn and the silk had a beautiful sheen that hadn't faded. It was the most expensive article of clothing that I owned and I loved it. Fortunately it still fitted me and I was delighted to have an occasion to wear it again. I'd also brought a tartan stole, in green Macpherson dress tartan, to wear with it. Jonathan and Gideon would also be wearing the clan tartan on the day, as having first checked with Deb that the hall was air-conditioned, both of them would be wearing their kilts.

On the morning of the big day, we were all up early. Jonathan and Gideon took the food and other bits and pieces that would be required over to the school and then returned to get changed. Meanwhile Deb, Mari and I helped each other with our hair and make-up. Deb looked amazing in a long, blue, traditional, Turkish dress which was beautifully trimmed and beaded. Once she was dressed, Deb left Mari and I to finish getting ready and went off to check on last minute details.

I helped Mari into her dress and zipped it up. It was emerald green, similar in style to Deb's, and it complemented her dark colouring perfectly. She was also wearing my mother's silver bracelet.

"You look lovely," I told her. "Are you looking forward to your special day?"

She smiled. "Thank you. Yes, I am," she said. Then she surprised me by giving me a hug. "I'm so glad you're here, Aunt Rachel."

I held her tightly for a moment. "I'm glad too," I said. "And I have something for you." I handed her the gift I'd got her.

"Wow, a present." Mari beamed and tore off the wrapping. She gave a little gasp when she opened the small box and saw the silver earrings. "They're beautiful. Thank you so much. But you didn't have to get me anything."

"I know I didn't have to, but I wanted to."

Mari went to the mirror and put on the earrings. She turned to me. "I love them," she said.

"I'm glad. They're in the shape of a Celtic knot and they were made by a Skye jeweller. I wanted you to have something from the island and I thought they'd go with Grandma's bracelet."

"Wow," Jonathan said when Mari and I finally emerged from the bedroom. "You two scrub up well." He glanced at his watch and smiled. "Almost worth waiting all this time for!"

"Cheeky," Deb said, appearing at Jonathan's side. She looked him up and down. "You look pretty good yourself. I do like you in a kilt." She kissed her husband on the cheek. "Give Gideon a shout and then we can take some photos of us all in our smart clothes."

A little while later we arrived at the school hall. Eitan, who was going to be master of ceremonies, was waiting to greet us. He looked great in a dark suit and white shirt which he wore without a tie. He shook hands with Gideon and Jonathan, kissed Deb on both cheeks and said something to her in Hebrew which made her blush. He embraced Mari and said something, also in Hebrew, to her. She beamed back at him as she replied.

He turned to me as the others went ahead into the hall. "Rachel," he said, taking both my hands in his. "You look beautiful." He kissed me lightly on the mouth and then offered me his arm. It felt wonderful, and somehow right, to walk into the hall like that with Eitan.

It was a very happy day. To start the proceedings off, a group of thirteen of the guests, as was traditional, and all chosen by Mari, lit a candle each. Then Eitan did a reading from the Torah. And from then and throughout the day, he did a great job of keeping everything on track.

After lunch Mari did her presentation. The night before, she'd given me an English version of what she planned to say. I had it with me to refer to. It was very moving. I was sorry my mother hadn't lived to see it. Jonathan's slide show and commentary on his daughter's life since she was a baby was both funny and poignant. The love and pride he felt for his daughter were obvious and I wasn't the only one with tears in my eyes as we all listened to him.

Then it was over to Gideon and me to get the ceilidh underway with the two songs. Nerves didn't overwhelm me and judging by the applause I guessed we must have sounded okay.

Gideon, along with a friend of his who played keyboards and a music teacher colleague of Deb's on violin, did a very reasonable job as a ceilidh band and Jonathan did the calling in a weird mixture of Hebrew and English, trying to keep everyone right in the dancing. It was hilarious at times with so many novices attempting the Eightsome Reel and the Dashing White Sergeant. After a particularly energetic Strip the Willow, in which Eitan was my partner, we both got ourselves a cold drink and went outside to find a shady spot in which to cool down and get our breath back.

We sat on an empty bench under a tree in the corner of the schoolyard. It was the first chance we'd had to talk at any length since the bat-mitzvah started.

"Your Scottish dancing is exhausting. It is fun, but it is exhausting." Eitan wiped his forehead with the back of his hand before taking a long drink of his cold beer.

"You coped very well," I said. "I was impressed."

"And I was impressed by you too," Eitan said. "Your singing, it was very good."

"Thank you. It's been a long time since I sang in public, but I enjoyed it, in spite of being nervous. Maybe I'll take it up again when I go home."

"So, you have decided? The UK is home?"

I shrugged, gave a small sigh. "I'm still unsure. I miss Skye more than I thought I would. I miss my friends. But I've have had a wonderful time here." I paused, looked Eitan in the eye. "And part of that is down to you."

Eitan smiled. "I hope that you think of me as a friend, and that you will miss me."

"Most definitely a friend and yes, I will miss you. I've enjoyed your—your company very much."

Now Eitan laughed, his huge, loud laugh. "My company— you mean the sex. I have enjoyed it too. And almost more than that I've enjoyed our discussions. As I've told you, you have passion, Rachel, real passion. Yours are the politics of passion and of conviction. That is good. You have a narrative going on in here." He tapped his forehead. "And it comes from here." He put his hand over his heart. "You're not caught by futile policies, or vested interest. You are—you are good." Then he took one of my hands in his and said, "You are a special woman, strong, beautiful, intelligent and very, very brave."

I shook my head, turned away slightly. "Thanks, but I don't think—"

Eitan put his hands on my shoulders, turned me to face him. "Only two women have ever made me think marriage could be a good idea, and you are one of them." He stroked my face and then held me close for a moment and I wondered if I'd heard him correctly.

"Oh," I said, when he sat back. "I don't know what to say."

"Don't worry. It wasn't a proposal, at least not yet. But, if you did decide to settle here then who knows..."

I was completely thrown by this. I could only stare at him.

"Oh, come here," he said. He touched my cheek, ran his fingers along my jaw. "I love your face. All that you are feeling, all the conflicts, they appear as light and shade." And, before I knew it, he was kissing me on the mouth.

I kissed him back. But then I pulled away. "Eitan, I don't—that is I'm not—"

"It was a goodbye kiss, nothing more. You leave for home in two days and I will not see you again before you go. I wish you well, Rachel. I hope you find the place you are looking for. I hope you find inspiration and that you paint beautiful pictures for the rest of your life. And, although it is painful for me to say, I hope your friend Jack sees what he means to you."

I gasped at this last part. "No, Jack isn't—"

But Eitan just carried on. "But remember, if you do come to live in this country, perhaps we could make it work."

In the end all I could do was hug him. "Thank you, Eitan. Thank you for, well, you know..."

"I know," he said.

"Just one thing," I said.

"What?"

"Who was the other woman, the other woman you could

have married?"

"Ah," he said. "That was Deb, but I made the mistake of introducing her to my best friend."

Chapter Thirty One

Jack

By the end of June the work on the house was just about completed. All I still needed to do was get it fully furnished.

I'd also helped Alasdair with bits and pieces of work on Rachel's croft. The few breaks I'd taken were to go on long walks, sometimes with Alasdair but always with Bonnie. The dog seemed to want to adopt me and kept appearing on my doorstep. I didn't mind at all. I enjoyed her company.

And on the walks I took photos. I enjoyed experimenting with different shots, trying out various focuses and exposures. There were a couple I was particularly proud of, landscape shots taken in Halladale. They were now framed and up on my kitchen wall.

But the photo I was most drawn to was one that Poppy had taken with my phone on the day we flew her kite. It was a shot of Rachel and me. I was standing behind Rachel as she held on to the kite, and I was holding her. I often found myself flicking through the pictures on my phone and thinking if only...

I missed her. I'd realised soon after Rachel left that the ache I was experiencing was more than just the feeling of missing a friend, even if I couldn't—daren't—put a name to it. I sought out excuses to be nearer her in some way. I got Alasdair to lend me her shepherd's crook and got quite adept at using it when helping with her sheep. I kept asking Morag for news of her. I walked with Bonnie, adopted Bonnie. Of course, I told the dog everything—about Ailsa, about Bridget, about Rachel. The dog looked pityingly at me. And then there were the dreams. Rachel and me together. Oh yes, I had it bad.

We'd spoken on a couple of occasions. The calls were sweet torture. It was good to hear her voice but I was sure she'd moved on. Moved on from Skye, from her unhappiness. She said she'd fallen in love with Israel and I also suspected she'd fallen for some guy, a friend of her brother, who'd she'd been away with. I hoped if I told her stuff from home, stuff about the croft, she'd get homesick. I made a bit of a fool of myself referring to ewe twenty-seven as the one who brought us together, truly cringe-worthy. But I was desperate. Desperate to see her, to be with her. Even although it was hopeless, even although I wasn't right for her, even although I was in a relationship. Yes, there was still that.

In July, I went down to Edinburgh. Bridget came round to the flat on my first night back in town. As was our custom, we went straight to bed, no chat, no preamble. The sex was good. It had always been good. As a couple, it was what we did best.

We'd been together for a couple of years. We met at some reception hosted by the Scottish Government. Bridget was there in her capacity as PR for the Minister for Legal Affairs. I was there as an unwilling representative of Lothian and Borders Police, standing in for my boss. We got chatting at the bar. She flirted. I responded.

Within a week we'd started an affair. Bridget was attractive, clever and fun. She was also married. She said she wouldn't discuss her marriage, other than to say that she loved her husband and would never leave him. She said she'd had other affairs and that she needed to be discreet for his sake. We got together at my flat whenever Bridget could get away.

This was fine by me. Neither of us was looking for a serious, live-in relationship. I'd had enough of close and committed. We weren't in love but enjoyed each other's company. This was a discreet, relaxed and grown-up affair.

Or rather it had been. Something changed when I told Bridget of my plans to buy the house in Skye. She'd been supportive when I'd had the heart surgery. She'd given me space and time to recover. She'd also been a good sounding board when I'd been trying to make up my mind about retiring. All in all she'd been a good friend. But my plans for Skye were a step too far. It didn't matter that I'd no intention of moving north permanently. She couldn't understand what I saw in the place and she couldn't understand that I didn't view my spending time away as a problem for our relationship. It was the only thing we argued about and it was an ongoing argument.

So, on my first night back in town, after our physical reunion, it was inevitable that we'd end up talking about my plans. We lay side by side in my bed. It was a warm evening but a light breeze coming in through the open window kept the bedroom cool. The curtains were open and I was watching the darkening sky. The sound of traffic and of voices drifted up from the street two storeys below. I was tired after the drive down from Skye and, of course, after our sexual exertions. I was ready to sleep and found myself hoping Bridget would go soon. She rarely stayed the night. I glanced at her. She was propped on one elbow, looking at me.

"Before I go, can we talk?"

I sighed, knowing what the talk would be about. "Bridget, please don't, not now. I'm tired."

"Then when? When, Jack? I tried calling you lots of times after you were home last. Your phone went to voicemail. You didn't reply to my messages or texts. I need to know what you're thinking. Are you still set on dividing your time between here and that—that hideout in the back of beyond?"

"Yes, I told you before. It's what I want."

"But you promised you'd think about it."

"And I have. I haven't changed my mind. I love the place, the peace and quiet, the landscape, the big sky. You should come and see it for yourself. You might like it."

"I doubt it. You know I'm a city person. I'm not into fresh air and cowpats. Besides, it's tricky enough for me to get away to spend time with you when you're here. I thought that when you retired it would be easier for us to be together, but we see even less of each other. Please, Jack, now the house is done up, couldn't you sell it?"

"Definitely not. That's not negotiable." I stroked her hair. "But I will try to divide my time more evenly."

"I hate that you're making me do this." Bridget pushed back the sheet and got out of bed. She began to get dressed.

I sat up. "Do what?"

"Beg, be needy. It's not me. I enjoy your company. I enjoy the sex. I've never had such a long lasting affair before. I'm better because of being with you, happier. James has even noticed."

"That's saying something," I said. "Why do you stay with him? He doesn't seem to notice you most of the time, happy or otherwise. From what you've said, he's hardly at home."

"That's rich! But I'm not discussing my marriage. I'm discussing our relationship. I at least need to know when you're likely to be around."

"I'll be here until the end of the week. Then I have to go back up. I'm helping a neighbour of mine look after the croft of another neighbour who's away at the moment. I promised to be back in order to let him and his wife have a couple of days away."

"God, listen to you!" Bridget, now dressed, paused as she rummaged in her handbag. "You've gone native. A crofter now, are you?"

"Hardly, it's just I promised Rachel when she went away that I'd help out. I enjoy it, looking after the sheep and the hens. It's quite relaxing in a way."

"Rachel? She must be a good friend if you're making promises to her, especially ones that demand so much of your time." Bridget brushed her hair as she spoke.

"Yes, she is. Rachel is a good friend. And it's not that demanding. Like I said I'm just standing in for Alasdair. He's the one with the real responsibility. Besides I owe Rachel. She was the one who put Poppy and me up at Easter time."

"Ah, that neighbour." Bridget dropped the hairbrush into her handbag and snapped it shut. "The one you couldn't stop talking about when you came back." Bridget gave a little gasp. "Wait a minute," she said. "That's it! That's the attraction. It's this Rachel person. She's the reason you want to spend so much time up north." I'd never seen Bridget this hostile.

"Don't be ridiculous! For one thing I bought the house before I met her. And for another, as I've just said, she's away." I tried to keep my voice calm, but my fatigue and the fact Bridget was right meant I was becoming increasingly annoyed and defensive. I got out of bed, began to get dressed.

"Ridiculous? I don't think so, Jack. Oh, I know you met after you'd got the house but now that you *have* met, I think she may well be what's keeping you on Skye. There's something about the way you say her name, the look in your eye when you talk about her. I should have picked up on it before now. And even if she's away at the moment, she'll presumably be back."

"I can't believe we're having this conversation. Rachel's a friend. She's a good person who's been through a lot, but hasn't let it beat her. I admire her, that's all." Only it wasn't all.

"Yeah, right," Bridget said.

"Look, nothing's changed as far as I'm concerned. I have the place in Skye. I will be dividing my time between there and here. We'll meet whenever we can. That's it. Trust me."

"You've not exactly got a trustworthy record, have you Jack? Not when it comes to women."

"Now that *is* ridiculous! Neither of us can claim fidelity as a strong point. You're married for Christ's sake. If anyone should be feeling jealous, it should be me. But I'm not, not in the slightest."

For a moment we looked at each other across the bed. Then Bridget said, "Will I see you again, before you go back north?"

"If you want," I said, my voice flat, my sigh barely stifled.

"I see," Bridget said. "When will you be in town again?"

"Next month, when Maddie's baby is born."

"Right, for the baby. And for me, Jack? When will you come to see me?"

I resisted the temptation to shrug, took a breath. I really didn't want to hurt her. But I knew it was over. All I had to do was tell her. All I had to do was be my usual fickle self. I just needed to find the right moment—and the right words.

"I see," she said again. "I'll be in touch. Please have the decency to respond. I'll see myself out."

Chapter Thirty Two

I didn't see Bridget again before I went back to Skye. I spent most of my remaining few days in Edinburgh with my daughter and my granddaughter. I tried not to think about Bridget. I also tried not to think about Rachel. That was even more difficult.

On my last afternoon in town, Maddie and I took Poppy and one of her friends to the park. It was warm and sunny and Maddie and I sat on a bench and chatted while the children played.

"So, what have you got planned for when you get back to Skye?" Maddie asked.

"I'm hoping to get more walking done, get up into the mountains over the summer while the weather holds. And I'll be continuing to learn from Alasdair about looking after sheep."

"Really?" Maddie laughed.

"Yes really," I smiled at my daughter. "I've been giving him a hand. He tells me I'm a natural stockman."

"I can't imagine you as a farmer."

"Crofter," I corrected her. "Actually, I'm a bit disappointed that Dun Halla isn't on a croft. I quite fancy having a few animals, some hens and some sheep."

"What about your other crofting friend—Rachel—it's her sheep you've been helping with isn't it?"

"What about her?"

"Have you heard from her while she's been away?"

"We've spoken on the phone a couple of times. She's enjoying her time away. I think she's finding Israel a pretty amazing place." I had to consciously try to keep my tone light.

"Are you missing her?"

I looked at my daughter, unsure how to respond. "A bit yes. Me and Rachel, we've become friends, I think, I hope. And when she gets back, and if she stays on Skye, I'd like to think we'll remain so."

"Oh, come on, Dad." Maddie linked her arm through mine. "Who're you trying to kid? You've got a thing for her. It's so obvious, whenever you talk about her, there's a—I don't know—it's sweet."

"No!" I said, so forcefully I made Maddie jump.

She withdrew her arm from mine. "Sorry," she said. "Sorry, I must have misunderstood."

She looked stricken. I instantly regretted upsetting her. "No, it's me, Maddie. I'm sorry." I put my arm round her shoulders and we sat in silence for a moment. And in that moment, I decided to be honest with my daughter and to be honest with myself. "You're right," I said. "I have fallen for Rachel. She's an amazing woman, very strong, kind, talented, bright—similar to your mum in some ways. But she's not interested in a relationship, not beyond friendship."

"How do you know? Have you asked her?"

"No, but she's very independent, and she's considering emigrating permanently to the Middle East."

"Only considering it. What if she doesn't go? What if she stays on Skye?"

I shook my head, leant forward, looked down at the ground as I spoke. "Not even then. Like I said, she's not interested in anything more than friendship. Besides there's—"

"Bridget!" Maddie sounded exasperated. "Bloody Bridget! That's not exactly going anywhere is it, Dad?"

I sat back, looked at my daughter. "What makes you say that?"

Maddie smiled at me, put her arm through mine again. "Apart from the fact she's married and apart from the fact you've stopped talking about her, I just know. I know Bridget's not—

she's not right for you. I know you. You start these relationships, you have fun for a while and then you get fed up. You and Bridget, it's lasted longer than the others. But you rarely mention her nowadays and when you do you look sort of strained and fed up. I'm guessing that for you it's run its course."

"Am I that obvious?"

"Yes." My daughter gave a little laugh and rested her head on my shoulder. "I've never seen you the way you are when you mention Rachel. You kind of light up and your voice softens. It's obvious she's special. Why not tell her how you feel?"

"Because I can't risk hurting her, not like I hurt your mum."

"Dad, we've talked about this. You've got to get over it, forgive yourself. Mum has—for goodness sake. She—"

"No, Maddie. No." I managed not to make her jump this time. "I can't take the chance, not with my history. Rachel's had more than enough pain in her life. She's only just beginning to recover. I won't risk hurting her. Rachel and me, it's not going to happen."

"Okay, but I think you're wrong. I think if this Rachel's half as bright and amazing as you say, she'd see all that other stuff is in the past. You should be honest with her, tell her how you feel. And—"

I tried to interrupt, but my daughter raised her hand to stop me.

"And you need to be honest with Bridget. You need to tell her it's over and you need to do it soon. Then, regardless of what you do about Rachel, you can move on, get on with your life."

I had to laugh.

"What?" Maddie said.

"Who's the parent here?"

Maddie laughed too. "I reckon I am. You're way too hopeless."

Maddie was right, of course. I was hopeless and I was in love with Rachel.

After I got back from Edinburgh and Alasdair and Morag had

returned from their few days away, Alasdair and I went for what had become one of our regular hikes. I really enjoyed these shared walks. Alasdair was a great guide. He'd been a geography teacher until his recent retirement, but his first love was geology. And he was an expert on the geology of Skye.

On this particular day, we'd seen to the animals early and set off immediately afterwards. We planned to climb Glamaig. This hill isn't one of the Black Cuillin mountain range, two of whose Munro level peaks we'd already climbed. Glamaig is one of the Red Hills, so called because their granite shines red at dawn and sunset. It may have been lower than the Cuillin peaks, but it was hard going. The hill sloped at forty five degrees from base to summit and was covered in scree. We stopped at regular intervals for my benefit. I reckon Alasdair could have got to the top with one short break at the most.

During one of our pauses, as we swigged from our water bottles and ate a few squares of chocolate, Alasdair smiled and said, "How's the heart holding up?"

"Fine, the stents are doing a great job and I'm definitely getting fitter. I think my cardiologist would be impressed." It was true. My Skye lifestyle was certainly improving my health. A year ago, before my operation, I wouldn't have believed how much better I could feel.

Once we reached the top, we found a patch of grass near the summit where we could sit and eat our picnic lunch. As we stood there, a sea eagle flew overhead. It swooped and then soared, riding the air currents, its huge wings hardly having to work at all. It was a magnificent sight.

We chatted as we ate. I asked Alasdair how the time away had been.

"It was good," he said. "Lovely to see our daughter, and we got quality time with the grandchildren. Morag and I are both very grateful that you were able to see to the animals. We'd deliberately not taken a booking for the holiday cottage at that time and the original plan was that we'd ask Rachel to look after the croft. But with her being away it could have been a real problem for us."

"I was happy to help."

"We're still close to all our daughters, even although we're separated by considerable distances. And we promised ourselves when we both retired we'd make a big effort to see more of them."

"Retired!" I laughed. "You may both have given up teaching but you've still got a lot on with the croft and the holiday let."

"We aren't ready for the rocking chairs just yet. We're letting go of our working lives gradually."

"Very wise. It's quite an adjustment."

"How are you finding it? It must be quite a change after life in the CID?"

"I do miss work. I don't regret the decision to retire, but it's unsettling and it can leave you at a bit of a loss. I'm glad I bought the house up here. That's definitely helped and I like that I can spend more time with my granddaughter but..."

"You've still got your own life to lead as well?"

"That's right."

"I just hope Rachel finds comfort visiting *her* family," Alasdair said. "I also hope her daughter eventually sees sense and makes it up with her."

"She was intending to visit her daughter on her way to Israel, wasn't she? Did you hear how it went?"

"Not at all well, I'm afraid. Rachel told Morag it had been very difficult, not least because Sophie announced she was pregnant but would be having an abortion. She somehow managed to blame Rachel for the fact she couldn't keep the baby."

"God, poor Rachel. That must have been awful." I hated the thought of the pain her daughter's actions must have caused her, hated the thought that I hadn't been around to comfort her.

"Yes ghastly. But she seems to be enjoying her time away in spite of its difficult start. You've spoken to her, haven't you, since she's been gone?"

"We've had a couple of phone calls. She's been doing a lot of interesting stuff. She sounded happy."

Alasdair smiled. "According to Morag, it's not just her brother's family and the wonders of Israel that are making her happy. She's got a new man in her life. What was his name?"

"Eitan," I said, only just managing to keep the sneer out of my voice. "His name's Eitan. He's a friend of her brother's. She's done a bit of travelling with him."

"Not just travelling," Alasdair said. "She told Morag they've become, you know, close, more than just pals. Morag's worried Rachel might decide to move to Israel permanently if it gets serious between her and this Eitan."

For a moment I couldn't speak. I felt like I'd been punched in the gut. "Really

Alasdair looked at me. "Are you okay?"

I shrugged. "Why wouldn't I be?"

Alasdair frowned, still staring at me. "Does it bother you that Rachel might emigrate?"

"She's become a good friend. I'd miss her."

"Does it bother you she's got this bloke?"

"No, it's just I wouldn't like to think he'd mess her about."

"Right," Alasdair said. "And that's all, is it?"

"Yes," I snapped. "Why?"

"Sorry." Alasdair, held his hands up. "None of my business. It's just it seemed like you were thinking of Rachel as more than simply a friend."

"Of course not," I said. "What a bloody ridiculous thing to say! I'm already in a relationship. There's someone in Edinburgh." I stood up, put my flask and the remnants of my lunch back in my rucksack. "Time we started back down." I didn't wait for Alasdair.

When he caught up, Alasdair apologised. "Sorry, didn't mean to step on your toes. I didn't know you had someone. Like I said, none of my business. But it's good that Rachel can count on you as a friend."

Alasdair looked so uncomfortable that I regretted being so irritable. "No, no, it's me who should be sorry," I said. "I don't know why I got so touchy. I honestly wish Rachel well wherever she decides to live." Only I wasn't speaking honestly at all.

And for the remainder of Rachel's time in Israel, I tried not to give up hope that she'd decide against emigrating. I'd meant it when I told Maddie that I wasn't the sort of guy that Rachel would be interested in and that I wasn't good enough for her. But I still wanted her living close by, still wanted her friendship.

I was impressed by Rachel's discretion in not telling Morag or Alasdair about Bridget's existence, but then I tortured myself with the notion that it wasn't discretion but plain lack of interest, and she hadn't thought it worth talking about.

During this time I also decided to go and see Bridget. She'd phoned me a few times since our last meeting. I took only two of the calls and we'd just talked round in circles. So I decided to have it out properly, face to face and for the last time. I had to tell her it was over.

Chapter Thirty Three

But Bridget had other ideas. Before I could even contact her to say that I'd be coming down, she appeared in Skye. It was late on a Saturday afternoon in the middle of August. I'd just got back from helping Alasdair with the animals.

It was also the day Rachel was due back in the UK. Alasdair told me she'd be staying overnight in Glasgow and would drive up to Skye the next day. I was glad she'd soon be home, but I also wondered just how long she'd be back for.

As I made myself a coffee, I tried to put all thoughts of Rachel out of my head. I sat at the kitchen table and did my best to read the paper. Bonnie settled down in her basket for a snooze but it wasn't long before she was barking, awakened by the knock at the front door. I knew it wouldn't be anybody local as they would just have walked in but the last person I expected it to be was her.

"Thank god!" Bridget said when I opened the door. "I thought I was never going to find you. Why on earth do you want to be here? It's the back of the back of beyond. And when did you get a dog?"

I stared at her. She was so out of context, my brain couldn't quite process what it was seeing. Bridget Barstow, in smart suit and high heels, was standing on my doorstep.

She pushed past me into the hallway. "I'll get my bags out the car later. Right now I need a G and T."

"Right," I said. "I don't think I've got any tonic—or any gin, come to that. I'll have to look."

"This way, is it?" She pointed down the hallway.

"Yes, yes—this way," I said.

She followed me into the kitchen. Bonnie got up from her basket and barked again. I told her to be quiet and to lie down. While I checked the cupboard, Bridget stood looking around. "Very nice," she said. "And an Aga. How chic."

"It's practical," I said. "Wood-burner, heats the radiators and the water." I closed the cupboard door. "No gin, whisky do?"

"It'll have to," she said. "I'm guessing the nearest shop's miles away." She sat down at the table.

I poured her a drink. "What are you doing here? How did you even know where I live?" I sat down opposite her.

She took a sip of whisky before answering. "Maddie," she replied.

"Maddie?"

"Yes, your daughter gave me your address. I phoned her in desperation. You were being so evasive. Even when we do talk, you don't hear what I'm saying."

"Why—why would Maddie give you my address?" I couldn't hide my anger.

"Don't be cross with her. I told her how difficult it was for me to get hold of you. She agreed with me that it would be a good idea if I came to see you. She said she was doing it as a favour to you, not to me."

"Did she now?"

"Look, I know it's a shock, me turning up. But there was a time when you'd have loved it that I surprised you like this. In fact you'd have had me in bed by now—"

"That was then. Before—"

"Before what?"

There was another knock at the door. The back door this time, and Morag walked straight into the kitchen, followed by Alasdair.

"Oh, sorry," Morag said, her eyes wide with curiosity and surprise.

"Yes, sorry," said Alasdair. "We saw the car. I did say we shouldn't bother you if you had a visitor, but Morag—"

"We're going to the Acarsaid for dinner," Morag interrupted. "Alasdair said you seemed a bit down. We thought you might like to join us."

"What a lovely idea! He does need cheering up, doesn't he?" Bridget said, standing up, hand outstretched to Morag. "Bridget Barstow."

Morag shook Bridget's hand. "Morag Mackinnon," she said. "And this is my husband, Alasdair."

After Bridget and Alasdair shook hands, I realised everyone was looking at me.

"Yes, right, dinner at the inn," I said, getting to my feet. "Yes, good idea. Bridget - surprised me. She's my friend from—"

Bridget laughed as she interrupted me. "Friend! I hope I'm more than that, Jack." She took my hand and leaned against me.

Morag and Alasdair exchanged a glance and then Alasdair said, "Right, good, let's go then. I'm driving."

Once we got to the inn, Alasdair went to the bar while Morag sought out a table.

Bridget looked around the walls at the nautical maps and the black and white photos of local crofts and crofters from years gone by. She took in the long, low-ceilinged room with its dark, heavy furniture, its inglenook fireplace and its small low windows. I knew what she was thinking before she spoke.

"Very cosy," she said, raising an eyebrow.

"Bridget," I said. "Don't."

"What?" she replied, smiling, untroubled by my irritation. "I didn't mean anything derogatory. It's perfectly pleasant. I just didn't think such places still existed. But then I don't really do rural."

"No, you don't."

"But you, you've gone native. You like all this?" She gestured around the room.

"I'm happy here if that's what you mean."

"Hmm," she said. "Are you sure about that?"

I was relieved to see Morag coming back. "There's a table through in the back," she said.

I can't remember what we had to eat. Even the whiskies which Alasdair insisted on buying me didn't help me to relax. Fortunately Alasdair was curious enough about Bridget to keep the conversation going. He asked her what she did for a living and had lots of questions about the workings of the Scottish parliament.

Bridget sat on the bench seat beside me, facing Alasdair and Morag across the table. She was much more tactile than I remembered her to be. She kept patting my hand or my arm, and every time I moved to make a space between us she kept shuffling back close beside me.

Then, as we drank our coffee, Morag looked across at Bridget and said, "So, how did you and Jack meet?"

"We were both part of a captive audience at a rather dull Scottish Government reception. We recognised each other immediately as kindred spirits." Bridget looked up at me and then turned back to Morag, smiling. "We fancied each other right away. That was a couple of years ago and we've been together ever since. Or at least we were until he started coming up here."

"You didn't live together in Edinburgh?" Morag said.

"No, no. I'm married. Jack and me, it's recreational."

I sensed Alasdair's surprise and I saw Morag's in the expression on her face. Bridget didn't seem to register either reaction. Again her hand was on my arm. "I'm just hoping I can persuade him to come back to Edinburgh. He's had long enough to get this ridiculous notion about living here out of his system. I need him to be much more available."

This was too much. I had to fight to keep my temper. I wanted to shout at her to shut up. Shout at her that our relationship was over. I glanced at Alasdair. He raised his eyebrows and gave a slight shake of his head.

"I'm going to pay the bill," I said, getting to my feet and stumbling from the table.

When I returned the others were finishing off their drinks and Morag said, "Ah, Jack, I was just telling Bridget about our neighbour, Rachel. She'll be home tomorrow."

I didn't look at Bridget. "Yes, Alasdair told me she'd confirmed her return date." I tried to keep my voice neutral.

"And now," Alasdair said, "If everyone's ready, I think we should go."

As soon as we were alone back at Dun Halla, Bridget started. We were in the kitchen and she said, "What's wrong, Jack? You've been in a right mood all evening. You don't seem pleased to see me."

I breathed deeply before I replied. "Look, Bridget, we've had a fair bit to drink, it's late, we're tired. Let's leave this till the morning."

"No, I—"

"I said, I'm not doing this tonight." I tried to at least keep my voice calm. "The bed in the spare room is made up. It's en suite, there's loads of hot water. I'll bring your bags in and show you upstairs. We'll talk tomorrow."

Bridget sat down on one of the kitchen chairs. "Okay," she said. "You win." She looked exhausted all of a sudden. I actually felt sorry for her. After all this was all my doing. But tomorrow, tomorrow she'd be free of me.

Half an hour later, when I got back from walking Bonnie, the house was quiet and no light shone from under the spare bedroom door. I went to bed and lay awake for much of the night. Punching the pillow and cursing myself didn't help. And neither did anticipating Rachel's return.

Chapter Thirty Four

I was up early next morning. My head ached, but my heart ached even more. There was no sign of Bridget. I didn't bother to shower, just got dressed and collected Bonnie and went straight out.

I headed away from the township, through the gates onto the common grazing and then out onto the peat moor beyond. It was a damp, misty morning, but the sun was out and the clouds were thin and high. I part jogged and part walked until I got to the foot of Ben Halla.

By the time I'd scrambled to the top of the hill my head felt clearer. The sun was already burning off the mist and it looked like it was going to be a fine day. I lay on my back on the damp, mossy summit and watched the wispy clouds drifting overhead. Bonnie ran circles round me, stopping periodically to lick my face. I had little in the way of specific thoughts and certainly no planned speeches, but by the time I stood up to head back, I felt positive and prepared for what I had to do.

Looking at my watch as I set off down the hill, I was surprised to see that it was almost ten o'clock. I'd been away for a couple of hours. There was no sign of Bridget when I walked into the kitchen. I decided to have a quick coffee before showering. Bonnie was lapping water from her bowl and I'd just put the kettle on to boil when there was a gentle knock on the back door. It opened and there stood Rachel.

Bonnie went crazy. She barked, whimpered, whined, jumped and wagged her tail.

As with Bridget's arrival the day before, it took me a minute to make sense of what I was seeing. I knew Rachel was supposed to be driving up from Glasgow that day but she shouldn't have been in Skye until late afternoon. I stared at her as she greeted the ecstatic dog. I was able to take in how great she looked. Her hair was down, coils of it around her face and neck, and its auburn shade had lightened with the sun. Her normally pale skin was now lightly tanned and the freckles on her face stood out. She was wearing jeans and a short orange cardigan that suited her perfectly. My mouth went dry and I didn't seem able to speak.

She eventually managed to calm Bonnie down and got her to sit. She looked at me. a puzzled smile on her face. "Jack?" she said. "You look shocked. I don't look that weird, do I?"

"Yes, I mean, no! You don't look weird. It's just it's a surprise to see you. I didn't think you'd be here till later on today. I thought you were planning to stay over in Glasgow after your flight yesterday and then drive up today."

"Right," she said, looking at me sceptically. "It's no big deal, really. I felt fine when I landed and I just wanted to get home. So I changed my plans and drove up straight away. I got back here just after midnight."

"I see," I said. "Well, welcome home. You look—great."

"Thanks." She smiled at me. "You look..."

"Sweaty, I know. I'm just back from a run. I need a shower, sorry."

"No need to apologise. I really just popped in to say hi and to collect Bonnie, if that's okay. I won't keep you. Besides I saw the other car parked at the front. I assume you have a visitor."

"That would be me," Bridget said. I turned to see her standing in the kitchen doorway. She was wearing my dressing-gown, her legs and feet were bare. I'd no idea how long she'd been standing there. She padded over to me and put an arm around my waist. "And you must be Rachel," she said. Then looking up at me, "Darling, you should have wakened me before you left.

It's just as well the dog barked, otherwise who knows how long I'd have slept!"

In the ensuing seconds, or maybe it was it only a split second, I knew I should say—must say—something, but I couldn't find any words. I didn't know where to start. Various thoughts crashed through my mind. I wanted to tell Bridget to shut up. I wanted to beg Rachel not to listen to her, to tell her Bridget was mad. But I knew that wouldn't be fair. Any delusions Bridget had were down to me. I also knew that my relationship status didn't matter to Rachel. I could only stand there looking at her.

She glanced from me to Bridget. Her eyes widened with surprise, or was it curiosity? I wasn't sure which. Whatever it was, it was momentary. "I'm so sorry for intruding," she said. "And for disturbing you. And, yes, I'm Rachel—Rachel Campbell." She held out her hand to Bridget. "I'm a friend and neighbour of Jack's."

"Yes, I knew who you were right away. Bridget Barstow—Jack's partner—pleased to meet you."

"Pleased to meet you too," Rachel said, shaking Bridget's hand.

As she let go of Rachel's hand, Bridget moved back close beside me again.

Rachel turned to me and said, "Thank you so much for looking after Bonnie. But now we'll leave you in peace." She signalled to the dog to come to her. "I'll call for her basket and other stuff later, if that's okay?"

I still couldn't speak, couldn't trust myself. I stared back at her. She was close enough to touch. I could smell her perfume.

"Jack?" she said. "Did you hear me? I asked if it would be all right to collect Bonnie's stuff later, only I'm on foot just now, I'll come back with the Land Rover, okay?"

I swallowed, found my voice. "Yes, yes that's fine. Or I could drop it off at yours if you like, later on this afternoon."

She smiled. "That would be great. Oh, and I also wanted to ask you to come to dinner on Saturday."

Dinner with Rachel, at her request, my mouth went dry again. I swallowed hard. "Dinner? On Saturday?"

"Yes, Morag and Alasdair are coming too. I wanted to thank the three of you properly for taking care of things while I was away."

"Ah, right," I said. "Thanks. That would be lovely." I told myself that being with her, even if Morag and Alasdair would be there, was better than not being with her.

Bridget cleared her throat.

Rachel turned to her. "And, of course, you'd be very welcome too, if you'll still be here."

"Thanks," Bridget said, taking hold of my arm again. "We'll see what our plans are and let you know."

"Of course."

As soon as the door closed behind Rachel, Bridget turned and walked from the room. I knew she was upset and I knew not to follow her. A short time later I heard the shower running in the en suite.

I decided to have a shower too and then to wait for her to come to me.

It must have been about an hour or so later that she did. I was back in the kitchen and on my second strong coffee. She was dressed and had her suitcase with her. She put it down at the door and then came and sat opposite me at the kitchen table. I could see she'd been crying. I poured her a coffee. "Strong and black," I said, pushing the cup towards her.

She put her hands around the cup and stared down into it for a moment. Then she looked me in the eye and said, "It's really over for you, isn't it? You don't want us to be together anymore, do you?"

I reached over the table, tried to take hold of her hand, but she pulled away. "I'm so sorry—but yes, it's over."

Bridget put her head back and sighed. Then she leaned forwards, put her elbows on the table and rested her forehead on her clenched fists. When she looked up her expression was angry. She hit one fist down on the table. "You shouldn't have come here," she said, waving an arm to indicate the room. She pushed her chair back and stood up. She moved round to grip the back of the chair. "You should never have left Edinburgh." She nodded her head in the direction of the window. "This isn't real, Jack. This isn't you."

"No, it is. It *is* me. I love it here."

She took a deep breath. She seemed calmer, her expression softer. "Look, I understand," she said, as she sat back down. "You've had a bit of a rough time. The heart operation and then adjusting to being retired. That's why I agreed to give you a bit of space. But you've had your adventure, your timeout—"

"No, no!" I said. "This isn't some late mid-life crisis, or a year out. This is me now, and from now on. This is where I want to be most of the time and I have plans."

"And they don't include me?"

"No—no they don't."

"But they do include that—that Rachel person?"

"No." I kept my voice even. "I'm not involved with Rachel. I'm no good at relationships—"

"I had no complaints. What we had, it worked for me. Please, Jack, if you came back, we could make it work. Maybe we could do a bit of travelling together—"

"Bridget—Bridget, please." I put my hand on hers. "Don't." A tear slid down her cheek. "Don't do this to yourself."

She pulled back. Her face flushed. Her fury obvious. "Do this to myself? It's you, Jack—you. You're the one being cruel. Can't you see I've fallen in love with you?"

"What?"

She shook her head. "Christ, what an idiot I've been." She put her head in her hands.

I'd never seen her like this. She was strong, single-minded, always calm and in control. I'd never seen her vulnerable or upset. I reached my hand out to her again, to comfort her. But she pushed me away.

"You never mentioned being in love," I said. "I thought it was just—"

"Just what? Sex?"

"Yes, mainly. But we've been good mates too. You helped me cope with my heart trouble, helped me decide about my retirement."

"And that's well and truly backfired. I encouraged you to give up work and inadvertently helped you to go on this mad venture. And as for heart trouble, it's me who has all the heartache now."

"I'm really sorry. I thought we wanted the same things out of our relationship. You told me you still loved your husband. You—"

"I know what I said and it's—it *was* true. I didn't plan to fall in love with you. But I did. And I'll have to get over it. You've moved on. It's Rachel now."

"No, I told you, Rachel's not—"

"Please, don't make it worse by lying to me. It was obvious when she was here just now. The chemistry between you, it was obvious." Bridget's voice was quieter now.

"Look, I don't know how to convince you, but there's nothing, no relationship between Rachel and me."

"You may not realise it but you're being dishonest, with me and with yourself. But whatever you're telling yourself, it's over isn't it, between you and me?"

"Yes, yes I'm afraid it is. I was going to come and see you, tell you—"

"Then I've saved you the bother, haven't I?" Bridget raised her hands in a gesture of submission. "I think I'd better go." She picked up her case and handbag.

"I'm sorry," I said. "I'm so sorry. Sorry you wanted more than I can give. I regret that you've been hurt, regret it's come to an end, but I don't regret a minute of the time we had together."

"Well that's just great, Jack," she said. Her voice was strained, full of sarcasm and bitterness She reached up and stroked my cheek. "You're a lying, cheating, pathetic bastard and I do have regrets. For one, I wish I'd never met you." And then she drew back her hand and slapped me hard across the face.

Chapter Thirty Five

I don't know how long I sat there in the kitchen after Bridget left. I should have been relieved, but I felt terrible. Bridget had been a transforming influence on my life over the previous two years. She was attractive, vibrant, opinionated and sophisticated and she was fun. I never meant to hurt her. I'd meant what I said to her. I had no regrets.

Eventually I dragged myself to my feet, told myself to get a grip, that I'd done what had to be done.

I called Maddie. I began by asking her how she was coping, given that she was into the last month of her pregnancy and that Poppy was still on holiday from school. She assured me she was fine, but she knew why I was really calling, and she apologised for giving Bridget my address. I told her I understood why she'd done it.

"So, she came to see you, then?" Maddie said.

"Turned up unannounced yesterday, stayed over—in the spare room—and this morning I ended it."

"Really, no room for doubt on Bridget's part?"

"No room for doubt. Bridget and me are over."

"It was the right thing to do, Dad."

"I know, but it feels—I feel—cruel. She didn't deserve to be—to be—"

"Told the truth, told how you really feel? Oh, she did, Dad. She deserved that at the very least. The cruel thing would have been to allow things to drift on. Life's too short to stagnate. Now you're both free, free to go on and find something real."

"How did you get so wise?" I asked, managing to smile.

"No idea, must have been in spite of you, I guess." And I could hear the smile in Maddie's voice.

After the phone call I felt a bit better and decided to go out and dig. And, after an hour in the wonderfully fresh air, pulling up the old turf in the garden, my spirits lifted even more.

As I prepared some lunch, I felt a surge of positivity. I was living in a place I loved. I was pleased with the renovations on the house. I was enjoying all my walks and climbs. I'd soon have a new grandchild. And Rachel was back on Skye. Life was good.

After lunch, I gathered all Bonnie's bits and pieces, bed, bowls, toys, lead and food and put them in the back of the car. When I got to Rachel's, the door into the porch was standing open, as was the door from the porch to the house. A lovely sound drifted out from the kitchen. Singing, Rachel was singing. I laid down Bonnie's stuff as quietly as I could, hoping the dog wouldn't bark and give me away. But as I stood in the doorway, Bonnie was nowhere to be seen.

Rachel was standing at her kitchen table kneading dough and singing along with the radio as she worked. I was reminded of the first evening we had dinner together and I'd heard her singing as she cleared up. This time the song was John Lennon's Imagine and she sang it beautifully. I was transfixed. I didn't speak until she was finished.

"Wow," I said.

She jumped and turned to look at me.

"Sorry," I said. "I didn't mean to startle you. I was enjoying your singing so much I didn't want to stop you."

She raised her eyebrows. I wasn't sure if she was annoyed or just embarrassed. "Right," she said, wiping her hands on a tea towel. "So, what can I do for you?"

"I brought Bonnie's stuff back—as promised. It's in the porch."

"Oh, okay, thanks." She looked at me, her expression serious. "I saw Bridget leaving."

"Oh, did you? She couldn't stay, she..." I hesitated, not sure if this was a good time to tell Rachel the whole story.

"Right," Rachel said. She pointed at the table. "I really need to get on."

"Yes, yes of course. I won't keep you."

"Sorry, I'm just trying to restock the freezer and also get ahead with stuff for the meal on Saturday. You'll be coming, will you, to my thank you meal?"

I didn't know if I was imagining it, but she didn't sound like she was bothered one way or the other. She certainly didn't seem as warm and friendly as she had earlier.

But I wasn't going to pass up the chance to be in her company. "Definitely, I'll be there."

"Okay, come for around seven. And thanks again for bringing Bonnie's stuff round." She gave a little smile.

Encouraged, I said, "Where is she by the way?"

Rachel smiled again. "She's sulking at not having my undivided attention after our separation, probably sneaked upstairs for a snooze on my bed."

The thought of Rachel's bed, of lying on Rachel's bed...

"I'm sorry, Jack, but I really do need to..." Her voice dragged me back to reality.

"Yes, sorry. I'll see you on Saturday. I'm looking forward to it and to hearing all about your trip."

She nodded.

And that was it. I left. I felt—what? Disappointment? Dismay? I realised I was probably over-reacting, imagining a distance between us. I'd been hoping that we'd get to spend some time together before Saturday. I phoned her on the Tuesday and suggested a walk at the Coral Beach, but she said she was too busy and made it clear she didn't want to prolong the phone call. Then I bumped into her at the Co-op in Portree on the Thursday and asked if she fancied a coffee, but she didn't. She was polite yet distant.

In spite of all that, I tried, during the course of that week, to rekindle the positivity I'd mustered before returning Bonnie's stuff to Rachel.

I remained sure about ending it with Bridget. That definitely felt right. And I spoke to Poppy on the phone and enjoyed her excitement at the prospect of having a wee brother or sister before very long.

The August weather continued to be settled. The days were bright and there was a good breeze blowing so the midges weren't active. I spent most of my time digging the garden, removing the remaining grass and preparing the soil for the new turf. Every now and then I'd pause in my digging to watch a boat out on the loch or a buzzard circling overhead. And I would breathe deeply and savour the incredibly pure Hebridean air.

But at times it was difficult to remain positive. My suspicions that Rachel had come back changed niggled away. She'd obviously just been being polite when she called in on her first day back and it was the same politeness that had prompted her to invite me for a meal. But that seemed to be it. The ease and the friendship that had felt so real between us before she'd gone to Israel didn't seem to be there anymore. Maybe she was going to emigrate. Maybe she was going to tell us of this decision at the meal. And so I tortured myself.

It was Alasdair who clarified things for me, to a certain extent at least. He dropped in to see me on the Saturday afternoon, the day of the meal. I was digging when he arrived but I put down my spade and told him to have a seat on the bench in front of the house. I got us both a cold beer and joined him.

"Sorry to keep you from your work," Alasdair said.

"No problem," I said. "I'm due a break. And it's always good to see you."

Alasdair looked slightly uncomfortable. "Morag thought I should come to see you before tonight."

"Oh?"

"She thought you should know—that is, be in full possession of the facts." He wiped his forehead and took a gulp of beer.

"Facts?"

"Yes, Rachel and your lady friend—they spoke. Had words."

"Rachel and Bridget, what do you mean?"

"The day Bridget left, she drove past Rachel. Rachel was walking on the track. Bridget stopped and spoke to her before she went away."

"Right. Rachel said she'd seen Bridget leaving, but she didn't mention that they'd spoken. I presume you know what was said?"

"Yes, I do. Rachel told Morag. She was quite upset."

"Oh, God what did Bridget say to her?"

"Bridget warned her off, warned her about you." Alasdair took another gulp of beer. "She told Rachel that you two had just broken up. She accused Rachel of being partly to blame, said she knew you'd been unfaithful to her with Rachel. Then she warned Rachel about you, told her she was foolish to get involved with you and that she should steer well clear. Said you couldn't be trusted, that you'd not even been faithful to your wife."

Alasdair paused, looked at me. "Sorry, Jack, about the break up and everything, but Morag—and me, we thought you should know what was said and then you could maybe clear the air with Rachel."

I was having trouble processing what Alasdair had told me. I was having trouble just breathing.

"You okay?" Alasdair said.

"Not really. No wonder Rachel's been keeping her distance these last few days."

"Och, you know Rachel, she'll not find it easy to say anything to you about it."

"What was Bridget thinking of?"

"Hell hath no fury," Alasdair said. "Don't worry, Rachel's probably over it. It's not like you two have actually been—you know—close in that way—a couple. And anyway she's so full of her big adventure in the Middle East she'll not have had time to dwell on it. We just thought you should know, but I'm sure it'll be fine." Alasdair drained his glass, handed it to me and stood up. "See you tonight then," he said, his relief at having said what he'd come to say was obvious.

"Yes, see you later, and thanks, Alasdair."

I considered not going to Rachel's that evening, considered making some excuse and just leaving her in peace. But I couldn't. I wanted to see her. I realised we probably wouldn't get a chance to talk, but, at least by going to the meal, I'd be keeping a line of communication open.

I arrived at Rachel's on the dot of seven o'clock. Alasdair and Morag were already there. The three of them were in the kitchen when I walked in. Alasdair and Morag were standing, each with a glass of wine in hand, chatting to Rachel as she put the finishing touches to the meal. The aromas coming from the Aga were amazing. Bonnie was there too and, in amongst us all saying our good evenings, she barked and jumped up at me in an exuberant greeting. I made a bit of a fuss of her and then told her to sit, which she did immediately.

"I'm impressed," Rachel said, glancing at the now quiet dog and then looking at me. "Alasdair will fix you up with a drink. Dinner's almost ready."

"Great, thanks," I said. "It smells good. Oh, and these are for you." I handed her the wine and the bunch of orange roses I'd brought.

"You didn't have to bring anything," she replied. "But thank you. I don't remember the last time anyone brought me flowers, not on a happy occasion at least, so thanks." She looked at me in the way I remembered from before she went away. A look so direct my heart and stomach did some sort of simultaneous clench.

"You're welcome," I said, not without difficulty.

"Drink?" Alasdair waggled a bottle of red wine and smiled at me in a way that let me know he knew how I was feeling.

"Oh, yes," I said.

Soon we were all sitting at the table enjoying a very tasty tomato and basil soup along with homemade crusty bread. This was followed by a truly delicious casserole of lamb shanks served with roast potatoes and what I guessed must be fresh peas, so full-on was their flavour. During the first two courses the chat was mainly local gossip with Morag and Alasdair bringing Rachel up to date with both Halladale and island-wide events. The atmosphere was pleasant and relaxed and I decided just to enjoy the meal for what it was, a shared evening with good food and good people. It wasn't the time for a heart to heart with Rachel.

"The peas are from Morag's garden," Rachel told me when I complimented her on the main course. "And the lamb's local. Which reminds me," she added, raising her glass. "Here's to all of you and thank you. Alasdair, you did an amazing job with the sheep. Morag, my hens are in great shape and the house has never looked tidier. And Jack, I know you did a lot too, helping Alasdair and looking after Bonnie. I really mean it, thank you everyone. I couldn't have gone away for so long without you all keeping things ticking over on the croft." She clinked each of our glasses in turn.

It was while we were eating dessert, a mercifully light and tangy lemon and raspberry cake, that the conversation turned to Rachel's time in Israel.

Morag had asked about the recipe for the cake and Rachel had said it was one she'd got from her sister-in-law. She said she'd learned a few new dishes while she'd been away and was keen to try them out. This led to a fair bit of chat between the two of them about Middle Eastern cooking and some of the new things Rachel had eaten while she was away. She also talked about the food her family had prepared for some sort of special birthday party for her niece.

"You must be finding Skye awfully tame since you got back," Alasdair said. "Are you finding it hard to settle back in?"

"In some ways," Rachel said. "It was, and I know this sounds over-dramatic, but it was a life-changing experience. I'm so glad I went. I saw and did so many amazing new things, and I learned a lot too."

"Well it's lovely having you back," Morag said. "I hope you missed us a bit at least."

"Of course I did. And I missed the croft and Bonnie and—oh, lots of things."

"Some of the photos are incredible," Alasdair said. "Thanks for emailing them. You'll have to talk me through them some time."

"I'd love to," Rachel said. "It'll give me a chance to relive it all."

"You seen them, Jack? Rachel's photos."

"No, no I haven't. But I'd like to." I turned to Rachel. "If you wouldn't mind." I felt ridiculously disappointed that she hadn't chosen to share the pictures with me.

"If you like. I wasn't sure you'd be interested, so I didn't..." She shrugged. There was that distance again.

And then, in response to questions from Morag and Alasdair, she went on to talk about her brother and his family, about life in Jerusalem, about the sights she'd seen and the impressions they'd made on her. Alasdair was particularly interested in her time on the West Bank and Morag wanted to know about her other travels, especially the trips she'd done with Eitan.

I could only watch, smile and endure it as she enthused about it all. She said she'd found it all fascinating and had learned a lot about this other part to her heritage. And, although I loved how animated she was, I dreaded what it might mean.

It was Morag who voiced the question. "So, will you be going to live there? Did you like it enough to emigrate?" Morag's expression was an exact representation of the fear I felt at what the answer might be.

"I don't know. I honestly don't know. There are things I need to do here first whatever I decide. And then I'll have to see..."

"But there's a possibility you might go?" Morag said.

"Yes, yes there is. But right now I just need time to reflect, think about what there is to keep me here, think about where's home and about where my heart lies."

Morag nodded. She looked as if she might cry. I knew how

she felt.

"Morag," Alasdair said, putting his hand on hers. "Come on now, don't get upset. Rachel's still here for the moment. Let's just enjoy her company. And even if she does go, good friends like you two, you'll never lose touch." He squeezed her hand.

Morag managed a smile. "Sorry," she said to Rachel.

"Don't be." Rachel smiled back at her. "Like Alasdair says, let's enjoy each other's company for now. Nobody knows what the future holds. But I promise you'll be the first to know when I do decide."

Over coffee, the light-hearted mood of earlier returned. On the surface at any rate.

Chapter Thirty Six

It was to be another two weeks before I saw Rachel again, other than just in passing. I badly wanted to see her, spend time with her, talk to her, apologise for Bridget. But I couldn't face her telling me she wanted no more to do with me. In some pathetic way, I preferred the uncertainty, the remote possibility that there might be hope for our friendship. So I let things be.

Again, it was Alasdair who gave me the kick up the backside that I needed. He called round late one morning to suggest a walk. He'd already prepared sandwiches and a flask. It was certainly another perfect day for being out, bright with a breeze.

We went walking on Trotternish up near the Old Man of Storr. It was while we were eating that Alasdair broached the subject.

"You cleared the air yet with Rachel?" he said, staring out towards the loch.

"No."

"You going to?"

"Yes—no—don't know."

"You should."

"I know I should! It's just—it's not easy—you know."

"I know, but it's Morag, she said I should speak to you."

"Oh yeah, Morag is it?" I couldn't help but smile.

"She's worried, you see, worried Rachel will leave. And she thinks she'll stay if you two make it up. She thinks you two—that you two should be together."

"Really, does she?"

"She does. She says Rachel needs to be told how you feel about her. She says you two had a good relationship before she went away and before that Bridget said what she said. She says Rachel misses you but would never admit it. She'd really like to see you two sort it out."

"Uh-huh," I said.

"Oh, for Pete's sake, Jack! *I'm* telling you! I'm telling you as a friend. Get this sorted. You two are crazy about each other. It's obvious. We can see it, Morag and me, and blooming Bridget saw it too." Clearly agitated, Alasdair got up and began to pack the lunch stuff.

"Look, Alasdair—"

But he raised his hand to stop me speaking. "No. You look. I'm not used to giving out this sort of advice. I'm no agony aunt. But you—you're hopeless. For someone who must have studied body language in your line of work, gone on instinct and hunches, you don't seem to be able to apply all that stuff when it comes to Rachel. Go and see her. You need to know where you stand." And with that Alasdair swung his rucksack onto his back and set off up the hill. We said no more about it.

But I did pay heed to what Alasdair had said. That evening I phoned Rachel. I hardly gave her a chance to speak. I said I wanted to see her, that I thought we needed to talk. I asked her to come to the house the next evening and I told her I'd cook. Before she could respond, I also said that if she didn't come, I'd leave it at that and not bother her again.

Her answer stunned me. "I thought you'd never ask," she said. "See you tomorrow. I'll be there around seven."

The next day was spent preparing—shopping, cooking and getting the house just right.

By six-thirty, everything was under control in the kitchen. I got myself a beer and sat outside on the bench at the front of the house. It was a beautiful pink-skied evening and I watched as the western sky became more deeply suffused with orange and red. I don't think I'd ever felt this nervous. And then I saw her approaching. Unlike the first time she came for dinner, Rachel had no need of wellies and waterproofs. This time all she needed was a little jacket which she had draped around her shoulders. She wore the same green dress she'd worn that first time, but this time her hair was up. She looked amazing.

"Good evening," she said as she came through the gate. Her smile seemed slightly wary, shy even.

I stood up, smiled back at her. "Good evening," I replied. "It's good to see you." I cleared my throat, surprised at how awkward I felt.

"And you, and it's good to see you're dressed this time."

This bit of light-heartedness on her part, unexpected but oh so welcome, made me laugh.

"Here," she said handing me her jacket and a bottle of wine and stepping towards the front door. "So, am I getting a tour of the house?"

We began in the kitchen. Rachel said she liked the steel and granite and how she envied my modern Aga. When we went into the living-room she gasped as she took in the windows on three sides. From the back window, she admired how good the garden was looking already and took in the view of Ben Halla and then from the front window she gazed out at the loch. She commented how strange it was to see these familiar views from this slightly different angle. She was particularly impressed by the long floor-to-ceiling window panels that made up nearly the whole of the gable end. She exclaimed at how amazing the north light must be during the day, but she did wonder about how it would be in winter. She said there was a reason that traditional Skye houses had small windows—the weather, especially the hurricane-force winds. However, she was impressed when I told her it was all triple-glazed and approved of my plan to hang heavy curtains in the winter.

The downstairs wet-room and upstairs bathroom also drew her approval and more expressions of envy. And, of course, the small guest room-cum-den located above the living room, which also had a north facing window, merited more exclamations about the quality of the light.

She saw right away that the remaining two guestrooms were well set up for when the family came to stay and agreed that putting an en suite in the larger one was a very good idea.

We finished in my bedroom. Yes, I felt awkward about showing this room to Rachel, but I guessed it would probably be even more awkward to leave it out. And anyway, Rachel appeared to feel no awkwardness. She stood at the foot of the bed taking in the black and whiteness of the room and said, "Wow! I like the design. Perfectly masculine—very you." I think I may have detected a slight blush, but it was difficult to tell in the fading light.

"Dinner?" I said.

We ate in the living-room. The table was by the west facing window. "This is the first time I've sat here to eat," I said. "I thought it would be nice to see the sunset."

"It is. It's lovely and I'm honoured to be the first to sit here with you." She smiled and raised her glass. "*Slàinte mhath*, Jack," she said. "The house looks great and I hope you'll be happy here."

"Thank you," I said.

As we ate, she seemed relaxed. I dared to hope, but it could just have been good manners on her part and I decided not to push things. I was content for now to be in her company, to eat together and to listen to her talk about her time in Israel. She was enthused about so many aspects of what she'd experienced. It was lovely to see, despite what it might lead to.

We'd just finished the main course when she asked about Poppy and I showed her a recent photo Maddie had sent me.

"She's a lovely wee girl, Jack. You're so lucky to have her and it won't be long until your new grandchild arrives, will it?"

"Any time now." I couldn't help grinning at the thought. "Maddie's at the fed up stage, just wants to get it over. I'm on standby to go down to Edinburgh at any moment."

"Sorry, sorry, Jack. I just need—sorry." She stood up. There were tears in her eyes. She made for the door. I stood up to go after her.

"Rachel, what is it? What's wrong." I caught hold of her arm and turned her to face me. She gave me that direct look, the tears now running down her face. I reached into my pocket and produced my handkerchief. "Here," I said. "I don't suppose you have one of your own."

She actually smiled as she took it from me. I don't know why. She wiped her tears. "Sorry, Jack. It was just the talk of grand-children, it upset me. Just ignore me." A fresh tear ran down her face

I reached out my hand and stroked the tear aside. "I could never ignore you, Rachel. I'm sorry I upset you."

She surprised me by putting her hand on mine. "It wasn't you that upset me. It's just that my daughter, Sophie, she's, she's not—oh God, Jack." She shuddered.

"It's okay," I said. "I know. Alasdair told me." I rubbed her arm as I spoke, took hold of her hand. "Come and sit."

It was almost dark outside and I flicked the switch for the lamps as I guided her to the sofa. We sat down and I put my arm round her. She rested her head on my shoulder and then she told me about Sophie, about their meeting in Glasgow and about the pregnancy and the abortion. As she talked she twisted my hankie in her hands, pausing occasionally to wipe her tears.

"I'm so sorry, going on about Poppy and the baby—"

"No." She pulled away from me and looked me in the eye. "Don't apologise. Poppy's delightful. I'm very fond of her and I'm sure the baby will be every bit as delightful. It's just, you know..."

I put my arm round her again. "I know," I said. "I know."

We sat side by side, silent for a few moments. When she spoke, her voice was quiet. "You're—you've become a good friend to me, Jack. It means a lot to me. I want—I want you to know that."

I covered one of her hands with mine. "This last couple of weeks, since you got back, I thought—I thought you'd had it with me—thought you didn't want any more to do with me."

"What? No! That was never the case."

"Alasdair told me about what Bridget said to you. Me and

her, it had been over for some time as far as I was concerned, I just hadn't had the courage to tell her till that day. I am so sorry she was rude to you and that she upset you—even if what she said about me was true. I wouldn't blame you if you'd had it with me."

Rachel shook her head. "Look Jack, I'm sorry about your breakup with Bridget. It can't have been easy for either of you. And yes, she did upset me. But only because of her tone and her accusations. What went on between you is none of my business. And anyway, she didn't tell me anything I didn't already know. You've always been straight with me. I didn't think any less of you."

"But you seemed distant. You didn't want to go for coffee that day we met in Portree and you didn't want to go for a walk. I thought you were trying to tell me—"

"No, no, that wasn't it at all. The coffee day, I really was in a hurry." She gave me that direct, searching look of hers, and her voice quietened as she continued. "And the day you phoned about going for a walk—well, that was the day I opened Finlay's letter. I had it in my hand when you called."

"Finlay's letter?"

"It's taken me all this time to open it. It's the letter they're encouraged to write, that soldiers are encouraged to write to their loved ones, to be..." she swallowed.

"To be opened in the event of their death," I finished for her. "God, Rachel, I'm sorry. I can see why you wouldn't have wanted—"

"You weren't to know. Besides, I almost asked you to come to the house when you called. I was feeling so sorry for myself. It was pathetic."

"Not pathetic, understandable. Why didn't you ask me to come?"

"Like I say, I felt pathetic. I didn't want to force my misery on you. You were up for a nice walk. I didn't want to bother you with my trouble."

"You were wrong. I would have come, supported you, and

certainly not regretted the lack of a walk."

She smiled, a small smile that broadened into a full on one. "A good thing happened too though, later that same day. Sophie called. I'd been going to phone her, to talk about everything, but I hadn't quite got my script sorted out. Then *she* called me. She wants to come up. Sophie wants to come up and see me." Rachel clasped her hands and took a deep breath. "She's coming to stay. She'll be here in September."

"Wow," I said, enjoying her happy smile. "That's great news."

And then my mobile rang. I glanced at the screen. "Sorry," I said. "It's my son-in-law. I better..."

Rachel nodded.

When the call ended I said, "Maddie's in labour. There are complications, baby's breech, it'll be a caesarean. She's asking for me. I better get organised then I can get away first thing."

"Of course," Rachel said. "It's time I was leaving anyway. Bonnie will be needing her walk."

At the front door, as she put on her jacket, she looked up at me and said, "I hope it all goes well for Maddie and the baby. Let me know when you have news."

"I will."

She put her hand on my arm. "And thanks for a lovely evening. There's just one thing before I go."

I looked down at her, at her lovely face. She was standing very close. Her eyes looked into mine. "What?" I asked, my voice hoarse.

"This." She reached up, put her arms round me and kissed me on the mouth. It was a long, slow, unambiguous kiss. I couldn't believe it was happening. I couldn't help but respond. When it was over, she ran a finger down my face and along my jaw. "I've wanted to do that for a very long time," she said. And then, before I could say anything, she was gone.

Chapter Thirty Seven

Rachel

As promised, Jack called to let me know he had a handsome and healthy grandson, William Baxter Paterson. Maddie was fine but was going to take some time to recover from the caesarean. So Jack planned to stay on in Edinburgh for as long as she needed him. He sounded tired, relieved and happy and I was very pleased for him. He promised to keep in touch and I told him I'd like that.

"And, I..." he said, just before our call ended.

"What?"

"I enjoyed how you said goodbye yesterday."

"Oh, yes?"

"Yes." I could hear his smile.

"Seemed friendlier than shaking hands. I hope you didn't mind."

"I most certainly didn't mind. It was very—friendly."

I laughed.

"Oh, and Rachel..." he said.

"What?"

"Wait for me."

"Wait for you?"

"Yeah, don't—that is please—please don't make any decisions, you know, about the future, until I get back."

"I'll be here," I said.

I wasn't sure why Jack was so keen for me to be around when he got back. Although I was glad he felt that way, I thought a new sexual relationship was probably the last thing he wanted. Yes, I wanted him, but I had no agenda. I understood Jack had other things on his mind and he had 'baggage', not least the fact he'd just come out of a relationship.

However, I had no regrets about kissing him. I'd wanted the kiss to happen. I'd gone to his house that evening intending it to happen.

Oh yes, my time away had changed me.

Being in so volatile, precarious and contested an environment as Israel, couldn't fail to make a person take stock, couldn't fail to define what really matters. And speaking to people like Hana, Jonathan, Deb and yes, Eitan, had made me question many of my long-held beliefs and attitudes.

Of course it was Finlay's death that had begun this period of profound change. I'd learned in the hardest way that life rarely works out as planned. Finlay had planned to leave the army when he was thirty and come home to live in Skye. I'd imagined him doing just that and married with a family. I'd also imagined that Sophie would forgive me for leaving her father and we'd become closer.

I hadn't planned to sit talking through the night to a wonderfully wise woman on the West Bank. I hadn't planned to explore my Jewish heritage and I certainly hadn't planned to be beguiled by Eitan or to consider emigrating to the Middle East.

And, perhaps most surprising of all, I hadn't planned on falling in love with Jack.

It was both an amazing and a delightful realisation, but it was tempered by all that I'd been through. So yes, I seized the day. Yes, I had hopes, but I had no definite plan. The uncertainty was at first exhilarating and then, simply and refreshingly, welcome.

But Jack going away when he did was probably just as well. I had a lot to think about, a lot of stuff to unpack and sort through.

My mood at the start of September reflected the changing of the season. Autumn had arrived; a time of letting go, dying back and of waiting quietly for renewal. I'd returned from Israel feeling more alive than I had since my student days. But I needed to pause, to gather my thoughts, clear the way ahead.

There was my mother's estate to finalise. Peter had been in touch just after I got home to let me know that everything should be sorted very soon. I knew the house would be mine, but there was the matter of the land. Crofting law was convoluted to say the least. However, Peter reassured me that it looked as if the croft would be reassigned to me. So now I could consider whether to continue working the land myself or let someone else take it over. But that decision depended on whether I was staying on Skye.

For now though, the sheep and hens needed looking after, along with all the other jobs that go with running a croft.

And, besides my work on the croft, there was also the rapidly approaching book launch for *Seamus the Sheep*. The plan was to launch in November in time for the Christmas market. I'd come home to a long checklist emailed to me by Lana. There were last minute tweaks, approvals and decisions to be made. The proofs looked good and I experienced the usual mixture of excitement and dread at the thought of publication.

I'd come home with so many ideas for developing my writing and art that I didn't know where to begin. But gradually my thoughts clarified. I chatted to Lana about an idea I had for a book about my time in Israel. I wanted it to be informative but not preachy or overtly political. I saw it as a book about displacement, exile and loss, both metaphorical and actual, and about how it's possible to remain rooted in the worst of circumstances and even to flourish and grow stronger. I planned to include some of the pencil sketches and photos from my visit and I'd intersperse them with personal reflections and observations. Lana liked my proposal and told me to get to it.

As for my painting, I got my old easel down from the loft and ordered some canvases, paint and brushes online.

I also caught up with some of my old friends, went to the book group, and contacted the conductor of the choir to discuss rejoining. And, of course, I spent time with Morag. I told her more about Israel and continued to reassure her that I'd no definite plans to emigrate. I decided against telling her about Jack and the kiss for the time being. It seemed too soon, after all neither Jack nor I knew where our relationship, if that's what it was, might be heading.

So as autumn settled in, so did I. My days returned to their previous routines and were mainly divided between caring for the animals, working on *Seamus* and, when the canvases and paints arrived, I made my first tentative steps at painting. I started small with a picture of my cottage, looking up the croft fields towards Ben Halla. I loved working with the autumn colours. The bracken was already shaded yellow and orange. The leaves on the rowan were just on the turn, its branches heavy with red berries, and the hedgerows were full of orange crocosmia and rosehips. Life was moving on.

I managed to find some time to tidy up the garden. Alasdair and Morag had done a great job of keeping the grass cut and the borders tidy while I was away, but there was still plenty of pruning, uprooting and transplanting to do. It was always hard to dig up precious plants but sometimes a move was necessary for their own good. Families of sparrows, pipits, goldfinches and chaffinches all visited the garden as I worked. Starlings bathed and drank in the birdbath, and a lone robin followed me, watching for worms as I turned the soil with the hoe. There was the last of the fruit and vegetables to harvest. I had a very good crop of blackcurrants and raspberries and spent one Saturday morning making jam.

It was indeed good to be back on Skye. After the heat and the beautiful, but parched, landscape of Israel, it was wonderful to breathe Scotland's cool air and to smell its damp earth. I came to a new appreciation of working outside to a sound track of gushing burns, tidal rushes, and the calls of the seabirds on the cliffs. I realised how much I'd missed the soft, muted quality of the island's light and colour.

I also found myself stopping often to stare at the magnificent Cuillin Ridge. Since my return, I felt drawn to these iconic mountains in a way I had never been before. I can't explain it, but it was as if they were telling me something, something I couldn't quite hear. They seemed to press on me like a reassuring hand, and the sight of them in their ancient steadfastness was comforting. When I walked the contours of the land on the croft or the hill tracks, on trails both me and my forebears had walked for centuries, I felt the deepest connection. Sometimes it felt as if every footstep reinforced my presence in time and space.

And Finlay was on my mind too. My grief hadn't lessened but it had changed. It no longer clawed and ripped and scourged. I was recovering from the violence with which my life had been dislodged from all its certainties. I'd been hollowed out by the pain but now it was a deep, sorrowful ache and it was containable. I seemed to be establishing a new root system and I carried my son with me, always, everywhere. But on Skye he felt especially close.

As I'd explained to Jack, I read Fin's letter soon after I returned, on the day Jack had called me to ask me if I wanted to go for a walk. It was early afternoon. I'd just finished checking the sheep. I paused and looked around me and Finlay was with me. His presence was strong. And I knew it was time.

I went indoors, straight to my desk drawer and took out his letter. Sitting at my drawing board, I read it.

Hey Ma,

I guess if you're reading this, I must have copped it. And I'm sorry. Sorry that I'll not get to take over the croft, or get to scoff your amazing roast lamb again or your magic bacon rolls - or see Hearts win the Scottish Cup. But mostly I'm sorry for YOU - because I know you'll say it's your fault. You'll beat yourself up, say-

ing stuff like 'I should have stopped him. I shouldn't have let him join up.' IT'S NOT YOUR FAULT. You couldn't have stopped me.

It's what I always wanted to do—to be a soldier. I love it, Ma. I love everything about it. I'm with the best bunch of guys, and I think we can make it better for the people we're here to help.

Whatever happened, it's down to me. I probably did something stupid, lowered my guard, forgot to check something, took a wrong turning.

I couldn't have had a better mum than you and I hope I made you proud. Remember me, but don't be sad. Enjoy your life, Ma, and make the most of every day.

I'll miss you.

With love from your boy,

Fin xxx

I read it straight through, then I reread it, pausing, pondering, tracing some of the words with my fingers. Then I held the paper to me, rocking as if it was a baby, and I wept for my son and for myself.

It was then that Jack called to ask if I wanted to go for a walk. I suppose I could have ignored the call, but it was Jack, and I didn't. I attempted to make my voice sound normal as we spoke. I would have loved to spend an hour or two in his company, outdoors, walking and talking with him. But at that particular time, I didn't trust myself not to break down. I was tempted to ask him to come to the house but I didn't want to prevent him having his walk, didn't want to bother him with my troubles. So I kept the call brief and declined his invitation.

But on that afternoon I did resolve that, during September, I would at last go through Finlay's things.

And then there was Sophie. Like I'd told Jack, she phoned me later on the same day. I was so surprised at first, I could hardly take in that it was her, let alone what she was saying.

I was still determined to see her and to try to put things right. I had planned to phone her. I'd considered calling in when I arrived back in Glasgow on my way home from Israel. But I'd decided against it. I didn't think surprising her would be a good idea. And besides, it was too important to be just tagged on to my trip.

But I'd never expected her to make the first move. The tone of her voice was polite, neutral. I was vaguely aware that she'd asked me a question.

"Mum, did you hear me?" she said. "I'd like to come up, come and stay for a couple of weeks around the middle of next month. Is that okay?"

"Yes, sorry, yes, I heard you. Of course it's okay. I was just surprised. You've not been here for such a long time. Why now? Not that it's a problem."

"I need to talk to you and I need to do it face to face."

"Oh, right, okay," I said. "That's good. It will be lovely to see you." My mouth was dry. I felt quite shaky.

"How was your trip? Did you enjoy it?"

"Good—yes—it was very good. I'm glad I went."

"You can tell me about it when I come up."

"Yes—yes—I will. I'd love to."

"Okay, then. I'm planning to arrive on the fifteenth, it's a Saturday."

After we'd said our goodbyes, I sat, the phone still in my hand, and tried to take in what had just happened.

Chapter Thirty Eight

I had mixed feelings about Sophie's impending arrival. Of course part of me was excited, optimistic even, about spending time with her. But another part of me dreaded it. I wondered if my daughter was coming to say a final goodbye, to ask me to stay out of her life permanently. But then, I told myself, she wouldn't need two weeks to do that and she could do it over the phone. Finally I came to the conclusion that it was to be some kind of last chance meeting, a make or break test. If it went well she'd stay for the fortnight, if it didn't she'd leave much sooner.

By the fifteenth of September, I was up to date with my croft work. The lambs had been separated from their mothers, and all but three of them had gone off to the auction mart. The preparations for the publication and launch of the book were on schedule and I'd also firmed up my proposals with Lana for the Israel sketchbook journal.

I continued to paint. Eitan had been right, it was wonderful to be at the easel again. And I completed a charcoal sketch of Jack and Poppy based on the photo I'd taken of them on the day we flew the kite. I certainly kept myself busy.

There'd been a few calls and texts from Jack. Baby William was thriving, Poppy was enchanted by her new wee brother and Maddie was recovering from the difficult birth. But with his son-in-law due back at work, Jack guessed he'd be in Edinburgh for a bit longer yet. We kept our conversations fairly light. We stuck to the facts of our days, the highlights, little frustrations and practicalities. It wasn't the time to take our talk into deeper, riskier waters.

But I did miss him. I missed his friendship, his ability to listen, and yes, I longed for more intimacy. I longed for his return.

It wasn't just Jack who called me. Jonathan and Eitan both got in touch as well.

Jonathan's call was to check how I was since arriving back and to ask if I'd considered the possibility of moving to Israel. I assured him I was fine but that I wasn't thinking of emigrating in the immediate future. I told him how right it felt being back. I also told him about Sophie's plan to visit and about the book launch and said that those things alone meant I couldn't leave Scotland in the immediate future even if I wanted to. I didn't mention Jack.

I didn't have the heart to be blunt about it. But I think Jonathan guessed I'd made my mind up. "You have to do what's right for you, Rache," he said. "Of course I'm disappointed you've not got the croft on the market and your plane ticket bought. But since you've not come out and said a definite never, then I'll settle for you being undecided. That way there's always hope."

Eitan was his usual direct self. "So, are you coming to Israel to live or are you staying on your island?" he asked, as soon as we'd said hallo.

"It's complicated. I loved being in Israel and I would love to return. But since I've come back here, things have changed. I've changed. And there are people here, that is, I've realised how much I love being here."

"Ah," Eitan said.

"What do you mean, 'ah'?"

"You're not coming to live here, and you're not coming to live with me. Your friend, Jack, he is the reason, is he not?"

"What? No! At least, not in the way you think. I meant my daughter, my friends, my work, my life is here. I'm fairly sure of that now. This is home." But Eitan was right of course. Jack was a significant factor in my decision.

"I am happy that things are resolved for you. I wish you well.

And I hope that you will return here some day. But now, tell me, have you done any painting?"

And that was that. We talked about my renewed efforts to paint. He was pleased and wanted all the details of what I was painting and how. He asked me to send photos. We talked about my other work and then about Eitan's latest projects.

Far from being offended by his unquestioning acceptance of my decision, I was grateful for it. I marvelled again at just how easy Eitan was to get along with. What you saw was what you got. I finished by telling him he was a true friend.

"As are you, Rachel. As are you. We will speak again soon."

I also heard from Hana around the same time. In her email she said how much she'd enjoyed meeting me. She said she'd looked at Skye on the internet and that she thought it was a beautiful place. The guest house was still busy and she was more convinced than ever that she was where she was meant to be, doing the work she was meant to do, with the people she was meant to be with. She reminded me what she'd said about working towards her dream and that until the dream could be realised the bread still had to be baked. She urged me to take the same approach in my own life.

I took Hana's advice. I got on with the small things, the everyday things, the possible and essential things. And, as I did, I hoped and I dreamed.

But I certainly didn't anticipate the shock of Sophie's arrival on that September Saturday. She was due to arrive in the late afternoon and I got increasingly nervous as the day wore on. I tried to keep busy, but couldn't concentrate on anything. Morag came round for a while after lunch, which helped, and Jack phoned to say he'd be thinking about me and that he hoped the visit would go well.

I'd just got in from checking the sheep when Bonnie began barking and I heard a car drawing up. I silenced Bonnie and glanced out of the window. Peter was getting out of the car. I met him at the porch door. Sophie walked up behind him.

"Peter!" I said. "Hallo. I didn't, that is I wasn't—"

"Expecting me. I know. Don't panic. There's a good reason for me being here. I insisted on driving our daughter."

"Oh?"

"Yes, it's a tiring journey at the best of times, but more so when..." He grinned and stepped aside. And there stood Sophie. A very obviously pregnant Sophie.

"Hello Mum." My daughter smiled at me.

I gasped, my hands over my mouth, tears in my eyes. And then my daughter was in my arms. "Oh, Sophie, Sophie," I said. I don't know how long we stood on the doorstep - hugging and crying and laughing. I didn't notice Peter returning to the car and fetching Sophie's luggage but I looked up when he did a theatrical clearing of his throat. He smiled at me.

"Sorry," I said, smiling back at him. "Come in, both of you, come in." I ushered them through to the living-room, still feeling dazed.

Before any of us sat down, Peter looked at me and said, "You look like you could do with a drink. Tea, or something stronger?"

"Tea would be good," I said. "I'll put the kettle on."

"No, you sit down, before you fall down," Peter said. "I'll get us all tea. You and Sophie need to talk."

I sat on the sofa and Sophie came and sat beside me. She turned to face me and said, "I'm sorry, Mum. I've been a bitch and I'm so sorry."

I took hold of one of her hands in both of mine. For a moment I couldn't speak. I shook my head, tears running freely. I looked into my daughter's eyes. She couldn't hold my gaze and looked down at the floor. With my free hand I gently tipped her chin up so she had to look at me. "I love you, Sophie. I'm so glad you're here. I've missed you so much."

"Oh, Mum," she said. A sob shuddered through her.

I took her in my arms and rocked and soothed her until at last she was calm. I released her and she sat back. "May I?" I asked, indicating her pregnant belly. She nodded and took my hand and placed it on her bump.

"I didn't want to tell you on the phone. I hope you understand. I wanted it, needed it, to be face-to-face, but I'm sorry for prolonging the agony for you, as well as everything else."

I shook my head. All that mattered was now, what was happening now. "When is it due?"

"The sixth of December. I'm twenty-eight weeks."

"I can't believe it," I said, as I withdrew my hand. "What made you change your mind?"

"Lots of things. I realised as the date for the termination got nearer that I wasn't going to be able to go through with it. I never really wanted to end the pregnancy, not deep down. I phoned Dad the evening before I was due at the hospital. He was amazing. He drove through to Glasgow right away, that same evening..."

"Did he?"

"He helped me see I was acting out of anger, and he also made me see that all those angry feelings were misplaced. All that stuff I said to you, it was ridiculous, unforgiveable."

"No, not unforgiveable, never that," I said.

"I was so angry at Fin dying. Blaming you, it stopped me falling apart. It was like if I didn't have someone else to blame, then his death was truly senseless, and down to him, to his decision to go."

"I see," I said. "And the stuff you said about you not being a wanted child, about the guilt you feel that Dad and I weren't happy—"

"I told her she had to let go of any such feelings," Peter said. He'd come back into the room carrying a tray and was followed by Bonnie. He laid the tray down on the coffee table, passed us each a mug of tea and sat down on one of the armchairs. "I told her how much you'd wanted her, that it was me who considered not going ahead with the pregnancy. I told her how amazing you'd been, coping with our parents and all the pressure to get married, how you carried on with your studies and made a home for us. I told her how very loved she was and is by both of us."

"Oh," was all I could say.

"And I also told her I don't want the pressure of being a hero. I told her I don't deserve to be seen in that light and told her the full facts about just how hopeless a husband I was. I told her you were always the strong one, the truly loving and unselfish one."

"Oh," I said again.

"Yes, Rachel, you were, *are*, amazingly strong. You stuck around for the children, even when you knew what I was up to. You kept the family together. And then later, you set Finlay free to follow his dream. You gave him your blessing. I didn't."

I could only nod. For a few moments we sat in silence, sipping our tea.

Sophie put her mug down on the table and turned to me. "I've been such an idiot," she said. "I never really doubted I was loved. I think, after Finlay, I think I went a bit mad. The anger was overwhelming. But I shouldn't have taken it out on you. Can you forgive me?"

I leant towards her, pushed a bit of stray hair back from her face and stroked her cheek. "There is nothing to forgive. You're my daughter. I love you, no matter what. All that matters is that you're here now. So please stop apologising and let's just enjoy our time together."

"Good," Peter said. "That's that sorted." He stood up. "I'll get away now. I'm staying in Portree tonight, but I'll call back in the morning before I head home. I can talk you through all the stuff to do with your mother's estate."

"Right, that's good of you," I said. But I didn't want him to go. I felt so grateful to him, what he'd done, his honesty with Sophie, bringing her to me. It was such a healing thing. I felt lighter. I looked at my daughter and then back at Peter. The relief, it was like when an agonising, gnawing pain stops. "Why not stay?" I said. "There's plenty casserole for three and both spare rooms are made up."

Peter shook his head. "Oh, no, I couldn't. This is time for you and Sophie. I couldn't impose—"

"You wouldn't be imposing. This is a special day for all three of us, for our family. I'd really like you to stay."

"And so would I, Dad," Sophie said. "Please stay."

Peter laughed. "Okay, okay," he said. "I know when I'm beaten."

It was a strange and wonderful evening, simultaneously surreal and heightened. It had been such a long time since the three of us were together in that way. We talked about all sorts of things, our work, my trip, Peter and Carla's recent holiday and lots of reminiscences about Finlay. We laughed and we cried. It was better than any therapy.

After Sophie went up to bed, Peter and I sat up for little while longer. I got us both a brandy and we talked some more.

"I hope I did the right thing, speaking to Sophie," Peter said. "I know you said you wanted to handle it yourself."

"You did absolutely the right thing. I got nowhere. I'm really grateful, Peter. It can't have been easy knocking yourself off that pedestal." I smiled at him.

He smiled back. "It was the least I could do and the least you deserved, you and our grandchild."

"We're going to be grandparents," I said, smiling even more.

"Yes we are," laughed Peter. "Come here, Grandma." And for the first time in years, Peter and I shared an embrace.

Chapter Thirty Nine

After breakfast the next morning, while Sophie went for a shower, Peter took me through the details of my mother's estate. I made us a pot of coffee and we sat at the kitchen table. It was all quite straightforward. The croft was now in my name. The house belonged to me and Jonathan. And Peter gave me a cheque for my share of the money Mum had left.

"So with that and the divorce settlement, you should be financially secure for the future," Peter said. "Will you buy a house of your own or stay on here and run the croft?"

"I'm not sure," I said. "My original intention was to get my own place, but now Mum's gone..."

"And you're staying on Skye, not emigrating?"

"Yes, staying on Skye." I couldn't help smiling.

"What are you grinning at?"

"Oh nothing, everything. It's just it's great to have reasons to stay. I don't want to be too far away from Sophie and the baby for one thing."

"And the other reasons?"

"The bad stuff I mentioned last time we spoke, all the bitterness and regret and how lost I felt, it's gone. I feel better. My time away, it was just what I needed. But now I'm back, I know Skye's where I want to be. And I've—I've made a new friend. He's—he's you know—"

"Oh my god, Mum's got a boyfriend!" Sophie had appeared in the kitchen doorway.

"Really!" said Peter.

"Why is that so amazing?" I asked. "But before you get carried away, no I haven't got a boyfriend. But I have made a new friend, a neighbour, Jack. He's a retired policeman from Edinburgh and he's bought Dun Halla Cottage as a holiday home."

"Jack," Sophie said. She nodded and smiled at her father.

"Jack," Peter said and he nodded and smiled back at Sophie. "Mum's new *friend*."

"Stop it, you two," I said. "He is just a friend." I knew I didn't sound convincing. I laughed and ordered a change of subject.

A little while later, I walked Peter out to his car. "It's been good to see you, Rachel," he said. "You're looking great. Your time away has obviously done you good, but I'm glad you're not leaving the country."

"Thanks," I said. "Not just for the compliments, but for speaking to Sophie and for bringing her here."

Peter shook his head. "It was time for some reconciliation, and time I took some responsibility. Thanks for the bed for the night and thanks for—for being you." And after a quick hug, he was in the car and away.

For the next fortnight Sophie and I hardly stopped talking. There was so much catching up to do, of the everyday anecdotal variety, and of the heart-to-heart variety.

There was so much I wanted and needed to know, not least who the father of the baby was, and if he and Sophie were still in a relationship. But I didn't want to rush things and, I sensed, neither did Sophie. We were cautious and gentle with each other, especially at first. We began with safe topics such as films we'd seen, books we'd enjoyed and my visit to Israel. Sophie wanted to hear about Jonathan and his family. She was also very knowledgeable about Middle-Eastern politics and seemed fascinated by what I told her about Hana.

I showed her the case Jonathan and I found, the one belonging to my mother, and she seemed very moved by its contents.

"I'm sorry," she said. "Sorry about not coming to Gran's funeral. It was—I was—"

I put my hand on hers. "It's okay. Really it is. And that re-minds me. I have something of Gran's to give you." I fetched the ring box from my bedroom. "Here, I think Gran would have liked you to have this."

"Gran's wedding ring," Sophie said as she took it from the box. "Are you sure you want me to have it?"

"Very sure."

Sophie put it on the ring finger of her right hand. "It's a good fit."

"Exactly," I said, smiling.

Sophie hugged me. "Thanks, Mum, thank you so much."

Being hugged by my daughter, standing there in my liv-ing-room, autumn sun streaming in the window, and feeling her pregnant belly pressing against me, was sublime.

And gradually, as the first few days of Sophie's stay passed, our conversations became more relaxed and more intimate.

Sophie was interested in the new book and studied the proofs closely. I was touched when she said how great it was that her baby had a Grandma who was so talented at writing and draw-ing for children. She was also interested in my post-Israel proj-ects and thought that my travel sketchbook idea sounded good.

She was enthused, too, by her own work. But one evening while we were still sitting at the table having just eaten dinner, she said she was thinking of going freelance after the baby was born. "I love it at the BBC, and I've especially enjoyed all the documentary stuff that I've been involved in for the last few years, but I want a bit more flexibility when I'm a mother."

"I know what you mean. But it isn't always easy working from home with a family around. Have you got any child-care arrangements in mind?"

"I haven't quite thought it all through just yet. Although..." Sophie hesitated.

"Although?"

"Although Steven has said he wants to be involved. He wants

315

to do some of the care."

"Steven? Steven is the father?" Sophie looked uncomfortable.

"Sorry," I said. "I don't mean to pry."

"You're not. It's all right. It's me being defensive. Yes, Steven's the father. You spoke to him on the phone, and you..." Sophie looked embarrassed. "You sort of met him when you were leaving my flat, the day you came to see me, before you went to Israel."

"Yes, I remember." I realised Steven was the guy I nearly knocked over in my rush to get away. But I didn't want to dwell on the reasons for my haste, and I was sure Sophie didn't either. "He sounded nice on the phone."

"He is. He's a lovely guy. But I don't—I don't know what to do about him."

"Oh, why?"

"I—I don't know. It's a bit of a mess. I'm a mess."

"Would it help to talk?"

"I wouldn't know where to start," Sophie said.

"How did you meet?"

"At work, end of last year. I was researching a piece about..." Sophie paused, looked at me, bit her lip."

"About?" I coaxed.

"About injured Scottish soldiers returning from Afghanistan." She looked at me again, gauging my reaction.

I didn't flinch as she obviously expected me to. "Right." I nodded. "Go on."

"I probably shouldn't have taken it, but when it was offered I couldn't help myself. I think I hoped it would bring Fin closer. I know that probably sounds crazy."

"Not to me."

"Anyway, Steven was one of the guys I was put in touch with. He lost both legs below the knee. Roadside bomb in Helmand. He was so kind about Fin. He understood and he was easy to talk to. After the research ended, we continued to see each other, went on a few dates, had a weekend away together. He even looked after me when I had a tummy bug, mopped up, me and the floor."

"A sign of true love," I smiled.

"Yes, I was impressed. So impressed I forgot that I'd puked up my last pill and had also missed a subsequent couple of days. And that's how..."

"That's how you got pregnant."

"It wasn't planned. We'd only known each other a short time. We weren't living together. We, or rather, I don't know if I can do a long-term, for better or worse relationship. I don't think I'd be any good at it."

"And Steven, how does he feel?"

"Oh, he wants it all, the full package, marriage, a house, the works. He says he loves me, has done from the start, wants to be with me forever. He was even prepared to stay with me if I got rid of the baby, even although it wasn't what he wanted."

"Wow, he sounds amazing and seriously in love. But you don't feel the same?"

"No... that is yes... I love him. It took me longer to admit it, but it was pretty much love at first sight for me too. He's good-looking, kind, brave, loyal, everything anyone could want."

"But?"

"But I'm—I'm scared, scared it won't work, scared we'll end up hating each other."

"Isn't it worth a try, if you love each other like you say you do?"

"I don't know. I just don't know, that's the trouble."

"And how is it between you at the moment? Is Steven still around?"

"We're in touch, if that's what you mean. I won't stop him seeing the baby. He'll be able to be a proper father. But I've asked him to give me a bit of space. We text and speak on the phone but that's it."

"Is the space helping you see things more clearly, work out what you want?"

"Not really. I do miss him, but..." she shrugged. "He's coming here to drive me back to Glasgow. He insisted, said there'd be no strings, so I agreed to let him. He'll come up the night before I leave, stay in a B&B and then take me back in the morning. So you'll get to meet him."

"Oh, right, well that's good." I so wanted to interfere, to do that motherly thing, to offer unasked for advice. I managed to resist the impulse.

"Thanks, Mum." Sophie reached over the table and squeezed my hand.

"What for?"

"For listening. Dad was the same. And neither of you told me what to do. You're great parents."

Sophie had tears in her eyes. Mine were running down my face. "Both of us?" I said, my voice a whisper.

"Yes, both of you."

We had other tearful times talking about Fin and sorting through his stuff. Sophie chose a couple of things of Fin's to keep. But we laughed too as we looked through old family photos and enjoyed reminiscing. It was all very healing.

We went to the cinema and to an art exhibition. We also visited Morag. She'd phoned me one evening to find out how it was going with Sophie. I told her the good news about the pregnancy and about how we'd cleared the air. She was of course delighted on both counts. She invited us round the next day and we had a happy afternoon, stuffing ourselves with tea and cake and listening to Morag's stories of what she and I had got up to as teenagers. Before we left, Morag invited Sophie to her and Alasdair's annual star party. It was planned for what would be Sophie's last night on Skye.

"Your mum's coming," Morag said. "We hold this party every year at the end of September. We have a bonfire and supper and a bit of a ceilidh to mark the end of summer and to welcome back the dark skies."

"Sounds like a great way to spend my last evening here. Thank you. Will it be all right if I bring a guest?"

"Of course. Who?"

"Steven," Sophie said. "Steven, he's my... he's a friend. He's coming to pick me up, to drive me home."

"Right, lovely," Morag said. She looked at me, an inquiring look. I knew what she was thinking, knew what she wanted to ask, but surprisingly for Morag she didn't ask it.

I called her later and filled her in on the situation with Steven. I also thanked her for her restraint in not asking Sophie about him. She laughed and said she'd understood my warning look.

"We know each other so well," I said.

"Indeed we do!"

At the beginning of her second week with me, I'd persuaded Sophie to sit for me so I could sketch her with a view to perhaps doing a painting at a later date.

And it was while she was sitting for me that she mentioned Jack.

"So, this Jack of yours, what's he like?"

I stopped sketching for a moment. "What brought that on?"

"Curiosity. I've told you all about Steven after all. I just wondered if I'd maybe be getting a bit more information about your guy." She smiled a knowing smile.

"He's not my guy. And there's not much to tell. We're friends like I said."

"How did you meet?"

So I told her. She was impressed.

"He sounds like a proper hero. How romantic!" She fluttered her eyelashes and grinned.

I shook my head. "You're as bad as Morag. She's been trying to pair us off since we met. There's no romance." But just thinking about Jack and how I really felt about him, I couldn't help smiling.

"I think you do protest too much. I can tell. Your face is giving you away. At the very least you fancy him. Come on, Mum, tell me. It's more than friendship, isn't it?"

"Okay, okay, bearing in mind you're my daughter, I will only say that yes, we have gone beyond friendship and it was just the once and it was just a kiss."

"I knew it!" Sophie grinned. "And is the 'going beyond friendship' going to move on to become a proper relationship?"

"I've no idea. Jack and me, us, the kiss, it was immediately before he left to go to his daughter. She's in Edinburgh. She's just had a baby. So we haven't had a chance to talk about what happens next."

"Right, I see. When's he due back?"

"I'm not sure. It depends how his daughter is."

"What would you like to happen next?"

"I think I would like it very much if Jack and I moved onto having a 'proper relationship', as you call it. But it's complicated. I suspect it's not what Jack wants."

"Have you told him how you feel?"

"No."

"Why not?"

"I'm scared."

"Ah," said Sophie.

"Yes, ah," I replied.

Chapter Forty

It was on the Wednesday morning of Sophie's second week with me that Jack called. It was the first time we'd spoken since Sophie's arrival.

"I just wanted to make sure things were okay," he said.

"That was nice of you. And things are more than okay."

"Oh? That sounds positive."

"She didn't go through with it. Sophie, she didn't have the abortion. She's still pregnant. She's going to have the baby."

"That's great news. I'm so pleased for you." I could hear the smile in his voice. "And you had no inkling that she was still pregnant until she arrived?"

I told him everything, the surprise about the pregnancy, Peter, Steven. I told him how unsure Sophie was of her feelings about Steven and how the future of their relationship was by no means certain.

"It seems to me it's not so much that she doesn't trust Steven, but that she doesn't trust herself," I said. "Do you know what I mean?"

Jack didn't reply. I realised how much I'd been rambling on. "Sorry," I said. "I'll shut up now."

"No, no. I'm sorry. I was thinking about what you said. I know exactly what you mean actually."

"Oh, right. So tell me, how's baby William and Poppy and everyone?"

Jack brought me up to date on how things were going at his daughter's. William was thriving and Poppy was an exemplary big sister. Maddie was recovering well from the caesarean and her husband, Brian, would soon be starting his paternity leave. He also said he planned to be back in Skye in the next week or so.

"That's good. It'll be good to see you. I've missed you," I said.

"I've missed you too, Rachel. Very much."

Not long after the call, I was in the kitchen making coffee for Sophie and me. I glanced out of the window and saw a car coming along the road and turning up the track to the house. Bonnie began barking. I didn't recognise the vehicle. But I recognised the young man who got out and stood looking around him. It was Steven. I silenced Bonnie and shouted to Sophie who was reading in the living-room. I went out to meet him.

"Hello," I said. "We didn't expect you for another couple of days."

He looked embarrassed. "Yes, I know, I'm sorry. I'm Steven, by the way, Steven Jackson."

"Rachel," I said, as we shook hands.

"Steven!" Sophie stood on the step. "What are you, why are you—"

"I couldn't wait, Soph. I've missed you so much. I had to see you." He walked towards her. The expression on his face left me in no doubt how much he loved my daughter. When he got to her, he took her in his arms.

I waited until they released each other. "Right," I called, waving. "That's me away. I'm having lunch at Morag's."

Sophie looked at me, puzzled. Then she smiled. "Ah, right, yes, of course. Bye."

"See you later," I called. A few minutes later a rather surprised Morag found me in her kitchen. I explained my predicament and was duly invited to make myself at home for the next few hours.

When I returned, Steven and Sophie were in the living-room. They were sitting side by side on the sofa. Sophie had her head on Steven's shoulder and they were holding hands. The fire had been lit and Bonnie was snoozing on the rug.

I told them I was going to check the sheep and that I'd make us all some dinner when I got back. Steven surprised me by asking if he could come with me. I glanced at Sophie. She smiled at me, a sort of shy, expectant smile. I told Steven that of course he could come with me.

As we made our way down the croft, with Bonnie running in wide circles around us, I noticed that Steven walked with a slightly swaying gait. "Sophie told me about your injury," I said. "The ground here is very uneven. Will you manage?"

"I'll be fine. The prostheses I have are carbon-fibre. They're pretty good, all-terrain jobs."

"I'm sorry," I said. "Sorry you were so badly injured and I hope you didn't mind me asking."

"Of course I don't mind. It helps if people are direct about it, sort of gets it out of the way. And thanks for your sympathy, but I was lucky to..." He stopped speaking, looked away.

"Lucky to survive," I said.

"Yes—unlike others, unlike your son."

"Mmm," I said. "But not easy for you."

"No, not easy, not at first, not for a long time. There was the guilt and the shame that I survived. And then there was the grief of losing my legs and my previous life."

"But now? Now you're okay?"

"I've come to terms with it, yes. And meeting Sophie, well, that's what's helped me most of all. And now with the baby coming. I feel even luckier."

We smiled at each other. The look we exchanged seemed to me to be full of understanding and I thought that I already liked this brave young man very much. He helped me fill the water troughs and put out the feed. He asked several pertinent questions about the sheep and helped me catch one of the ewes whose feet I wanted to check.

"I'm impressed," I said, as he flipped the ewe onto her back so

I could carry out my inspection. "Did you grow up on a farm?"

He laughed. "No, I'm a city boy but I spent a lot of my summer holidays at my grandparent's farm in Argyll. My uncle has it now and I still like to help out now and again."

It was when we were walking back to the house that Steven asked the question.

"Would it be all right with you if I asked Sophie to marry me?"

I gasped and my hands went to my mouth. I stopped walking and turned to look at him. He stopped too. He smiled. "I hope you're shocked in a good way," he said.

"Not shocked. Pleasantly surprised… delighted."

"So it's all right then? To propose?"

"Yes of course. You didn't have to ask me. But it's nice that you did." I wished that I could assure him of Sophie's acceptance.

"Good. And it's okay, I know she might say no. I've mentioned marriage before, although not a proper proposal with a ring and everything, but she's never been interested."

"And you think she'll be interested now?"

"I don't know. But I do know that these last two weeks while she's been away, it's been awful not being able to drop round and see her. I love her so much." He paused, cleared his throat. "I have to give it one last try. I've booked us into a hotel in Portree tonight. It looked suitably luxurious on its website, with a good restaurant. So I've got a ring and a list of reasons why she'd be daft not to accept, and tonight over dinner I'm going to do it. I'm going to propose properly."

"Good for you. And I do hope she says yes. She told me she loves you and how right you are for her. It's just she's scared it won't work out, that you and her will fail, end up hating each other. I'm afraid the relationship between her father and me has left Sophie with the very scars I tried to prevent from happening."

"Hmm, life can be messy, can't it? But if there's one thing I've learned after my injuries, it's that life's also too short and too

324

precious to be ashamed or guilty or afraid. You have to go to it, embrace it and live it."

I nodded. "You're so right. It's what Finlay, my son, said in his letter. You know the one you soldiers write to your family in case..."

"In case we don't make it home."

"Yes. And you and him, you're both right of course. I've recently come to understand that for myself and I just hope Sophie does too."

After we got back to the house, Steven told Sophie that he was taking her away for the night. She seemed very happy to go and much later that evening I got an excited call from my daughter to tell me she was now engaged. She pretended to be cross that I'd been in on the secret and there was laughter and tears from us both.

"So," Sophie said when we'd regained our composure. "That just leaves you now, Mum. I've been honest with myself and with Steven. I've made my leap of faith. It's your turn now."

Chapter Forty One

Sophie and Steven went home to Glasgow the next day. They came to see me before they set off and we had a very pleasant lunch together.

Sophie apologised for leaving a couple of days earlier than planned. She said that since they'd decided to move in together, they wanted to use the remaining time they had off work for Steven to get all his stuff over to her flat. It was lovely to see her so excited and I assured her that I really didn't mind.

It did feel slightly strange to be on my own again once they left, but I was far from sad. Relief and gratitude were what I felt. To be reconciled with my daughter was utterly wonderful. And although I'd often thought about it, I'd never imagined that the circumstances would be so amazing. To have Peter bring her to me, to have his support and understanding and to have talked so honestly, to see Sophie pregnant and then so happy with someone who I could see was such a good man, it was overwhelming, it was healing, it was exquisite.

On the day that Sophie and Steven left and throughout the following day, I would find myself stopping what I was doing mid-task. I'd become lost in contemplation of what had happened, not just recently with Sophie, but all that had happened to me since the night I almost gave myself up to the river. The disorientation that grief had wrought in me was gone. It wasn't a bright new dawn. It wasn't a renewal or a restoration to how I was before Fin's death. Grief, at least for me, wasn't like that. I was changed and permanently scarred. The loss of my son would always be with me. I would forever be a bereaved mother and part of me would be forever sad. But I was better. I was re-rooted, reoriented. I was hopeful.

I didn't see or speak to anyone until the Saturday afternoon. I wanted, needed, time alone. Time to get used to the repositioning of my life.

I thought about Jack. Of course I did. I looked forward to seeing him again. I remembered what Sophie had said about it being my turn to be honest about my feelings and about leaps of faith and I wondered...

It was Morag who broke the silence. She phoned just after lunch. She'd seen Sophie and Steven driving off. She'd noticed they hadn't returned. Her curiosity was now uncontainable. Alasdair had apparently told her to leave me be for a day or two, but now, under the pretext of confirming my attendance at the party that evening, she felt she must call.

I said I would indeed be there and that I was looking forward to it. I also told her what had happened with Sophie and Steven. She shared my delight.

Later, as I got ready for my night out, I realised I really was looking forward to it. I was ready for company. It would be good to see all the neighbours and old friends who attended this annual event. It wasn't the kind of party you'd dress up for as most of it took place outdoors, so I just put on clean jeans and my favourite green, cashmere sweater.

Bonnie watched me put on jacket and boots, and wasn't impressed when I told her she wasn't coming with me. Her hopes of an evening walk dashed, she went to her basket as I left to walk over to Morag's.

It was a perfect evening for the party. The air was frosty but the sky was clear and the stars were out. Quite a few people had already arrived. There were groups, both sitting and standing in Morag's living-room and kitchen and there were more people outside in the garden.

Alasdair met me in the kitchen, which was already filled with the delicious smells of the party supper. He offered to take my jacket, but I told him I wanted to go outside. "The bonfire's impressive," I said, watching the flames through the kitchen window as he poured me a glass of mulled wine.

"It is, isn't it? It took me a couple of days to build, but it's definitely worth the effort." He handed me my wine and raised his own glass in a toast. "Cheers and congratulations on your forthcoming grandchild. Morag told me the good news about you and Sophie, and about the baby."

"I'm only just beginning to take it all in but it's a lovely feeling."

"You're looking well, Rachel. And, dare I say it, happy." He smiled at me.

"I feel well and I *am* happy," I said.

Once outside, I stood for a few minutes staring into the flames of the bonfire and enjoyed its warmth. I also took a minute to look at the stars and do that thing of pondering my own insignificance, which for some reason I found rather comforting. I also admired all the little lights and lanterns that Morag and Alasdair had hung around the garden. The atmosphere was magical and felt full of possibilities. But it wasn't long before I was spotted and dragged away from my introspection. I was soon mingling with the other guests and chatting to various neighbours and friends. Our talk was accompanied by the background noise of a fiddle and a guitar being tuned, signalling that the ceilidh part of the evening would soon be underway. I felt so completely at home, and at peace with everything, that when Morag appeared at my side and asked if I'd be willing to sing a couple of songs to get things started, I readily agreed.

"That's great," she said. "I wasn't sure you'd want to."

"A few months ago, I definitely wouldn't have. But now it feels..."

"What?"

"It feels good. It feels—right."

Morag hugged me and I hugged her back. "You've come a

long way," she said, as she let me go. "It's great to see you looking so well and so happy. I was afraid I'd never get my best friend back."

"I was very lost for a while, but yes, I'm back."

"And now, you better go and speak to Ken and Robbie about what you're going to sing. They're tuned up and ready to go. I'll chivvy everyone to come outside and I'll get Alasdair to introduce the three of you in about ten minutes."

"Yes, ma'am," I said.

I decided to sing the same two Burns' songs I'd sung at Mari's bat-mitzvah. I'd begin with *Ae Fond Kiss*, that beautiful song of yearning for lost love. Then I'd sing *The Silver Tassie,* a song close to my heart because of the poignancy of the words, the words of a soldier bidding farewell to his sweetheart before going into battle.

It was at the end of Alasdair's introduction, just as Ken the guitarist began to count us in, that I saw him. He was standing beside Morag and was looking right at me. Jack was back.

Somehow I managed to start singing. And, once I began, I focussed only on the music. I didn't dare look at Jack, not while I sang about love. Ken, Robbie and I slipped from the first to the second song with only the shortest of pauses between. It was only as the applause greeted the end of the second song that I allowed myself to look at Jack. He hadn't moved and he was still looking at me as he joined in the clapping. Alasdair stepped forward to ask everyone to take their partners for some dancing and announced that Strip the Willow would be the first dance. As Alasdair was speaking, Jack came over to me.

"Wow," he said. "That was beautiful." His voice and expression were gentle and soft. It was so good to see him.

"Thanks." My own voice had faded to a hoarse whisper. I cleared my throat. I was also aware of Morag. I could see her out of the corner of my eye. I knew she was watching us.

"It's lovely to see you, Rachel." He smiled and stroked my cheek with the back of his hand, pushing a loose strand of hair back from my face. For a moment we just stood looking at each other. For a moment I felt like teenager at a school dance. I struggled to speak, struggled not to give Morag the satisfaction of grabbing him and kissing him, kissing him long and slow.

I swallowed, tried to steady my breathing. "Good to see you too," I said. "When did you get back?"

"Today, late afternoon. Morag called me a couple of days ago to let me know about the party. She seemed very keen for me to be here, and when Maddie heard about it, she said it was time I left her to it and to get myself back here. So here I am."

"Here you are."

"Shall we go inside, get a drink?" he said.

"Good idea."

Everyone else was still in the garden, dancing or chatting, so we had the kitchen to ourselves. Jack poured me a glass of wine and got himself a beer. We sat facing each other at the kitchen table.

"Poppy was asking after you. She wanted to know when she could come to see you again."

"Oh, that's nice. I'd love to see her again too. How is she? And Maddie and the baby too, of course."

"All doing well. William seems to be a good baby, sleeps a lot, and Poppy's a great help to her mum, no sign of jealousy."

"It must have been hard to leave them."

"In some ways. But..."

"But?"

Jack reached across the table and took hold of my hand. "I wanted to get back to see you."

"Oh," I said.

"That kiss, before I left, it made me think."

"It did?"

"It did. It made me think you might want to—to be more than friends."

"Oh," I said again. And again I was struggling to speak, struggling just to breathe. I hoped his desire to see me wasn't so he could make his feelings clear, so he could tell me he didn't want to be more than friends. I needed to know, but I didn't want to hear it. For a moment we just looked at each other.

"Look, Jack," I said, as the back door opened.

Morag came into the kitchen. "Sorry to interrupt," she said. She smiled at us both. "Some folk are getting hungry, so I thought I'd better get the food set out."

I jumped up. "Of course," I said. "Let me help."

As Morag and I began to transfer the hot food into serving dishes and onto the table, Alasdair appeared. He greeted Jack with a handshake and ushered him through to the living-room saying, "Come and tell me what's been happening with you."

"You two getting along okay?" Morag asked, as we got the supper dishes set out.

"Yes, fine," I said.

"It's just I got the feeling I might have interrupted a heart-to-heart."

"No, no. You didn't interrupt anything. It's fine, we were just catching up on news."

"If you say so." Morag looked sceptical. "Right, I think that's everything. I'll go and let everyone know to come and get it." On her way to the door, Morag turned back. "I won't be offended if you and Jack want to get away early, if you want to talk or—or anything."

"Morag, please!" I said. I couldn't hide my irritation. I was annoyed because she was right. I was desperate to be alone with Jack.

"Okay, okay. Just saying." Morag disappeared out of the door.

The kitchen gradually filled with people. Jack stood, tucking into a bowl of chilli and chatting to a group of our neighbours. I stood with another group of neighbours and half-listened to a discussion about lamb prices and the cost of animal feed. When I'd finished my plate of pasta, I made my excuses and fetched my jacket and boots. I'd decided to go back outside.

I was by the bonfire looking up at the stars when Jack approached. "So, can you remember any of their names?" he said.

"Probably not." I kept my gaze on the flames, but enjoyed being near him.

"I think I should test your recall. Do you fancy a bit of a walk?"

Now I turned to look at him. I struggled to keep a grip on my feelings. Told myself how ridiculous I was being. But it didn't make much difference. It really was like being a teenager again. I managed to keep my voice steady. "Okay. Can Bonnie come too?"

"Of course. As long as she doesn't help you with the answers." He smiled that smile. I tried to look cool and calm.

We said our thank-yous and goodbyes to Morag and Alasdair. Morag was obviously delighted Jack and I were leaving together, but Alasdair steered her away before she could say anything embarrassing.

I failed the star test miserably. My mind was so concentrated on not making a fool of myself by blurting out my feelings for Jack, that I made a fool of myself trying to identify the stars and constellations instead. It didn't help, as we stood side by side looking up at the royal blue sky, that Jack put his arm around my shoulders and put his head close to mine as he directed my gaze heavenwards.

"Either I'm not much of a teacher, or you're not a very good student," Jack said. He offered me his arm. I took it. It felt good. We set off walking again. "I'm not ready to give up on you yet," he said. "But I think we'll require some more night walks."

"Sounds good to me," I said, smiling into the darkness.

We were almost at Jack's house. Our pace had slowed. Bonnie was running in circles, rounding us up. "Would you like to come in for a nightcap?" Jack said.

Again I kept my voice calm. "That would be nice."

Once inside, Jack poured us a brandy each. He also filled a pudding bowl with water for Bonnie who'd already curled up on the rug in front of the Aga. "Come through," he said.

We sat on the sofa. At first we sipped our drinks in silence. A companionable, comfortable silence. The fire had burned low. Red coals glowed behind the fireguard. Two table lamps cast a soft light.

"How are you, Rachel? How are you really?" Jack had turned to look at me. The urgency in his voice surprised me. I couldn't help but return his gaze. His expression was serious, concerned.

"I'm fine. Very well, a lot better than when we first met."

"Happy?"

"I think it's more contentment, an acceptance of how things are along with hope for the future."

"And have you decided where your future lies?"

"I'm not emigrating, if that's what you mean."

"No?" Jack looked at me. I'm not sure whether I saw relief or disbelief in his expression.

"No."

"I suppose the prospect of your grandchild has influenced your decision."

"I suppose it has, but I'd more or less decided before I knew there was going to be a grandchild."

"Really?"

"Don't you believe me?" I smiled at him.

"Yes, sorry, of course I believe you. It's just—"

"What?"

"You seemed so happy when you got back. You seemed changed, as though you'd found what mattered to you, found your way again. I felt sure you'd want to return to Israel, establish a life there, maybe settle with that guy, Eitan."

I was tempted to laugh at this last part, but the seriousness of Jack's look stopped me. "You're right. I did come back changed. I went to Israel to try to make sense of the past, but what I actually found was a sense of my future. Israel was like—was like a prism. It showed me all the component parts of my life—all separate and clear. I arrived there feeling lost, dislodged, hollowed out by all the—the changes. I soon realised my uprooting had already happened. I didn't need or want any more displacement shocks. Jonny and Deb, they've put down roots where they could flourish. My mum did it too, coming here to live with Dad. As for me, what I want, what I *need*, is to re-establish, reposition my life here."

Jack nodded, seemed deep in thought for a moment. He sipped his brandy before he spoke. "I've been doing a bit of thinking about the future too, making some decisions."

My curiosity only just outweighed my trepidation about what Jack's plans were. "Oh, right. What sort of decisions?"

"Like you, my life had got out of place. Nothing like the trauma you've had to face, but I've been through a few transitions. The heart thing, the retirement thing and then the end of me and Bridget. And there's the grandfather thing too. I've had to adjust my view, face up to some hard truths about myself, work out what's important." He took another mouthful of brandy and sighed as he laid down his glass.

"And now? Where are you now?"

Jack leant forward, looked at the floor as he spoke. "I've faced up to what a rotten husband I was. I've also realised that I'm way past wanting short-term affairs and that I'm no good at long-term. So it's best I don't get into any more relationships."

I stifled a gasp of pain, covered my mouth with my hand. I was glad Jack wasn't looking at me.

"I've also faced up to the fact that I'm not immortal," he continued. "Life is finite and I intend to make the most of the time I've got. And to do that, I want to spend more time here on Skye."

"Oh, that's good," I said. I couldn't hide my relief. At least I'd still get to see him.

He glanced round at me. He had that sceptical, curious look again.

"It's good, after all the work you've done on the house and everything. It's good you still want to be here," I said.

He returned to looking at the floor. "I initially thought I'd only come up from time to time and that I'd prefer to be mostly based in Edinburgh. I thought I needed all the city stuff. I thought I'd spend lots of time with the family. But Edinburgh doesn't excite me—not now—not without the job. And, like I said before, I don't want it to become that I'm just living through my daughter and her family. No, Skye, it's become very—very special to me. I feel alive here. I love the walking, the dark skies—everything. It's where I want to be most of the time." He drank the last of his brandy and turned to me. "I'm sorry, Rachel. I don't usually talk like this. You must be bored stiff. I'll fetch your jacket."

It was then that I realised it was now or never. I remembered what Sophie had said about me getting this sorted. I was also aware of Eitan and Morag and what they'd be urging me to do. But in the end it was me, just me, the me I was now.

"No, Jack, no," I said. "I don't want to go." I put my hand on his arm. "I want—I want to go to bed with you."

Chapter Forty Two

Jack

When I'd arrived at the party that evening, Morag had directed me straight to the garden. I spotted Rachel right away. I'd enjoyed just watching her as she chatted in Gaelic with two musician guys. Then when she sang, I couldn't take my eyes of her. Her singing was beautiful. She was beautiful. I smiled as I remembered her kiss. Watching her, my resolve to remain no more than friends weakened. Should I tell her how I really felt? Obviously I'd reassure her I wasn't looking to get into a relationship, but maybe it would be good to be honest and then put it out of the way.

But, later, when I broached the subject of the kiss, she'd looked uncomfortable. She probably hoped I'd forgotten about it. It was just as well we were interrupted by Morag. So I decided to stick to plan A. I'd suggest a walk and a nightcap in order to enjoy some precious time with her. And I'd leave it at that. No more hopeless relationships for me.

And now, Rachel had gone and said what she'd just said. I stared at her, momentarily paralysed by shock.

She was so close, so beautiful, the smell of her perfume so heady. She looked back at me, her expression now one of horror. "Oh God, Jack, I'm sorry. What must you think of me, propositioning you, especially after what you've just been saying. Please, forget I said anything."

"No, no, it's just you took me by surprise. I mean, I want to go to bed with you, of course I do. It's just I'm not, I don't—"

"Jack," she said.

"What?"

"Shut up." And then she reached her arms up and around my neck and kissed me. And I kissed her, on the mouth, on the neck, on the mouth again. She began undoing my shirt buttons and there was more kissing. I caught hold of her hand and led her upstairs to the bedroom. She kicked off her shoes and then removed her socks, sweater and jeans. All I could do was watch, still in shock.

"Your turn," she said, standing in front of me, dressed only in her underwear, an incredibly sexy smile on her face. She watched me, as I took off my shoes and then struggled with my buttons, belt and zip. My co-ordination seemed to have deserted me. I felt like a teenager. It felt like my first time.

"Allow me," she said. She undid the rest of my shirt buttons and I wrestled it off. She ran her hands down my chest and brushed it with her lips as she undid my belt and trousers. I managed to stumble out of them, along with my socks. And then she was in my arms and I was pushing her back towards the bed. She lay down and raised her arms up to pull me to her.

"Are you sure about this?" I said to her with the little bit of voice I still seemed to have.

"Oh, yes," she said, pulling me on top of her.

I was lost, lost in Rachel, lost in her touch, her scent, her murmurs and gasps, lost in the feel of her skin and in her eyes as she watched me, caressed me and kissed me. I don't think I'd ever felt so much hunger for, or tenderness towards anyone, until that night. At last, we stopped and lay spent and satisfied in each other's arms.

Eventually I managed to speak. "Like you said when you kissed me, I've wanted to do that for a very long time." I stroked her face.

She looked at me, her smile still very sexy. She raised one

eyebrow and traced her fingers across my chest. "Oh?" she said. "Really? Since when?"

"Oh, probably since you stood dripping all over the carpet in Morag's holiday cottage, after I fished you out of the burn."

She giggled—yes—giggled, something I'd never heard her do before, and it sounded so good. "It wasn't as instant as that for me," she said.

"No?"

"No. I didn't fancy you until you until much later."

"Oh." I felt ridiculously disappointed.

"It *was* the same night though, the night we met. It was when said you'd throw in some toast with the second cup of tea." She giggled again.

I laughed too. And then I kissed her. "I can't believe you're here, here in my bed. I was prepared to settle for friendship."

"So was I. Or so I thought."

"What changed?"

"As I said, when I was away, lots of things changed."

I felt a surge of jealousy, a tug of dread. "Eitan, did he—did he change you?"

She frowned at me. "Yes, he did and yes, I slept with him. He even made an open-ended, somewhat lukewarm proposal of marriage."

"Oh, did he?"

"He did. My time with him, it was all part of the magic of being away. We disagreed on lots of stuff, politics mainly, but he's a good guy, you'd like him."

"Hmm, I'd probably want to smack him one."

She smiled. "Just like I could happily have smacked your Bridget that day she left."

"She's not *my* Bridget. But she was right about me. I did let her down and I wasn't—I did cheat on my wife. So—"

"Stop!" Rachel had rolled onto her front and was leaning over me. She put her fingers on my lips. "When I was away, I realised how much I missed you, realised what you meant to me.

I didn't think you'd be interested, but I did have to acknowledge to myself that I was in love with you."

"Oh?"

"I love you, Jack. Bridget, Eitan, your marriage, the past, the future, they're not for tonight. We have a lot of talking to do, but not now. Let's just enjoy being here tonight, together. Okay?"

"Okay." I pulled her in towards me and kissed her long and hard. "Just one thing, though."

"What?"

"I love you too."

New Year's day, almost a year since Rachel and I met. There was a Hogmanay party last night in the Halladale hall. We all went. Maddie and her family, Sophie and hers. They left earlier than us of course because Poppy and the babies needed to be put to bed.

Rachel's still asleep here beside me, but I can hear that Maddie, Brian and the kids are already up and about downstairs. I'm sure, along the track at Burnside cottage, baby Miriam will also have awakened Sophie and Steven.

I look at Rachel. I still find it hard to believe that she loves me as much as I love her. When I can no longer resist, I stroke her cheek. She stirs, opens her eyes and moves into my arms. We enjoy the perfect start to a new year.

It's been good having our families to stay over the festive season, a good chance for everyone to get to know each other. Maddie and Sophie seem to approve of Rachel and me being in a relationship although like Morag, they want us to go further and to move in to together.

For us though, for Rachel and me, there's no rush. Even although I find it difficult to trust myself, Rachel says she has no such difficulty. She says she's always trusted me. She says I saved her life. We do spend a lot of time together. We sleep together. We have a loving relationship. It's what we want.

But I do have a plan. After Sophie's wedding in the spring, after she and Steven move up and take over the running of the

croft, that's when I'll do it. I'll pack us a picnic and we'll walk to
Waternish point and that's where I'll ask Rachel to marry me.

Anne writes contemporary fiction for people who enjoy a good story which informs, entertains and satisfies. There's usually a liberal dash of romance thrown in.

For more about Anne Stormont and her writing
visit http://putitinwriting.me
Anne can be contacted at annestormont@putitinwriting.me

Also by
Anne Stormont

Change of Life

A tale of life. A poignant mix of sadness, hope and love.

Be careful what you wish for…

Wife to Tom and mother to four adolescent children, Rosie feels taken for granted as she juggles family life and her work as a teacher. She longs for a change.

When she hits a teenage boy with her car, her life veers into unpredictable and uncharted territory. The boy is Robbie - and Rosie discovers he is part of a terrible secret that Tom has kept from her for seventeen years. Then Rosie is diagnosed with breast cancer.

Rosie leaves home and begins the fight for her life. Meanwhile heart surgeon, Tom, learns what it means to be a husband and father. He struggles to keep his family together and strives to get his wife back.

'A good convincing voice that had me identifying with the characters from the outset.' David Wishart, Novelist

'It's a real emotional roller-coaster of a read. I was completely involved in the characters and their lives.' Romantic Novelists' Association.

8298142R00205

Printed in Great Britain
by Amazon.co.uk, Ltd.,
Marston Gate.